"An epic of apocalyptic f[...]
rock-hard realistic. A caut[...]

—[...]s Rollins,
New York Times bestselling author of *The Judas Strain*

"Part Michael Crichton, part George Romero, Jeff Carlson's *Plague Year* is deft and compelling, full of high-altitude chills." —E. E. Knight,
National bestselling author of *Valentine's Exile*

"Frightening, plausible, and action-packed, *Plague Year* is one of the best debut novels in years . . . Jeff Carlson packs riveting storytelling with a lot of fresh ideas."

—David Brin,
New York Times bestselling author of *Kiln People*

"A grim and fascinating new twist on the post-holocaust story, unlike anything I've read before."

—Kevin J. Anderson,
New York Times bestselling co-author of *Hunters of Dune*

"Jeff Carlson is a terrific writer and *Plague Year* is a marvelous book, full of memorable characters, white-knuckle scenes, and big ideas. Get in on the ground floor with this exciting new author." —Robert J. Sawyer,
Hugo and Nebula Award–winning author of *Rollback*

"*Plague Year* proposes a frightening new nanotech catastrophe, and uses it as a crucible to explore the best and worst of human nature. Tightly written and well-told."

—Robert Charles Wilson,
Hugo and Aurora Award–winning author of *Spin*

PLAGUE
YEAR

JEFF CARLSON

ACE BOOKS, NEW YORK

THE BERKLEY PUBLISHING GROUP
Published by the Penguin Group
Penguin Group (USA) Inc.
375 Hudson Street, New York, New York 10014, USA

Penguin Group (Canada), 90 Eglinton Avenue East, Suite 700, Toronto, Ontario M4P 2Y3, Canada
(a division of Pearson Penguin Canada Inc.)
Penguin Books Ltd., 80 Strand, London WC2R 0RL, England
Penguin Group Ireland, 25 St. Stephen's Green, Dublin 2, Ireland (a division of Penguin Books Ltd.)
Penguin Group (Australia), 250 Camberwell Road, Camberwell, Victoria 3124, Australia
(a division of Pearson Australia Group Pty. Ltd.)
Penguin Books India Pvt. Ltd., 11 Community Centre, Panchsheel Park, New Delhi—110 017, India
Penguin Group (NZ), 67 Apollo Drive, Rosedale, North Shore 0745, Auckland, New Zealand
(a division of Pearson New Zealand Ltd.)
Penguin Books (South Africa) (Pty.) Ltd., 24 Sturdee Avenue, Rosebank, Johannesburg 2196,
South Africa

Penguin Books Ltd., Registered Offices: 80 Strand, London WC2R 0RL, England

PLAGUE YEAR

An Ace Book / published by arrangement with the author

PRINTING HISTORY
Ace mass-market edition / August 2007

Copyright © 2007 by Jeff Carlson.
Maps by Meghan Mahler.
Cover photo of mountains © Adam Jones/Image Bank/Getty Images.
Cover design by Judith Lagerman.
Interior text design by Laura K. Corless.

ISBN: 978-0-441-01514-6

ACE
Ace Books are published by The Berkley Publishing Group,
a division of Penguin Group (USA) Inc.,
375 Hudson Street, New York, New York 10014.
ACE and the "A" design are trademarks belonging to Penguin Group (USA) Inc.

PRINTED IN THE UNITED STATES OF AMERICA

10 9 8 7 6 5 4 3 2 1

For Diana

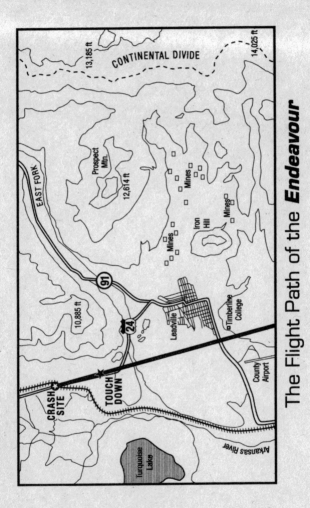

The Flight Path of the *Endeavour*

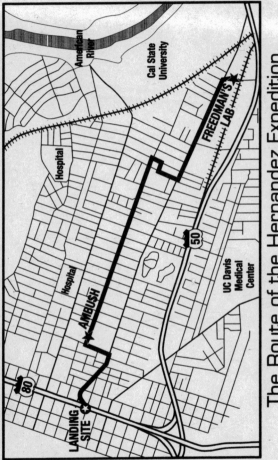

The Route of the Hernandez Expedition

1

They ate Jorgensen first. He'd twisted his leg bad—his long white leg. The man hadn't been much more than a stranger, but Cam remembered five hundred things about him.

It was a weakness.

Cam remembered someone who never cursed, who kept his credit cards and driver's license for some reason. He remembered a hard worker who exhausted himself the day that he fell.

Later there were others Cam had actually talked with, where they were from, what kind of jobs they'd had. Talking made the days easier, except that ghosts seemed very real after you'd sucked the marrow out of someone's finger bones, and Cam got extra portions because he volunteered for wood detail even when the snow drifted up over the roof.

Each night stretched longer than his memory. Erin refused to have sex more than it took to get warm, and then there was nothing to do but pick at his blister rash and listen to the nightmares and slow whispers that filled the hut.

He was glad when Manny banged on the wall and yelled.

Erin shifted but didn't wake. She could stay down for

twelve, thirteen hours at a stretch. Others pushed up on one elbow or raised their heads, mumbling, groaning—screaming when Manny pushed through the door and let in a river of cold air. Fresh air. It washed Cam's ghosts away.

The kid was short for fifteen, barely five-three, but still had to duck the ceiling. They were lucky they hadn't scavenged enough material for anything better. They probably would have built high out of habit. This low space was quick to heat and they planned to drop the roof another twelve inches before winter rolled around again, use the extra boards for insulation.

Manny said, "There's someone in the valley."

"What?"

"Price wants to light a bonfire."

"What are you talking about?"

"Someone's in the valley. Coming toward us."

Cam reached over Erin to shake Sawyer, but Sawyer was already awake. His arm tensed under Cam's palm. The fire, down to coals, threw just enough light into their corner that the profile of Sawyer's newly shaved scalp looked like a bullet.

"In the valley," Sawyer repeated. "That's impossible."

Manny shook his head. "We can see a flashlight."

The high California Sierra, east of whatever remained of Sacramento, consisted of surprisingly straight lines. Ravines and drainages formed slashing V shapes. Every mountaintop grew to a pyramid or slumped away as flat as a parking lot. Painted by the sweet glow of the stars, the sight gave Cam hope—that it was beautiful, that he could still recognize beauty.

Even better, it must be April or even May and would finally get warm enough that he could escape the stinking hut and sleep outside.

The toes Manny had lost didn't prevent the kid from set-ting a quick pace, weaving around the fields of snow they hadn't yet carried to their crude reservoir. Cam and Sawyer kept close on his heels. This peak was no bigger than the back of God's hand and they knew every barren inch of it, hunting day and night for the few rodents and birds that lived along the tree line, scouring it clean of plant life.

They'd been up here now for most of a year, maybe longer. It was definitely spring again, they knew that much, no matter how confused their best calendar might be.

They'd been up here too long.

Jim Price had everyone from the other cabin hauling firewood to a low ridge, even his woman, Lorraine, who'd miscarried just three weeks ago. Cam couldn't recall whether Lorraine had limped before or not. So many of them moved awkwardly now.

Price himself stayed by the woodpile, pointing, hollering, marching alongside one man briefly before hustling back to help another guy load up. "Here you go, let's go!" Unfortunately some of these people needed cheerleading. In Cam's opinion, at least half of Price's supporters were fractured, beaten souls who had latched on to the only available father figure. At forty-six, Price was twelve years older than anyone else on the mountain.

Sawyer plunged into the busy line, leading with his stubble-dark head. Talking louder than Price, he grabbed at people's sleeves and blocked their way as Cam strode out to where they were making three piles. Big piles.

Manny followed, pointing with his entire arm. The kid's voice was unmistakably eager. "Down there."

Cam stared out across the valley instead. The people on the next peak had built three bonfires, just flickering orange sparks from here, but an obvious signal.

"See him?" Manny asked, then yelled, "Heyyyyy!"

Some of the human shadows around them also cheered. There was little chance this sound would penetrate the vast, black valley, but a sense of hope and wonder welled up in Cam again.

About a mile below them, a wand of light strobed wildly over the rough terrain—electric light like a star.

Cam said, "He must have started across this morning."

"You think someone could make it that far in a day?"

"Longer than that would kill him."

Price bustled over with a tin soup bowl of embers, hugging it against his chest with one hand and waving his other arm grandly at each of the few stragglers he passed.

Jim Price had a compact, barrel-shaped torso that in daylight sometimes gave him the illusion of plumpness. In the dim shine of the embers, his face was all hollows and cheekbone. Across his chin, a prominent hourglass pattern disrupted his beard, scarring from the last time he'd gone below 10,000 feet with a scavenging party. His grin was unbelievable, even frightening, but Cam must not have looked any better because Price lowered his eyes when Cam stepped in front of him.

Cameron Luis Najarro had been below the barrier four times as often and his brown skin was mottled with burn blisters. His eyebrow and left nostril. Both hands. Both feet. He kept his coarse black hair at shoulder length to cover a badly disfigured ear.

"One fire," Cam said. "One fire's plenty, and make it smaller. Where the hell are we going to get more wood?"

"He must have a way to protect us!" Price glanced at his hut mates, chopping his hand through the air again, and some of them nodded and mumbled. Some of them had been listening to his pompous crap all winter.

"Don't be stupid. If he did, he'd camp for the night instead of risking a broken leg. Remember what Colorado said."

"That was five months ago!"

Sawyer moved closer, both arms tight by his sides, his chin tucked down into his chest. "We can't afford the wood," he said.

Price didn't even look at him. He had never understood Sawyer's body language, so much more subtle than his own. Facing Cam, Price made a wagging, dismissive gesture and said, "You tell your little bed buddy—"

Sawyer decked him, one jab sideways across that big mouth. Price fell in a heap and fumbled his soup bowl, throwing orange meteors over his head. He scrabbled and kicked in the dirt as Sawyer paced forward, stiff, deliberate. Then Lorraine lurched between them, keening deep in her throat, spreading her arms wide in a very Price-like gesture.

"One fire," Cam said. "Please."

A few of them went back into their cabin. Everyone else pressed tight around the bonfire, roasting themselves, blocking the light. Sawyer was obvious about staring at Price over the yellow flames, and Cam almost said something but didn't want to embarrass his friend. He and Sawyer hardly talked to each other anymore outside their hut unless Erin was with them—and he was sick of playing peacemaker.

Across the valley, the other fires were put out.

"They don't have forests to burn either," Sawyer announced with mean satisfaction, but Cam felt a spike of disappointment, misplaced fear. It was as if the dark of the valley lunged up like a wave and smothered those people.

After the last of their batteries had died, after they'd lost the calm, redundant, twenty-four-hour military broadcasts out of Colorado and the underground shelters near Los Angeles, there had been two suicides. Almost 10 percent of their population. Both women, of which there were only six left.

Cam had no idea how many people survived across the valley or how bad winter had hit them—nothing except that they were there. Cam's group had never possessed binoculars or a real radio, just a glossy red CD boom box. He'd tried faking Morse code with a pocket mirror and reflected sunlight, thinking they could teach each other, but even if communication had been possible there was nothing the other survivors could do for them except say hello. Nothing except keep them sane.

Isolation cinched tighter around their hearts every hour, and they had become as much of a threat to themselves as their environment was, contorted by despair, strain, and mistrust. Ferocious hunger and guilt.

Maybe they were all poisoned by the same thought. Sawyer said, "I wonder what they've been eating."

Jorgensen was easy. That gimp leg made him totally useless. He'd crashed down a stairwell while they were scavenging insulation and more nails from the ski resort lodge, clumsy with exhaustion. They'd been rushing nonstop for days because the first snow came early. They could have just left him there but chose to be heroes, dropping most of what they'd collected and hauling him back instead. Cam didn't remember even discussing it, which was strange and awful and hilarious, considering what they did to him six weeks later.

But they needed to be heroes.

Every person on this mountain had left family and friends behind in the first mad scramble to get above the invisible sea of nanotech.

The flashlight vanished into thatches of whitebark pine, too small to be considered forest, then soon reemerged. Plant life thinned dramatically well below their peak, reduced in clearly visible bands from trees to brush to hardy little flowering weeds. Not enough air, water, or soil. The few pines and firs scattered above the timberline were nearly indistinguishable, all of them bent, pretzeled, abused by wind and snow.

The jouncing beam of light disappeared again behind a rise in the land. A minute passed. Five. Cam had hiked through there repeatedly and tried to picture it in his head. No sheer drainages, no slides, nothing to delay the man.

Sawyer said, "He's slowing down."

"Come on." Cam moved into the night with his friend, and Jim Price muttered something. A few people laughed. Sawyer stopped, looked back. But Cam slapped at Sawyer's shoulder and Manny had left the fire to tag along, and that seemed enough to get Sawyer walking again.

The three of them ventured down a wide, shallow ravine that formed a natural funnel to their peak and was the easiest access through a series of granite ledges and crumbling ridgelines of old basaltic lava. Picking confidently through the rocks and packed earth, Cam felt as if he'd physically *evolved*. Sweeping his eyes left and right to make the most of his peripheral vision, he smashed his toes only once.

A chipmunk piped and they all froze, listening. The rare sound wasn't repeated.

The grasshoppers sang and sang and sang.

They found seats at the base of a ragged pinnacle of lava they thought they'd identified on their best topo map, marked at 10,200 feet. Normal fluctuations in atmospheric pressure meant the barrier shifted daily, hourly, and it was only smart to minimize their exposure.

Cam said, "Maybe he does have some way to stop it."

"You don't make nano-keys out of dirt." Sawyer rarely spoke of who he had been, who and what he'd lost, but he'd argued like an engineer when they were building their huts, pointing out drainage and foundation problems. "Even if there was someone over there who knew what they were doing, I seriously doubt they have any real equipment."

"Maybe they brought it up in the beginning."

"If he had a defensive nano that worked like antibodies in individual people, he would've stopped for the night like you said. And the only other option is to go on offense, build a hunter-killer that'd go out in the world and eat all of the little fuckers that have been eating us."

Cam turned from the dark slope downhill to look at him.

Sawyer was staring at the ground instead of searching below. He said, "This crazy son of a bitch wouldn't have to carry a weapon like that over here, he'd just release it."

Manny stood up. "There he is."

A ray of light burst over round boulders and skeletal brush no more than two hundred yards away.

"Heyyy!" Manny screamed. "Heyyyyyy!"

The grasshoppers quit for one instant, then started up again in full chorus. *Ree ree ree ree.* The mindless noise seemed to synchronize with Cam's heartbeat and interrupted his thoughts. The bugs were like a sea of their own, rising higher every day, triumphant, unstoppable.

Manny danced, all his weight on his good foot. "Hey! Hey!" The kid windmilled his arms as if to break apart the darkness.

"Here, *over here*!" Cam hadn't intended to start yelling himself, but his breath went out of him in a rush. Blinking back tears made his eyes sting and he half choked as he whirled on Sawyer. "You said SCUBA gear might protect somebody."

"Right." The long shadow of Sawyer's face split with a grin. "There's lots of dive shops on mountains."

"I just meant . . ." Cam turned downslope again to hide his face as one fat drop squeezed free, streaking his skin with cold before sifting into his beard. "Maybe they have bottled air like medical supplies, that could work."

"Right. Except for your eyes. Open wounds. Bug bites."

Cam involuntarily touched the still-healing burn blisters on his nose. His body itched with a hundred minor scratches, especially his hands.

Every cut, every breath, was a doorway.

"It doesn't matter," Sawyer said. "Even if he was driving a limousine up here with enough air for everyone, that wouldn't solve anything."

Of the few known facts, it was certain that the machine plague first got loose in northern California—San Jose, Cal Berkeley, someone's garage—and there hadn't been time for much warning. Otherwise their desolate peak might have been very, very crowded.

Last they'd heard, Colorado was dealing with 14 million refugees, food riots, and a rogue element of Air Force recruits carrying automatic weapons.

Colorado should pull through. The Rocky Mountains offered hundreds of square miles at safe altitude, a few towns, ranches, ski villages, National Park structures. Several areas still had power jury-rigged from hydroelectric plants, and just below the barrier were dozens of towns and even small cities for easy scavenging. Similar high country like the Alps and Andes would keep the human race alive.

A future existed. Cam just hadn't believed he would be part of it. Unless their group had incredible luck hunting throughout the summer and fall, he and Sawyer had calculated that the only way they'd survive another winter would be to dismantle the other hut for fuel and kill and freeze most of the others immediately after the first snow.

2

Cam heard the newcomer breathing about the same time that his crunching footsteps reached them. The man sounded like a tortured wolf. They huddled together like children. Not even Manny shouted, and Cam realized that the grasshoppers had fallen silent again.

The newcomer almost marched through them.

His light stabbed into Cam's eyes, diamond hard— Then he stopped, panting, sinking to one knee. He clawed at his face, at the bandanna and ski goggles over his mouth and eyes.

"Please water," he gasped.

They swarmed him, babbling, helping him to his feet, hauling him up toward the fire. Cam got the flashlight, a smooth weighty rod, the metal hot where the newcomer's hand had been. It felt like magic, like strength. Cam noticed that the man wore a ludicrous pink parka lined with fur and a little fanny pack, like he was some rich old lady out for a stroll. Had he chosen it for its visibility or were the people across the valley short on decent winter gear?

"Water," he said again, but they'd brought none. Stupid. Spasms hit the man before they reached the fire and he fought them, moaning, trying to get at his pants. They didn't understand and he shit himself bloody.

Manny cried out—"Aaah!"—a sharp noise like a bird in a net. Cam met Sawyer's glinting eyes in the dark. Until the man exhibited symptoms, it had been possible to hope that he really was bringing them doses of a new-generation nano that would serve as a vaccine, protecting their bodies from within, despite his crude armor of goggles and mask. But he was infected.

They knew only what they'd heard from Colorado and what they'd experienced themselves. Sawyer theorized that the nanotech had been a prototype of a medical nature, so obviously made to work inside a body, while others insisted it must be a weapon.

It didn't matter.

The important thing was that the nanos burned out at high altitude, because of a design error or an intentionally engineered hypobaric fuse.

It didn't matter.

The microscopic machines were carbon-based and disassembled warm-blooded tissue to make more of themselves.

Like a super virus, they spread both by bodily fluids and through the air. Like spores, they seemed capable of hibernating outside a host anywhere except in thin atmosphere. And this machine plague had multiplied exponentially until most of the planet was barren of mammals and birds.

Inhaled by a human or animal, inert nanos passed into the bloodstream before reawakening and tended to cluster in the extremities. If they gained entry to a body through breaks in the skin, such infections usually remained localized—but only at first. Even the tiniest contamination multiplied and spread and multiplied again. Again and again. The body would heal if it didn't sustain too much damage, which meant they'd been able to dip into the invisible sea and raid the nearby resort as well as a village of cabins and condos farther down the valley. But if you got too weak, you couldn't make it back up.

Almost as bad, the transition to safe altitude shocked an already-exhausted body with cramps, nausea, migraines, even hemorrhaging and diarrhea, as hundreds of thousands or millions of dead nanos clogged the bloodstream. Cam had seen one woman drop stone dead of a stroke; three cardiac arrests; an exploded retina; and he had never known anyone to stay below the barrier longer than six hours.

The newcomer must have been beneath 10,000 feet for most of a day, running and climbing. He seemed now almost to lose consciousness, his boots dragging as they carried him.

He had been eating well. He was soft in places that they were only hip bones or ribs.

In the sharp white beam of the flashlight, Cam saw blisters peppered over the man's neck and hands, oozing blood and worse. A sudden phantom of ash sloughed off into Cam's face. Maybe he imagined it. Unfortunately their level of medical ability was pathetic. They no longer possessed even basics like disinfectant or aspirin. Cam had full EMT training, a requirement for all ski patrol, and during the slow winter he'd taught everyone interested—but none of them were up to cutting somebody open to stop internal hemorrhaging. If the newcomer was that bad off, his survival would be a roll of the dice.

Cam hoped the man would live long enough to say why he'd come. He deserved at least to fulfill his mission.

Near the fire the others got in the way, crowding around, Price shouting a formal greeting that he'd obviously rehearsed. "All this time we've been alone! All this time we've waited!" The noisy idiot had been a real estate developer with several rental properties in the area, and if he excelled at anything, it was making presentations.

"Let the man rest," Cam said, and Price immediately took the newcomer's elbow and pulled on him.

"Yes," Price said. "Yes, you can have my bed!"

It made sense, their hut was nearest, but Cam didn't trust Price not to use the situation to his advantage. To make it political. Manny had clearly come to alert Sawyer and Cam on his own rather than being told to do so. They might still be asleep if the kid hadn't had to move out of their hut after bickering with his bedmates all winter—and not for the first time, Cam was glad to have a spy in Price's camp.

He followed everyone to the low door, and Sawyer growled, "Want to crowd in with them?"

"No. That guy's going to sleep forever."

Sawyer bobbed his head once and Cam was struck again by his friend's resemblance to a bullet. Even Manny had more of a beard now that Sawyer had grown obsessive about shaving, nicking his long cheeks with blunt old razors and a knife honed on granite, scraping his prematurely receding hair down to black sandpaper. Cam thought this was wildly fatalistic behavior for someone so intelligent about the ways that nanos got into the body.

He tried to smile. "Let's go warm up, okay?"

Sawyer stared at him, maybe angry, then glanced left and right to see if anyone else had heard.

He didn't try to catch up with Sawyer in the cold moonscape between the huts. Dumb way to break an ankle.

There was nothing he could say to change things anyway.

Sawyer paused at the door, his face turned up, and Cam spotted the pale dot of a satellite cruising across the rash of stars. He looked away.

The walls of their hut were thick patchwork, like a boys' fort. They'd had only hammers and two heavy-duty Forest Service chain saws to work with. Yet it had withstood the weight of the snow, the force of the wind. The raised cover they'd designed for the hole in the roof functioned well, keeping their fire dry while allowing at least some of the smoke to escape. Cam had regarded their accomplishment with fierce pride for all of one week before claustrophobia eroded that good feeling.

Half a dozen voices protested as he and Sawyer pushed into the reeking gloom. Barely twenty feet by ten, most of the space was occupied by four wide beds: flat wood frames softened with blankets. Crammed into the remaining area were two holes in the ground used for food storage, a rock fire pit, a woodpile, a pee pot, water containers, backpacks, and half-built box traps and other gear—and eight more unwashed people.

Erin was awake and murmured, "I'm freezing," but Sawyer stamped over to the fire and left her to Cam.

He reveled in the distraction.

They feasted on their own pungent body heat, moving slow to keep the thin, filthy covers airtight, teasing each other into a well-practiced frenzy. Her first. His rough fingers. Her bottom lifted off the hard bed as she rocked her pelvis up, up. Then she drank him, wanting whatever nourishment it was worth. She let him hold her ears and thrust.

They were smarter about pregnancy than most—hands and mouths only. Always only hands and mouths, except for eight times after Sawyer found a partly used box of condoms in a ski locker. They still whispered about those couplings, three heads together, eager, wistful, Erin stretching slick and limber between them.

Yes, sometimes there had been six hands together. A few times. Six hands and nothing more. It was their only escape. Cam's father wouldn't have spoken to him for a thousand years if he found out, but his father was dead. The world was dead. Why should anyone care now?

During the eternity that blizzard winds had forced them inside, however, some of their hut mates hadn't kept their eyes to themselves, the same dumb assholes who'd been unable to fashion a marriage of their own. Jealousy fueled nasty rumors despite everything that Cam and Sawyer had done for them—

"You're hurting me," Erin said. And smiled.

Once upon a time Erin D. Shifflet-Coombs must have been gorgeous. Her eyes were the color of gems, Anglo sapphires, and Cam fantasized often of what her rear and long thighs had looked like in tennis shorts, expensive skirts, soft rumpled sweats. If the two of them had gone to his parents' home for dinner, his father would have puffed up like a bullfrog and pressed Cam for details all night with hard, manly nudges.

Arturo Najarro had named his sons Charlie—not Carlos—and Tony, Cameron, and Greg. The boys were sixth-generation American and only Mom spoke more Spanish than *mas cervasa*.

Erin had been a college girl, a junior, majoring in business communications at UC Davis and up with five friends for a little weekday snowboarding. Now she refused to cut her hair, insisting that it helped keep her warm, and her face was permanently lost in a sandy blond tangle. Sleeping beside this mane had probably started Sawyer's new shaving habit.

There was no question that the changes in Erin's appearance had contributed to the change in her heart. Her jawline was a ripple of old blisters and her thighs were melted, anorexic. Worse, the smile came at the wrong times.

Over breakfast she actually laughed. "But why?"

Cam had brought her to his favorite cliff, favorite because no one else ever came here; they couldn't stand the view; the town nestled along the creek far below looked too much like their past, a square-cornered grid of color amidst the panorama of dusky forest, black lava formations, and dull granite. Typically the two of them ate with Sawyer but he had never come to bed last night and was gone when they woke.

She said, "If this guy doesn't have some kind of antidote—why would he hike over?" The corner of her mouth curled up. "Do you think they threw him out?"

Cam shook his head. "They wouldn't have used all that wood setting so many fires."

Four ravens circled less than a mile to the south, riding a thermal. He watched to see if they'd dip into the valley or come toward his peak, though they never had much meat on them. The last catch had been scabby, molting, no doubt lured below 10,000 feet on a regular basis by swarms of insects.

What remained of the ecosystem was badly out of whack, with only lizards, snakes, frogs, and fish left to whittle down the surging insect populations. On his most recent trip below the barrier, Cam had glimpsed what looked like threads of smog farther down the valley. Bugs. So far the high altitude had kept biting species away, except fleas, and until recently their scavenging parties down the mountainside had been protected by winter cold. No more.

There wasn't any wind today and the morning sun felt strong enough to bare his skin. The sensation was so clean, so erotic, that goose bumps broke out over Cam's entire chest, which Erin mistook as a reaction to cold. He had to tickle her before she'd even roll back her sleeves. Then she pulled off her shirt without looking to see if anyone else was around, which sent a thin chill through him. The huts offered zero privacy, and she had been having sex with two men for most of a year, but Erin Coombs was never an exhibitionist. In fact, she used to brave the elements she hated so desperately just to avoid peeing in the common pot. *The tinkle*, she said. *Everyone looks.*

It upset him that suddenly she seemed uncaring. Too many of them were less than they had been, numbed by experience. Cam felt more attuned to his surroundings and to himself than ever before. He felt raw and aware.

He had grown as pale as a Latino could get, but Erin was pure ivory, except the purplish scars. Cam snuck glances at her body and small breasts as they shared a sticky mush of bone meal, bitter lichen, and gritty specks of the rock from which the orange fungus had been scraped.

When he jammed his bad tooth she kissed him and kissed him, skin on warm skin. It was as good a moment as they'd ever had.

He kept one arm tight around her shoulders as he studied the opposite peak. She watched his face. Finally she gestured across the valley and said, "Take me with you."

3

The newcomer told them his name was Hollywood and only Price had something to say about that: "Oh yeah, I knew people there!"

Cam thought Hollywood frowned. Tough to say. The young man had been partially eaten alive from the inside, and wet agony drew his expression in too many different directions. Blotches and rash had sprouted over his temple. Adding to the deformation were swelling bug bites, including three disgusting, whitened clusters on his neck and cheek. Cam tried to imagine how many hundreds of insects it took to inflict such damage.

"I'm here to bring you all across," Hollywood said. The hut stayed silent. He frowned again, gazing up from his bed at their crowded faces. Barely nineteen years old, in good shape, he was Japanese, black-eyed, black-haired—and pure surfer-boy California, drawling his vowels, tipping his chin up to emphasize every pause in his speech.

Cam couldn't help but think of his brothers, dark-skinned yet no different than the Joneses next door. Here on the Coast, a great nation had truly worked as a melting pot, many cultures blended into one by unprecedented freedom and wealth.

"I mean across the valley," Hollywood explained. "We've got a doctor, some farming stuff. And like, way more space."

Erin said, "Why?"

"Just lucky." He had a brave grin.

"I mean, why do you care so much you'd risk your life?"

He had a deliberate shrug, too, though the motion made him wince. He must have pictured this scene over and over in his mind. "We couldn't just leave you here."

Sawyer said, "Is there a two-way radio?"

Cam glanced around, surprised. That was a question he'd expected from Price. What did it matter? Colorado wouldn't send a plane even if there was somewhere to land.

Hollywood nodded. "Yeah. Shortwave."

"CB or ham?"

"Ham, I think."

"How many of you are there?" Sawyer continued, too quietly, and Cam decided that the radio questions had been an attempt to disguise his real intent. Cam tried to signal him but Sawyer seemed blind to everything except Hollywood's expression.

"Nine," Hollywood said, "including me."

Less than us.

Sawyer couldn't leave it alone. "You have food? Houses?"

"There's a cabin with like an apartment in back and a big propane tank. It got us through winter. And we want to grow as much food as we can, you know, that's why we need your help. There's only four other grown-ups."

Sawyer's hand twitched, closed shut.

"Actually we're totally impressed you guys made it, stuck over here on this little peak. You must have raided down below the barrier all the time, huh?"

Too many faces turned away and Hollywood's gaze shifted over them, worried, wondering.

Cam said, "Yeah, we're pretty tough."

Hollywood grinned again. "We couldn't just leave you here."

* * *

After Jorgensen they murdered Loomas—Chad or Chuck or whatever Loomas, sales manager, hairy-chested like a dog with a fat platinum ring on his fat finger. Cam distracted the lazy *hijo de puta* with a shout as Sawyer rushed up from behind and put a hammer in his skull. Loomas whined, down on all fours. Always whining. Cam hurt his foot and both shins kicking the man until Sawyer pushed him back and finished it.

Carving the body was much harder. Their new wealth had to be set aside, portioned out exactingly. Sweet fat and salt.

Jim Price was next on Sawyer's list, but Cam hoped to avoid a war. No one liked Loomas, whereas Price was undisputed leader of the largest faction on the mountain, even loved by a few. So they were trying to invent a fair, random lottery that they could secretly control when the last of the batteries died and Nancy McSomething cut herself from wrists to elbows.

Then Mrs. Lewelling jumped off of Cam's cliff. Maybe she thought they wouldn't be able to reach her.

Something inside Pete Czujko burst on the way back up from a scavenging trip, fighting knee-deep drifts of powder. He bled out over eight long days, watching them, the knowing fear in his eyes gradually dulling.

Timmerman died of pneumonia.

And after a worthless expedition through cabins they'd already picked clean, Ellen Gentry keeled over within seconds of hitting safe altitude. A stroke, they thought. *A stroke of luck*, Sawyer said, laughing and laughing.

Seven bodies were enough meat to get them through.

"What if it's a trap?" Sawyer walked up behind Cam, glancing at the ragged skyline to the north.

"So you are talking to me." Cam's first instinct was to disguise his relief, curious, and he regretted the joke immediately. Lately Sawyer had been hearing double entendres in everything and it was stupid to antagonize him. Stupid to have to apologize. Stupid waste of energy.

Cam turned back to his work, breaking the frozen crust of a snowbank with a telemark ski—a surprisingly functional tool.

Sawyer took another step as if he intended to keep walking. But he was trying to catch Cam's eye. "This guy could be lying," he said. "What if the people over there are having themselves a cattle drive?"

Cam regarded the virgin snow beneath the deep, broken skin of dirty ice. It was like a metaphor for something that he was too tired to realize. Yet the snow was not as pure as it appeared, compressed by melt and gravity, and he jabbed the ski down again.

"Think about it." Sawyer knelt beside him and they shoved loose hunks onto the blanket that Cam was using in place of a wheelbarrow. "We get there too weak to stand. Even if there are only four adults, they bash us all in the head."

"No."

"Maybe keep a couple women."

Cam looked left and right. Broken rocks against the pale sky. Price had delegated six people to help him but they were hauling small blanketloads to the reservoir, a natural pocket in a bed of lava that they'd built up on one side. Much closer, Erin basked on a stretch of sun-warmed granite, having complained of light-headedness.

Cam kept his eyes on her, kept his voice down. "No. No way they're planning something like that. Too risky. Too much work. Hollywood barely even made it across."

"But he did."

"Some of us won't."

"Right. Better for you and me if they don't." Sawyer was casual, picking up two corners of the blanket and motioning for Cam to do the same. "We're going whether it's a trap or not. I just need you to be ready for it."

"The only reason to send him over is if they really do need help trying to rebuild."

Sawyer shook his head once.

"If," Cam said, but the thought was too ugly to articulate.

If they did make it, what sort of future would they create? Murderers and cannibals. Were they worth Hollywood's sacrifice or better left to die here?

Albert Wilson Sawyer could be as selfish as a rat, violent if he perceived a threat—all of which made him the perfect survivor. Sawyer's will and intelligence had kept them alive through the harshest conditions. The chance to partner with him had proved extremely fortunate. The loyalty Cam felt for his friend had become reflex, and yet Sawyer's strength would be a crucial weakness if he was unable to stop striving, stop fighting, creating threats that hadn't existed until he imagined them.

Cam glanced toward Erin again and beyond her, across the valley. A profound and dangerous sadness had settled over him and he almost told Sawyer how much he regretted what they'd become.

The end of the world was buried on page four of the *Sacramento Bee*. Cam wouldn't have noticed except that his buddy Matt Hutchinson was a politics junkie. Two years of college had done something to the dude's brain. Hutch watched shows like *Crossfire* and *60 Minutes* and always had a new outrage to talk about, a web site he'd discovered, a magazine article he'd folded into his pocket and insisted on sharing. Peculiar behavior for a ski bum. There were many reasons people moved to the Bear Summit area, but a strong connection with the machinations of the twenty-first century wasn't one of them.

The place was nowhere. In winter the permanent population barely topped four hundred, another thousand or more vacationers fluctuating through each week, mostly Saturday–Sunday. Come summer that resident population dropped to four dozen. The nightlife consisted of a pizza place with no liquor license, one bar with one pool table, and a corner room of the only gas station with six arcade games from 1997. The cable went out regularly, sometimes the electricity and phones, too, and at least once each winter the roads closed.

Cam humored Hutch because watching his friend get worked up was always a good time. The guy actually talked back at the yammerheads on his shows. Cam preferred sports. Every day, everywhere, everybody seemed to be bombing and raping each other and poisoning the water and ripping up forests in city-sized hunks. It was depressing.

He figured he was in for more of the same when Hutch whacked him with a rolled copy of the *Bee* in the cluttered ski patrol HQ and said, "Have you heard about this shit?"

"Oh yeah, Hutch, the mind boggles."

"You don't even know what I'm talking about."

So he skimmed most of the first few paragraphs while he buckled his boots, the paper spread on the bench beside him. Four fatalities in Emeryville and Berkeley, four others sick, possibly more; whatever was killing them had first been misdiagnosed as a voracious bacterial infection— But then Bobby Jaeger planted his butt right smack on top of the paper to futz with his own boots, and Cam punched him and they both laughed. Then Bobby took off before Hutch could corner him too.

Cam also stood up. He didn't like to be late for First Walk, as they called it at this resort. Once all of the poles and markers in his section had checked out, he was free to sneak in a run or two before the chairlifts opened to the public. The mountain was an intriguing combination of wide-open views and secret thickets and gullies, and sometimes the new sun was so bright, the quiet so crisp, that he felt like a kid again.

Cameron Najarro wasn't carrying any crosses to speak of. Money was a minor issue and he hadn't been laid in eight months and Mom always made him feel crappy for living so far away when they talked on the phone, but like all true athletes, he found it good to lose himself. No experience surpassed that of the animal mind, of being muscle and only muscle. Snaking through trees in fresh powder, charging down a mogul field— he cherished speed and balance and mental clarity.

He was twenty-three years old.

"Hutch, dude, sometimes you're such a buzz-kill," he said as they clumped down a narrow hallway to the ski racks.

"So what do you think?"

"I think you're totally morbid, man. It's a beautiful morning, let's enjoy it before the storm hits and we're stuck digging out the kiddie slopes." The snow had been superb all through March, and the forecast was two more feet starting that afternoon.

"No, really," Hutch said. "Remember that meningitis scare a few years back? All our tax money spent screening for anthrax?"

Cam shrugged. Tabitha Doyle was crouched at the base of the racks, thumbing the edges of her new Dynastars, and he wanted to have a smile ready when she looked up. He knew his chances were marginal. Among the locals, guys outnumbered women more than three to one and there were plenty of better-looking faces than his own. And Tabby had just gotten out of a relationship. And of course Cam was the token colored boy on the crew, which wasn't saying much, but skiing was a white man's sport and even in his third year at Bear Summit, he still got funny looks. Some women just didn't want to deal with that. Tabby wasn't even pretty, really, her small face dominated by constantly chapped, puffy lips. But it was good to stay in practice.

Hutch kept raving. "Why doesn't the state have a networked medical database, that's what I want to know."

"You guys talking about that epidemic?" Tabby asked.

Cam shrugged again. "Hutch is pretty worked up."

"Hey, me too," she said. "See the news this morning?"

"Just the paper." Hutch had brought it along, like he was going to read his horoscope on the chairlift. "Four dead."

"Thirty-eight," Tabby said.

That afternoon, Army and National Guard units began to enforce biological-warfare protocols across the Bay Area, grounding all flights and closing the freeways, instructing people to stay put, stay inside, windows shut and air-conditioning off. Cam's mother and three brothers and year-old niece Violeta and everyone were inside the vast quarantine area.

He got an open line on his seventh try, lucky seven, and talked with his mom for forty minutes until she made him hang up. She felt perfect, she said. She wanted him to pray for his brothers. She'd been trying to reach them with no success and could see smoke on the horizon and sometimes there were sirens—and the TV had shown maps of the East Bay marked red over Greg's neighborhood in Concord.

Jewish mothers were supposedly the worst, but Cam's mom was an old Spanish Catholic lady and used guilt like a pocketknife. She had a blade for every occasion.

The last time she spoke to her third son, she was gentle.

Jesus had obviously had good reason, she said, for making Cam *mi pajarito vagabundo*—her wandering little bird—and she was glad he'd moved so far away. He had to stay there, because above all it was important to carry on the Najarro family line.

Hutch wanted to drive east down into Nevada, and most people did, but Cam couldn't bring himself to leave his phone. He heard nonexistent rings and even picked it up a few times. And two days later, as containment efforts broke down, rumors spread that the machine plague itself died at high altitudes. Some of the hundreds of sick people who'd dodged the roadblocks had headed for the mountains, and an army pilot had depressurized his plane to knock out an infected trooper who started acting dangerously. Reports conflicted as to what elevation was safe, but nothing could stop the savage exodus that began—nothing except the crowds themselves, hundreds of thousands of civilians and soldiers fighting through each other, through abandoned vehicles and wrecks and shrieking cripples.

Nothing except thirty-plus inches of snow across the Sierra range, by then in its third day of blizzard conditions.

Sawyer began to move, the blanketload of ice and snow between them, but Cam was still staring across the valley and whacked his shin on a rock and stumbled. They looked at each other. Then Sawyer nodded once, as if Cam had spoken. "I want to show you something," Sawyer told him.

"Let's dump this in the reservoir first."

"Now, while no one's here." Sawyer abruptly lowered his end of the blanket to the ground. Cam bent to keep the snow from spilling. Sawyer frowned at him and said, "Why are you even knocking yourself out like this?"

"A few of us will stay."

"Then let them worry about it." Sawyer headed downslope.

Cam followed, glancing at Erin again. She hadn't moved from her warm slab of granite and probably wouldn't for hours if left undisturbed. "We might have to come back to this peak," Cam said. "We might need them later. It's the smart thing to do."

Sawyer just grunted.

Half a minute later Sawyer paused, then moved behind a boulder. Cam turned to see Doug Silverstein trudging along two hundred feet below them. Silverstein was six-four and had been skinny when they first met. Now he was a weird scarecrow, and looked utterly bizarre embracing a stiff, curly cloud of netting ripped from screen doors. Grasshopper hunting. Sawyer let the man hike out of sight before he started off again.

The western end of their high island narrowed into a long, slanting ridge like a diving board. Beyond it, a maze of peaks and valleys tumbled oceanward, falling in elevation until a dinosaur spine of foothills bumped up and formed the horizon. Only the straight lines and switchbacks of the few visible roads gave any sign of the civilization that had once existed in the lowlands, a string of power lines, a far-off radio tower.

The dirt on the ridge had been holed by marmots, large cousins of the ground squirrel, mostly stiff red-brown fur and tail and tough leg muscle, as quick as a wish. All of the burrows that Cam could see appeared abandoned but they'd placed three of their clumsy box-traps in the area anyway. He hadn't been out here for several weeks because Manny took genuine pleasure in being in charge and because they didn't want to scare the marmots off with too much foot traffic. He hoped Sawyer wanted to show him fresh spoor or new digging or signs of young—or, more likely, some proof of total extinction, given Sawyer's mood.

Cam smelled sage and pine pollen. He turned his face into

the wind, then noticed the discoloration across the valley to the south. "Jesus Christ. Is that what you wanted me to see?"

Sawyer looked back, confusion evident on his face. Cam gestured and Sawyer cast one short glance.

Random patches of brittle dead brown and gray marked the evergreen forest below, huge patches, each more than a mile wide. Cam tried to make sense of the scale, his thoughts confused by a cold surge of fear. *All this struggle for nothing—* "Are the nanos doing that?"

"Beetles. Maybe termites." Sawyer shook his head. "If the nanos were self-improving to the point that they'd learned to disassemble wood, they'd have come up over this mountain by now. Let's move."

Cam took two steps, slow and careful, unable to look away.

Eventually erosion and landslides would wipe out any trees the bugs had missed. Eventually that valley would become a sterile mud pit. Eventually . . .

He marched after Sawyer. In twenty yards they'd reach the limit of their world. Seemingly at random, Sawyer stopped. Then Cam saw that he'd laid his hand over a milky vein of quartz. Sawyer measured out three paces, then glanced back upslope before kneeling at a rock. An ordinary stone. From beneath it he pulled a package wrapped tightly in black plastic.

Cam's first thought was *food*. His second was to be glad, grateful. Guilt arrived late and he also looked back upslope, thinking of Erin, of possible witnesses, of salted Spam or rich and gooey beef stew. He closed his eyes to the Christmas promise of rustling, opening—

Sawyer had a revolver.

Jim Price was loud like always. "Colorado said they almost had a cure! Them and the space station! They were very close!"

Cam surveyed the crowd of faces, twenty-two in all. Their entire population had gathered here in the dusty flat outside Price's hut, even Hollywood, who rested against the wall in a cocoon of blankets. But everyone looked identical. Long months of deprivation had imprinted each face with a death mask.

Body language had become the best indicator of what someone was thinking—body language, and position. Price's supporters had gathered tightly around and behind him, making what could have been a circle into a teardrop shape.

It was interesting that they stood opposite Hollywood.

Price flapped his arms. "A cure could come anytime now! Colorado has universities, military, and the astronauts are—"

"Don't hold your breath." Hollywood spoke no louder than the breeze, tired, maybe bored. His uncharacteristic lack of enthusiasm made it clear to Cam that he'd been repeating this argument all afternoon. "The broadcasts out of Colorado are saying the same thing you heard five months ago. Like they need a little more time. Like they need more samples."

"We're still better off waiting!"

"Could be forever."

Along with two couples and several loners, Cam, Erin, and Sawyer made up the fringe of the gathering, Manny hovering nearby. Most or all of these people would go, Cam thought. In comparison to the rigid, defensive stance of Price's group, their postures seemed more natural.

That this was a minority shouldn't have surprised him.

McCraney had busted his glasses nine weeks ago and would need a hand-holder, because the best replacement they'd found barely let him see ten feet. George Waxman had lost an eye to the nanos last fall and refused to venture below the barrier since. Sue Spangler was six months pregnant, big now, too big to make it even if she'd wanted to take the risk—and her lover, Bill Faulk, had good reason to stay. Same for Amy Wong and Al Pendergraff and their infant son, Summer.

Standing beside Price, Lorraine directed a burst of words toward her own faction rather than the group at large. "We'll never make it across the valley. Look at him, he barely got here and he's not half-starved!"

Cam said, slowly, "There's nothing on this peak for us. Not a group this size. Not more than a few people."

"Let 'em stay," Sawyer muttered.

"Hollywood needs at least a couple weeks' rest before we go. We can strengthen up, eat most of our supplies."

"No," McCraney said.

"We need those rations!" Price took one melodramatic step forward and Faulk and Doug Silverstein moved to back him.

Emotion wrenched through all the impassive faces, ugly, urgent. Waxman and one of the loners backed off quick, but Cam strode into the center of the gathering, strong with adrenaline.

He was never more aware of the difference between his skin color and all of theirs than in moments like this—it actually seemed to have weight, especially on his face, his broad cheekbones—and he wondered fleetingly what showed in his expression. If they would misinterpret his fear.

"Listen to me," he said.

I found it in that luxury cabin with the deck overlooking the river, Sawyer had told him. *Remember that?* The place was a goddamn paradise, twenty feet of sofa cocked around a stone fireplace, double-pane glass, a giant oven, and two water heaters fed by propane tanks. They'd stumbled through jamming ski gear and canned goods into already-heavy backpacks, blotting the polished oak cabinets with flecks of skin and red fingerprints. *Things were getting tight*, Sawyer said. *That fuck Loomas had started hoarding food, Price was talking about elections again. I figured a .38 and two boxes of shells might be more help than a few extra packets of Saltines.*

"There is nothing here for us." Cam kept his voice soft and level. "We've barely lasted this long. You know that. Trying for the next peak is a gamble, but it's our only choice."

Price jabbed his index finger at them. "You can leave, we won't stop you! But you can't eat all the food!"

Cam wanted to hate him. It would have been easier. Yet these were good people, mostly, the cream of the crop by definition. Fighters. He had bled with them, shared utensils and huddled for warmth with them. Their sins were the same. So it was right to try to save them.

It was a way to save himself.

Cam needed to balance all of the wrong that he had done. If he could start over, live better, he might have some chance at forgetting everything that had happened up here against the cold, open sky.

But Price looked over his shoulder to face his own faction, exactly as Lorraine had done. "Nobody is eating more than their regular rations!" he shouted.

Another of the loners, Bacchetti, stepped to Cam's side before even Sawyer or Manny. "Our food," Bacchetti said, grungy teeth flashing through his mess of beard. Cam hadn't heard the man speak in days, had long since written him off, and now his heart leapt with strange pride.

It was a weakness, a distraction.

Price kept yelling. "That food belongs to everyone!"

"Right!" Sawyer was just as loud. "Bacchetti and me and these guys have been killing ourselves hauling supplies up this mountain. We deserve to eat heavy."

"Vote! Let's vote!"

"We're eating heavy, Price." Sawyer shifted his weight forward and Doug Silverstein bent his tall frame in response—

Cam pushed between them with his hands out. Silverstein gave way but Sawyer was unyielding and Cam shoved him, frantic, swiping his fingertips down Sawyer's chest. He could not feel the gun under Sawyer's clothes.

Price's breath smelled of bitter stomach acids, but Cam leaned closer and said, "Come with us, Jim."

"Let 'em stay," Sawyer growled again.

"We can make it," Cam insisted. "Hollywood's already scouted out the easiest trail. It will take us less time than he needed. Okay? There are always a few rain showers up here in springtime. We'll wait until then."

Low-pressure systems had pushed the nanos down almost a thousand feet by Sawyer's estimation, and they'd always gone scavenging during the worst weather. The dangers of hurrying over ice and slick rock in darkness and cold, the possibility of avalanches, of getting lost—it was all worth reducing their exposure.

"We have to do this," Cam said. "Don't you get it? If more than four or five people stay here, you'll be eating each other by December."

4

Ruth spent her time at the window, day after day, hours at a stretch. Commander Ulinov had ordered her to stop, had pleaded and even joked with her, his attitudes shifting as smoothly as the cloud masses wrapped around the blue Earth below, but the International Space Station was a narrow, sterile world. Ruth needed more room to think.

Besides, making each other crazy was about the only fun available to them.

The lab module had a viewport only because its designers intended to conduct free-space fluids and materials tests, and Ruth had long since retracted the twin waldos bracketing the window to improve her view. No one was interested in pure science anymore.

Prehistoric darkness blanketed the nightside of the planet. Ruth watched patiently, dreaming. Sunrise still enthralled her, although from low-Earth orbit it came every ninety minutes. Each new dawn reminded her of inspiration.

"Dr. Goldman!"

She flinched as Ulinov's voice boomed through the lab. Lately he'd taken to surprising her—not difficult when he could float noiselessly through the neck connecting this module to the main station—the same way her step-dad had attempted to retrain his terrier after Curls began eating the couch. Shock treatment. Lord knew her reaction was irrational but Ruth found herself behaving exactly like that dumb dog, making a contest of it, and she no longer doubted that Ulinov was also playing this small game. The amount of time he spent tormenting her was too great. Their sparring had become the careful flirtation of commander and subordinate, skirting iron-fast rules against fraternization, and the attraction must have been more difficult for him because of his reluctance to undermine his own authority.

They were hard on each other, strong for each other, and it was wonderful to have any chance to feel amused. Ruth kept her face turned toward the viewport, baiting him.

"What can you be thinking?" Ulinov demanded. "What haven't you seen through that hole a million times before?"

The interior of the lab module would have been impassable in gravity. Her gear extended in bulky towers from three of the cube's six surfaces, bolted down between the original equipment and computers. It was a monochromatic jumble— off-white walls, gray metal panels. He expertly threaded his way toward her and touched his foot against the ceiling to correct his spin.

Commander Nikola Ulinov was large for a cosmonaut, his rib cage wide enough to hold two of Ruth, and his square face had spread to epic proportions due to the redistribution of body fluids that occurred in zero gee. He apparently thought his size gave him a psychological edge and often crowded her, like now.

His odor was how Ruth remembered Earth, a full and textured smell. Good, real. Inviting. She finally glanced at him, wondering why he still bothered to act the gruff Soviet bear.

He seemed to notice and tried a new tone. Truly he was more of a wolf, nimble and cunning. He spoke quietly now: "*Tovarisch*, must I cover this hole? Will I assign someone to watch you? Why are you not understanding the importance?"

The warm spark of mischief in her heart faded. Maybe that was best. "I've done all I can."

"India transmitted new schematics only yesterday—"

"I've done all I can here."

He said nothing. He never did after she insisted she'd been beaten. It was a good trick, letting her stew in her shame and frustration. She used to blurt promises to work harder. Now they hung together in silence.

At last, Ruth risked another look. Ulinov's wide brown eyes were aimed not at her but out the viewport, where a vast corona of yellow-white illuminated the dark curve of the planet.

"The snow's melted enough," she said. "Colorado should be able to clear a stretch of highway for us."

He was gruff again. "There will be no returning to orbit."

Ruth nodded. *Plague Year*, they were calling it now, changing the calendar, changing history, and the decision felt right in so many ways. Everything was dead and new all at the same time. It had been a very different life eleven months ago when she rode the last shuttle launch out of Kennedy Space Center, the final launch. The supply rockets put up by the Europeans a week later didn't count.

"We are remaining as long as we can," Ulinov said. "The president ordered us with good reason."

And you want to stay a part of your war, she thought.

Ulinov's motherland, like so much of the planet, must now be unimaginably empty. The remnants of the Russian people had fled to the Afghanistan mountains and to the Caucasus range, a sheer jag of rock thrust up between the Caspian and Black Seas, where they were entrenched in a confused, ferocious struggle against the native Chechens and refugee hordes out of Turkey, Syria, Saudia Arabia, Jordan, and Iraq. It might have been worse except the Israelis had airlifted south to Africa and the high peaks of Ethiopia.

Peace had at last come to Jerusalem and the Middle East.

The space station still received sporadic broadcasts from the Russian population, demands for orbital surveillance or American military support or, sometimes, wild declarations of bloodthirst directed at their Muslim enemies. Ulinov transmitted high-res photos every day, weather and orbits permitting, and diligently relayed each request for supplies—and he had sworn his allegiance to the United States.

As daylight lanced through the viewport, Ruth touched his shoulder. Foolish. Reaction sent them both drifting slightly. She increased her grip to keep them together. The surface of his jumpsuit was as cold as his self-control, but his gaze flicked to her hand and then roamed her face. His expression softened.

Ruth spoke first. "Zero-gee working conditions aren't an advantage if I don't have what I need. I'm past the limit of what I can achieve with reconstructions. Badly translated reconstructions."

In the rush to get her away ahead of the invisible tide, ground crews had misplaced her samples of the nano. Most likely someone hadn't understood why they were loading human body parts. The machine plague was most easily and safely preserved inside chunks of frozen tissue.

She said, "Colorado's using an old electron probe and India lost a lot of software. The breakdowns they're sending are incomplete."

Ulinov seemed to shake himself, then pulled free from her. "Every time you report progress."

Ruth didn't know what to do with her hand. "Sure. I'm still learning." She gestured at her equipment, then jaunted to the machining atomic force microscope, which had always reminded her of a stout dwarf standing at attention. Its smooth body terminated at what would be the shoulders, where low collars protected a working surface—the broad cone of its "hat" contained computer-enhanced optics and atomic point manipulators. They'd had to install the MAFM sideways across the lab, and Ruth had spent so many hours at the device that she oriented herself alongside it by habit, though doing so meant that she and Ulinov no longer shared a local vertical. Impolite. Ruth barely noticed, staring at the MAFM's blank display grid.

Lord knew it was wrong to admire the genius behind the

nano. This invisible locust had laid waste to nearly 5 billion people and left thousands of animal species extinct.

Plague Year. It wasn't just human history that had crashed. The savage effects to the environment would be centuries or more finding balance again, if that was even possible. In many ways Earth had become a different planet and they were only beginning to see what would happen to the forests, the weather cycle, the atmosphere, the land itself.

"If you are still learning," Ulinov began, trying a new angle with her, but Ruth said, "The design technique is extremely innovative. I could putz around with my models for another five years if you want."

"This is a joke."

"No." She tried to be gentle with the truth. "Colorado's electron probe is barely strong enough to disassemble a nano of two billion AMU, much less reverse-engineer it, and the glitches in India's programs make their schematics almost useless. This machine may be the best equipment left in the world."

"But yet you have stopped your work."

"Uli, I've done all I can here." Ruth had never felt this way toward the same person, real warmth shot through with resentment. It made her nuts. The decision to stay in orbit was not his to make, but Ulinov had always been an outspoken proponent of keeping the ISS crew on-station as long as possible, when he could have added his voice to hers instead.

She understood his position. She respected his commitment and his code of honor, and honestly believed these traits were her own best strengths. It was the basis of their attraction and at the same time it was probably what would keep them apart.

Their little slugfest might have gone on longer except that they'd already been knocking heads for weeks now, ever since the snowpack across the Rockies began to fade.

He left. She kicked back to her window. Watching the patchwork of Earth's surface roll past engaged enough of her brain that she soon reentered a practiced state of meditation, allowing her subconscious to chew over the locust's design. It almost felt as if she was outside on EVA, alone in the vacuum, sketching diagrams like constellations and pacing through those intricate shapes, pulling sections apart for closer examination.

Ruth Ann Goldman hadn't entered the field of nanotechnology because it promised to revolutionize manufacturing, cure all disease, eradicate pollution, and even scrub the sky clean of greenhouse gases, although she'd always dazzled interviewers with such possibilities before the recruiter from the Defense Department came along and she quit publishing. The truth was more basic. Ruth had an IQ of 190 and was easily bored, and developing functional machines on the nanometer scale proved challenging enough that she often forgot herself.

At the turn of the millennium, top researchers had been thrilled merely to push, etch, chemically induce or otherwise manipulate atoms—individually or by the millions—into tubes, wires, sheets and other inanimate forms.

While Ruth was still an undergraduate, sneaking into the lab at night to indent HEY GOOD LOOKIN or ELVIS LIVES onto her colleagues' test surfaces, those first crude tubes and wires were fashioned into processors that would power a hyperquick new generation of computers.

By the time she'd acquired her Ph.D., those new computers and related advances in microscopy had been used to construct actual nano-scale robots, albeit moronic ones capable only of expending energy as they meandered aimlessly in a sterile bath.

The most arrogant scientists and most hysterical pundits had long compared nanotech to playing God, but Ruth found this analogy rather goofy—and ironic, that anyone would confuse an ability to direct change on the molecular level with the capacity to create universes. Nanotech was precisely the opposite, a fine, exacting degree of construction—nothing more.

Ruth chose to focus her efforts on recognition algorithms—brains, essentially. Assembling microscopic robots still posed a catalogue of interesting hurdles, but the groundwork was well established and every Jack and Jill in the world wanted to put together a machine twice as fancy as the next guy's. Ruth didn't see how that mattered. Without direction, the most elaborate robot was only a curiosity, not even usable as a paperweight.

She used her certainty and her considerable powers of sarcasm to obtain grant money and a platoon of grad assistants of her own, then settled in for a lifetime's work.

It helped that she was a patient, obsessive freak whose idea of time off was to wedge herself under the sink in the men's room and wait there in order to scare the bricks out of a rival. She had one affair with a fellow lab rat, more convenience than genuine lust, and banged her stepbrother too at Hanukkah. Meanwhile her efforts earned sixteen patents and ultimately saved her life. She was thirty-five when the man from the Defense Department waltzed through security into her office.

Government operations tended not to be as flashy as private labs, and Ruth was sufficiently self-aware to realize she'd thrived on the attention that came with publishing her accomplishments. It was fun being hot stuff. She also had qualms about working for the military, clichés about destroying rather than creating, but the man from the Defense Department was either a romantic or a well-schooled actor. He envisioned Ruth as a bold and clandestine vanguard, kind of like Batman, equipped with billion-dollar equipment and more computer power than most small nations, poised to counter the attacks and accidents of enemy labs and garage scientists in colossal duels of talent versus talent.

He also offered the chance to craft micro- and zero-gravity experiments at the taxpayers' expense. It had long been theorized that freedom from Earth's pull would benefit nano design, as it had so many structural sciences. Ruth saw a fat opportunity to stay ahead of the pack. *Yes*, she said, and enjoyed five months of incredible resources as well as her first NASA classes before the machine plague erupted in California.

The locust was not military, despite the rumors. Nor did Ruth believe the three or four terrorist fronts who'd claimed responsibility, one of which hastily retracted its statement as the infections spread beyond control. Even if a fringe group possessed the necessary gear and training, the design was far too complex if the goal had been mere devastation.

The locust resembled a long, viral hook rimmed with cilia, rather than taking a more basic spherical or lattice shape—and nearly a third of the locust's capacity remained unused. The machine as they knew it seemed to be only a prototype, with room left for additional programming. The damned thing was biotech, organic, built to fool the human immune system. Also, a weapon would have been created with a life-clock to keep it from proliferating without end. Instead, the locust had a fuse that was as useless as a control outside of lab conditions.

The magic number was 70 percent of a standard atmosphere. At that pressure, locusts self-destructed. Unfortunately, 70 percent of atmosphere occurred at 9,570 feet elevation, and normal changes in air density meant that the locusts routinely functioned as high as 10,000. On August 19th, a pristine and sunny day, Colorado had recorded infestations up to 10,342 feet.

Ruth considered 70 percent to be a somewhat peculiar number. Her guess was that the design team had rounded up from two-thirds to avoid the clumsy math of 66.6 percent—and Lord knew how many lives that had saved. At high altitudes, each percentage point covered a lot of ground. Two-thirds of standard atmosphere would have put the barrier well above 11,000 feet.

It was a small clue to their thinking, part of an overall trend toward brutal efficiency. The locust was brilliant work, representing both conceptual and engineering breakthroughs that exceeded anything Ruth had done to win so many accolades.

She would need to confront the machine plague face-to-face if she was ever going to master its secrets.

5

Mission Specialist Wallace, Bill to his friends, unstrapped from the exercise bike as soon as Ruth entered the med/life sciences node. The timer still showed twenty-seven minutes, but he pushed up from the seat and pulled off the wrist cuff and didn't wipe it clean.

That short rip of Velcro and two chimes from the heart monitor were their only conversation.

The interior of the ISS offered less room than a four-car passenger train, though it was squashed into a maze of separate areas. They never managed to avoid each other completely. Wallace was an ex–Navy defensive back with too much time on his hands, and Ruth found that nothing cleared her head like a good sweat, and exercise aboard the station was limited to the bike and an adjacent pulley system. She might have come here regularly for no other reason except that the drawers and storage units that made up the walls were dotted with red and orange emergency labels, and some of the European medical supply cases secured to the ceiling were hazmat yellow—and in this small, metal world, she was always starved for color.

Bill Wallace was no one's idea of a recruiting poster. He had hair like rust and freckled cheeks pockmarked in adolescence by machine-gun acne, yet he'd been close to breaking the American record for hours in space before their long exile and, like Ruth, kicked ass at his job. He was an entire engineering team unto himself, electrical, mechanical, a fact that had kept him aboard the ISS when three of the seven-member crew were evacuated by the shuttle *Discovery* to extend the available oxygen, water, and food for Ruth's benefit.

He pushed closer without speaking or even bothering to telegraph his intent with a gesture. It didn't matter. They'd performed this dance a hundred times. Ruth moved aside and Wallace rudely bumped past.

She almost hollered right in his ear, anything for a response . . . except she'd learned the hard way that such pranks only deepened his silence.

Ruth jaunted toward the bike. Passing over it, she caught hold by jamming the toes of one foot under the cushioned seat, then used her other foot like a pincher and pulled herself down. Momentum twisted her hips, however, and she whacked her butt on the backrest, ruining what might have been an excellent stunt.

She would miss flying, somersaulting. It was a simple joy laced with many shades of guilt, frolicking during the apocalypse—and she would pay for it. Back on Earth she might be wheelchair-bound for a time. Muscle and bone degeneration were very real threats in zero gravity, and even special diets and nonstop exercise regimens could only slow that process.

She glanced after Wallace before strapping herself down, an uneasy reflex. Silly. He would never hurt her, if only because he'd been ordered to regard her as his superior. All of the astronauts took as much pride in their discipline as she did in her work.

Wallace had actually been among the crew members who volunteered to vacate the station, hoping to rejoin their families, but Control had deemed him too essential to long-term operations. That wasn't the problem. No higher compliment could be paid to a man such as Wallace, and his wife and

daughter had been crammed aboard a Florida National Guard
plane along with other VIPs and made it to Pikes Peak in Colorado, 14,000 feet above sea level. They were presumed dead
in the holocaust that swept the makeshift fuel depots last
spring, yet had still been given a better chance than most.

It was a packet of carrot juice that turned him against her.
The whole thing was incredibly dumb, but they'd all been
packed into this small hell for too long. Ruth could count
more personality conflicts than there were personalities. Astronaut A didn't like the way Astronauts B or C reorganized
supplies, while B had gotten weird about singing country
songs and argued with A, D, and E each time he disturbed
them, and C thought D smelled especially bad and resented A
calling him an idiot, et cetera.

Their day-to-day existence was one of grim stagnation and
Ruth had rigged two juice packets to burst in hope of lighten-
ing the mood, if only for a moment. Planning the trick had
been a delight. Too bad Wallace got both of them. She hadn't
realized carrot was his favorite but he took it personally, and after they vacuumed up the second sticky cloud he'd ripped into
her about safety violations and the possibility of damaged
electronics.

Ruth flinched suddenly when a low thump sounded close
to her and then another, hands or feet against the walls. The
heart monitor blipped in alarm and she twisted, bound by the
bike's Velcro straps.

Derek Mills, *Endeavour*'s pilot, neatly stopped his approach by jamming himself in the passageway with one outstretched hand and one outstretched foot.

Mills should have been good-looking. His brow and jaw
were strong and smooth. But she didn't like his carefully neutral expression or the way that he stole glances at her white
cotton undershirt. Ruth managed to hide her chest with her
elbow as she wiped at her forehead. "What?"

Mills had thought the juice bombs were a riot. He'd flashed
his perfect teeth at all of her jokes, chatting her up at every
chance. He'd even stashed his share of the tubes of chocolate
pudding and brought out these treasures in random moments

for just the two of them—an odd, forced intimacy, taking turns pressing their lips to the same small plastic opening.

He quit being friendly because he was a true believer in the space program, like most of the crew, and Ruth insisted now on grounding them, maybe forever.

"Radio," he said, then turned his back on her.

She passed through a dark, chill section of the ISS and was suddenly aware of an aching throughout her body, a deficiency as real as scurvy. Mills thought this shell was their final glory. Ruth just wanted to see trees and sky again.

Communications was a mess, a nest. Slips of paper torn from logbooks and packaging had been affixed to the walls in uneven groups, inked with names and frequencies and locations from all over the globe. It was a living record of the plague year. Many bits of information had been X'd out, and most of the rest had been altered at least once—and yet no slip of paper was ever taken down.

Ruth squeezed in. Ulinov ordered this passageway cleared almost weekly and had even removed the offending supply cases himself many times, but the blockade always rematerialized. There was just too much extra gear aboard.

She found Gus listening to bursts of static, so loud she didn't say anything. He fingered his control panel with one hand and rubbed at his bald spot with the other, as if he were his own good-luck charm. Then he saw Ruth and waved and shut off the white noise. Apparently he'd been walking through channel after empty channel.

"There you are," he said. "Pop on this headset for me, we're gonna set you up hush-hush, big news maybe, let me get ya dialed in through a satellite relay."

"Hi, Gus."

Communications Officer Gustavo Proano, left aboard to appease the Europeans, was the only crew member who'd grown more free with his thoughts during their endless wait. Force of habit. Trilingual, with a smattering of Farsi and Portuguese and learning more, Gustavo had more friends than anyone else alive, friends all over the world.

Ruth still hadn't figured out his habit of blockading himself in. He was the most gregarious person aboard. Maybe subconsciously he was trying to protect his radios.

He waved again, hurrying her, and jabbered into a microphone too fast for anyone to answer. His English had a pronounced New York accent, but the blabbermouth personality came through in any language, even those where *hello* and *how are you* were his entire repertoire. "Leadville, this is the ISS. Leadville, come back, I gotcha contact waiting."

Ruth clipped on the earpiece and realized her hair was growing long again, starting to curl. Good. An astronaut's buzz cut made her look like a monkey.

"Leadville," Gus said. "Leadville, Leadville . . ."

During the late 1800s, at the height of the Gold Rush, Leadville had been a boomtown of thirty thousand frontiersmen attracted to central Colorado's rich silver mines. In the twenty-first century, shrunk to just 3,000 residents, the modern claim to fame had been that at 10,150 feet elevation it was the highest incorporated "city" in the United States.

Now it was the U.S. capital, and a rough census put the area's population at 650,000.

NORAD command shelters under Cheyenne Mountain had originally housed the president, the surviving members of Congress, and the most prominent men and women in nanotech. The subterranean base sat far below the barrier but was equipped with a self-contained air system to protect against radiation or biowarfare, and most of Ruth's communications had been with NORAD until the locust got loose from a laboratory inside the complex.

"ISS, this is Leadville," drawled an unfamiliar voice, calm in her ear. "Stand by."

Gustavo chattered, "Roger that. You wanna power down?"

"Stand by."

The partial evacuation of the NORAD base had reduced their working capacity by a full order of magnitude, just as the original plague had done. Once there had been more than a thousand researchers nationwide, then hundreds, finally mere dozens—and aside from India and a displaced Japanese team on Mt. McKinley, Alaska, no one else was even trying. Across the Alps, the Germans, French, Italians, and Swiss were embroiled in war with starving refugee populations and each other, lost like the Russians, and the Brazilian scientists in the Andes had stopped broadcasting before the end of the first winter.

Ruth reached for the lists of contacts plastered over the nearest wall but stopped short of disturbing them. So many names and places had been crossed out, she wondered how Gus could stand the constant reminder. Gruesome. Yet clearly something in him was satisfied by surrounding himself with data, and with physical barriers.

"Hey, hello, am I on?" This new voice spoke almost as fast as Gustavo, trained by months of power shortages.

"James," Ruth said. "I hear you."

"I have—"

The other voice on the ground intervened. "This is a secure call, ISS communications. Please clear the channel."

"Roger that." Gustavo turned and winked at her before he swam toward the exit. So far, she'd chosen to share every piece of news with the rest of the crew, classified or not. She felt they deserved it. Why keep secrets anymore? The soldiers down there only bothered because it gave them something to do.

Ruth opened her mouth to speak but there was a low, menacing click. Gus had identified the sound as recording equipment and it raised gooseflesh up the back of her neck.

She yearned for clean air, a horizon, new faces, but felt it would be sinful to envy anyone on the ground. She was among the safest and best-fed members of the human race.

They had been informed that the situation in Colorado was stable, yet Ruth caught hints of a different truth in these conversations—unexplained delays, obvious shortages, names that seemed to have permanently disappeared. She'd tried to chitchat, digging for more, but was usually interrupted and once had been cut off entirely. Power conservation, they said. Other times, the scientists she spoke with deflected her questions or ignored her outright. Why?

If she'd known any of them, if she had any friends there, she might have pressed. But their relationships were as narrow as the thin umbilical connecting her headset to the radio.

James said, "I have good news and I have good news."

"Well I always say hear the good news first." Ruth tried to make her smile show in her voice. Too many of these contacts were litanies of despair.

She had actually met James Hollister at a convention in Philadelphia, years ago, and had a vague image of thick glasses and a great Moby Dick of a desk-belly. Her memory of his published work was stronger. He'd led a new approach in nanobiotic medicine, using synthesized amino acids to pierce bacterial membranes and thereby kill infections. That was a field related to the current problem only in the loosest sense, but James was no dummy and had brought a unique perspective to their efforts to build an anti-nano nano. ANN.

He'd volunteered for this coordinating position to free up others with more appropriate skill sets, and Ruth was glad. She talked to him six times out of ten and no one else made jokes anymore, not even sorry little puns like *good news, good news*.

"We've redesigned our engine," he said, "pushing burn efficiency up almost 5 percent."

"Great." Chemical science was his specialty, after all. "I suppose that's great, James, but what does it matter? We can just enlarge the ANN if we need more capacity."

Silence. Static.

She almost didn't say it. "You're wasting time, getting fancy. We have a functional rep algorithm. We can go as big as we want—5 percent, 10, it doesn't matter. I thought we agreed to focus on discrimination."

"Ruth, we needed something we could point to, something real. LaSalle's bug tested solid and the president's council is talking about reassigning everyone to him."

"What! Did he run real-world or in lab conditions?"

"Lab, if it matters."

"Of course it matters! We test out in controlled conditions, too. What did you tell them?"

"I told them our burn efficiency was up 5 percent."

This time it was Ruth who didn't answer immediately. Then she laughed. "Okay, I guess that is good news."

There had never been a consensus on how to deal with the situation. Everyone wanted to destroy the locust, of course, but at present there were no less than three competing proposals—and twice that many concepts had been discarded in the past months. A shortage of equipment meant much of their work was theoretical anyway, and nanotech developers in any field tended to be both visionaries and a bit wiggy about their favorite ideas. The end of the world hadn't changed that.

The end of everything had probably made it worse. Too much was at stake, and the name of the person who defeated the machine plague might become greater than Muhammad or Christ.

"LaSalle's an idiot," Ruth said, and her earpiece rattled with two thumps, maybe James shrugging.

Or maybe it was whoever else was listening.

She didn't care. She said, "I guess he's still shouting from the rooftops that discrimination is a waste of time?"

"He's got half the council agreeing with him."

"James, there's no way it can work otherwise. He can't ignore the issue just because it's inconvenient."

Any real-world nano had to overcome three major hurdles, and integrating each solution into a functioning whole was in a sense the fourth and most difficult challenge.

First was how to power something so abysmally tiny. Ruth's teachers had called this the Tin Man Problem—if we only had a heart. Dozens of possibilities existed using synthesized fuels, proteins, live current, heat. The trick was to dedicate as little capacity as possible to energy storage and/or generation.

Second came the Scarecrow—if we only had a brain. Nature's oldest, most fundamental intelligence was based on chemical reactions like those of RNA and James's amino acids, simplistic and neat, enough for some biotech, but it was a real chore to bestow the faculties of awareness and decision upon machines this size without crimping their operational speed.

The third problem, known in polite company as the Wicked Witch, was how to create enough nanos to accomplish a goal of any worth. Manually assembling one gear composed of five hundred atoms could take a person sixty hours, depending on the material and equipment used. Automation might accelerate the process but it wasn't economically viable, spending millions of dollars to build factories to build the nanos.

A leading school of thought had been to bed the Scarecrow with the Witch. Nanos capable of fulfilling instructions should also be able to assemble more of themselves. Their function was their form. Once again, the infinitesimal scale had hindered efforts to master this approach, but crude kilo-atom prototypes had been doing it since before Ruth entered college.

No single aspect of the locust was revolutionary. What made it so efficient was how well it had been put together.

For a power source the locust used the body heat of its host, which required only a few receptors at key points in the locust's structure. As for a brain, the locust's creators had overcome this hurdle by dodging it altogether. The machine was remarkably straightforward. It infested warm-blooded tissue because it was unable to function in any other environment, and it assembled more identically limited yet aggressive creatures because it had been told to do so. Period. Everyone agreed that the locust as they knew it was just a test model, and yet Gary LaSalle wanted to adopt this method for his ANN.

What a joke. *Igor, fetch me a brain!* Ruth must have taken her ribbing too far, though, because two months ago LaSalle had quit talking to her on the radio.

He was right that the locust functioned quickly because it lacked complex instructions, but the man was a complete boob if he thought they could sweep the planet clean with an

ANN lacking discrimination. The job was too big, the battle-field too varied. More importantly, out there in the world, below 10,000 feet, the locusts had no more hosts and would be in hibernation. They were inert, inactive targets and even a slowly replicating ANN would eventually destroy the vast majority.

The idea was simple: release their best work, then wait and watch. But who would be the savior?

LaSalle's ANN, more like a chemical reaction than a machine, was composed of oxygen-heavy carbon molecules intended to bond the locusts into nonfunctional, supra-molecular clusters. Fast and dirty. James had helped pioneer the process, "snowflaking," before declaring it unstable—and yet LaSalle's ANN remained the smallest and the quickest to replicate, a fact he'd constantly harped upon when he was still trying to enlist Ruth's help.

Another faction, perhaps the most ambitious, imagined a parasite ANN that would deliver new programming to the locusts, take advantage of the locusts' extra capacity, and turn the damned things against each other. This group was still cranking out diagnostics and computer simulations, however, and no one else believed they'd advance beyond the planning stage.

Ruth belonged to the third team, which consisted mostly of techs with military and government backgrounds like her own. They had constructed a hunter-killer whose entire life cycle was based on disassembling locusts. A true weapon. It would burn a portion of a locust for fuel while using the rest to build more ANN like itself, and this design had been the early front-runner until the president's council grew understandably desperate.

There was one big problem with all three concepts.

In creating more of themselves, locusts pulled both carbon and some iron from the tissue of their hosts; and as a substance, each locust was hardly distinguishable from any other life-form.

One very big problem. ANN designed to target locusts in mass would also attack human and animal cells.

"Show them your figures again," Ruth said. "If LaSalle's bug lumps together every speck of organic carbon in the world, everything else that's happened so far is going to seem like a roller disco in comparison."

"Roller—?"

"We'll all be dead, everywhere."

Her earpiece thumped once more and she wondered if James was smiling, pacing, shaking his head. She wished she could see his face. His voice, like always, conveyed only quiet strength. "The council has a way to protect us from any ANN," he said, "in case something goes wrong. Incorporating the hypobaric fuse into every design is mandatory now, even if that sets everyone back."

"A fuse won't stop LaSalle's bug from affecting plants or insects or whatever else is left below 10,000 feet. Any environmental balance the planet still has will be shot! We need an ANN that can discriminate."

"Actually the other good news is somewhat related."

"What? Then what are you getting me worked up for?" Ruth's grin was real but she forced a laugh for his benefit. "Zap me the file, this is perfect!"

They had the beginnings of a brain. Another member of their group had proposed targeting the hypobaric fuse itself rather than locusts in general, using this unique structure as a marker. Unfortunately, so far their best-developed program was less than 30 percent effective in a pressurized capsule where decoys and debris outnumbered hibernating locusts only two to one.

"It's better than that," James said. "The FBI got a team into Denver. They think they have a new lead."

Ruth flexed her arms and legs, an involuntary surge of excitement. She struck the wall with one knee and set herself rotating, and jammed her palm against her headset to keep it from pulling off. "When? How?"

"They just cleared enough highway to start flying again—"

She nearly interrupted. *How much highway?* The shuttle required more than twice the landing strip of most airplanes.

"—took a group into town and pulled more computers

from the field office there, the public library. They think they have full records on manufacturers' sales now."

Before the plague there had been forty-six university nanotech labs nationwide, seven private groups, and five more working for the government. That number had not included Ruth, or at least two other covert federal operations she was aware of—nor had it included perhaps a dozen independently funded labs who were also keeping their heads down, mining the public data but not sharing their own advances.

Only thirteen companies had manufactured microscopy and nano-fabrication equipment, however, and such big-ticket items hardly sold like the stock shares of those companies.

Even before the locust burst through the quarantine lines around northern California, FBI data crunchers had unearthed two private groups in the region. Agents swept through those labs and the six more operating publicly in the area, confiscating everything, even the few lab techs who could still be found.

Too bad only some of those people reached safe altitude.

Evidence everywhere had been lost or destroyed. No one was even certain that the locust had been built in the Bay Area. It could have gotten loose in transit or during a buy. No one ever came forward to explain. That wasn't a surprise—anyone claiming responsibility would have been lynched—but not a single alarm had been raised even in the first forty-eight hours, when the problem might have been contained.

The general belief was that the locust's design team had died as soon as it got loose . . . and by the reckoning of most survivors, they probably hadn't died slow enough.

There was no punishment hard enough for this crime. No human language even had a word to describe what had happened.

But the goal of the search for the locust's designers, at least in Ruth's mind, had never been revenge. They wanted insight, answers, a key to stopping it.

She said, "Tell me you found the lab." But even James would have been shouting.

"It's just a lead," he said. "Hardware."

"Are they sending someone after it? Where?"

"They're still costing out fuel and bottled air."

"But this could be everything we need! Original schematics, customized gear, even clues to what happened to the design team!"

James didn't reply for several moments, maybe letting her calm down. Maybe wishing, like her, that it could be true. He said, "No one's convinced it's solid information yet."

"Tell me."

"Three years ago Select Atomics delivered a fabrication laser to a Stockton location that can't be accounted for."

Ruth had never been to the West Coast but had grown familiar with the area, at first from watching news coverage, then from interviews with the FBI and NSA. Every survivor associated even vaguely with nanotech, even security guards and janitors, had undergone extensive debriefing as the intelligence agencies combed for potential leads, names, rumors.

Based on the pattern of infections, the authorities' best guess was that the locust's designers had worked in Berkeley or Oakland in the congested urban heart of the region.

"Stockton," Ruth said. "That's east of the Bay Area near Sacramento, right? Near the foothills of the Sierras?"

"I know what you're thinking. But you have to realize—"

"Get a plane out there! As soon as we can."

"Ruth, you have to realize that the laser could have been taken anywhere. Even if they were in Stockton, things got crazy in a hurry. The freeways were traffic jams. Half the city burned. And it was snowing something like two inches an hour everywhere above 6,000 feet."

She shook her head, the earpiece hurting her ear. "The original team might have made it."

"Ruth—"

"Some of them might have made it."

6

Sawyer prowled back and forth across the shallow drainage that led up to their peak, moving laterally, as if the small markers of rock they'd built at 10,000 feet were an impassable fence. He wasn't interested in good-byes.

Cam gathered with the others on the ridge where they'd lit their signal fire for Hollywood. Faulk, who was staying, had agreed to burn two armloads later in the day. Much later. Sunrise remained a great yellow promise beyond the ranges to the east, and in the frost-hard twilight even whispers sounded sharp and loud. It was April 14th, Year One. Plague Year. The broadcasts out of Colorado had served as a reliable calendar for Hollywood's group, and he said the radio had just begun to talk about the future that way—and the idea caught on here immediately, for obvious reasons, Cam thought. A new start.

"Throw a bed frame over the pile," said Doug Silverstein. "That should keep it dry long enough to really get it roaring."

Faulk nodded. "They'll know you're coming."

To the west, gray clouds emerged from the lingering night and absorbed the familiar shapes of the nearest mountains, earth and sky bound together by charcoal sheets of rain. The damp, erratic wind was fragrant with oxygen.

Sawyer's voice whipped over them—"M'on!"—and most of their heads turned. He pumped his balled fist up and down and Cam remembered, strangely, making the same gesture to truckers from the backseat of his dad's car when he was a kid, baseball on the radio, horsing around with his brothers in the tightly packed space. He smiled. They had shrieked like idiot hyenas whenever a trucker hit his horn for them.

Erin was smiling, too, the only other face not tight and brooding. Cam shook himself. He knew her weird cat's smirk only meant she was thinking, but he didn't want anyone to see the two of them standing there grinning. Jesus. He waved back at Sawyer in a slow arc meant to convey patience.

Wait. This is important.

The center of their gathering was a knot of handshakes and embraces, private words. It was the greatest display of emotion Cam had ever seen on this high, barren island, and he wished he was more a part of it. He wished so many things.

It didn't matter that they'd already enacted this same ritual two days ago, when the skies clouded up and spit hard for half an hour, or that everything had been decided for more than two weeks now. They all wanted to touch the few who were staying—Faulk, Sue, Al, and Amy Wong. Amy's three-month-old boy, Summer, was passed among a dozen people who cooed and murmured to him and scratched at the puffy down jacket that served as his swaddling clothes.

Cam hadn't gotten a chance to hold him and hadn't fought for it, either. Summer gave him the willies. Babies should cry. Summer only stared, oblivious even to this morning's commotion. Cam suspected brain damage. Their diet had been dangerously short on protein, and Amy had gone beneath the barrier twice before she knew she was pregnant. The nanos might have affected that part of her body or attacked the baby directly, or both.

Below, Sawyer moved past the line of rock markers and Cam's thoughts vanished in a jolt. It shouldn't have been frightening, that dark silhouette against the rough slope of grays and browns, but they had survived long enough to develop a new set of instincts. Nothing belonged down there. Nothing human.

Watching him, Cam hesitated, then turned suddenly and shouldered in toward the heart of the crowd. He needed to say something. Anything. He was pleased when Erin grabbed his hand and came along.

It felt as much as ten degrees warmer inside the gathering, shielded from the wind. Their jackets whistled against the others' GORE-TEX skins, a sound that Cam associated with busy weekends at the resort. His past had never seemed closer.

Amy and Lorraine were crying softly, heads together, holding Summer between them; but Sue studied Cam's approach with dry, steady eyes, both hands on her pregnant belly. He couldn't read her expression. No one else had noticed him yet. Price was clapping people on the shoulder like a football coach, out of words for once, and both Hollywood and Doug Silverstein fidgeted with bundles of yellow twine that they'd cut into lengths of roughly two feet.

"We really appreciate this," Faulk said, for the hundredth time, and Hollywood nodded and shrugged.

Their plan was to tie markers on trees near berry patches and snake pits and anything else of use down to 7,000 feet or more, to decrease the time that Faulk and Al Pendergraff would spend below the barrier on future scavenging trips.

"Really," Faulk repeated, and Cam cleared his throat. They all turned. Hollywood looked relieved but the others just stared at him with the same careful intensity as Sue.

Beside Cam, Erin ducked her head.

He put his hand out and Faulk took it immediately. And that was all. He and Pendergraff repeated the handshake and Amy smiled through her tears, and Sue even kissed his cheek as he bent to hug her around her big belly. After everything they'd been through, it came down to a civilized exchange of gestures.

* * *

He never saw any of them alive again.

Seventeen days hadn't been enough for Hollywood. The boy still hunched slightly over his right side and couldn't seem to move his left leg forward all the way, resulting in a swaying waddle even worse than Manny's lopsided gait. Manny had long since grown accustomed to his missing toes and walked or ran with an easy skipping motion.

Leading everyone down from the peak, the two of them looked like a drunk penguin alongside a windup toy with a bad spring. They were the youngest members of the group, at nineteen and fifteen, and had a certain eagerness in common.

Cam wanted to believe that was a good thing.

Hollywood admitted he still felt some pain. If it wasn't already mid-April, they might have let this rainstorm pass and given him more time . . . except California's short wet season was ending. They couldn't risk it. They'd all thought this winter was worse than normal, though Sawyer just laughed at Cam's idea that the planet was cooling because all the cities and factories and everything were shut down. In fact, now that they knew it was still early in the year, the truth was this winter had been comparatively mild. This might be the last rain.

Cam had encouraged Hollywood to exercise while he was still bedridden, leg lifts, simple arm motions. It helped flush the system of dead nanos. That Hollywood hadn't known this, that he'd made the trek in good weather, was evidence that the people across the valley had rarely if ever scavenged below the barrier. They hadn't needed to. They were rich. So Sawyer's suspicion of a "cattle drive" must be groundless.

It must be.

The tension in Price's hut had been as thick as the smoke stench and body odor, and surely didn't help Hollywood's recovery, yet Cam never suggested moving him upslope. Price's group needed goading. He'd figured that if his regular visits made them uncomfortable, so much the better. He came by every day to talk about landmarks in the valley and the easier, bigger life on the other side.

After just six days Hollywood insisted on walking again, gingerly, bent over like an old man and holding his arm close the way that a bird would tuck in a broken wing. The boy had clearly been rushing himself; rest was their only treatment for internal wounds; Cam should have said something but didn't have the heart to keep him tied down. More than that, he wanted everyone to witness Hollywood's tenacity.

They fed him weeds and lichen and greasy, stringy scrub-jay, sweet crunchy grasshoppers. They made a great present of the last can of fruit cocktail.

If he suspected, he said nothing.

Sawyer had climbed back to the piles of rock at 10,000 feet and stood gazing up at them, his face lost behind his hood and mirrored ski goggles and a black racing mask.

"We should stay together," Hollywood said. "It's safer," and Cam felt someone bull past him to the front of the group.

Price shouted, "Everyone sticks together!"

Sawyer gave no indication that he'd heard, no sound, no movement. They couldn't even tell where he was looking. Price flapped his arms and opened his mouth again, but Cam spoke quickly over Price's navy blue shoulder. "So what do you think, what's the air pressure?"

"The barrier's down at least five hundred feet, maybe six or seven." The racing mask muffled Sawyer's voice but he made no extra effort to be heard. "There'll be pockets of high pressure, though, fluctuations. Suit up now."

One thing the resort lodge and cabins had had in abundance were goggles and other ski gear, gloves that pulled way up over jacket sleeves, fabric masks. Equipment designed to repel snow could not be proof against a sea of nanos, of course, but today it was especially crucial to delay and minimize infections.

They had never gone more than three hours before feeling the machines inside them, at which point they'd always started back for safe altitude if they weren't already climbing.

Today, by that time, they would still be descending.

According to their topography map, the other peak was seven and a half miles due north, down and across and up—and it would be impossible to zip straight over. The roads in the great valley ran mostly west and east, and Cam had estimated that a man on foot would total twelve miles or more as he switchbacked up and down the steepest slopes, avoiding cliffs and hard terrain.

He tightened his gogs and glanced toward the low, oncoming clouds. He wondered again why storms hadn't washed the world clean, at least the mountain areas. Common sense suggested that rain and snow would press the nanos to the ground, then carry them downhill. Sawyer said he didn't understand the rule of scale. Nanos weren't little people. Airborne particles of that size barely noticed the finest drizzle or the thickest blizzard, and gusts of wind and the impact of a storm's first raindrops would stir up pockets of grounded nanos. Bad weather probably swept away a good percentage of the invisible machines, yet brought just as many or even more up from the lowlands.

"Wait." Erin laid her hand on Cam's hip. She'd set her goggles on her forehead and her eyes were a rich violet in the gloom. Several loose strands of her hair, flagging on the breeze, reached out from her hood to Cam's face as she stepped close. Her smile felt funny when she kissed him.

She was warmth and softness. He moved his hand up under her jacket but was frustrated by its tight fit, and ran his palm down to her crotch instead. She rocked her hips forward to increase the pressure.

All around them, fifteen other human beings were engaged in similar embraces or slugging water from canteens or urinating there on the dirt. Keene had squatted down in a last attempt to move his bowels. After crossing the barrier, they'd keep their armor shut regardless of the body's needs. No one wanted the nanos inside their clothing, exposing any cuts or bug bites.

In a way, this was farewell. There wouldn't be another chance to feel bare skin until they reached the other side.

Cam wanted to say *I love you*, but it wasn't true. *Need* was

a more honest word. There had been times when taking care
of Erin had been the only thing that kept him going.

He said the words anyway, like a prayer. "Love you."

"Yes." Her smile broadened so much that the corners of
her eyes crinkled. A real smile. "I love you too."

Then she went to Sawyer, glancing back over one shoulder.
But her smile had become that crooked little smirk again and
Cam pretended to look elsewhere. He watched her gesture
silently, watched Sawyer push his face open, goggles up,
mask down. His friend had quit shaving the day after Hollywood came and seemed like someone else now with a patchy
beard rounding his long face.

Cam wished he'd gotten the last kiss. Didn't everyone save
their favorite for last?

He turned uphill, thinking that the stay-behinds would
have come to the top of the drainage to watch them go. Yet he
saw nothing, no movement anywhere except a fleeting dust
devil and one quick arrow of a bird.

Anger stabbed through him, not pity. Faulk and Pendergraff
should have been running downhill for early juniper berries
and fresh greens, for lizards and insects slowed by the cold. He
knew they weren't busy double-checking their rain traps or
putting out every spare container because he and Manny had
already done that for them . . . He supposed they'd gone to
their hut, reeling from the emotional shock, surrounded now
by a new and equally dangerous sea of total isolation.

Somehow Cam was certain they would haunt him much
longer than any of the people he'd eaten.

7

Shuttle Pilot Derek Mills shifted his body or grabbed for a new handhold each time Ruth matched his local vertical, a reaction that she thought spoke volumes. Not that the derision in his voice wasn't clear enough.

"You don't know what you're talking about," he mumbled. "It's not like landing a plane."

Ruth bit down on her first response. *If you're really planning to stay up here forever you'd better learn to breathe vacuum, buddy.* Instead, she turned to the others, glancing back and forth across the hab module, making a show of raising her eyebrows and sort of shrugging with one upturned palm. The new Ruth was quite ladylike and certainly not inflammatory.

Too bad that rotating after Mills had put her at an odd angle compared to everybody else. They'd all grown accustomed to entering a new section of the ISS and finding someone standing on what appeared to be the ceiling or a wall, but only Gustavo readily conversed with people before wheeling around to share their alignment. The mind balked at making sense of facial expressions turned sideways or bottom-up.

No one acknowledged her attempt at eloquence and she felt a dull frustration as ungiving as the walls. The pale, elongated habitation module was about the size of a racquetball court, just large enough for both Mills and Gus to put five feet between themselves and anybody else, Gus claiming the deep end, Mills hovering by the only exit.

Ruth would have preferred to meet inside the *Endeavour*—the power of suggestion might have helped her argument—but Mills discouraged anyone from entering the shuttle, which he'd made into his private quarters. Ruth understood. She felt the same edgy possessiveness about her lab and had decided not to risk adding to the pilot's discomfort. But she was never going to convince him to take his last flight.

She looked at Ulinov. His frown was a warning. Ruth chose not to notice and said, "I know it won't be a cakewalk without ground support. We can still get down."

"You wanna ditch her?"

"—ditch the shuttle!"

Mills and Wallace spoke at the same time. It might have been funny if each of them hadn't interpreted her words in the worst possible way.

Contingencies existed, she knew, for crews to parachute from a damaged or malfunctioning shuttle if it could first be brought to subsonic speeds. There was even a massive lake just two miles west of Leadville—she had been studying a lot of film—and Ruth supposed they could intentionally strike the water to avoid the dense refugee population camped throughout the region. Of course, her computers and MAFM might not fare so well.

"No way," she said. "The shuttle's worth too much. We can use the highway north of the city, there's a stretch that runs straight and mostly flat for almost three miles."

Mills said, again, "It's not like landing a plane."

"But there must be—"

"Why do you keep thinking you know more about our jobs than we do?" Deborah Reece, M.D., Ph.D., sniffed in a way that gave both her words and the set of her chin a haughty, imperial manner. The bitterly dry air had left Doc Deb's sinuses

in a state of permanent irritation and for months now she'd
been a walking phlegm-farm. Ruth had suggested that decon-
gestants might be the answer, but Deb replied that her body
was generating mucus for a good reason—to protect her ag-
gravated tissues. So she oozed. Constantly. It was just gross.

"Look," Ruth said, trying again, "sooner or later we have
to leave. We have to go down."

Ulinov's frown never changed. "The president ordered us."

"Orders are to beat the locust. Your orders are to support
me in any way. That's all that's important."

"So quit wasting time," Deb said behind her.

In the beginning Ruth had been vaguely glad to have another woman aboard. She'd even smiled when Deb and Gustavo became an item. Then Gus broke it off in a storm of
silence. The two of them got back together, swore it was over,
reunited again. Ruth recognized the pattern. They just needed
something to do.

Maybe what happened next was inevitable, given the close
quarters and their complete separation from any normal soci-
ety. Deb had bounced to Derek Mills. Back to Gus.

Ulinov tried to stop it. He talked to each of the men and he
made jokes about American customs and he threatened to in-
form Colorado. Sexual promiscuity went against all their
training, and rightly so. It had turned each of them, in different ways, into the components of a time bomb.

Ruth was hardly conventional, and she was not a prude. In
her junior year she had been among the girls in the dormitory
who stripped down to their underwear for most of spring se-
mester after the air-conditioning blew out. Some years later,
on an apartment balcony just three floors above the Miami
traffic, she had given her stepbrother a hand job with SPF 45
coconut sunblock. More and more she had taken to contemplating the line of Ulinov's shoulders and the breadth of his
hands, the smooth, ruddy bump that was his lower lip.

Amazing, that six people hurtling around a dying planet in
a tiny metal shell could find new ways to torment themselves—
but whether Deborah Reece with her blond hair and her neat
little hips had acted out of boredom or a physician's urge to

heal, the truth was that Wallace had burrowed deeper into his grief as Mills became distracted and hostile. Poor Gus, always a churning supply of words, developed a stammer in Deb's presence.

"Wasting time, you, do you have an appointment?" he asked. "Let Ruth say what she has to." Gustavo had folded himself into the corner like a crab, shying away from open room, and Ruth worried how he'd react back on Earth, exposed to miles of sky and land. It made her appreciate his support all the more—

Deb snorted and kicked toward the exit. Mills, blocking her path, grabbed new handholds with a neat pull-and-push movement that carried him aside to clear her way yet also backed him farther from the group.

"Stop." It was risky, but Ruth had nothing left except a blunt assault. "You'll be back," she told them. "You'll all be able to come back here again."

Mills looked directly at her for the first time, a mix of emotion cutting across his face.

Ruth said, "I can beat this thing, I swear it, but I need to be on the ground." Then she lost eye contact with Mills as Deb moved between them, and fought to keep from raising her voice. "We'll have spaceflight again in no time! There was hardly any industrial damage, they'll want the most experienced crews . . ."

Deborah turned to stare and missed her handhold, but Mills caught her waist—and despite everything that had or hadn't happened between the doctor and the pilot, neither reacted to each other's touch. The ungodly echoing drone of the air circulators made their silence all the louder.

Too far. Ruth had gone too far and she knew it, and she'd barely touched the surface of what she felt was the real problem—their pride, their vanity. She should have been flown down to join the other scientists in Leadville a month ago or even earlier, as soon as the snowpack could be cleared, yet Colorado had kept them in orbit for the same reasons that the astronauts wanted so badly to stay, prestige, power, a reasonable fear that the human race might be trapped in the mountains forever and only look at the moon and stars with fading memory.

She also had no doubt that the crew was terrified of being without purpose. Couldn't they see that they'd actually have more value on the ground? Engineers, pilots, radiomen, doctors, these were everything that would allow Ruth and her colleagues time to defeat the locust.

Ulinov broke the quiet, thumping his big palm against a supply cabinet. "We are following orders to stay," he said.

Ruth shook her head. "There's nothing more I can do here."

"What if you are wrong?"

"I, but— What if *you're* wrong?"

"New data comes up every hour. Tomorrow they may find what you need, what only works in zero gee." His frown wavered as he watched her face, but then he struck the cabinet again. "I decide," he said. "I tell you no."

Seventeen days hadn't been enough for Ruth. Since learning of the FBI's new data pinpointing the locust's birth, she'd ramped up her campaign to sway opinions in Leadville, making as much of a nuisance of herself as possible for someone in orbit. Unfortunately, at best she was 250 miles above Colorado. At worst there was an entire planet between them. And the men and women down there had no reason to engage in a conversation they didn't want to have if they could win simply by not talking to her.

Yesterday her fears and frustration had reached a new pitch.

Yesterday, Gus had intercepted a series of transmissions between Leadville and a C-130 cargo transport on its return flight from California. They'd done it. They'd sent a team of Army Rangers west in search of the lab where the locust had been created—and the soldiers had remained in Stockton for more than five hours after their air tanks ran out, refusing to accept failure. One young man had been partially blinded. All for nothing. They hadn't found a single clue and Ruth could still hear the last words of the recording Gus had played for her, the terse exhaustion of the soldier's voice: "No go, it's no go."

What if Leadville chose not to risk more men, more equipment, more jet fuel? What if they stuck to the conservative path that had trapped her up here for so long and let their greatest opportunity slip away?

Ruth decided she'd been working on the wrong people. It was too easy for everyone on the ground to ignore her—but if she could convince the astronauts, everything changed.

There wasn't anything Leadville could do to stop them from abandoning the ISS.

Derek Mills had fled to the *Endeavour*, and Ruth cornered him there. He sat in the low, cramped flight deck, strapped to his chair, the rattle of his laptop's keyboard masking her approach through the interdeck hatch behind him.

She froze halfway out of the floor. He'd dimmed the uplights but didn't seem to notice her shadow laid over the console before him, until she knocked and quickly moved closer.

Mills tilted one glance up at her, his jaw set. Ruth didn't bother with words. She passed him the bound sheaf of photographs she'd wanted to share back in the hab module. The station's cameras were incredible stuff, worthy of James Bond, able to count the legs on a bug.

She'd clipped the picture of the Leadville county airport to the top of the stack because she wanted to stir his interest. She needed to engage him with the challenge of it.

Two bulldozers and several hundred people both in and out of uniform were expanding the lone runway, fighting into the hill on the south side because a big DC-10 had sunk into the mud fifty yards beyond the north end. They were also bringing in a crane to deal with the wreck, but it was having trouble maneuvering through the jam of other aircraft.

Mills barely looked at the picture and he did not look at her. He held the stack out for Ruth to take back.

"I know it's not enough room," she said.

A ten-minute drive from town, the county airport offered less than 5,000 feet of runway. It was never intended for large commercial flights, much less space shuttles careening down at 220 miles per hour. If they'd begun construction the previous spring, Ruth supposed there might have been something usable by now—but she didn't have the right to blame them for being too busy.

"It's never going to be enough room," she told him. "Not before we're out of air."

Mills jiggled the stack with an irritated grunt, about to drop it. Ruth reached in quickly but was careful to touch only the top picture, peeling it back.

"Here," she said. "We land here."

From above, the terrain around Leadville resembled a giant bathtub that had been filled with clay and left under the shower for eons. The Continental Divide ran nine miles east of the city and curled around to wall it in on the north as well. Just six miles west of downtown stood another immense range, and most of the area within this vast, bent tub was a jumble of hills and lumps and gullies, scoured by the unimaginable amounts of rain and snowmelt that formed the headwaters of the Arkansas River.

A railroad track and two-lane highway ran north together along the river, until the highway dodged east into Leadville, where it split in two. From town, Highway 24 shot north again to rejoin the railroad in a wide marsh basin.

Colorado roads tended to swerve through the shapes of the land, but this basin covered four square miles and some tired draftsman must have simply laid down his ruler. The highway cut straight through.

"It's perfect," Ruth said. "We can come in out of the southeast like we were hitting Runway 33 at Kennedy."

Mills finally looked her in the face.

"The angle's almost exact," she said. "Look at it. And the prevailing winds are out of the north just like you'd want."

"This hill at the south end could be trouble," he answered, and Ruth fought down a hopeful laugh and let him continue. He held the photos in both hands now. "The road isn't wide enough, either," he said. "What is it, sixty, seventy feet? The wingspan is almost eighty."

The runways at Denver International, where Leadville planned for them to touch down eventually, were twice as wide as Highway 24 yet still only half the breadth of the strips at Kennedy Space Center. All in all, if they did try to land without permission, without ground support, Denver International might be slightly less risky than Highway 24—but then what? The Mile-High City wasn't high enough. They could only hit Denver if there was a plane ready to fly them up to Leadville.

Ruth moved closer and tapped one finger on the photo. "We can overshoot that hill," she said. "There's plenty of room."

"There's a bridge over this fucking railroad right in the middle. No way. It's fifty feet wide at the most."

She had been relieved that the tracks ran under the highway instead of vice versa. Obviously you didn't want to squeeze the shuttle beneath a train trestle at any point during a landing—but Ruth had figured that the overpass was no different than the highway itself. "What's the problem, the guardrails? Our wings will clear them easy."

"It's not like landing—"

"Yeah, yeah, it's not a plane, stop saying that! I know more about this than you think. If you come in on target we'll zip straight down the center. And if you're off a bit, the nosewheel can pull us back in line."

The approach was everything. The shuttles had long been compared to flying bricks. They were not only clumsy in atmosphere—unlike conventional aircraft, the *Endeavour* would be unpowered during touchdown. Essentially the machine became a hang glider that was too heavy for the updraft of its body and stubby wings. Worse, the shuttles had no go-around capability. A pilot who didn't like what he saw did not have the option of goosing his jets and regaining altitude to circle back. Once committed, it was do or die.

"You'll have to pull off the best fucking touchdown in history," she said, making herself use his favorite swear word and afraid it sounded forced.

He didn't answer. Ruth hoped he was visualizing his approach. Derek Mills was something of a hotshot, or had been a year ago. That was why he'd been sent up here, like all of them, and she knew he'd kept himself as sharp as possible, running simulations, talking through an occasional exercise with Leadville. Maintaining hand-eye coordination had been his excuse for playing video games instead of cleaning or doing inventory.

Mills shook his head before he spoke, then swept his hand over the photo from left to right. "There's a rainstorm coming out of California right now, and another one behind it."

He had been prepping for the situation himself!

Ruth felt a wave of adrenaline and involuntarily bent both arms into her chest as if to contain the feeling, aware of that wild laugh bashing at her insides again.

Mills was the key. Building a majority vote would be impossible, given her relationship with Doc Deb and the hard discipline shared by Ulinov and Wallace. But if she could tempt Mills onto her side along with Gus, it would be three to three and she'd have the tiebreaker. She'd have the pilot.

He said, "We can't do anything in weather."

"It'll pass." Ruth could almost feel his desire, feel him wavering. Should she say something more?

"That's just the top of the checklist," he continued.

Her heart wouldn't quit. She was afraid to let him fall back on the methodical caution that NASA had ingrained into his thinking, but she'd already played her best card, the legend he could become among fliers everywhere.

"The big problem is FODs." He said it as one word, *fauds,* Foreign Object Debris.

"Birds won't be an issue here like at Kennedy."

"I'm thinking cars. People."

"I've got more pictures," she said. "You can see there's almost no traffic at all. And they'll know we're coming. It's ninety minutes minimum for reentry, right? Or as much as we want if we announce before we leave the station."

Mills flipped through the next several photos, stopped when he reached the shots of the other tiny airports in Eagle-Vail and farther north near Steamboat Springs. Ruth wished she hadn't said anything about an early announcement. Was he worrying over what Ground Control might say? His *career*? Leadville could block the road and force them to stay . . .

"If we give them an hour," she said, "they can walk a thousand people over the highway picking up every piece of everything. You know they'll do it. They'll have to."

"I guess."

She wanted to add that it was unlikely that more than a handful of soldiers would precheck the Denver runways. Leadville just didn't have the suits or the canned air for a larger effort, but she wasn't going to be the first to say *Denver*. She didn't dare distract him.

"I guess if we force their hand," Mills said, "they'll use all the resources they have anyway."

"Yes."

"I could use a fucking beer."

The unsteady laugh escaped this time, but she knew it was okay. Mills would think she liked his joke. He flashed a grin and Ruth realized what she had to say next, *I'm buying*. Could she build him up enough that Ulinov and Wallace wouldn't sway him back to their side?

Ulinov scuffed through the interdeck hatch directly behind them and banged one hand against the ceiling to catch himself as Ruth turned, blinking, confused to find her fears manifested.

How long had he been listening?

"You," Ulinov said. His broad face was a deep bloody brick color, so much uglier than his frown that at first she didn't even see his expression. Then she noticed his stance. He had not secured himself with one easy grip. He'd wedged himself to the floor by pushing back from his handhold, ready to launch himself with both feet.

It was a combat pose.

Ruth managed to force a sound past the earthquake of her heart. "Look—"

Ulinov dismissed her with one shrug of those beautiful shoulders. He addressed Mills, his English as bad as she'd ever heard. "You, I think better. Professional knows better."

There was a noise beside her as Mills shifted in his seat and Ruth wanted to look, maybe encourage him with a gesture. But there was no way to pull her gaze from Ulinov.

"Your photographs," Ulinov said. "Now. Pushing them over."

She said, "It was me—"

"No." His shoulders twitched again. He didn't even want to hear a confession.

How long had he been listening? Fuck. The only way to salvage anything would be to take the offensive, act like a nano. Fuck fuck fuck. She had to be relentless. "Commander—"

"Enough. Do your orders." Ulinov sounded more tired than angry now, and might have relaxed a fraction.

"The war you're trying to fight. Ushba. Shkhata." She named the peaks where the Russians had failed to hold a line against their Muslim enemies. "You can help them more by putting me on the ground before we lose our best chance to beat the plague. Otherwise they'll fight forever."

"What is it wrong with you? Do your orders."

"They'll fight until they're all gone, Uli."

"No. There is no mutiny."

Strange that the word hadn't even occurred to her. But it was accurate. *Mutiny.* "That's not, I was just . . ."

Ulinov watched her wind down before he turned to Mills. "Push me the photographs," he said. Then he looked at Ruth again and said, "You do not come back to the shuttle."

Her pulse refused to calm and chased so rapidly through her thoughts that she felt disassociated from herself. She'd retreated to her lab after Ulinov escorted her from the *Endeavour*, both to placate him and because she didn't want to show herself to the others. Because she hoped to find some safety and comfort.

It might have been better to face them. Here there was only the rattle of her own fear.

Ruth knew how she could force an evacuation of the ISS.

There wasn't any other way. The Russian Soyuz docked to the station as an emergency lifeboat wasn't something she could pilot herself. The whole crew had to leave together or not at all.

She intended to dig under the insulation somewhere away from her lab, create a pinprick pressure bleed. The damage would be attributed to a micrometeorite strike. Wallace had already gone on EVA twice to repair their solar panels. The concept of total vacuum was an illusion. There were constant hazards, dust and debris, human garbage left in orbit.

All the more reason to get out of here, before a random strike killed them all.

Ruth had decided the curse of guilt was an acceptable price—and it would not be a small burden. No matter what the crew thought, she respected the knowledge and effort that had gone into establishing a permanent human presence in space more than most of her own work. Partly that was a casual respect for any challenge successfully met. Mostly it was in recognition of the Cold War notion that Earth was much too fragile a basket in which to place all of humankind's eggs.

The locust was more proof than anyone needed that they'd better spread throughout the solar system and farther if possible as soon as they got the chance, before a disaster even worse than the plague left humankind extinct.

But first they needed that chance.

Ruth tore through her personal effects in search of a tool and laughed at a box of tampons. Four pencils. Nothing. She tried to jaunt across the lab without clearing her foot from the open locker door, and momentum flung her down against a bank of computers. She whacked her thigh, then her forearm, and hurt her neck straining to keep her face from the console.

Somehow she bounced in the direction she'd intended to go, toward the hatch. She caught herself there. She didn't think she'd suffered worse than bruises, but the shock of it had cleared her head. She rubbed her leg.

She had to wait, of course. The timing would be suspicious if it happened right away—

The thump of hands and feet ignited her heart again. Someone was coming. Ulinov? He'd already shown an uncanny ability to predict her actions.

Ruth backed away. Her eyes went briefly to the viewport.

But it was Gustavo who filled her tiny space. "The radio, your friend James," he yammered. "They said yes!"

"Yes . . ."

"It worked! Everything you've been telling them, the ANN, getting you on the ground, they said yes!"

He stuck out one hand in congratulations and Ruth grabbed him instead, shouting right in his face. "Aaaaaaaah!" There were no words to express the depth and complexity of her triumph.

She was going back to Earth.

8

Chair 12 had an alien look against the broken mountainside. All of the lifts at Bear Summit were painted dark green, to blend with the environment, but nothing could soften the giant straight lines of these structures. Cam always felt an ambiguous thrill when he emerged from the gorge between the base of their peak and the highest point of the ski area. In another life this had been among his favorite places. Now it was strange and deadly.

The big metal box that housed the gears perched fifteen feet in the air, looming over a glass-faced attendant's booth. Two hundred identical, evenly spaced chairs dangled from a cable that ran along both sides of a series of massive poles, plunging out of view beyond a ridge and the first pine trees of any height.

The chairs rocked against the gray sky, heralding the storm, creaking, weeping. Sometimes when the wind was right this sound had carried over their peak for hours.

Cam looked away and turned to Erin, close beside him. She was also staring. "Watch your feet," he said. Nosing up from the hardpack were low veins of granite, mostly smooth but peppered with toe-catching nubs and hollows.

He tried not to think about the nanos that must be puffing upward with every step, unseen dust. Grasshoppers sprang out of their path constantly, the same tans and grays as the dirt and rock. There were more of them now than ever and their irregular bursts of motion made the ground seem unstable—constant flickers at the corner of the eye.

Sixty yards ahead, almost racing each other, Sawyer, Manny, and Hollywood marched three abreast. Erin had protested when Sawyer pulled away from her, but Cam was glad. They needed pacesetters. The bulk of the group seemed to be hanging back, and this ridge they were traversing was the easy part. They'd come just three-quarters of a mile, heading west into the damp wind.

Cam glanced over his shoulder. Bacchetti wasn't far behind but everyone else actually seemed to be moving slower, faces tipped up, all eyes on the chairlift.

Lorraine caught her foot and flailed into the ground. Cam lost sight of her as most of them bunched around, yet he could see that she didn't get up again. He started back to help and Erin said, "Cam, no."

The storm clouds had muted both the sudden dawn and the few colors of this world. His polarized goggles, designed to highlight white-on-white features in the snow, made the forest below seem almost black. Then he pushed into the blues and reds of everyone's jackets and saw that Price had pulled Lorraine's ski mask down from her cheeks.

"Christ, what are you doing!"

"She has to breathe," Price said, and Cam dropped to one knee and grabbed at her, tugging the mask up again.

Her eyes were wide behind her goggles and he thought she was hyperventilating. She knew how serious her mistake had been. A flap of jacket sleeve hung from her left elbow and on the rock between them was one thin looping spatter of blood like a signature, dark as oil.

"We're still safe here!" Price said, and McCraney added, "There's no way we've hit the barrier yet."

"How do you feel?" Cam asked. "You think it's broken?"

"Let her breathe!"

Lorraine shook her head and Cam took her wrist, feeling for any deformity beneath her sleeve, working all the way up to her shoulder. Then he shook his head too. "Do you hurt anywhere else? No? Good. Somebody bring us a hunk of ice."

Price didn't move but Doug Silverstein turned away.

"Hold on," Cam said. "I need a few pieces of that rope."

Silverstein handed him the entire bundle, then hustled up-hill toward a field of snow.

Cam had two canteens in his backpack and removed one, dumping it over her arm, trying to flush out any nanos she'd embedded there. Price was probably right that they were above the ever-shifting barrier, but Cam had learned to be pessimistic.

"Who's got a spare hood or something?" he asked.

He tied her sleeve shut, covering the rip with an extra pair of gloves, as Silverstein returned with too much ice.

"I thought this was to keep the swelling down," Silverstein said. "She won't even feel it through her jacket."

"She will." Cam met her eyes. "Hold it there as long as you can, okay?" Lorraine nodded and her mask worked, like the words *thank you* were percolating up. Cam stood and turned his back. "You'll be all right," he said.

Sawyer hadn't waited and Manny had gone with him, but Hollywood was standing right where Cam had last seen him, head bent over a crummy gas station map he'd folded down into one square. Erin hadn't moved either, except to sit and rest.

Cam jogged through another burst of grasshoppers. He nearly ran. The urge to escape Price and the others was that strong. It might have been better if he'd stayed in the midst of the pack, herding them, but there was a limit to how much responsibility he would accept.

They would catch up. They had to.

Erin rose to her feet and Cam saw her glance past him at the others. She had always been very attuned to his moods. His and Sawyer's. "Thanks for waiting," he said, and gave her butt a swat, and she took his hand for a moment until their pace made it clumsy. His breath felt hot in the thick hair of his beard, matted against his cheeks and neck by his mask.

"I guess I'm still not convinced," Hollywood said as the two of them approached. "It really seems like we're gonna lose time heading out this way."

Cam shrugged and kept walking. Hollywood turned to follow, lowering his map, and Cam was glad he left it at that.

There was no point in arguing anymore.

Ahead, trudging after Sawyer and Manny, Bacchetti reached a swath of loose, shattered boulders that spilled for a thousand feet from a hump of stone above Chair 12. Cam and his buddies had called this rock the Fortress of Solitude, after Superman's secret hideaway. They'd had names for every gully and cliff on the mountain. Smoker's Hole. The Cock Knocker. Paradise.

Cam entered the rock field with Erin and Hollywood exactly where Bacchetti had started across, but the markers here were hastily assembled piles rather than the neat stacks they'd erected at 10,000 feet. Twice he lost the trail. The uneven jumble was all granite, split into square-cornered blocks as small as a fist and larger than a car.

He paused to orient himself, unsettled, even frightened, and saw that Sawyer and Manny were already at the lift.

Chair 12 topped out at 9,652 feet, which meant Bear Summit had been able to advertise itself as the highest ski area in California. This was almost true. "B.S.," as the locals called it, sat unquestionably lower than Heavenly in Lake Tahoe, which claimed a wedge of terrain up to 10,067, but that section of Heavenly lay a stone's throw across the Nevada state border.

Cam had also skied bigger and better mountains. Extreme terrain at B.S. was limited to a half dozen ravines, but that was okay. He knew each run intimately, the best jumps, every powder stash. Working at a small-time resort also meant crowds were a rarity—and Bear Summit hired people that the ritzy, brand-name places in Tahoe wouldn't touch. People like Cam.

"Watch it," Erin said, over a sudden clack of rocks, and he glanced back to see her gripping Hollywood's arm as the boy regained his balance.

Cam looked forward again and almost fell himself when the slab underfoot shifted. Then a ghost turned his head.

He expected to see grasshoppers but there was nothing there.

Before the winter he turned thirteen, Cam Najarro had seen snow only in movies and TV shows. Until then, it was almost possible he'd never been farther above sea level than the tops of various roller coasters and Ferris wheels.

Money wasn't the issue. Cam and his brothers were sixth-generation Californian, an eternity by white standards, and their grandpa had been the last to slave in the orange groves and garlic fields for lousy cash wages. Their father was a college graduate who had been promoted to district manager of an office supply chain before succumbing to early heart disease. He made a point of taking his family on weeklong vacations each year. He usually packed them into their Ford station wagon on holiday weekends as well. It was important to him that his sons understand there was more to the world than their own urban neighborhood. He did not want them limited in any way.

For much the same reason, he never allowed them to wear their older siblings' hand-me-downs, though that would have meant less overtime for him. And if his decision made for birthdays and Christmas mornings of more underwear and socks than new toys, at least the Najarros looked good.

Their father treasured pride and appearance above all else.

For him, the highlight of each day had been to sip one beer in the living room of their three-bedroom home, which he invariably described to his own brothers as "right on the ocean." In English. Always in English. Maybe Cam was never offended by Bear Summit's half-truths because his father indulged in the same habit of exaggeration. The city of Vallejo, where they lived, actually sat deep inside the San Francisco Bay—and in any case, three blocks of commercial properties lay between them and the flat, listless green murk of the delta.

Their father loved the ocean like he loved them, almost

formally, and from a distance. He did not fish or swim. He would have drowned since he never took off his shoes, much less unbuttoned his shirt. He just liked to look and listen and maybe walk in the sand. That alone was victory to him, having grown up landlocked in a cow town near Bakersfield.

He couldn't have realized he was restricting his sons' perspective in exactly the way he'd worked so hard to avoid. Their vacations ranged north or south for hundreds of miles, but always along the coast that he found so exotic—the Santa Cruz boardwalk, Disneyland, the Pismo Beach pier. He raised a generation of lowlanders who would keep their eyes and their own dreams facing west toward the Pacific.

Cam was the only one to break free.

Hollywood quit moving as soon as they emerged from the rock field and waited for Price and the others, raising one arm, calling, "This way! You got it!" Erin hesitated, but picked up the pace again before Cam could grab at her. Good girl.

Almost nothing remained of the ski patrol shack that had sat alongside Chair 12—a concrete pad, steel struts they hadn't been able to tear free. Every other scrap of material had been lugged up the mountain to build their huts, and looking at the raw foundation aroused an odd, melancholy satisfaction in Cam.

He'd done the best he could.

His father only took them to the mountains to show up a coworker. A white coworker. The boys went berserk, sledding and hucking snowballs for ten hours a day while he took pictures of them having fun. Later in the week he insisted on splurging for ski rentals and lift tickets.

Cam was soon lost in the confusion of the bunny hill, although in retrospect getting separated had been at least 50 percent intentional. For someone with three brothers, even biking down to the store for milk was a competition—and Cam was always the odd man out. His two older brothers tended to gang up and his kid brother Greg was three and a half years younger, not much help and often a hindrance.

The other boys spent their morning bickering and showing off and started racing, which wasn't so bright since they lacked the ability to turn. Or stop. Rocketing downhill in straight lines, they eventually smashed into a blond six-year-old and spent their afternoon on a bench in the patrol office.

Cam returned to the car late, shivering with excitement and cold—they were all wearing jeans—and happily infuriated his brothers with his tales of success. The next day they shunned him. That only gave him more time to get hooked.

He didn't ski again until he was fifteen, after one of his friends got a driver's license—after his father was in the hospital. The Najarro boys were expected to find part-time jobs upon reaching high school and Cam burned through his savings before February, buying better gear than he needed and fewer lessons than might have been useful. More than the new alpine environment, more than the senseless joy of hurling himself into gravity's pull, he loved the individual nature of the sport, no opponents, no audiences, no scores kept. It was his alone.

First year out of high school, already a strong intermediate skier if not particularly smooth, Cam worked seven brain-numbing months in a phone center and was up for a minor raise when he quit in December. That season he skied sixty-one days at nine different resorts. Each night he had to ice his shins, bruised so deeply by his cheap boots that he walked like a cowboy. The nail on his left big toe fell off in March. But it was too late. He'd met powder hounds who thought it was the height of cool to brag about such bodily damage.

Cam found a job as a lift operator and later earned a spot on the maintenance crew just by showing up every day, which was a little too much to expect of most B.S. employees. The kids partied hard and it didn't help that management had hacked wages and benefits to a minimum.

Next year B.S. gave the shaft to the ski patrol as well, and there were plenty of openings. He jumped at the chance.

* * *

They reached Chair 12 as the clouds pushed overhead and the air got still. The ringing screech of the chairs quieted. It was almost like the lift had been waiting for them.

An omen. But what did the silence mean?

Cam experienced the opposite phenomenon, as if all that noise went straight into his head. As they passed downhill of the attendant's booth and the heap of earth that had served as the off-load ramp when buried in snow, both he and Erin glanced up at the string of chairs. If only. But they kept walking.

The diesel for the backup engines hadn't lasted a month.

Most people drove east down into Nevada to escape the plague, including his friend Hutch, which of course proved to be the worst decision possible. There couldn't have been more than three hundred souls left in Bear Summit when the newscasts said it might be safe at high altitudes—but by that point, the Sierra range was in its third day of blizzard conditions.

Cam stayed in his duplex at 7,500 feet with his TV and his phone, until after midnight on the fourth day when he woke to stinging pinpricks inside his left hand.

He called home one more time. All circuits busy.

The blizzard had stopped but the road was nine inches deep, deeper on either side of the single lane that some hero had plowed the day before. Navigating this narrow trail might have been too much for Cam if he hadn't half memorized the highway's constant turns, few dips, and blind corners. He drove the same stretch to work six days a week and, as the joke went, the mark of a true local was the ability to get up to the resort in any conditions, by Braille if necessary, scraping a fender against the iron reflector poles set every forty yards for the plows.

White road, white embankments. Trying to maintain his depth perception, he snapped his lights from low beam to high to low again, a crude sort of radar.

Odd silhouettes cavorted into his path, three bucking shapes with too many legs. Cam braked. His truck skidded and he rode down on the monsters. Deer, the things were just deer. They fled before him, giant eyes rolling in his headlights, until the embankment fell away on one side and they ran off. Downhill.

He passed two abandoned stalls, nearly getting stuck himself as he edged past the first.

The streetlamps of the condominium village threw a surreal pink glow across the low clouds, visible long before he inched into the valley. Then he saw lights on the ridge too among the luxury cabins. Were people staying put up there? The ridge was only a few hundred feet above the road . . .

He kept driving. He was not surprised to find only a few vehicles in front of the resort's main buildings, transformed into white dunes by the snow, but it confused him to see just fifty cars parked farther up beside the mid-mountain lodge.

It was dark here, totally black when he shut off his headlights. Somewhere between the condominiums and the resort, a power line had gone down. He didn't think to worry about it. The mid-mountain lodge sat at 7,920 feet and the hideous itch in his hand would not stop, new tendrils worming through his wrist.

He stumbled inside and found seventy-one people. Of them, he recognized only Pete Czujko and two guys who'd worked in the cafeteria. The rest were tourists, vacationers. Outsiders. They were all infected, wild with panic and the freakish pain and desperate to figure out how to get higher.

Bear Summit's small fleet of snowmobiles and Sno-Cats were gone. Diesel generators, rescue gear, the CB radio and patrol walkie-talkies, everything. Even the gift shop had been gutted. The chairlifts could operate at two-thirds speed on auxiliary diesel engines, yet whoever rode off with the Sno-Cats had also made a mess of draining the fuel from Chairs 11 and 12, punching holes into the bottoms of the tanks, wasting what they couldn't carry. While Cam had hidden in his cabin with his fear and his grief, others had worked to ensure their survival.

The missing locals. They must have seen that a majority of the vacationers and other refugees would end up here, and decided they'd be better off in the cabins along the ridge above the condominium village. Some of those homes would be empty, the fat cat owners trapped below the snowline. With propane tanks and well-stocked cupboards, those cabins were ideal for long-term survival—except that the ridge topped out at 8,100 feet. If the plague rose any higher, the locals had nowhere left to go.

Cam might have been over there himself if he'd been more popular. But there wasn't anything to do but start hiking.

The new snow was hip deep and the temperature, with wind chill, hovered just under twenty degrees, though it was warming as a high-pressure front moved in. Uphill lay only darkness. Three people refused to leave the lodge. Several girls, Erin and her friends, wore only slacks and stylish little cowboy hats. There were nine children, a couple in their seventies, an enormous woman named Barbara Price who simply would not put down her show-quality beagle, three Korean tourists able to communicate only in pantomime.

But there wasn't anything to do but start hiking.

Hollywood still had his map out yet didn't say anything more, which Cam appreciated, and somehow he'd gotten Price and the rest to hurry up. No one was too far back when Cam and Erin quit following the ridge westward.

Scoured by the wind, the crest of the ski run was soft barren dirt and gravel. They walked through parallel tracks of deep, sliding prints left by Sawyer, Manny, and Bacchetti.

Hollywood had come a different route, powering straight up to their peak, and probably would have done so even if he'd known the area. That was just his nature. But they had learned that it was equally fast—and safer—to hike out to the resort and use the wide-open runs and the jeep trails that in winter served as Sno-Cat tracks. When there was enough snow they'd skied down, of course, on telemark equipment since the boots were soft enough to walk in, the skis light enough to carry back up.

Delicate flowers clung to the hillside, vibrant red pride-of-the-mountain, white phlox. Cam went out of his way to avoid stepping on them and felt encouraged.

He could see the mid-mountain lodge now, a pine shake shoe box far below. Much closer, Bacchetti had caught up with Sawyer and Manny as they cut a steady diagonal across the slope. Then the rain finally hit, reducing the three figures ahead to phantoms of green, blue, and blue. Were they waiting? No, he saw Manny leap over a dry jag that would soon fill with water. Against Cam's hood, the patter of drops sounded like words.

He shouldn't have been surprised to stumble over Tabitha Doyle. A bulge in the hill tended to funnel hikers into the easiest route, and he'd passed directly through this low spot twenty times or more.

Sawyer must have kicked Tabs because she'd moved, the familiar fetal position uncurled into a spread-eagle pose, her distended jaw gaping now through the stained orange hood of her ski patrol jacket. Cam's eyes were drawn as always to the clawing hands. Dissolved in a way that bacteria and the elements alone could never have done, Tabitha's finger bones seemed to have melted in several places.

Of the sixty-eight people who hiked up from the lodge into darkness, sixty-five escaped the machine plague even though it rose with them as the storm cleared. They experienced burn out, reinfection and burn out again as the air pressure fluctuated.

One man just sat down. Another blundered off despite their yelling, the rocking beam of his flashlight visible below them for an eternity. Barbara Price lost a paint can of blood when the whimpering beagle chewed open her face and hands.

Halfway up, a sliver of moon cut through the clouds. They were carrying the children by then and Barbara Price had collapsed four times, and the Koreans were singing a repetitive curse that Cam began to think he could understand.

Huddling out of the wind with two nameless shadows at the base of Chair 11's ninth pole, slumping against the frosted metal, he had not immediately recognized the angry, high-pitched buzzing that reverberated up the hill. Snowmobiles. Headlights appeared in the east, nearly level with him, a swarm of false stars occulted by trees and bursts of snow. The missing locals. They had abandoned the luxury cabins and made their way around the valley's ridges, wallowing in the powder, defeated by the mountain's steepness until they reached the flat, open trails of the Sno-Cat tracks within the ski area.

He was too full of hurt and cold to feel anything more when an avalanche snuffed out the roaring convoy.

Tabby's bent skeleton was like a gatekeeper. She'd survived the collapse of a snow cornice known as High Wall and died alone here, two hundred yards above the other locals, almost certainly the last person to fall short of elevation. So close. In the safety of his hut, warm with Erin, Cam often regretted never burying Tabs—but below the barrier it would be idiotic to waste the time.

He helped Erin over the creek bed and glanced back for the others. One shape had fallen to his knees. McCraney. Cam recognized the striped jacket. He watched to make sure he stood up, and Erin touched his hip.

Her eyes seemed colorless behind the bronze visor of her goggles, yet her anxiety was obvious. Not even Sawyer pretended to be unaffected by this part of the mountain.

They held hands again as they descended.

The thirty-one snowmobiles hadn't rusted or lost their sheen at all, except where unearthed trees had caused dents or the machines had bashed against each other inside the rumbling fist of snow. The glossy metal shapes looked like the parts of a shattered merry-go-round, red and purple and blue, thrown among the cracked trunks and groping root fingers of dead pines.

Cam and Pete Czujko had rifled through the frozen corpses long before spring thaw, digging into pockets and backpacks and saddlebags. Later they'd returned to drain the oil/gas mix that these two-stroke engines used for fuel. The bodies were still intact then, although Cam had seen a snapped elbow, a badly dislocated neck, and assumed the rest had breaks beneath their clothing as well. He'd guessed right. Fragments of bone and unmatched limbs now lay scattered everywhere.

What disturbed him most was the final frenzy of the nanos. Until a host body lost some minimum of temperature, the damned things continued to multiply.

Tabby's melted hands were not the worst, nor was the fused rib cage of another skeleton. One little skull, likely a child's, had a lopsided jack-o'-lantern stare. Its teeth were impossible, leaning out like barbed fangs, and the left eye socket had been eaten away to nearly twice normal size.

The sixty-five people who reached safe altitude were joined in the icy dawn by two survivors from the snowmobile convoy—Manfred Wright, budding star on the regional junior ski team, and a sheriff's deputy bleeding from her lungs.

But sixty-seven was quickly reduced to fifty-two as those with the worst internal injuries died, including all except one of the children. The nanos had destroyed their smaller bodies. Barbara Price would likely have survived her bite wounds, barring infection, but nano infestations in her cheek had spread to her sinuses. She could scream no louder than a moan, and lasted six days. Her husband Jim was dangerously silent for weeks.

At first they tried living at the top of Chair 12, cramming into the patrol shack, but waves of nanos repeatedly forced them to climb again no matter the time of day or the weather.

Exposure shrank their number to forty-seven, many weakened by altitude sickness and despair. Dehydration was a threat to them all and wasted a diabetic woman.

Cam and Pete found themselves in leadership roles by default. They were wearing uniforms. A man named Albert Sawyer also pointed out that they must be more familiar with the area and its resources than anyone else. Sawyer was a real pragmatic. It was his idea to wait for the next storm to raid the lodge, no matter that they were mad with hunger. It was his idea to use the nanos' only flaw to their advantage.

Chair 12 made every difference in their fight to live. They patched the fuel system, then dared to ski down to the main lodge and fired up Chair 4, relaying cans of diesel across the mountain—and food and gear and lumber.

By spring they were fairly well established. Accidents, pneumonia, and a suicide had compacted their population to forty, which made things easier. With rare exceptions, the survivors were young and determined. They understood this world now. Cam even had a girlfriend. Erin Coombs might never have attached herself to him if she hadn't mistaken his name and the hue of his skin as Italian, but she must have felt committed to her decision. By then, the camp was already dividing.

Jim Price rallied support for himself, like a politician, with a series of proposals. His first was work assignments, popular because most people felt they were doing more than anyone else. He organized a sing-along and a "remembrance meeting." He interceded in arguments, in discussions, in everything.

Two of the Koreans had been among the first casualties, and the third was their first suicide. The only black man lasted through their efforts to build the huts, but laid open his calf with a grazing touch of a chain saw and died of blood poisoning. After that, Cam and Amy Wong were the sole non-Caucasians.

It shouldn't have been important. Too much of the human race had been decimated to worry about cosmetics . . . yet Cam suspected his skin color was another reason why so many people turned away from him to Price.

How many cultures had been lost forever? If they did reclaim the planet, what would humanity look like?

There wasn't time to brood. The canned goods faded fast and they spent their days scavenging, and found plenty to eat if they would only work for it; confused, crippled rodents; one deer; lush new spring greens sprouting from the earth. No one even whispered of the bodies down in the avalanche field, which rotted away with the melting snow—and they'd buried all of their other dead. By summer, however, they'd picked the mountain so clean that nothing ever grew there again. And as winter returned, their only option was to raid below the barrier on a regular schedule.

They ate Jorgensen first.

9

The red Chevy long bed pickup, perched on the falling hillside, always made Cam think of television. It embodied that image of rugged power that a lifetime of commercials had hoped to project. They'd pretty much beaten the crap out of it, scraping off the paint, grinding the undercarriage over rocks and bumps, exceeding the load recommendation by a thousand pounds—and the truck had never failed them.

Somehow that made Cam proud. He kept glancing at the distant vehicle as he led the others through the mud and loose boulders above the worst of the avalanche. Manny leaned over the hood, furiously scrubbing grit from the windshield, and Bacchetti held his arms and body up to shield the gas tank from the rain as Sawyer wrestled with a plastic five-gallon drum. Water in the fuel lines would kill them.

This slope was constantly decaying, sometimes in house-sized chunks, or they might have tried to fashion a road through. But they had to take what the mountain gave them.

The downpour increased, beating into a fine mist on Cam's shoulders. Sloppy brown puddles rippled with impacts.

Behind him someone made an outraged noise. "Huh!"—it had to be Price—and Cam glanced up again to see the truck moving. On the way back from scavenging trips they were always crazy to reach altitude and left the vehicle pointed upslope. Sawyer was carefully jockeying back and forth on the narrow flat, getting the nose around, as Manny stood at the downhill edge with both hands up, signaling how much space was left.

"Wait! Wait!" Price pushed to the front as soon as they hit solid ground, Nielsen and Silverstein moving with him.

Cam left Erin and jogged after them, but his heel skated in the muck and his knee twinged. His bad knee. He slowed and made himself concentrate on placing his feet.

Bacchetti was already in the truck bed and Manny hopped up as the group closed in, Price still hollering, "Wait! No!"

Nielsen got to the vehicle first, thumping against the driver's side as he stumbled around to the hood. The white corona of the headlight exploded across his filthy yellow jacket, glinting in a bead of moisture tucked inside his nostril. Nielsen's mask had pulled down and Cam said, "Hey—"

"I'm driving!" Price shouted. The handle on the door rattled as he tried it twice. Locked. "Get out!"

"*Your mask*," Cam said, and Nielsen wasn't the only one who cupped his face with his palms and pushed up.

Price slapped at the window. "I'm driving!"

"No." The fogging glass had reduced Sawyer's hood and goggles to a strange silhouette.

"It's my truck!"

It was, actually. This full-size long bed was one of the few worthwhile vehicles in the lodge parking lots that they'd been able to get started. An incredible number of refugees had bothered to lock up and take their keys, and either died with these crucial bits of metal or lost them altogether.

Price threw his arms wide. "Just because you rushed down here! Just because you got here first!"

"You wasted too much time leaving those goddamn markers," Cam said, harshly enough to divert their attention. Hollywood stood by the rear bumper, his head cocked uncertainly, and Cam lowered his voice. "Someone had to get it turned around."

"Then tell him to get out!"

"Jim, we know this road better than you anyway."

The truck's overloaded shocks responded poorly to the rough trail. Each time the tires hit a large bump or dip, the truck bed swayed like a boat sliding down between two waves, and Cam thought it was only a matter of time before someone fell overboard.

They'd crammed all four women into the cab, although it only had bucket seats for driver and shotgun, which put twelve men in the long bed. Even sitting half of them on top of each other left barely enough space for the rest to stand. It was safest in the middle and at the front, where Price and Mc-Craney leaned over the cab with their hands out, but Cam had deliberately climbed in late on the passenger side. The uphill side. In most places the jeep trail was merely a flat strip bull-dozed out of the mountain, vulnerable to erosion, and if the truck slid in the mud or if part of the trail fell away, he wanted a chance to jump free.

Sweat had pushed through the skin of his back and under-arms as they hiked but now his body temperature dropped, pockets of wet and cold seeping through his GORE-TEX shell.

They rode into a calm hallway through a stand of fifty-foot pines, then back into the rain.

Then they reached the mid-mountain lodge. The parking lot was hardly glass-smooth, warped by a thousand freezes and thaws, but the jouncing of the truck bed settled into a mild vi-bration as they sped through the disorderly gathering of cars.

"Watch out—"

"Stop pushing my goggles!"

As Sawyer accelerated, the few men on their feet leaned in for balance, grabbing at the men who were sitting down, and Bacchetti and another guy shoved back. Hollywood cried something that Cam heard only partly. "You together!"

There was more grabbing at every turn and Sawyer revved the engine through each straightaway, no matter how short.

Price struck the roof of the cab. "Slow down!"

"Jim, let him concentrate!"

"I said slow down!" Price beat on the roof until Sawyer stabbed at the brakes, decelerating from thirty-five to ten in the middle of a long, easy turn. To Cam it was a clear warning and demonstration of power. Price obviously thought otherwise, rapping again with his fist. "That's bet—"

Sawyer gunned the engine, two jolts, rocking them backward. Hollywood wasn't the only man who shouted in protest but Cam was struck again by the disappointment in his voice. "What is he doing?" Hollywood cried.

Sawyer pushed it to fifty or more as the highway slanted straight down for a quarter mile. Cam thought the rain had let up, but it was impossible to be sure inside the corona of spray blasting up from the tires. His sodden face mask tasted of bitter old human stink.

Around a tight corner they passed a jam of three vehicles, then the entrance to the condominium village. Clusters of tiny yellow flowers on the roadside drew Cam's gaze and then there was an acre or more of living color. "Look," he said.

Sawyer slowed and left the highway. Cam hadn't noticed the CORLISS RESERVOIR sign, but recognized this turnoff.

"Don't turn, don't turn! What are you— This road is a dead end!" Price raised one fist to strike the roof of the cab again and Silverstein said, "He's right, the reservoir's just a few miles down and then it's a parking lot."

Cam was glad for his mask and goggles. He knew his guilt was on his face. Would Sawyer stop if Price threatened to push him over the side? But Price was banging on the cab, and Nielsen was trying to find room to turn forward, and Hollywood had leaned over and placed his hand on Keene's shoulder as Keene hugged his belly with both arms.

It was Manny who drew everyone's attention to him. "Cam? Where are we going?"

The truck entered a series of turns and the hazy sun shifted to one side and back again, their goggles darkening and clearing in a pattern that reminded him of pendulums.

Manny said it again, "Cam?"

The urge to silence the boy actually carried his hands out from his body several inches.

Manfred Wright had aged in ways that Cam both mourned and respected as necessary, yet still didn't grasp some fundamentals of human relationships. Cam often believed that this was a kind of self-defense on Manny's part, a willful retreat to childhood. His thoughtlessness had become a threat, however, and Cam realized that Sawyer had been very right not to trust the kid with their plan. Manny would have told Hollywood, who would have told Price, all with the best intentions in mind.

"It's a dead end," Silverstein said.

Price was also quiet, almost hoarse. "What are you guys trying to do?"

Cam knew he needed to say something. There had to be a right word, but then a handful of fingers bunched in his jacket underneath his daypack. Nielsen.

"Let go of him," Bacchetti said, growling.

The horn blared again. "Two minutes!" Sawyer ducked out his window and slapped on the door. "We'll be there in two minutes and you can have the truck if you want it!"

No one else spoke for an instant and Cam's relief was mixed through with gratitude.

"David's infected," Hollywood told them, still bent over Keene. Keene kept his arms tight into his belly and rocked his upper body back and forth as if nodding *yes*.

But they had all turned toward Sawyer's voice.

"His hand," Hollywood explained.

Sawyer hit his door again, impatient with their lack of response. "Just another minute and you can have it!"

Silverstein was the first to spare a glance back at Keene. Then he looked forward again and yelled, "You're wasting time! This is a dead end."

"We're saving time!" Cam said. "Look at the map. The highway runs west almost fifty miles before there's a junction in the right direction, and it's all turns. That's at least two hours, maybe more, and if it's blocked you'll have to drive back up here again no matter what."

"*What!*" Price echoed his last sound in a squawk.

"We hike down."

The few roads in the greater valley tended to run laterally west-to-east, because there was a limit to how steeply cars could climb and because there just weren't many destinations in the area. East of Bear Summit, Highway 6 went nowhere except down into the Nevada desert, and westward for forty-six miles lay only campgrounds and orchards and three small towns. Eventually 6 did bend down to meet Highway 14, and eventually 14 branched into Route 47, which ran north up to Hollywood's peak—but Cam and Sawyer had estimated the total mileage to be ninety or more.

He said, "Even assuming 6 is clear all the way down, and it won't be, you'll spend two hours just to get to 14. But there's only three and a half miles between the highways from here. We can cut cross-country. Forty minutes."

"It'll take longer than that! That's crazy!" McCraney looked at Price. "There's a reason there's no road down there!"

"We can go places that cars can't," Cam shot back.

"But then what?" Silverstein asked. "Then you're on foot."

"We find another car, or hike straight up. Staying on the highway just because it's there is going to get you killed."

Price said, "Everyone voted! Everyone already voted!"

They'd actually conducted their ritual twice, as if a show of hands would somehow change the layout of the valley. Cam had raised the same objections only to be shouted down, but Sawyer hadn't even tried to change anybody's mind. He'd watched and he'd listened and he'd given Cam one silent nod when Price made a spectacle of tallying the votes for the first time.

Cam looked at Hollywood now. The boy had also argued against using the truck initially and Cam had expected him to weigh in on their side, but he said nothing. Maybe he was trying to picture the map in his head.

"We all went over it a hundred times!" Price pointed at

Nielsen and Atkins and McCraney as if counting them. "We all measured it out! One hour! It's only one hour down!"

"The roads will be blocked, Jim." The snowline had been 6,000 feet, which might have kept the roads clear to that level—except for four-wheel drives and locals with plow attachments, snowmobiles, National Guard tanks. It would only take one pileup to stop them.

Price flung his arm like he was throwing something away, his only acknowledgment that Cam had spoken. "It's stupid to hike now if we don't have to! Save our strength!"

"You'll die out there," McCraney added, as if the truck were a fortress or a submarine, as if David Keene had not been breathing the same air as everyone else.

The randomness of the attacks had always been nearly as terrifying as the speed and force with which the nanos consumed a host body, and Cam knew it was only a matter of time before the plague awakened inside them all. A very short time.

Neat wooden signs appeared in clusters beside the road, showing stick figures making use of garbage cans and restrooms. Then they rode into an asphalt meadow occupied only by a Subaru wagon. Beyond a surprising expanse of dark and utterly still water, rock shapes jutted into the sky.

Sawyer left the engine running and pushed through the door with his green pack in hand. Cam hopped over the passenger side across from him.

Silverstein was the only one who joined them on the ground, immediately placing himself between Sawyer and the open driver door. There was a bustle of motion and shouting from the women inside the cab, and Bacchetti fought with the jam in the truck bed.

Cam gazed up at them. He'd told himself that once they were committed, everyone would see that it was unrealistic to think they could just coast on over.

Most of them hadn't even moved.

"Sawyer was right about you," he said, hoping to spark some reaction, anger, anything, and Keene half rose as Bacchetti stepped down beside Cam. Manny had also come up on one knee but paused there, glancing from Cam to Hollywood.

"I have to go back," Keene said. He gripped his left wrist with his other hand. "Take me back."

The commotion inside the cab quieted as Erin lunged out on the driver's side, bumping Silverstein from behind. The other women must have resisted getting out so violently that she couldn't even open the passenger door.

She stumbled into Sawyer's embrace and Cam watched him lead her away from the group, readjusting her face mask and goggles with a minimum of efficient gestures.

"I have to go back!" Keene thrust both arms up in a wild shoveling motion, never letting go of his wrist.

Price yelled, "If these bastards hadn't wasted our time—"

"Hollywood," Cam said. "You of all people, you know we're right. We'll be on the trail you took in forty minutes."

"You can't," Hollywood said. He might have been answering Cam. Then he patted Keene's shoulder and said, "You know we can't drive up again."

"My hand," Keene whispered.

"That station wagon might have keys in it," Silverstein said, waving across the parking lot, and Price finally dropped to the ground and threw himself inside the truck cab.

"Hollywood," Cam repeated. "Please."

Price shut the door with a bang and shifted into gear.

Cam stepped back, and every inch between them felt like a huge gulf, widening fast as the truck began to roll away. Yes, Hollywood had every right to resent him. Diverting from the highway had been a nasty trick, but it was Price's stubbornness that was to blame for the deception—

Maybe it was just that the boy's leg hurt. Maybe Hollywood had realized during their short hike that he didn't have the strength to walk all the way again.

Price braked beside the other car, but Keene didn't move and Silverstein said, "Check it, you better check it now."

Hollywood jumped down and was at the Subaru's door in two paces. He tried the handle, then cupped both hands on the glass and pressed his goggles close. He straightened up, shook his head—and as Cam moved toward him, Hollywood stepped back to the truck and reached for it like a ballplayer touching base.

"Let's go with them! I want to go with them!" Manny lurched toward Hollywood through the crowded bodies, even though the other side of the truck was closer. "Sawyer always knows what he's talking about!"

"Don't be stupid." Silverstein caught Manny's arm.

Cam's amazement at this reaction vanished as McCraney also grabbed at Manny and Nielsen rocked over on his butt to block the kid's path. These men were so threatened by any alternative to their thinking that they would fight to keep others from making a different choice. Safety in numbers, maybe.

"Your foot!" Price yelled through the driver's window. "You can't walk on that foot, Manny!"

"He's in better shape than most of you," Cam said. A mistake. Manny had jerked free, but now Silverstein hooked his skinny waist and McCraney used both hands to secure the kid's left arm. Scaring them, threatening them, had only increased their resolve.

Manny pushed away from Silverstein, and Cam thumped his hand against the truck. "Let him go!"

Price yelled at Hollywood. "Get in, move it, we're—"

The gunshot felt so loud that Cam stumbled back from the fight, impaled by the sound.

Sawyer stalked toward them with his tarnished revolver held up in one fist. There was no need to point it at anybody. McCraney shoved Manny away, and Silverstein only kept an arm around the kid in a reflex effort to keep him from falling.

Words were also unnecessary, but Sawyer seemed to relish the moment. He thrust his weapon overhead as if testing its weight and its power. "Get your fucking hands off him," he said.

10

The wind in the trees sounded like clean ocean surf. It soothed Cam despite reminding him of his father, his brothers. The pervasive roar was loud enough to drown his worrying and this small surrender became easier with every step.

He was tired.

Sawyer kept up a merciless pace. Sawyer had his anger and his vision to feed upon, but Cam was tired. His knee hurt. His snow pants were hot and still heavy with moisture.

Sunlight rippled through the canopy of whitebark pines, cut into distinct rays that swarmed with gnats and flies. His boots made tiny sounds beneath the wind's surf, the clack of pebbles kicked together, the snap of twigs. The rain-softened dirt absorbed all else.

His four companions might have seemed more obtrusive if they were marching down in a group instead of single file, but following Sawyer through the trees was easier than deciding on individual paths. Cam heard Erin's breathing whenever he got close—whenever rocks or a deadfall slowed their parade or, more rarely, when she shied away from a tight squeeze and paused to find her own course. Mostly there was only the working beat of his heart and the monotone wind—and the bugs.

Black flies droned around Cam insistently, attracted by his heat or smell or color. No amount of waving could disperse these fat dots. They beat against his goggles and face mask with the weight of raindrops.

The flies were loud but for the past ten minutes Bacchetti had been louder, mimicking their engine buzz. "Vrrrve! Vrrrrrve!"

Finally, Sawyer stopped and swung his head around as they bunched up. Bacchetti outweighed him by thirty pounds, even wasted to the bone, yet Sawyer merely said, "Shut up."

The grasshoppers were fewer here in the trees than farther up the mountain, before the storm, but Cam had noticed several veins of ants. One dark mass boiled around a flailing millipede. Another exploded up Sawyer's calf when he stepped in the wrong place, and Cam shoved past Erin to help his friend sweep his leg clean before the jittering specks got inside his clothing.

Six times now Sawyer had dodged left or right. Cam could only guess why except during the fourth detour, when he heard the dry, warning shake of a rattler. Already he'd spotted two nests of snakes, babies coiled together for warmth—and it was unnatural for these creatures to be exposed. Maybe all the good crevices and overhangs were taken.

Maybe on a hot afternoon this land would crawl.

The lizard population was unbelievable. Chilled by the passing rain, small gray bodies hunched within every patch of sunshine. They clearly preferred rock but sometimes covered fallen logs and bare dirt as well. They scurried from Sawyer with astonishing speed, a low wave front of motion, yet quickly expended themselves and merged with the still earth again.

Cam studied the land to distract himself. The sensation in his left hand was undeniable. Shaking his arm would not disrupt the ever-worsening itch and it would not keep the nanos from spreading, but the only other option was to do nothing. So he snapped his wrist downward again and again. This threw off his balance, and he nearly toppled when he stepped on a pinecone.

His fear was real but not overpowering. Not until he noticed Sawyer's green shape pacing back uphill—

Erin had sat down. Cam opened his mouth to yell but Sawyer stopped in front of a break in the pines. Their map hung open at his side, creased folds of white.

Manny slogged by and didn't pause, moving to join Sawyer. The kid's limp was clearly more pronounced.

"Go," Cam said to Erin. "Let's go."

But Sawyer and Manny returned as Bacchetti caught up.

"Look. Everybody look." Sawyer crouched and spread the map on the ground. "We're drifting too far west."

You're the one who said it had to be you in the lead, Cam thought, yet resentment was more than petty; it could be dangerous.

He bumped Manny to move in by Sawyer's shoulder. Manny was preoccupied anyway, digging into his boot with both thumbs, punching at the heel. Maybe the kid had only cramped, but the nanos had an unfortunate tendency to bunch up in scar tissue, attacking the parts of the body that had already been weakened. Cam always got it first in his hand or his ear.

A red grid covered the map, showing square miles, each block messy with brown contour lines of elevation, yet Cam located their intended path in a glance. They'd scratched big X marks into the lighter patterns of abrasion in the waterproofing.

Sawyer touched his gloved finger beside a tight, hooked contour nearly a full square off-course.

"God." Manny stopped working at his foot. "Oh God."

Cam said, "That's the crest we're on?"

"Right."

They had been led three-quarters of a mile farther west than necessary by an undulation of ravines that ran oceanward rather than directly down into the valley, allowing themselves to be channeled by the shapes of the mountain.

Cam shut his burning hand into a fist. "I'll walk point with you, watch the compass while you keep an eye on the map."

"Right." Sawyer stood up and Cam rose beside him.

Manny also broke into motion again, frantically squeezing his foot and kneading his ankle.

Erin said, softly, "Can't we just sit for five minutes?"

Cam bent and took her arm.

She went inside herself. Cam wasn't sure how much time had passed since they'd worked down from the ridge—fifteen minutes, maybe; the sun was no higher than midmorning—but already Erin had bumped into him twice when he slowed to read the compass. She was tapping some reserve of energy.

Cam needed that second wind himself. They'd tromped through a hundred yards of wilting stalks before he remembered it was spring. This field of Mule's Ear looked as if autumn had come. The yellow flowers, usually the size of a silver dollar, were just incomplete nubs—and the long, fleshy leaves that gave the plant its name had browned. Many were dry enough to crackle beneath his boots despite the storm runoff that made this meadow an uneven carpet of muck and puddles.

He'd seen no bees or butterflies this year, and wondered if the ants and reptiles had devoured every hive and slow-moving caterpillar. He wasn't sure that a lack of pollinating bugs would doom these plants. Maybe a fungus was also to blame, or mites, or aphids . . .

Cam had nearly grasped the tremendous interlocking gestalt of it when mosquitoes gathered at the bottom edge of his goggles, a sudden fog probing for entry.

He slapped the spindly black cluster and twisted his mask. "*Christ—*"

Sawyer jumped and almost fell, turning to look back at him. Thirty small shadows clung to Sawyer's face, his fabric mask stained with a wet comma over his mouth.

"What?" Sawyer said, and Cam reached out. Sawyer blocked his arm, the map flagging out from his hand in stiff paper zags, but none of these movements dislodged the bugs.

The bloodsuckers themselves were a minor threat, no more

than an irritation. It was the bites that could kill. Each puncture might also drive nanos into their skin.

Cam mashed his gloves against his chin and forehead and turned to Erin. Her hood bristled with thin bodies like hair. Behind her, Bacchetti was already rubbing busily at himself. Manny lifted both hands before his eyes in disbelief.

"Oh shit," Sawyer said.

"Run." It was all Cam could think of. But they stood there for another instant, water chuckling somewhere among the dying plants. He bent to wipe his thighs and saw that inky living hair attached to his boots as well.

He stared, as Manny had.

The mosquitoes' egg cycle must have been broken long ago. They lived no more than a few weeks, and the females needed blood to become fertile. Could they have adapted in such a short time to feed on soft-skinned frogs and salamanders? That seemed impossible. This entire species should have been wiped out except for some remainder of the breeds whose eggs lay dormant in mud until wetted by flooding.

Spring runoff. Christ. And Hollywood had probably suffered enough bites to fertilize five hundred females, each capable of birthing a thousand more—

Cam killed twenty with his hand and it meant nothing. He straightened up into a haze of bodies, squinting against their high, brittle whine. "Run." He pushed Erin and she stumbled, crunching through two yards of Mule's Ear. "Run!"

Manny bounded away, milling his arms, and they all broke after him. The mosquitoes were black snow.

Cam screamed when the blue jacket ahead of him disappeared, but then he saw another figure and changed course. He fell. He jumped up and Manny staggered into him, coming sideways across the slope. Cam began to shove at him, but Manny resisted. They went in different directions and Cam ran another forty yards before he realized that Bacchetti, to his left, was also moving laterally across the floodplain. West, into the wind.

Maybe it would be enough to push off the bugs.

He saw flashes of green and red disappear over a low rise,

Sawyer and Erin. They might have yelled for him. He scrabbled after Manny to the top of the embankment.

They thrashed into the brush and lowest branches, shielding their goggles and masks with their forearms. These pines were different than any Cam had seen for twelve months, with thin needles and fragile orange soft cones that showered pollen over him. Each impact squashed mosquitoes by the dozens and chased away hundreds more.

He saw Bacchetti's blue jacket and then spotted Erin ahead, a red figure working toward the sparsely wooded face of a hill. The wind would be stronger there.

Adrenaline was a poor substitute for real stamina. Cam made it to the slope, but the incline knocked his feet out from under him. He began to crawl. Then Manny helped him stand again and they struggled up.

At the crest, Erin lay on her side, heaving for air. Sawyer was still standing. There was nothing beyond them except more forest and rock bumps. Cam saw himself as a distorted blob in Sawyer's mirrored lens when Sawyer stepped toward him, patting at his face and chest, killing the few bugs that still clung to him. Bacchetti was more clumsy, his efforts like punches.

"We have to keep moving," Sawyer told them.

"The ridges," Manny said, panting. "Stay on the ridges."

"Right. If we can. Definitely keep away from water."

"You think we're near the road?"

Sawyer shook his head, untangling the torn map. He crouched and pinned the folds to the ground with his arms.

"We must be close," Manny insisted.

But all the distance they'd hiked eastward again had been lost. They might even have run farther west than they'd been before. At least they had also fought a good ways downhill, north. The lodgepole pines and abundance of undergrowth were proof that they'd reached a lower altitude, more vivid to Cam than numbers on a map—6,600 feet. That was the benchmark nearest to the point where Sawyer's tracing finger stopped.

"Maybe here," Sawyer said.

The new sound on the wind didn't register with Cam at first. They would need to head northwest to avoid the flood-plain and the worst of the mosquitoes, but Highway 14 wasn't more than a mile off. They could find a car.

A car. Cam turned his head. "Is that—"

The horn cried and cried again, a mockery of the coyotes who had once sung here. Then the howling became bleats.

"That's Morse," Manny said. "Ess oh ess."

Three short, three long, three short. The pattern was obvious once the kid had pointed it out.

"Right." Sawyer laughed and rubbed his forehead. "I don't know what the hell Price thinks we're going to do for him. Look." He slid his finger two and a half miles west, upwind. "Somehow they got onto this logging road."

Cam said, "But it goes through."

"Unless it's blocked. Or they crashed." Sawyer teetered noticeably when he rose to his feet. "It doesn't matter," he said. "We can't help them."

11

There were surprisingly few bones in the forest, mostly just birds like elaborate little carvings. Their best theory was that every creature had tried to hide away. Squirrels and rabbits and fox had gone underground, while deer and coyotes disappeared into thickets. Birds had tucked themselves into brush and treetops only to be blown free later by the wind.

Humans had experienced that same burrowing impulse.

Each of the first six cars they came upon was a mass coffin, the stick shapes in their matted, stained clothing invariably bunched together against the doors or in the floorwells. The smell would have been worse except that during the first spring, bugs had slipped in through vents and doorjambs, stripping the rotted flesh and often the upholstery as well.

Sawyer dragged the remains out by their legs or skulls or punched them deeper into the car, whatever was easiest. Keys dangled from every ignition—but every engine had been left running, heat on, lights on, radio on.

Four of the six vehicles were locked. At first Cam had giggled at the absurdity, yet his head swam each time he bent to find a rock and he nearly cut open his jacket when he broke the third window, too weak to disengage himself from the momentum of heaving his crude tool into the glass. He stared back at himself from the fourth window. Even hefting ten pounds of asphalt pried from the road's edge, his posture was tight and defensive, shoulders hunched, head bent, as if making himself smaller would help in any way.

He understood locking the doors.

Every vehicle was a bitter frustration and Manny wasted time trying each ignition again after Sawyer had given up. Sawyer was all business, in and out, cranking each key three times. Only three times. Then he walked away.

The blacktop let them maximize every stride rather than fighting rocks and mud. They were also now on nearly level ground, the bottom of the valley, halfway there. Moving too slow. It was as if they were old now, bodies bent inefficiently.

Highway 14 was not a parking lot. At 6,200 feet, this road had been under several inches of snow, yet Cam imagined the lack of cars was due more to the fact that most people had been drawn off by Highway 6, farther down the valley . . . but if they couldn't get an engine running soon, their only option would be to continue on foot up the northern face. Hollywood had said Route 47 was blocked in at least two places, anyway, but if they could ride all the way to the first obstacle . . .

Erin slumped against him, as heavy as dread. They'd come upon another vehicle, an old brown pickup half in the ditch, and Sawyer simply let go of her.

A fly smacked into Cam's fogged lens. He blinked, awareness opening and closing in him like a lighthouse beacon. It hurt. He burned. Molten barbs swam through his hand and his wrist. The same fire distorted his ear, pushing the tissue apart.

Erin tried to sit and he clubbed uselessly at her side. Then Manny bumped past. Erin's weight peeled away from Cam and he staggered, trying to soften her fall but desperate to stay upright himself. He looked at the others for help.

Sawyer had dragged a freakish little body from the pickup.

Cam stared, realized it was a dog, and Erin managed one word hardly different than breathing. "Rest."

Bacchetti's boots scuffed into Cam's field of vision and the

big man grumbled, encouraging the truck just as he'd talked to
the flies. "Rrrrrr. Rrrrr—" He coughed.

"Help," Cam said. "Get her up."

Bacchetti had already settled into a wide, braced stance.
He might have been a little nuts but Cam was glad for his presence, glad for his strength and his loyalty—so it confused
him when Bacchetti sidestepped away, until he heard other
boots.

Together, Cam and Sawyer heaved their lover into a sitting
position. Her eyes rolled open and the band of skin framed by
her goggles crinkled in a familiar way. She was smiling.

"I can't carry you," Sawyer told her. "I won't."

"Please," Cam said, maybe to both of them.

He'd studied the town so often from his favorite cliff that
he thought he knew where he was going. The Forest Service
and CalTrans shared a lot on the northeast side, a complicated
zoo of chain-link fence populated with a limited variety of
green trucks, orange trucks, and orange plows. They could get
an engine running there for sure. It shouldn't be hard to find.
This place only had eight streets, a three-by-five grid set off-
center on Highway 14, plus several curling back roads lined
with old cabins and giant modern homes.

"Sick?" Erin said. *Six.* A wooden sign on metal stilts read
WELCOME TO WOODCREEK, POP. 2273, ELEV. 6135.

Bacchetti continued to help Cam each time Sawyer tried
another car, stepping in to keep Erin upright, but the big man
had stopped making his engine sounds. He coughed whenever
he did. He coughed constantly now.

The fucking things were in his lungs.

Regret filled the core of emotion that Cam maintained inside himself, banked against his despair in the same way they'd
learned to protect the embers of their cookfires. Bacchetti had
been the real surprise, the surprise hero, and Cam hoped somehow he would make it.

Woodcreek seemed remarkably well preserved. Two homes

had burned and there was a jeep rammed up on a guardrail, but anyone who'd died here had hidden themselves away.

The ghosts came out as they reached downtown. Their feet echoed down every road, and shadows paced alongside them in the dusty storefront windows.

Then Sawyer got a van to turn over. Tucked between a deli and an antiques shop, the white Ford would not idle, dying again and again. He pumped the gas and tried shifting into neutral or first, giving the van more time than the last three cars put together. But it just wouldn't catch.

They detoured left when they wanted to go straight, avoiding a huge nest of rattlers sunning in the street. The thick, brown, ropy bodies held their ground when Manny waved his arms and yelled in a pleading voice—"Go! Move!"—and the ghosts began to talk.

They were not alone in Woodcreek.

The mumbling and whispers became real words as Cam hurried Erin into an intersection, Bacchetti dragging on her other arm. He actually looked the wrong way first, tricked by the silhouettes in the glass of a real estate office.

McCraney's urgency was clear. "Heard him—"

"—doing, you know, we don't—" Hollywood saw them and lifted both arms overhead. "*Hey.*"

Cam shouted back, "Hah!"

They were seventy feet off, standing in a bunch on the sidewalk. He recognized Silverstein and Jocelyn Colvard and that was as much counting as he could manage. All twelve seemed to have made it.

Price had been right. Jim Price had made the best choice. Yes, these people had gotten stuck farther west of Cam's group—they must have, or they would've driven into town an hour ago—but while both groups had hiked roughly the same distance, the miles that Price covered on foot had been the last part of the logging road and then the easy surface of Highway 14.

Even better, Price hadn't wasted time trying to get any cars started. It must have been obvious, doors open, bones scattered, that each vehicle had already been tested. Every failure and disappointment had been a help to them.

The surge of gladness in Cam carried him forward despite Erin's weight and she moaned, "Stop."

He knew that she hurt. He knew she wanted to sleep. It was smarter to keep moving. The others would need to come up the street to reach the CalTrans station, but he wanted to see their eyes. That was worth fifty steps.

Erin let her legs go limp and Cam and Bacchetti sagged together, holding her up. "Stop," she said.

"Get back!" Sawyer yelled behind them.

Cam felt his thoughts open and close again, and realized suddenly that Hollywood had not raised his arms in welcome. The boy had made himself larger as a warning.

The knot of people on the sidewalk shifted, retreating, leaving three men in front like fence posts. Price. Nielsen. Silverstein. An open doorway stood at Nielsen's elbow and above it jutted a touristy Old West sign. THE HUNTING POST.

Price held his rifle down alongside his leg as if its heft was too much for him, and Silverstein's long torso had kept the outline of his weapon from showing. Only the tip of its muzzle poked above his shoulder. Nielsen's hands were oversized, a pistol in each, the barrels like stiff ugly fingers.

"Get back," Sawyer called again, to Cam, and Silverstein screamed, "You get back! Stay away from us!"

Cam had never heard Doug Silverstein speak in any way except a controlled manner, not even during their worst arguments, and the hysteria made him seem like an imposter.

There was more. Silverstein was shorter, hunched to one side. Price made a familiar slashing wave yet stayed silent.

These were not the same people Cam had left on the mountain.

Hollywood's voice held no trace of the confident madman who'd crossed this valley for them. "Just go away," he said. He sounded lost. He sounded old.

Sawyer ignored him. "Put 'em down, Price."

"Get out of here!" Silverstein brayed.

Then Bacchetti coughed and there was an answering hack from someone at the rear of the other group. A weak, wet rasp. It could have been enough to reunite them. Their suffering was the same. It had always been that way.

But Sawyer yelled again, "Put the guns down!"

Caught between them, Cam was afraid to move or speak. Motivation came from a sharper fear. Sawyer and Price, here, now, had only one conclusion.

Sawyer and Price had too much hate between them.

Cam flicked his gaze over his shoulder, shaping words inside his crowded head before he reconsidered making himself a target. Manny had followed them down the block and stood ten yards back. Sawyer was still in the intersection but stepped close to a blue mailbox with his revolver.

"Come on, hey," Hollywood said, louder now. His intent must have been the same as Cam's, but the poor deluded asshole had never understood the depth of the fear and resentment among them. They had tried to conceal it from him, yet Hollywood had also willingly ignored a thousand clues.

The boy repeated his words, "Hey, hey," and his voice seemed to stir Price, who directed nonsense at Sawyer.

Price said, "Took too long, killer."

The bewilderment in Cam resolved into a fleeting memory of Chad Loomas, the second man they'd murdered and eaten. But they had all eaten. They had all wanted the stew. What had Price been telling Hollywood, redirecting the blame?

"Killed her," Price muttered again. Cam had misunderstood, deafened by his own guilt. *Lorraine.* Price must be talking about Lorraine; *too long* meant hijacking the pickup truck.

He looked for her but the people behind Price were too similar, all hoods and goggles. Apparently she was missing. "I helped her, Jim, her arm, remember?"

"Spic."

Cam hadn't heard that curse since the end of the world. In all their time together, all their confrontations, no one had ever condemned him out loud for the color of his skin—and it meant nothing now except that whatever remained of Jim Price had been burned down to something base and primitive.

"You goddamn spic, you faggots, you killed her." Price waggled his right arm, his rifle. "Faggots," he said.

Something happened behind Cam. He saw Silverstein and Nielsen react together. Silverstein pulled his rifle from his shoulder and pushed it forward like a spear, as Nielsen lifted both pistols.

Cam moved. He yanked hard on Erin's arm as he turned and Bacchetti came with them, one step, two.

Sawyer stood behind the mailbox now, his revolver leveled.

"Get away, get away!" Silverstein screamed, and Hollywood said, "Come on, hey, just let them—"

Sawyer fired first.

12

Bacchetti stayed with Erin and Cam. Otherwise they would have fallen. Erin managed only a cramped, kicking motion as they began to run, and Cam put his boot down on her ankle. Then Bacchetti hauled her forward and Cam regained his balance. That first gunshot still had yet to roll beyond their hearing.

They were twenty feet from the end of the block but it looked like forever, a wide, flat-walled canyon. Sawyer's revolver barked again and stamped a hundred details into Cam's mind; screams behind him; the square shadows of the buildings painted on the street. A rifle cracked and Nielsen's pistols stuttered *pop pop pop pop*—

All three of them instinctively ducked and Bacchetti dodged sideways, pushing Erin into Cam. The noise felt like a solid thing, each slap backed by a crazy weave of echoes.

The corner building was brick. They ducked past it and fell together as the noise disappeared. There were still human sounds—hysteria, the ragged screech of someone hurt—but the shooting had stopped.

Unsteady even on his hands and knees, bumping against

the rough brick, Cam looked for Manny first. He saw Sawyer across the intersection on this same crossroad, crouched against a shop wall, a barbershop, busy with something in his lap. Reloading. Cam's face mask had pulled down over his chin and he reset it as he poked his head around the corner.

Silverstein had come several paces after them, still holding his rifle away from his lanky torso. He lurched stiffly, trying not to disturb the nano infection in his gut. "Get away!" he screamed. "Getaway getaway!"

Price didn't appear to have moved, rifle leveled. Someone near him ran into the hunting shop. Everybody else was down, either wounded or making themselves as small as possible, bright jackets like human confetti strewn over the asphalt.

Some of the confetti moved, crabbing away, kicking in agony.

Manny was a blue figure between Silverstein and Cam, his goggles ripped from his thin, bloody face. The kid had been smart enough not to run for Sawyer's corner, even though he'd been closer to that side of the street. Most of the fire must have been directed back at Sawyer's gun, but at least one stray round had caught Manny nevertheless—or maybe he'd been too slow, too easy, hopscotching on that bad foot. Maybe Nielsen had targeted him in frustration when Sawyer escaped. Maybe Price had done it from spite.

The kid was alive. His body was bent as if he'd been thrown from a great height, chest down, hips turned on their side, but he was alive. He looked like he was still trying to run or maybe dreaming of running. Both legs worked pathetically and he inched one blue-sleeved arm over the filthy road.

In his heart, Cam said good-bye.

"Getawayyy getawayyyy!" The yelling was more frightened than frightening, and deprived Silverstein of any element of surprise as he paced closer. Silverstein had lost his mind.

Sawyer knew exactly what he was doing. Sawyer had always known. He looked across the intersection at Cam, hefting his revolver and pointing with his free hand. He walked two fingers, then tapped down on them with the weapon's short barrel.

Club him if he comes up your side of the street.

The clarity of the idea, just the act of communicating, gave Cam focus. He slipped out of his daypack. The canteen in it was no more than ten pounds, but it was the only weapon he had. He balled his hand around the top of one shoulder strap to give himself as much reach as possible, then glanced back for Erin, not sure what he would see.

Both she and Bacchetti were in ready crouches and she bobbed her head once, the way Sawyer always did, like once was plenty. Cam nodded back. He knew then that he genuinely loved her.

"Getawayyy!" The warning cry sounded no closer.

Cam dared to lean over, peering through the chink between two bricks. Silverstein was still reeling around the beast in his stomach but he'd altered his direction, patrolling a line across the street instead of continuing to advance on them.

Cam's eyes went to Manny again, left out there like a bloody sack of garbage. It should have been Price. It should have been Sawyer. The idea resounded through him with no sign of madness, quiet and clear and definite.

It should have been Price and Sawyer.

Most of the people lying on the ground were rising now, and clustered around the two figures who remained prone. One of them was alive, a woman named Kelly Chemsak. She sobbed when Atkins and McCraney hoisted her up. The other casualty was Nielsen, the big gory splotches on his torso turned purple by his yellow jacket. No one wasted any time on him. Jocelyn grabbed a pistol trapped under Nielsen's shoulder as George Waxman emerged from the hunting shop with two shotguns.

Hollywood was backing away. Cam noticed him first as motion separate from the group, a good distance behind everyone else. Then Hollywood turned and ran. He ran back the way that Price's group had come, away from Cam, away from them all.

Heads turned. Silverstein turned.

It was an opportunity. "Go," Cam said, heaving himself into the open. He didn't have enough left to help Erin.

His knee buckled on the first step, nearly dropping him.

Bacchetti and Erin went past immediately, leaning on each other, and the best that Cam could do was an uneven skipping like Manny.

He heard Price shout. Halfway there. But the first shot came again from in front of him.

Sawyer had leaned out around his corner and put two quick bullets down the street, then two more as Erin and Bacchetti made it to safety beyond him. Cam swung his arm into Sawyer's chest as he dived for the sidewalk and they fell in a tangle.

"*Watch it!*"

"Stop—" But he had no breath in him.

Sawyer crawled back to the edge of the barbershop, even though looking out to shoot meant exposing himself to their fire. Cam could never have done it. The voices and scuffling down the block might have been retreating or charging closer, a hundred feet away or only five. Why not just run away? Why force a standoff in this place as the nanos chewed through them?

He saw his answer in the outline of Sawyer's figure against the brick building across the intersection.

Sawyer had taken a bizarre interest in fashion during the past week, showing Cam and Erin different jackets from their stash of extra clothing. *It's new, it'll keep you drier,* he'd insisted, but Erin loved her soft-worn puffy red coat and Cam had been unwilling to give up his old ski patrol jacket—his orange jacket, designed with visibility as one of its main functions.

Sawyer's green jacket and brown snowboarding pants had camouflaged him well in the forest. He was no less noticeable than any of them here, yet he had prepared himself as best he could. He had anticipated a need to run and hide.

Cam leaned toward his old friend across the cement.

Sawyer didn't react, focused entirely in the opposite direction. Sawyer rocked his head past the edge of the barbershop and brought his revolver up—

"Don't," Cam said, catching his other arm. "Jesus, don't."

"*Get off me!*"

"Just let them go."

"Fucking stupid, *go where*? Go where, Cam?" Sawyer shifted closer, back behind the corner, lifting his hand as if to keep the .38 from Cam. It was also a position that would allow him to bring the revolver's weight down like a hammer. "Goddammit, I could've gotten a couple more! They probably took off by now!"

Cam stayed very still, staring up into Sawyer's mirrored goggles. He was so busy doing this that he barely registered the news that the others had fled. Good news.

Sawyer said, "Next time we might not see them coming."

Cam nodded, but the motion was only reflex. *Agree with him.*

"You have to help me!"

"CalTrans. Let's just get to the CalTrans station."

"You have to help me," Sawyer said again, lowering the gun. After another moment he shifted away from Cam and peeked around the corner. Then he stood, in stages, grabbing at the shop wall. And when he was up, he held out his other hand.

Cam didn't hesitate. It was difficult to follow a chain of logic through the shock and pain crammed through his body, but he saw little choice except to run off like Hollywood, and then what? Price would shoot him on sight, now or later, here or on top of the mountain. Sawyer was right about that—and maybe Sawyer had saved them by firing first. It was good to think so. Yes. Sawyer had saved him.

He held on to this decision in the same way that he clung to Sawyer's hand, pulling himself up.

There were four bodies sprawled in the street now, Manny and Nielsen and two others, and he had seen Kelly Chemsak wounded. That left eight, maybe fewer if Sawyer had winged anyone else, and David Keene had been infected early, so he would be weak . . . They might not be outgunned by more than four or five people . . .

The reversal in Cam was swift and powerful. This wasn't who he wanted to be. It would be a very small tragedy compared to everything else that had happened, but there was a way out of this box. There was a third alternative.

"I need a gun," he said, with just the right reluctance.

Kill Sawyer. Kill Sawyer now and shout it to the others, that should be enough to end this war.

Erin's groaning turned his head, yet his gaze caught on Sawyer's mirrored face and Sawyer bobbed his head once, ignoring her sounds. "We both need rifles," Sawyer said, "in case they come at us from a distance."

He gestured with his revolver for Cam to start walking, but Cam found it impossible to turn his back. Sawyer depended on his own paranoia the way that most people used their hearing or their sight. Sawyer needed an ally, but he might have decided that Cam was unreliable. He might just drop Cam here in the street with the rest of the dead and go on alone.

Cam made a show of hobbling on his bad leg and reached for Sawyer's shoulder. Sawyer stepped closer. His sweat smell was strong and evoked memories of bed.

"We can do it," Sawyer told him. "We're going to make it."

Breath went in and out of Manny in rapid huffs. Cam saw blood high on the kid's back and on his thigh, dark stains beneath his jacket and pants.

"It's us or them," Sawyer said. "It's that simple."

Manny lay facing the other way and Cam felt relief, then shame and horror. Were the kid's eyes open? Was he listening to them? Cam expected him to roll over at any moment, and then what would they do?

The next body was Silverstein, shot in the back. In fact, Nielsen seemed to be the only one who hadn't been trying to run away. Nielsen embraced the sky, arms open like a bird, but Silverstein had collapsed facedown with his rifle at his feet.

Cam pushed off from Sawyer and took three steps before he remembered he was exaggerating his limp. He almost glanced back. He bent, and closed his good hand on the smooth wooden stock—

"You have to help me," Sawyer insisted.

Kill him.

"I was part of the design team that built the nano. Cam? I was one of the people who built it."

He paused, tensing to spin around as he came up.

"Cam? Listen to me."

Silverstein wasn't dead, either. Life wasn't like the movies, *pow,* one shot in the belly and you're gone. The resiliency of the human body was amazing. Sometimes it would continue to fight even when the will was gone.

Doug Silverstein had lost consciousness and his lungs gurgled badly, but he might last for hours. He might wake here, alone, as the machine plague devoured him.

Cam shifted his rifle to the man's head. He couldn't have said when he'd started crying.

"No! You'll just let them know where we are!" Sawyer grabbed his shoulder. "Are you listening to me? We were going to beat cancer in two years, we were that close. I swear. We had everything right in the pipeline."

"What . . ."

"Just get me to the radio. I swear. I can show Colorado how to stop it, but you have to help me."

"What are you talking about?"

"I built the nano, Cam. I built it and I'm probably the only person alive who can stop it."

13

Sawyer rarely spoke of who he had been, who and what he'd left behind, but that was not unusual or any cause for suspicion. Many of them had abandoned their pasts.

Sawyer had always taken an authoritative stance regarding the plague but he seemed to be knowledgeable about the workings of almost anything mechanical, diesel engines, radio reception, and he had argued like an engineer when they were building their huts, pointing out drainage and foundation problems.

Cam had never worried about it, not even during the lightless days of winter when his mind stole away from their reeking hut and came back remembering the wildest fantasies as actual memory. Everyone talked about the plague. Everyone had theories. His long-lost buddy Hutch had read enough articles about nanotech to spout impressive factoids as they watched the first confused reports on TV. Manny offered plausible ideas based on nothing more than comic books and *Star Trek*.

There was no question that Sawyer seemed smarter about

the problem than anybody else, but Sawyer had always been smarter than everyone about everything.

Kneeling in Doug Silverstein's blood, Cam rejected all of the easy questions. Four thousand feet into the invisible sea was no place for an interrogation. *Colorado,* Sawyer had said. *Radio.* That had been his first demand of Hollywood, seventeen days ago, *Is there a two-way radio?*

He knew Sawyer would say and do anything to save himself—but this, this would be such a crazy lie, such a risk, all or nothing.

The crafty son of a bitch knew exactly how to play him.

Cam looked up. Sawyer hadn't moved from his side, waiting on a verdict.

"Hurry," Cam said.

Sawyer nodded and strode away toward Nielsen's body and the gun shop. Cam might have shot him then. Instead, he rummaged through Doug Silverstein's pockets for extra ammunition, and the man jerked at his touch. It should have been awful.

It was nothing.

Cam had regained his feet before Sawyer stepped out into sunlight again, cradling two pistols and another rifle. Then they shuffled back up the street toward Erin and Bacchetti.

"You ran," Cam said. How else had Sawyer reached safe altitude? Without a head start, he would have been trapped in the cities or on the chaotic highways with all those millions of others. "You ran instead of trying to help."

"I had nothing to do with it getting loose."

"But you ran."

"Everything that, everyone . . . It wasn't my fault."

Cam pressed him again. "You said you can stop it."

"I swear. I've worked out a way to turn the nano against itself. Here." Sawyer touched one of the pistols to his head. "*Archos* is a highly adaptable template, that was the whole point. We can rework—"

"Why didn't you stop it before?"

"Right. On the goddamn mountain? You don't build nano keys out of dirt."

"Before. Why didn't you do anything *before*."

"There wasn't time! It's not something we're going to bang out in an afternoon! I didn't get any more warning than anyone, I swear it. It wasn't my fault."

Cam said nothing. They'd nearly reached the corner, and he didn't want Bacchetti to overhear.

Sawyer was for real. Sawyer was telling the truth. He was more than canny enough to bury a secret of such magnitude— they would have killed him if they knew—but he had never been much of an actor, letting his contempt and superiority show even after those traits became a danger to the survival of their threesome.

Cam had hated him before. Cam had mistrusted Sawyer enough that, ultimately, he had been ready to silence him with a bullet. It was the anger of love betrayed. In many ways their bond had been the most intimate of Cam's life, past or present. They were family in every way that counted.

He knew he'd carry the bastard if he had to.

Cam and Bacchetti hooked Erin's elbows around their necks, dragging down on both wrists, and she walked with a new determination just to relieve the stretching and tearing of her gut. Somewhere inside she had ruptured.

He supposed the cure wasn't as close as he dreamed. She wasn't falling just short of the finish line. *It isn't something we'll bang out in an afternoon.* Still, her suffering was a waste. He and Sawyer could have come across the valley alone, perhaps with Hollywood to guide them.

Of course that was exactly what Sawyer had fought for. *Let 'em stay.* He'd said it again and again.

Cam was the one who convinced the entire group to try.

We'll never make it. He barely got here and he's not half-starved! Whose voice was that? Lorraine. Dead for no reason. She could have stayed on the mountain, too. They all could have stayed if they had only known.

Two blocks to the CalTrans station. Two blocks and Erin could sit and rest.

Sawyer ranged ahead, shoulders cocked like a man pushing into a stiff breeze. Cam wondered how bad he had it. Not bad enough. It was insane but he wanted Sawyer to look at her. The back of that green jacket was an insult, and Cam tried to hurry her moaning weight forward. "Wait," he said. "Hey!"

"Oh—" Erin made a mournful sound.

Sawyer should have told her. She should have stayed back above the barrier. The bastard was right to consider himself more valuable than the rest of them put together, too valuable to risk, and Cam saw the sense in skipping a general announcement. Price's reaction would have been hysterical, a trial, a sentence. But Sawyer had chosen not to keep Erin and Manny safe.

"Heyyy!"

Sawyer stopped and turned with one fist up, his index finger extended. Cam thought it was a threat before he saw that Sawyer was merely shushing him like a schoolteacher, the oddness of the gesture due to his face mask.

Erin had pulled her mask off. Erin had shaken her head violently when he tried to reset it. Erin smiled, lolling her head toward Cam because Bacchetti was two inches taller than him and held her up higher on that side.

Erin had a relationship with pain that Cam had never understood, and he hated her gruesome little cat's smirk.

"God, I'm sorry," he told her.

At least Bacchetti's coughing hadn't grown worse. Cam was optimistic that the big man might survive.

One block to go, after they got past the bank on the corner. This big concrete cube had been one of the easier landmarks from his cliff. One block and then a left past the gas station.

Sawyer reached the intersection first and paused at the tall edge of the bank, working the bolt of his rifle. Then he leaned his head around the corner directly into the concussive blast of Waxman's shotgun.

Some or all of Price's group had chosen not to flee into the woods after Hollywood. Some or all of them had circled around to the CalTrans station as Sawyer and Cam found weapons—and Jim Price had posted guards while he got a vehicle started.

Price had made the better choice again.

Sawyer's head snapped away from the corner of the building in a huge fan of concrete dust and his body followed like a poorly designed flag, tangled and limp. He lost his goggles and one flap of hood and Cam thought his face was gone—

gone it's gone it's all over

—and Cam stumbled backward even as Sawyer flopped into the gutter, his left arm sprawled over the sidewalk.

Erin hung on to Cam, choking one elbow around his neck, as he let go of her and brought up his rifle. But when he shifted forward again, the change in momentum was too much. She tugged lightly at his daypack as she slid off.

Sawyer was alive. Sawyer had bent his left arm in and pushed, lifting his chest from the ridge of the gutter.

Before Cam reached him, a rifle cracked somewhere up the street and a fleck of black leapt from the asphalt near Sawyer's boot. They could see his legs! Cam threw himself down, dropping his weapon, grabbing the back of Sawyer's jacket. His infected hand came free but he pulled Sawyer nearly two feet, out of sight of anyone around the corner.

Blood curled in the gray concrete powder that covered the side of Sawyer's face, speckled with green fibers from his hood, yet he seemed more dazed than seriously wounded. The worst was two divots on his temple. Cam saw bone or white tendon at the bottom of these small, shallow wells. The shotgun blast must have only grazed him, deflecting first off the wall of the bank, and Cam guessed that Waxman was at the edge of the gun's short range. The end of the block. The pellet blast had widened and weakened, which was why the dust cloud had been so big and why the top of Sawyer's skull wasn't pulp.

Cam pulled his pistol and fired two shots past the bank at

an angle that hit almost directly across the street from him. It should be enough to slow anyone advancing on them.

The shotgun roared back, then the rifle twice.

More gunfire erupted farther up the block and Cam bent his head around as fast as his pains would allow, wondering if somehow Bacchetti had outflanked Price and was trying to chase the other group back this way. Time had become elastic. He was afraid he'd lost several minutes. Yet Bacchetti stood right behind him, over Erin, revolver up in one hand.

Sawyer had given Bacchetti the .38 but Cam suspected it was empty. He knew Sawyer didn't share his faith in the big man.

The new gunfire had a weird rhythm, methodical, paced, rather than the tight frenzies of attack and answer. It also consisted entirely of pistol shots—and there were other sounds mixed in, ringing metal, flat pops.

"Priiice!" He knew what they were doing. "Priiiiice!"

He put another shot across the street, helpless to stop them. He couldn't even look around the corner.

The other group had obviously found a working vehicle. The other group was ready to go and they were now disabling the rest of the motor pool, shooting out radiators and tires.

"Tell me where to find your lab," he said, cleaning Sawyer's wounds. He was no longer afraid that Waxman or anyone else might charge their position, and he emptied most of a canteen over Sawyer's head, scrubbing with two fingertips as Sawyer flinched. Then he risked three quick drinks himself. Each mouthful was sweet beyond understanding, and almost certainly laced with poison. Inert nanos carried into his belly would soon awaken, but the dust-and-damp fragrance had been too compelling to resist.

"Tell me." He was careful with his voice.

If something else happened, if Sawyer didn't make it, at least he could tell Colorado where to look. The lab would have computers, files, something. The radio broadcasts had implored survivors in the West for any clues.

"Just to be safe," he said. "You have to."

But Sawyer's brown eyes were as flat and guarded as his mirrored goggles had been. "I don't think so."

"Jesus Christ, I'll help you! Swear to Christ!"

The blaze at the CalTrans station spread fast. Greasy black smoke lurched up in two thickening towers, and Cam heard the fire crackle and laugh as they limped away. Gas tanks detonated in a random array of claps that rolled over the valley walls, sounding out every inch of elevation between them and the afternoon sky.

They walked.

They walked apart, Sawyer striding into the lead again, and Cam tormented himself with the question. *Tell me where to find your lab.* If his thinking wasn't so fragmented, he would have asked it earlier. It should have been the first thing out of his mouth after Sawyer confessed.

It was a measure of what they'd become that he dropped Erin just to give Sawyer a hand with Nielsen's body, stripping the yellow hood and cheap goggles. He actually looked back at her then—her gogs were high-quality Smiths—before he thought to check Doug Silverstein and see if his gear was any better.

Not far behind them, exploding vehicles threw the fire from one block to the next like a giant kicking his way through town. They were forced west, then cut north again ahead of the holocaust.

Beyond the center of Woodcreek, the terrain canted upward and pine trees closed in on the gravel road. The homes here were small and old and comfortable. They passed a fat SUV tucked under a carport, then a driveway with a 4Runner and a sedan. Then the road ended and they hustled through someone's overgrown yard. No doubt they could have searched for keys, gotten an engine started, but then what? Work their way around the fire just to catch up with Price?

Hollywood had come across on foot. Hollywood had told them Route 47 was no good. Getting into a car was a trick, a trap. Sooner or later Price and the others would be forced to leave their truck and angle back this way again on foot from farther up the valley.

The rifle was too heavy, but Cam kept his pistol.

The north side of the valley, facing the sun, bristled with more plants and trees than the mountain they'd hiked down, and the lush spring growth would keep the fire from racing after them. They were safe from that danger at least.

They climbed.

They climbed, and the giant raged behind them. Cam let his tattered spirit roll upward on the booming of a propane tank. He let himself go away from here. He reached for the distant rim of the valley where the earth quit and the sky fell on forever. There were other minds gathered there at the highest points, watching for him. If Hollywood's people hadn't heard the gunshots, which seemed unlikely, the explosions told the story. The smoke would be visible for fifty miles.

They climbed to judgment.

They climbed on distended muscles and broken feet. They climbed carrying acid and coals inside their bodies.

A wrinkle in the terrain brought them out of the trees and into a brown meadow and suddenly the ground leapt up in dark, fluttering sheets. Ten thousand grasshoppers. The four of them reared back, pelted by tiny, kicking bodies—and Erin fell, folding and squeezing her innards. It destroyed her. She bled out in a rush, a horrible soup that spilled out of her pants.

In some ways it was a mercy, but like Silverstein, like Manny, she retained a flicker of life even after this incredible trauma. She stared up at Cam as he pulled off her goggles, her gem blue eyes wide and confused.

He brushed the twitching bugs away from her face and out of her long hair because there was nothing else to do. He thought to kiss her, but then the bloody froth poured from her mouth.

* * *

They climbed and the mountain was everlasting. They climbed like drunken men, careening off of trees, bumping shoulders. They passed an empty canteen and Cam scuffled another ten yards before he realized he was in front. He swayed and nearly toppled when he raised his eyes from the slanting rock face.

Someone was ahead of them.

Cam put his hand on his wide chest pocket, on his pistol. He turned into the late, low sun as Sawyer tottered up behind him, rubbing at his yellow hood with one black glove. Were they high enough yet to run into Price again? Maybe. Maybe they were almost at the top, they didn't know, they'd only tried to place themselves on the map twice since fleeing Woodcreek— No. The opposite side of the valley was clearly higher. How much higher was tough to judge, but Price wouldn't have crossed their path so soon unless he'd come laterally across the mountain.

That should have felt like good news. They weren't going to sneak up on anyone, not with Bacchetti wheezing, not with their bootsteps echoing from the castle shapes of granite, and they couldn't afford to search for a different route to avoid an ambush. A crippled man with a shotgun could have held them off until they were crippled themselves.

It had to be Hollywood, which had to mean they were on the right course. Good news.

But Cam was beyond anything good.

They climbed. They climbed over a jumble of car-sized boulders and Cam went first, testing the footing. At the top of a loose drainage, he held his burning arm down to Sawyer like a rope.

They climbed too slow.

Sawyer knocked himself over, beating at his temple. Cleaning and armoring his wounds might have minimized the infestation, but the machines were in him just the same.

Cam leaned down and summoned a voice. "Tell me where."

Sawyer snapped his head like a dog shaking off wasps. Cam wasn't sure it was an answer.

"Tell me. You son of a bitch."

Sawyer lifted one shredded glove. That was his only response. He lay there panting until Cam pulled him up.

They climbed and Bacchetti matched their pace for three hundred yards on his hands and knees, convulsing and choking. Cam glanced back too many times. The man probably wouldn't have made it even with assistance, but they would never know. Cam chose to stay with Sawyer.

They climbed above the sun.

At this elevation, the gradual mornings of spring were capped by sudden afternoons, and the mellowing light had eased down into the west. Soon it would be canceled altogether by a saw-toothed ridge.

They climbed and their sight dimmed as the day settled into dusk. They climbed through a field of dirt-browned snow and ice, the first they'd encountered. Cam knew this meant something. Wrapped in stars, his consciousness shot through with hard pinpoints of white, he didn't realize that there were three of them again until he kicked into a silhouette and, when he tried to pick Sawyer up, the shape of the body seemed unfamiliar.

Hollywood had scratched open his round face before he passed out, maybe trying to stay awake. In the starlight his blood was black and glossy, and only hinted at the raw furrows he'd clawed through the rash on his cheek.

"Hey," Cam whispered. "Hey, get up."

They were almost there. He was sure of it. On this side of the valley, snow remained only in the highest reaches. The sun had destroyed the rest, and this gravel moonscape was the same as home. They were almost there.

Hollywood had won. Hollywood had succeeded, twice, at a punishing odyssey that they wouldn't have even attempted without his example—and there was no question that it would have gone faster if they were better people. If they hadn't bickered and lied and killed.

More than anyone, this young man deserved his help.

"Sawyer," Cam said, looking around. "Hey."

Sawyer was already beside him, clacking through the gravel on his knees. He blundered past Cam and pushed a chunk of rock into Hollywood's teeth.

The boy's eyes bulged open, shining glints in the dark. "Glaah! Glah!"

Cam screamed, too, putting his arms in the way. "*Stop*—"

"He fell." Sawyer reeled away from them, hefting the rock again and then driving it down onto Cam's wrist.

"Stop, *stop*, you don't have to—"

"He fell. He fell and hit his head but we carried him up. We carried him all the way."

"We could! We could have done that!"

Sawyer panted against him. "We have to. To be the good guys. In case Price makes it. His word against ours. And we're the good guys. We carried their friend."

"We could have. Oh Jesus, we could have."

"Price wanted to take over. Remember that. It's what we have to tell them. Price grabbed all those guns and planned to take over."

They climbed to the barrier. They climbed with Hollywood between them, dying or already dead, draining blood down the front of his jacket, and then an invisible wall slammed through them in bits and pieces.

The pain did not miraculously cease. Too much tissue had been disintegrated. Too many machines had filled them.

Cam shrieked and hit the ground, unaware of the impact. He had known that transition would be awful but he had never been so thoroughly infected.

He flailed against the ungiving rock, crabbing upward, a spasm of nerves encumbered by thick, strengthless muscle. Clots and blotches rose beneath his skin and merged, expanding, piling into reefs of blisters. He climbed, but his foot was trapped beneath Hollywood's weight, and his leg held him like a leash. He did not know this. He did not understand that his progress had stopped. He tried to climb—would always climb—and screamed again as his own blood abraded him from scalp to toe.

Sawyer rolled close, thrashing in the same animal frenzy, though he made no sound except a strangled, nasal grunting.

The voices that answered Cam were from above.

He would never guess how long it took the footsteps and flashlights to reach him. Long enough that the overall agony settled again into specific burns and aches. Long enough to worry that it was Jim Price, that Price had reached safety hours ago and would now kill them both.

Long enough to wonder if it mattered.

Sawyer was still in the grip of a massive seizure, grinding his teeth as his head drummed against the gravel.

The strangers descended together in a halo of light, and cutting beams stabbed out at Cam and played over his trembling, stained body. The tall figures stayed back. They murmured among themselves, quick, guttural, alien. Then they broke apart and encircled him. He saw the beveled shaft of a baseball bat, the gleam of an ax . . .

Realization cut through his delirium.

Sawyer's original fear had been right, as he had been right about so many things. The situation here was no less desperate than on their own peak. These people had sent Hollywood across to bring back food. His strange enthusiasm, his urging and his promises, everything made sense now. *Cattle drive.*

It was a fate that they deserved, but Cam rasped up at the faceless shadows. "Wait. Me." Then the empty black of the valley swept up and claimed his mind before he could say more to convince them to spare Sawyer's life.

14

The shuttle's trademark sonic booms rattled over the high mountain basin like cannon fire. Moving fast enough to compress air at the front of its nose and its wing, *Endeavour* sent twin shock waves through the Colorado sky.

James Hollister looked up. He had been watching the crowd.

This basin formed a vast natural amphitheater in roughly the outline of an egg, its oval floor two miles across and three long. Canyons, sinks, and gullies creased the surrounding hillsides and James estimated the total surface space to be in excess of fifteen square miles.

The northern and western slopes were mostly empty—bald humps of green wild grass and rock. Along the eastern face, however, people stood shoulder to shoulder, horizon to horizon, like a great bison herd of Native American legend.

James had always possessed a flair for numbers but this mass defied him. It was unreal. It was hypnotizing. And its voice was an inconstant rumble, louder now that the *Endeavour*'s far-off thunder had split the clear blue afternoon.

"I don't see them—"

"You think they're okay?"

Some of the camera crew near James had turned south, shielding their eyes from the sun. That wasn't the right direction. It was too soon. *Endeavour* would still be turning into its approach path, hidden from everyone down in this basin.

James looked back at the teeming crowd. He stood at the broad end of the egg, the southeast end, on top of a low knoll set beneath the mountain's bulk. Highway 24 wound north from Leadville and took one last bend directly below him before shooting straight across the basin, riding its eastern edge to avoid the heart of the marsh. "Front-row seats," he'd told Ruth, and she'd laughed. Actually he would have preferred another location farther north. All they'd see from here was the shuttle's tail. *Endeavour* would pass nearly overhead and come down a quarter mile beyond him.

VIPs couldn't be expected to walk far, of course. Four dozen vehicles sat at the base of the knoll—army trucks, sport utility vehicles—and there was another camera crew down there, watching this much smaller crowd watch the highway, recording their presence here today. Fine and good. The problem was that James had been classified as Very Important himself. Major Hernandez refused to let him hike beyond this little bump. Hernandez had fought to keep him from coming at all, in fact, but the security chief lost out, with only a few well-placed words from James, because all of the bigwigs he'd contacted had been dead set on coming themselves.

If nothing else, the *Endeavour*'s landing was an event. It was historic, even in the midst of the plague year.

Perhaps three hundred thousand people had come on foot to witness the attempt. James figured they must have started out this morning, despite the still bitter cold. Most of the half-million refugees around Leadville lived in the snaking valleys and hills east of town, in the hundreds of old mine shafts and in shelters built from tailings and debris. No car rides for them, and the nearest camps were four miles away as a bird flies.

As the shuttle flies.

James shifted from one foot to the other, like he was trying to balance his fleeting smile to keep it from falling off. He knew with absolute certainty that Ruth had been complaining the whole way down, not because she'd told him that the ride up had been a slap in the shorts, but because the vocal, wise-ass style was her trick for dealing with stress. A wonderful trick.

They had become good friends. James often rested his hand on the comm equipment when they talked and was slightly embarrassed now to see her in person, as if she'd know somehow and misinterpret the gesture.

Ruth had flipped—literally flipped, she said—when he relayed the council's proposed schedule: two more weeks. At first they'd only planned to wait out a spring rainstorm coming in from California, but James had taken the opportunity to spread a few second thoughts.

Oh, the battle had not been particularly fierce. The convoluted hierarchy of displaced officials was packed with fat egos who strove daily to stay relevant, and James had had zero trouble stirring up a battalion of congressmen to holler for resources to protect their brave astronauts. For all their excitement about committing to the inevitable, they were equally nervous about a disaster. Nobody wanted to be held accountable, and replaced, if something went wrong.

That was fine and good, as far as James was concerned. No need to tell Ruth who'd shaped their fears together into a ball and started it rolling. She could tough things out for a little longer if it meant she'd get back to Earth in one piece.

He accepted that to most survivors, the true benefit of bringing down the *Endeavour* was only an abstract. Maybe they didn't even believe in it. The general populace was too busy scratching out an existence and the leadership was wholly preoccupied with more immediate threats and with the subbarrier scavenging efforts.

James had faith that Ruth would jump-start their efforts to develop a functional ANN.

James knew she might be their last chance.

During her long exile she had pursued her own concepts for all three ANN still in development, trying to stay sharp, stay busy, and the entirety of her files had never been transmitted because broadcast time was limited. Fresh thinking might be all they needed to advance their research. Her gear alone would be invaluable, with extreme imaging and real-time fabrication that exceeded anything in their hodgepodge collection.

The crowd rumbled again. The lights had come on.

James stared out across the basin and admired his handiwork. What had been a narrow, backcountry highway was now something more worthy of what they demanded of it.

It was April 27th. The highway had been ready for six days. If construction hadn't gone so well, no doubt some grandstander would've proposed waiting for Memorial Day or even the Fourth of July. The NASA folks and Army Corps of Engineers had exceeded all expectations, and James was inspired to see so much accomplished with so little. For fifty-five years he had been an optimist, but this new life was short on pluses and positives.

The work crews had shown the best of everything human. Ingenuity. Cooperation. They'd ripped the targeting systems out of three M-1 tanks and built a decent radar system on the mountain above him, patching into a radio tower there to use existing power and signal lines. There was also a fully manned AWACS plane in the air to ensure accuracy. As for the highway itself, the army had widened and reinforced the railroad underpass. Embankments had been pushed up, leveled, and packed along the entire three miles—much of it by hand—to provide emergency overruns as well as wide spots for fire trucks, medical trucks, military trucks, and the PAPI equipment.

The Precision Approach Path Indicator lights were assembled in two groups, one most of the way up the basin, the other much closer to James. Each batch consisted of red and white beacons, as well as generators that had been topped off an hour ago. Some bright boy hadn't wanted the fuel tanker sitting out there next to the road.

Calibrating the PAPI system must have been a hassle, though. It was just basic math to figure the layout, of course, but the actual lights were a mismatched selection torn from the high school football field and from the fleet of aircraft parked on the small county strip south of town. The last thing anyone wanted to do was confuse the shuttle pilot. PAPI was a visual aid that showed him if he was in the correct glide angle, depending on whether or not the reds and whites matched up.

They had done all they could. The last delay was due only to the weather, again, as they waited for mild head winds and a good high-pressure front to settle in. James had seen helicopters struggling at this altitude, and the shuttle would also have minimal air resistance to ease its descent. Would it be enough? Funny, he'd only become unnerved after everything was ready—

Endeavour came in steep and fast.

Screams filled the basin, a treble howl. James flinched but didn't look away from the gleaming craft. They thought it was crashing, he realized. The space shuttle descended at an angle of nineteen degrees, more than six times the glide slope taken by commercial airliners.

Slowing, its blunt nose up in a flaring maneuver, *Endeavour* plummeted below the near horizon of white peaks.

The spacecraft was magnificent. It was their past.

James Joseph Hollister, respected scientist and middle-aged bachelor, raised both fists and screeched like a beer-blitzed college kid. Another trick he'd learned from Ruth. He yelled for her. He yelled with her.

Endeavour ripped past in a blink and was below him, its black underbelly becoming the off-white of its fuselage.

"Shit I missed it!" one of the cameramen shouted.

The pilot was top-notch. He hit the narrow highway directly in the middle. The stubby white bell of the *Endeavour*'s wings came down like a dress, a ball gown, unmistakably broader than the road by a good fraction on either side.

Smoke exploded from beneath the shuttle's body upon touchdown. Still nose up, its stout body swayed left on its rear tires and James jerked his arms down as he leaned to his right. "Come on, come on," he chanted.

Endeavour dropped forward and embraced the ground finally, but continued to drift toward the left edge of the road. The drag chute snapped out and wagged violently, a huge gray blossom.

At speeds in excess of two hundred miles per hour, the shuttle reached the bridge while James was still caught in his dance. He'd become quite a student of the technology during the past weeks, and had spoken reassuringly to each of his bigwig contacts about carbon brakes and nosewheel steering capabilities. He had been repeating that same mantra to himself all morning but now he kept begging, "Come on—"

The pilot brought his hurtling craft back from the left margin, back from the dirt embankments and disaster.

It was that excellent reflex that doomed *Endeavour*.

There had been an inch-and-a-half drop from the highway asphalt to the concrete slab of the bridge, the result of a repaving effort three years prior. Army engineers noted it while making their improvements. For a car the bump was marginal, barely enough to slosh a cup of coffee, but they had recognized that the shuttle's weight and phenomenal speed would amplify any defect, and smoothed the surface with fresh tar. NASA pad rats had approved the work and warned the ISS crew.

Endeavour hit the new patch with its nose wheel slightly cockeyed. Even so the accident was one in a thousand. The front end bounced heavily and the wings were carried up on a gust of wind. The pull of the drag chute increased the drift.

On a normal runway there would have been room to correct. Instead the shuttle, lurching to the right now, clipped four inches of its starboard wing through the boxy cab of a yellow Colorado Springs fire engine. The roof and doors of the vehicle tore away in a brilliant shower of glass and plastic shards. *Endeavour* lost only a few white panels of its heat shielding.

Impact, however, brought the nose of the spacecraft farther to the right. *Endeavour* plowed through an ambulance and another fire truck before it cartwheeled over the embankment.

15

Ruth was the only one who panicked. Gus had her unbuckled before she even realized they'd stopped moving. Her inner ear and every muscle spun with the forgotten sensation of *down* as terror shot through her laboring heart, which seemed to be trying to jump free from her chest.

"Get out, Gus, we have to get out!"

Down felt all the more wrong for the sideways tilt of the shuttle's crew cabin. She grabbed at him as she flopped forward, weak and clumsy. Her faceplate clunked against his orange pressure suit. They were all fully armored, in case *Endeavour*'s long wait in vacuum had resulted in subtle damages and the pressure blew out; in case it became necessary to reroute for Denver International, deep within the invisible sea; in case any of a dozen scenarios that the NASA team had game-planned.

The voices in her helmet were quick, deliberate, too much overlapping jargon to process: "Evacuate not responding control med med power-off."

Gus dragged her toward the side hatch, bumping after Deb. Fortunately the floor tipped in that direction.

His mouth moved and she realized that two of the words resounding through her head were his. "Hang on," he said, but pushed her away.

Deb had stepped onto the interdeck ladder, and Ruth caught one of the struts. Deb kept climbing toward the flight deck.

Ruth looked after her, shocked that she would move away from the exit. She would block the way for Ulinov and Mills and Wallace to get down. "What—" Each shallow breath was an aching. Her breasts and ribs felt like a badly used drum. Reentry had been rough but she was pretty sure the whole shuttle had rolled a few times at the end.

Impact, Mills had announced on the radio. One word. Ruth guessed there hadn't been time for more.

It had been nothing but guessing since she strapped into her chair down here for the initial burn, ninety-some minutes ago. You'd have to be superhuman not to be scared. Mills had kept up a running commentary for their benefit, but Ruth, Gus, and Doc Deb had been relegated to the crew cabin beneath the flight deck, blind in a box, an elevator in an earthquake.

Ruth was definitely not superhuman. There had been a time, at the height of her success, when she would have accepted a bet to do this alone in radio silence or even strapped outside on the wing, damn it, but that brash steamroller of a girl had left her, giving way to claustrophobia and fear.

Deborah gasped on the radio: "Derek, oh—"

"Get back down that ladder." Ulinov might have been asking for tea, his voice as composed as Mills's had been.

Impact.

Once upon a time, postlanding operations had involved well over twenty specially designed vehicles and a hundred experts whose first action was to test the shuttle's exterior for toxic and/or explosive residual gases such as hydrogen and nitrogen tetroxide. The astronauts remained inside while a Vapor Dispersal Unit fanned away potential hazards, and soon afterward Purge and Coolant Vehicles began a more thorough job of making the shuttle safe. The payload bay especially, where Ruth's records and nanotech gear were stored, tended to fill with fumes.

Leadville had only a jury-rigged wind machine and civilian firefighting trucks. The NASA team had been anxious about dealing with a successful touchdown.

Ruth was inside a bomb.

One spark from a sheared wire, or the terrible heat of the engines—it was crucial to escape the vehicle that had saved them. There was no chance *Endeavour* would be obliterated in a titanic ball of flame, since most of the excess fuel was burned off during reentry as a safety precaution, but a flash fire would still roast them well enough.

Gus opened the hatch and Ruth shoved against him as the massive coin of the door dropped down, sticking out from the side of the shuttle like a round plank. Normally it would have been ten feet above ground but the *Endeavour* seemed to have ridden up a hill, so that although this side of the craft tipped down, the gouged earth dropped away to match. Below them were green shrubs, torn and smashed— The peeled-apart tire of a car— And two men in black firefighter jackets, yelling and waving their arms—

Ruth shoved again but Gus stayed in the opening to deploy the thermal apron, which would protect them from the hot exterior tiles. And in those unbearable extra seconds, the conversation in her helmet at last penetrated her lunatic fear.

Ulinov: "Evacuate Dr. Goldman now."

"Your leg." Deb again. "Bill?"

"I'm busy."

"Get back down that ladder."

Deb said, "I need help up here."

"No. Evacuate now."

"Okay, go go go," Gus said, and he went through. The two firefighters had been joined by a soldier and an EMT in white, all of them shouting and waving.

The bravery of these men was striking. *They had run toward the bomb.* Without equipment, without any of their plans intact, they had run into danger for her.

Deb's voice was matter-of-fact. "I have three wounded on the flight deck, one critical."

Ruth could have saved herself. She should have. It was

exactly how they'd trained for this moment—yet she hesitated at the brink of safety.

Like the first responders on the ground outside, the ISS crew had gambled everything for her. They had sacrificed their families and their homes. Gus and Ulinov had abandoned their countries just to serve her. If she left them now, she might never recover from the decision. The impulse to sabotage the space station and force this landing, no matter that she hadn't acted on it, had damaged her in ways that could never be erased.

For one instant Ruth gauged the balance inside herself, but there was never really a choice.

She turned back inside. The men below her wouldn't be able to help, not immediately. Lord knew where the shuttle had come to rest but clearly it was a disaster outside. They might need several minutes just to reach the hatch.

Ruth slipped and banged her faceplate against the interdeck ladder. Her body didn't work right. It was unbelievable that she'd ever been so heavy. The ladder leaned over her like a wave and she was forced to wedge both hands and one foot into the rungs before raising her other leg to keep climbing.

"Ruth! Ruth, jump!" That was Gus, apparently on the ground now and looking for her at the side hatch.

She froze with her head above the floor of the flight deck. She saw glass and dirt blasted over the cockpit—wet crumbly brown *dirt*—and heaved herself up on a new flood of adrenaline.

Riding copilot, Bill Wallace leaned past what looked like two bodies to reach the pilot's panel. Derek Mills had been rolled up in his seat, up despite the downward-tilting floor, by a crumpled shaft of metal jammed through the windshield. It was the twisted roof of the ambulance that the *Endeavour* had carried over the embankment.

Blood covered Wallace's arm, some of which must have been his own. Shrapnel had flayed open the elbow and shoulder of his insulated orange sleeve, wounding the arm he'd extended to complete his work. Emergency power-off. A complete shutdown of every onboard system was their best chance to prevent a fire and the man left with this responsibility had never formally trained as a pilot.

"Hurry!" Ruth screamed at him, at herself, at all of them.

"Go back down. Evacuate." Ulinov was still in his seat, directly beside Ruth at the rear wall of the flight deck. He had also taken shrapnel. His faceplate was partly masked by opaque chips and Deb slapped his gory knee with one hand, hanging on to his seat with the other. The adhesive patch she'd put on his leg bulged as if there were other patches folded beneath it, pushed against his torn skin, a crude but effective pressure bandage despite the bulk of his suit.

"Get him out," Deb said to Ruth, gesturing. "Try to hold him so he doesn't fall down the ladder."

Ulinov waved them off. "Your orders are to—"

"Do it," Deb said, imperious as ever, before she left Ulinov for Wallace. There hadn't been time yet for Deb to work on Mills, and Ruth realized that he must be dead. The metal bulk nestled into his lap and chest had hit him hard enough to bend his seat.

"I gotcha," Ruth promised Ulinov, grabbing his armrest with one trembling hand.

Maneuvering on the crowded deck was like a puzzle. She hauled her legs out of the access hatch, then did her best to slow Ulinov as he left his chair and squeezed past her.

"You go next," Deb told Wallace, probing at his shoulder wounds, but Bill Wallace stayed in his seat. He slapped at a computer, either because it wasn't responding or to clear away the debris, but he never even turned his head.

Ruth hurt her back when Ulinov lost his footing at the top of the ladder. Bracing her feet against the wall on either side of his torso, she clenched his arm with a strength that seemed entirely mental. His blood had rubbed off onto her sleeves.

Ulinov collapsed at the base of the ladder, on the floor of the crew cabin. Ruth stepped on him and fell.

They crabbed out into the awful white sun together and Ulinov swan-dived from the round plank of the hatch. Ruth screamed, but caught her breath. He hadn't fallen—he'd jumped, turning to protect his leg—and the knot of people below them had become a group of forty or more, uniformed in black or olive drab or blue or white. Ulinov's big orange body knocked down a wide swath of them.

The men had their arms up for her, too. Nearly every face was bearded, which looked strange, rough, animal. Ruth knelt to minimize the distance but slipped off before she could kick outward. Three guys dived to break her fall.

No one bothered to set her on her feet. Half a dozen arms clamped around her boots and armpits and elbows, hoisting her up, and a confusion of silhouettes in caps and firefighter helmets bobbed above her faceplate as they carried her.

"Wallace," she said. "Wallace!" But the radio chatter in her ears was only a confusion again.

Someone at her left shoulder tripped and they dropped her, two bodies slamming into her midsection. She might have grayed out. She lost her thin breath altogether.

Then she was upright, suddenly, propped on the low bumper of an army jeep. A rangy Santa Claus in dirty paramedic whites squinted at her through sun-darkened wrinkles and bushy eyebrows. His hands fumbled with the seals of her helmet. Ruth stared past him. But the panorama of sky and mountains was too big for her and she deliberately lowered her eyes, reeling, even as curiosity forced her to glance up again.

They were about a hundred yards from the *Endeavour*, north up the highway, and she froze as she realized the mountain face was alive with bodies. Lord God. There must be *miles* of people up there watching—

The shuttle had gone off the highway between her and the impossible crowd, its path marked by the wreckage of two or more fire engines. Other emergency vehicles had come up the road to that point, lights winking, horns blaring, trundling through the swarm of firefighters and soldiers and NASA pad rats.

Then they pulled off her helmet and the radio chatter in her ear was replaced by a less immediate, more chaotic hubbub of yelling. Ruth winced at the sun, and the sweet fragrance of the air made her close her eyes.

Savoring it, she remembered Derek Mills. *Impact*. His last word, warning them. She looked up.

"Dizzy?" the medic asked, putting his palm to her cheek and thumbing down on the skin beneath her eye. "You're not bleeding, are you?"

"It's just his," she said.

They'd seated Ulinov next to her while she was catching her breath. Two medics, one also in dirty whites and another in combat fatigues, had knifed open the leg of Ulinov's suit to wrap gauze over his thigh. Another busy cluster of medical personnel had formed at the back of an ambulance across from them, and Ruth caught glimpses of an orange suit. Gus.

"Are they out?" she asked. "The astronauts?"

"I think—" The medic jerked and lifted his head.

Then the rifle shot reached them. Ruth wouldn't have noticed the distant clap amidst the engines and hundreds of voices, except that his motion alerted her and the general din instantly went quiet.

She thought to wonder how the medic had heard a sound before it existed. Then he took his hand off her cheek and reached for his side. Blood seeped there through the medic's grimy white shirt. His beard parted with a question.

Then he sagged away from her as the voices roared. People everywhere belly flopped onto the ground or ran for cover behind the many vehicles, hiding from the great eastern slope. The mountainside itself undulated as three hundred thousand refugees fled in conflicting, colliding masses.

"Sniper!" yelled the soldier kneeling before Ulinov, seizing Ulinov's arm to haul him down.

Ruth didn't make sense of it, didn't realize that her bright orange suit was the target, even after a ricochet whined off of the jeep's hood not two feet away. She gawked at the riot surrounding her until Nikola Ulinov hit her in the side.

His bulk drove her into the asphalt like the heel of God's boot and snapped both bones in her forearm.

16

Leadville had become a fortress. The barricade across its northern border choked the highway into what must have been the world's only traffic jam.

Ruth and Ulinov were hustled into the ambulance after Gus, and their siren cleared a lane through the emergency and military vehicles for a mile and a half—not far beyond the spot where the *Endeavour*'s tires first hit ground. But at the knoll that James had dubbed the front row, other sirens interceded and blocked their way, three civilian police cars and two military police jeeps. Another ambulance came up on their tail while they waited and Ruth assumed that it held Doc Deb and Wallace.

Gus blabbered, "Do they know who we got in here? Tell 'em who we got here, go, go, let's go."

No one else said anything, except for the EMT working a protective brace around the sleeve of Ruth's suit. "Lie down, you're very pale," the woman said, but Ruth couldn't look away from the windshield. The ambulance driver had shut off his siren and made no move to force his way into the stream of olive drab trucks and black Suburbans bumping down onto the

highway. Both of the MP jeeps had long machine guns mounted
in back, gunners ready, and all of the cops had weapons in
hand.

Ruth realized several things about the "front row" that
James hadn't mentioned on the radio. This knoll was distanced
from the main body of the mountain by a shallow ravine filled
with fencing and soldiers. Presumably the blockade went all
the way around. Also, this side of the knoll paralleled the bigger slope, so that no one up there would have a good view of
the people down here—or a good shot. It wasn't so much the
front row as it was elite seating, separate and protected.

They had expected trouble.

A trace of that wild panic hammered through her blood
again but was muted by shock and utter exhaustion. She'd
burned out. There wasn't anything left. Ruth sat with her
snapped arm in her lap, listlessly roasting inside her suit. The
air was so fresh, even in the close quarters of the ambulance,
that she was aware of her own moist heat rising from her
round metal collar. In another time and place, the stink would
have been humiliating.

Less than a minute passed before they were moving again.
Another army jeep skidded up behind the cops and MPs
blocking the way, and a man like a lean wire flung himself
from the passenger seat. He wore army green but a cap instead
of a helmet, and was unarmed except for a pistol on his hip.
None of the military police saluted him, yet the debate only
lasted ten or twelve words. The MPs pulled one of their jeeps
off the road.

"Oh yeah, wow, I like that guy," Gus said.

The lean man waved at their ambulance driver, then turned
and hustled to his jeep. His driver weaved aggressively toward
two of the vehicles still coming down from the hill, cutting
them off, and the lean man popped up in the passenger seat
with one hand jutting forward to deflect a military truck.

They didn't get far. The road bent around the knoll and
then dropped into a riverbed, sheer hills closing in on both
sides. The dozens of vehicles slowed and backed up across
what amounted to three lanes, all pointed southeast, using the

shoulder and nosing out onto any level patch. Ruth wanted to laugh—it was goofy, feeling nostalgia for a jam of red taillights—but again she experienced only a tick of emotion beneath her weariness. Hard gravity had flattened her butt and compacted her innards, and drew open an aching space between the ends of the broken bones in her forearm.

"What a mess," Gus said.

The lean man stood on his seat again. Ruth waited dully for him to go ballistic, screaming the other vehicles off the road into the reed marsh and lazy water. Instead, he looked back at their ambulance and lifted both hands in a shrug. He was Hispanic, late forties, trim and hard with a formfitting uniform to show it. He had a dark bar of a mustache but no beard.

He looked left and right, contemplating the hills overhead, then ducked over and grabbed a walkie-talkie. Ruth bent forward to look herself. She saw hundreds of people trudging down the slope on their left, a solid mass in the bright sun, and there were dozens more gathered along the bank upriver.

She felt more than a faint spark then. Not hearing the rifle shot until after the bullet hit the medic, that would stay with her as long as she lived. There would always be a small absence of sound chasing after her.

"Okay, now what?" Gus said, jarring Ruth to get a better view himself. "What a mess. Who planned—"

"Gus." Ulinov had his eyes closed.

"Why is there shooting?" Ruth asked the driver, blurting her fear like a child, but it was the female EMT who answered.

"A lot of people lost everything." She was Ruth's age, and no better washed than any of them. Grease had wicked her long brown bangs into points. "They want to get even."

The ambulance inched forward. Ruth turned this statement over in her mind just as ponderously.

She said, "What?"

"Some people just want to get even."

"I didn't build the locust! *I'm* trying to stop it!"

"Might've been rebels," the driver put in, uselessly revving his engine. He was only a kid, his facial growth spotty except for a hanging tuft on his chin.

Ulinov spoke one word again. "Rebels."

"Got us boxed in fucking good right now, waste the whole government if they wanted." The kid revved and revved, knuckles flexing on his steering wheel.

Somewhere there were helicopters thumping.

"I'm trying to stop it," Ruth repeated.

"I just meant—" The EMT shut up, like the gray-bearded medic had done when he took the bullet.

Thunder swept toward them from downriver, closing fast, sheets of noise that intensified into a single bass vibration. The ambulance shook. So did Ruth's heart. *Rebels.* The setup had been perfect. Start a panic, pack the leaders into a kill zone— Gus shouted and Ulinov reached for the rear doors as if to jump out—

The gunships went overhead, upriver, at least two of them, then swooped around and thudded back again. They were covering the slow wedge of trucks and Suburbans.

It was a disproportionate response to a lone rifleman, even to protect the president if he'd come. The fuel cost alone would be awesome. The response was also improbably quick. They must have readied the chopper crews before *Endeavour* even grazed the atmosphere and Ruth wished fleetingly, honestly, that she was back in her lonely little cell aboard the ISS.

This time she did laugh, one short huff.

Betrayal, disillusionment, she had no name for her tired anger. She'd long suspected that the situation down here wasn't as stable as she'd been told, carefully worrying over the few reports of raiders and food riots, but if James had ever hinted at civil war, she'd missed his clues. What else didn't she know?

They jockeyed around the next bend and the reason for the jam was obvious. Ruth knew the barricade existed, from orbital photographs, but her eye had skipped over it easily. She had wondered at its size, yet accepted that Leadville's security needs were extraordinary. The harsh fact was that there wasn't enough food or shelter for everyone who'd reached elevation, and it was mandatory to protect the labs and the nanotech experts who were the one hope of reversing the situation.

She had rarely considered what it would be like on the

outside. She didn't have to. She was one of the chosen. She always had been. Now she stared at the wall, following the helicopters with her ears, as the ambulance nudged forward a few yards at a time.

It would be such a waste for her to be killed out here.

The up-and-down terrain slumped into a saddle between the short hill on their right and, on their left, a more gradual rise that eventually thrust up into Prospect Mountain, one of the rounded white peaks east of Leadville. In this rare low spot, their highway merged with another that had come out of the northeast along the river. It was a textbook defensive position. Cars had been stacked three deep and three high across the gully, civilian cars, many stripped of their tires and seats and possibly their engines and wiring as well.

This colorful pile of steel was beyond anything required to divert the refugee masses up the eastern slope, of course. It would withstand artillery, though it didn't look as if an assault of any kind had ever come. No wonder. A tank had pulled forward from the one gap left in the wall, where it probably functioned as the gate, its stout barrel raised cross-river in support of the helicopters.

Twenty soldiers stood at the entrance and stopped each vehicle, if only briefly. Why? Was there a password? She supposed there must be. How else could you keep out infiltrators who looked like you and talked like you?

Impeded by the tank, traffic jostled for position. Directly ahead of Ruth, a black Suburban butted against the lean man's jeep and he beat on its tinted driver-door window with his walkie-talkie. Horns bawled, helpless, stupid, but she still heard some of his confident voice.

The soldiers at the gate waved the lean man through without hesitation, before his driver had stopped—and when he gestured they let both ambulances pass as well.

Leadville was the stuff of postcards and paintings, even disregarding the majesty of its mountain cradle. The pride taken by its tourist board had been deserved.

The main body of town covered slightly more than one square mile on a shallow, concave plain just west of a sweeping mess of upheavals and canyons with names like Yankee Hill and Stray Horse Gulch. Eastward, the mayhem of land rose onward until it finally broke at 14,000 feet and plunged away toward Kansas.

There had never been many trees at this elevation—absolutely none, now, all burned for fuel during the first winter—and Leadville was a gathering of red brick. The white spire of a church jabbed heavenward. Anchoring main street were two heritage museums, the courthouse, and a well-preserved opera theater built in 1870, and the low buildings and wide boulevard would always have the shape of a frontier town. It didn't matter that these structures, and the shops and breakfast cafes, had been turned into command centers for civil, federal, and military staffs. It didn't matter that sandbagged firing positions cluttered the sidewalks.

This place, already so laden in history, would survive to repopulate the continent and become America again. Ruth swore to herself. Her days, her nights, her life, anything. She would make it happen. These people had fought too hard.

Gus touched her leg and she leaned away, squeezing both hands into fists despite the horrible grating in her arm.

"Look," he said. "Look at that."

But she had already seen. Red, white, and blue bunting hung from the streetlights and storefronts, and she noticed a podium on the courthouse steps as they sped past. A victory parade. A celebration in the face of starvation and madness.

"We made it," Gus said.

Ruth nodded but couldn't talk, too busy, too keyed up, all senses locked on absorbing her surroundings.

She had never cried in front of them.

The jeep led their little convoy around the back of a modern hotel, which seemed strange, but she saw another ambulance parked in the lot already. She stared at the three-story building. Some new reflex in her was desperate to get *inside* again. Inside meant clean, calm, alone. Inside meant safe.

"My name is Major Hernandez," the lean man told them, as medical staff bustled around the open doors of the two ambulances. "We're going to get you out of those suits and have the doctors look you over."

It was a chaotic moment for an introduction but he made it work, looking for Ruth's eyes as she sat deep inside the ambulance, then trading a curt nod with Ulinov. Ruth had the impression that he made everything work, but he wasn't her idea of an officer. He wore no decorations or pins. His only insignia was a single nonreflective black oak cluster on one side of his collar—and she recalled how the MPs had acted, making way but not saluting. Of course. It would be stupid to identify command in a war zone with snipers in the hills.

Hernandez was also shorter than she'd realized, no bigger than Ruth, yet stood undisturbed by the rush of white uniforms. The medical staff had wheelchairs, a gurney, and two men held IV bags overhead, shouting, but they went around him exactly as the traffic jam had dodged around the tank.

The gurney and IV bags, probably blood plasma, went to the other ambulance—for Derek Mills or for the wounded medic?

Ruth opened her mouth but Major Hernandez continued, his tone practiced and reassuring. "You'll probably see some old friends inside. We have NASA's best physicians waiting."

Ulinov was lifted down into a wheelchair as Gus crawled out on his own. Ruth tried to follow, with help from the EMT inside the ambulance, and she fell against the woman. Raging adrenaline had carried her up and down the *Endeavour*'s interdeck ladder, but at a real price. Her body had no more strength left than a bag of jelly rammed full of sticks and stones wherever it hurt.

Then the gurney rolled past again in a knot of bodies, bearing an orange pressure suit. Mills had made it!

Deborah stood at the rear of the other ambulance, resisting the nurse who was trying to ease her into a wheelchair beside

Ulinov. "Let me go with him—" Deb had her smooth jaw tipped up in that haughty, aggressive way.

"Easy." Hernandez pushed an open palm at her. "We have the best teams right inside. Let us take care of you too."

Ruth grimaced. Her own heart was slamming, badly over-taxed by Earth's gravity, and her system hadn't been ruptured. The injuries Mills had suffered must be twenty times more dangerous because of that strain.

She was grateful to be set in a wheelchair herself.

"There are some people who need to see you," Hernandez said, and Ruth looked up and was confused to find him addressing Ulinov. "I'll hold them off awhile if you like, Commander."

Ulinov shook his head. "You have the shuttle secure?"

Hernandez turned smoothly to Ruth, as if the question had been hers. "Yes. Your equipment is all safe, Dr. Goldman. We've pulled everything out."

He made another spare gesture and they were wheeled toward the glass entrance. Ruth watched Ulinov's face, wondering at his exchange with Hernandez. Why was it important for them to talk to *him*?

Too much else was happening. "Is Derek going to be all right?" she asked. She didn't want anyone to think her only concern had been for her gear.

Hernandez paced alongside her without answering, and Ruth realized that he might not know the name. She glanced up again to clarify. His frown was genuine, affecting his dark, direct eyes. "I'm afraid your pilot is dead," he told them.

Ruth shook her head. "But I saw—"

Deb, close behind, cut her off in a clipped tone that Ruth took to be accusing. As if she could have known. "Bill has puncture wounds over his left hip, arm and shoulder, blunt trauma to the abdomen and thigh. He's hemorrhaging."

And yet Bill Wallace had stayed at his console to complete the emergency power-off.

Ruth moved her head again, unsure what she was denying, if anything. She would need to rediscover that kind of courage and dedication in herself.

17

She fell out of a dream and clutched at the narrow hospital bed with her good hand and the awkward club of her cast, digging at the mattress, pressing into it with her bare heels.

The dark wood ceiling was no part of the ISS. Ruth breathed in and took stock of herself.

Strange, how the mind persisted in making sense of things, even unconscious. Her body would be a long time adjusting to gravity again and as she rested her brain had worked furiously, whirling up on uneven tornados of fear.

Voices buzzed at her door, which was probably what had woken her. Not the noise itself—the ceiling creaked regularly, and a woman coughed and coughed in the room behind her—but even asleep Ruth had been waiting.

She needed to see a friendly face. She just hoped James hadn't brought too much of a welcoming party with him. She would be a long time adjusting to crowds again, too.

What took you so long? Ruth glanced left and right to see if it was night or even morning already, thinking to impress him with a cavalier remark. Unfortunately this room had been divided in two with raw sheets of plywood, and the window was on the other side. No clock. One sixty-watt bulb in a ceiling fixture meant to hold four. She knew she was lucky to get any privacy at all, but a touch of claustrophobia made her feel like she was still caught in that falling dream. She might have slept for an hour or for a hundred years.

Her bladder was full, a heavy boulder pressing hard. They'd made her drink as much as she could hold. But this divided space had been the living room in one of the hotel's business suites, dark walls, light trim, and there was no toilet. All she had was a bedpan, and the men at the door seemed to be coming in.

"—telling you."

"And I'm telling you, Doc. Not a chance."

The bedpan! Her nurse had left it in full view, on a blue patio chair that was this cubby's only other furniture. Ruth half lunged for the pan but there was only one hiding place—under the sheets with her, where it would form an obvious lump. Better to leave the damn thing out as a conversation piece.

They were still at the door, maybe trying to wake her. That would be like James. He was very sly, and very polite, though she didn't think she'd heard him yet.

"I said no. Now get out of my way."

"It's for your benefit as well."

Maybe that was how he sounded off the radio. Ruth almost called out, *I'm awake*, but touched her hair and frowned. She must look awful, dirty and dazed and puffy with sleep, her short curls matted into spaghetti. Lord knew they should be beyond anything so trite as appearances—except that she was the new girl, after all, and those dynamics would play a part in her success or failure. She needed to establish herself correctly.

There was a lot going in her favor, a reputation of past achievements, the mystique of being from the space station, the fact that the science teams here had hit a wall.

Some people would resent her for those exact same reasons, of course. She was used to that. Some people would want any excuse to distance themselves from her, to spread doubt, to keep or increase their own support, and a bad first impression might be all they required to begin their little campaigns. These were brilliant minds. No one was capable of more cutting ridicule.

She was practically naked, damn it, clad only in a T-shirt and undies. James should have known better than to bring anybody before she was ready!

Ruth tried to heave herself into a sitting position. Her broken arm made a lousy stilt, though, locked into an L-shape by the thick plaster, and a shiver of pain shot all the way up through her shoulder.

It would have been so much better to endure three or five hours of parades, speeches, medals, baking inside her photogenic orange pressure suit up at the podium with the astronauts and every big cheese in town. After that she would have been the undisputed king. Queen. Whatever.

Swooning, Ruth swept her good hand over her legs and smoothed her blankets like a dress.

She had asked four times for painkillers but they refused, afraid to make her heart or respiratory system work any harder. Now she was glad. She had grayed out again when they reset her bones, spasming away from her own arm, but this meeting would be hard enough to pull off looking like an abused mouse. At least she wasn't dull with morphine.

Ruth looked up and smiled as footsteps came into her cubby, but it wasn't James. It couldn't be James. She'd only met him in person once, years ago, and the man in front seemed about the right age, mid-fifties . . . but James was originally from Seattle. This guy had decked himself out like a cowboy, hat, jeans, string tie on a chambray work shirt. He was clean-shaven.

The second man was too young to be James, and Arabic, apparently a doctor. He wore a surgical mask and held an extra one. They had been arguing at the door about whether or not the cowboy would also cover his nose and mouth.

The cowboy stuck out a small hand. "Miz Goldman. Glad to see you're awake."

Ruth looked at the doctor first. She couldn't afford to get sick. His brown skin looked stained around his eyes, bruised by exhaustion. "Do you feel up for this?" he asked.

No. "Absolutely."

"Not a germ on me, Miz Goldman," the cowboy said easily. "I came straight to your room here and didn't touch a thing."

She took his small hand, regretting the care that had made her hesitate. He was unquestionably someone in power. "I just like to follow the rules," she said. A soft pitch, to see how big of a whack he'd take at it.

"Good." He smiled without showing teeth. "Always good."

The young doctor said, "Five minutes?"

"Might be longer," the cowboy answered. "Don't you worry."

Ruth made sure to agree with him, half-consciously matching his clipped way of talking. "Really. We're fine." *Except I'm going to pee myself.* She hoped they couldn't see that her thighs were tight together but felt like she was on display up on the raised bed.

"Go on, Doc," the cowboy said. "I can find my way out."

The doctor glanced once at the mask in his hand, then shook his head and left. They had taken blood from her, and urine and mucus, to test her immune system among a hundred other things like kidney function and protein and calcium levels, and Ruth worried that the results had been poor.

She turned back to the cowboy. He glanced at the plastic chair but remained standing. She didn't think a bedpan would deter him. He just didn't want to sit lower than her.

"I'm Larry Kendricks," he said.

"Wonderful to meet you." She was sincere.

Senator Lawrence N. Kendricks, Republican, Colorado, occupied one of seven prized seats on the president's council. Ruth had been scheduled to appear before this ruling body in two days, after the public ceremonies, after settling in, but maybe the crash of the *Endeavour* had changed things. Maybe Kendricks had always intended to see her directly, yet chose not to prearrange it on the radio for everyone to hear.

"Sorry I couldn't afford the rooftop luxury suite," Ruth said. She meant it as a joke, meant to be charming, but Kendricks thought she was playing him.

He lifted his chin and his broad white hat in a slow, serious movement. "Should be able to do something for you there," he said. "Get you a window, at least. Anything else?"

"No, no, they've been great. It's perfect."

"Well, the plague year's been pretty rough on us here, you

understand. We're working with what we have. But the right people always get taken care of."

He watched her, and she nodded.

"I want you taken care of," he said. "Anything you need. We all have big, big hopes."

"Yes."

"Everything is riding on you people."

Ruth nodded again, trying to keep her face clear. She couldn't risk his thinking that her disgust and anger were directed at him. Damn. One careless remark, and they'd instantly dive-bombed into this grim exchange.

She was too tired, too uncomfortable. Her bladder actually hurt more than her broken bones.

He said, "You sure you're all right? How's that arm?"

Ruth met his gray eyes, wondering at this shift back to small talk. But he'd already made sure she knew who was in charge. At least he wasn't heavy-handed about it.

She said the obvious things. "They're taking good care of me. Really. I appreciate it."

His outfit, the hat and string tie and everything—he probably would have been laughed at in Washington, but this was his native ground and a good percentage of the survivors were locals, maybe a solid majority if you counted the refugees out of Arizona and Utah and the Midwest. Much of the surviving military had also been based in this state.

Ruth didn't think there had been any elections, or would be, yet every politician worth his name wanted to be popular. And it must be easier, playing the caricature. People wanted the traditional and the familiar to steady themselves against the brutal tide of change.

"Well, I should let you rest," Kendricks said. "Doctor's right. I just had to meet you myself."

"Thank you for watching out for me." She almost said *sir*.

Kendricks made no move to leave. He offered that thin smile again. "Now, see, Miz Goldman, a whole pack of folks have been telling me you were a bad apple."

Ruth considered surprise but went with an answering smile instead. "I guess I can be really stubborn."

He moved his head again in that slow, lifting nod. "There's not going to be much room for that here. We need team players. We need everybody on the same page."

This was why he'd come.

"I understand, sir, it won't—"

"We need everybody cooperating. Everybody does their part. That's the only way we've kept so much together for so long." He paused, maybe waiting to interrupt her again. "You got an eyeful today, what happens when some people go off on their own, working against each other."

A memory reared up inside her, of the menacing clicks on the radio that Gus had identified as recording equipment. It raised the hair on her arms and neck.

It was the same feeling as that instant of silence before the rifle shot pressed into her ears.

Ruth made her head go up and down, a nod. "Yes."

Kendricks repeated it. "Yes." Like they were sealing a bargain. He patted the rail of her bed, hammering in the word, then creased his lips again with a meaningless smile. "Get some rest. Get some food in you. Tomorrow or the next day we'll start you working again and you can show us your magic."

The feeling stayed with her after he was gone, after she'd peed, after she'd curled up on her side and closed her eyes with the unwashed blankets balled against her chest like a ragged teddy bear. It was a phantom pressure closing in all around her and she could only think of one escape—someone who'd carefully flirted with her for months.

She knew where to find Ulinov because Major Hernandez had continued to do an exemplary job of making them feel at home, and because her nurse had been excited and talkative to have such celebrities on her watch.

Ruth had asked why they were in a downtown hotel and learned that this building was VIP care. The only hospital in the area had been more of a clinic, with only forty beds.

"Your friends are doing great," the nurse had told her. "We have a great staff and great equipment."

It was a rare case of too much wealth. Both military and civilian medical gear had been flown and driven into the area, in the first days of the plague and later after salvage operations— and anyone with medical experience or education had been given a place inside the safety of Leadville's barricades.

Wallace would remain in what had been the hotel restaurant under intensive care and Deb and Gus, kept for observation, were directly behind Ruth with the woman who coughed and coughed.

Nikola Ulinov had been wedged into a cubby like hers across the broad hall. Ruth only made it that far because she'd been resting and because she leaned on the walls like an old woman. Less than one in five of the ornate lamps were on, and the carpet had been ripped up so that wheelchairs and gurneys rolled easily. Ruth might have sat down on the unfinished wood floor to collect herself before going in, except she didn't want to get caught and sent back to bed.

She needed a friend very badly.

He was there, propped up on what looked like sofa cushions, reading from a sheaf of papers. He was alone. Ruth had expected to find Kendricks visiting, or another council member, but she didn't care what they wanted with Ulinov. Not now.

His eyes dropped to her bare legs and paused on the front of her T-shirt, and she was glad. She was too conscious of her stiff left arm hanging off her shoulder like something from a marble statue. His leg was elevated, slung up at the knee and at the foot. What a pair.

"Comrade," she said. It was an old joke between them.

"Sit. Your face. You are white."

Wonderful. "Comrade, can I squeeze in with you?"

"There is no room—" His bull chest, clad in an ugly green army undershirt, took up all but a few inches of the narrow bed.

"I'm very cold."

A man in the other half of the room groaned, barely separated from them beyond the divider of plywood. Ruth didn't care. She could be quiet. All she really wanted was to lie with him, to be held. Neither of them had strength for much more. A soft word. A touch.

She pushed off the wall and went to his side.

Ulinov looked at his stack of papers, tucked it down by his elevated leg. He turned toward her again to say something and Ruth leaned in, her gaze lowering to his mouth, feeling the first true glow of excitement at her own boldness.

He tipped his head back from her.

She didn't beg, exactly. "Don't you . . . Uli . . ."

"This is not a time," he said, his accent thickening as it always did when he was upset.

"I just don't want to be alone."

"I am sorry."

Her surprise hurt, too colossal to fit. It had gone on so long between them, the hesitant flirting, the looks, and finally they were free of being commander and subordinate. They were free to do whatever they liked and he didn't want her.

How had she been that wrong? She was not a romantic. When her mind wandered, her thoughts revolved around her work. Could she really have only *imagined* that the slow-building tension was mutual? Yes, they had argued, and yes, Ulinov had always been two-faced, or three- or four-faced, trying any mood that might help him. Maybe what she thought had been restrained interest on his part had only been another trick to earn her obedience.

No. Ruth touched his arm, leaning close again so that the hem of her shirt raised to expose her thighs and underwear.

"I am sorry," he repeated. But he looked.

There was something else. A reason for rejecting her. Because she'd been tagged as a "bad apple," and he didn't want to be associated with her? *You coward, you stupid coward, we could have been fantastic together.* But she didn't say it. This armed camp that had been Leadville, this maze of intimidation and deceit, was too complicated for her to burn any bridges.

She might need him later, so she tamped down her anger and her embarrassment. She forced a smile.

"Okay," she said.

18

Nothing else on Earth was like Ruth had expected it either, not even James. When they did meet, the next day, she initially mistook him for another politician. Her memory was of thick geek glasses and a desk-belly, but he'd had laser surgery two years ago and nobody in this place carried extra weight.

He looked good. His cheekbones were high and compact above his white mask and his well-trimmed beard, and he appeared to be using the same setting to chop his bristly brown hair as well. At least that was a hint of lab rat mentality, efficiency taking priority over appearances. The one-inch carpet of beard and hair gave him a no-nonsense look that was reinforced by a plain beige sweater. It was an image he'd cultivated, unassuming, inoffensive.

James Hollister had turned into a politician in every sense of the word. He was both a general administrator for the nanotech teams and their liaison to the president's council. He rode herd on thirty-eight disagreeable geniuses, quelling their disputes, enforcing a rotation of the equipment, and meanwhile championed their interests above every other problem faced by Leadville without excessively irritating the bigwigs above him.

He walked these many tightropes with confidence.

Ruth was attracted to his poise before she knew most of this. She was also much different than she'd envisioned, more alone, more needy—but the father-daughter thing was too strong in her head. She had leaned on James for several months now, going to the radio for guidance and for praise.

Just getting a hug was super. He smelled clean. She might have clung long enough to make him uneasy, then babbled the words she'd held back from Kendricks. "There's a war going on out there! How did— What's happening?"

But James didn't want to talk seriously, another change. To this point their entire relationship had been nothing except scheming and big ideas. He murmured pleasant things. "Your pilot was incredible, they're talking about a plaque or something," and pulled his ear and touched his index finger to his mouth and shrugged. Ruth swallowed her questions.

They might be listening.

She was released the next morning with a quarter-full bottle of calcium supplements and a handful of aspirin. She had been invaded by a gynecologist, and attacked by a dentist who made her gums bleed, and an optometrist had briefly tested her eyes, and they needed her bed. An ATF assault group had been brought in with gunshot wounds and the peculiar subdermal rash caused by nano infestations.

Major Hernandez personally escorted Ruth out into the vast, crisp light of the open sky, along with James and no less than nine soldiers in three jeeps. James seemed to know Hernandez well, asking after someone named Liz, and Ruth was glad. The two of them were a lot alike, she thought, assured, methodical.

It was good to know that there were still good men.

Yet it felt damned surreal, listening to them chitchat as the jeeps rattled south through residential streets.

"Come by tonight for a drink," James told him. "And bring

your lady. I can definitely scrounge up a little more of that boo juice if you've got another can or two of sardines."

"You know if I find that still, I'll have to confiscate it," Hernandez said, with a glance back at his gunner.

"Just don't look too hard, Major."

The optometrist had given her sunglasses, giant bug-face aviator shades that she'd donned immediately after James rolled her wheelchair outside. Daylight stung her eyes, muting colors, burning the edges off of the high white mountain peaks.

Ruth stared all around.

The original residents had done everything possible to help the mass of refugees, putting them up in living rooms and sheds and garages, in campers and tents and horse trailers. The locals were definitely not city folk. Everyone had outdoor gear and camping equipment and, briefly, it had been enough. A majority of the displaced population ended up in the hills east of Leadville, but Ruth could still see the results of the locals' resolve and generosity. Open lots and backyards remained full of improvised shelters. She noticed very few people, though. Why? There could hardly be an economy, jobs, anywhere to go . . .

They reached a checkpoint, a low wall of cars stacked across the street, two machine guns and a full platoon. Then they left the heart of the fortress, turning out onto a small highway that formed Leadville's southern border.

James and Hernandez shut up and Ruth hunched over her cast. She'd already been shot at once, and Hernandez hadn't brought along two extra jeeps just to impress her.

Thousands of bodies worked at the long slope rising away from town, scraping the mountainside out into level terraces. For housing? Ruth couldn't make sense of it. Several hundred more people clogged the highway, walking in both directions, a bizarre pilgrimage, moving pushcarts and wagons by muscle alone. There were no horses left. In fact she had seen no animals at all except one bird, maybe a hawk, drifting far overhead.

The lead jeep hit its horn constantly. Some of the heavier loads were slow to move aside, though, and the three vehicles managed only ten or fifteen miles per hour, weaving, braking. Ruth saw people with boxes and backpacks, with shopping carts.

They were carrying dirt.

She understood then, but it was easier to turn her head to James than to face the envy and numbed hope of these filthy strangers. "What are they doing?"

"The soil here is lousy, especially up off the valley floor. It's nothing but rock and hardpack."

"But the riverbed is . . . two, three miles from here?"

He just nodded. They turned off the highway after a hundred yards, into another checkpoint, then followed an empty road up the hillside. Ruth looked over at the excavation project and wondered how they would irrigate the cropland they'd built. Surely not by hand, bucket by bucket.

The space and resources dedicated to the nanotech labs were better than she'd feared. Timberline College, a small outdoor and environmental studies school that had often used the field as the classroom, was as large as the hotel and resembled a Swiss chalet. Stout white walls, high windows framed in dark wood, heavy beams jutting out beneath a roof steep enough to prevent snowfall from accumulating.

The courtyard was a jumble of RVs and trailers and aluminum sheds, but this clutter seemed unnecessary, since the two- and three-story building could easily house thirty-eight scientists, their fifty-four family members, and at least most of the security detachment—but the soldiers lived outside, even Hernandez. It was a tactical decision, putting themselves between the scientists and any potential threat. Reaching along the hillside were coils of wire and bulldozed gun positions.

When the jeep stopped, Major Hernandez offered one hand and helped Ruth out. He had brought a collapsible wheelchair that looked newer and better padded than the heavy, rigid frame she'd been using. "Thank you," she said.

He smiled for the first time before turning back to his men.

James pushed Ruth inside, where he'd secured a ground-floor room for her. It was almost the same white as her lab aboard the ISS. The view was of the hectic courtyard. Her gaze went instead to an off-color rectangular patch that marred the wall adjacent to the window, where a blackboard or a painting had hung for years. The furniture was practically nonexistent, a mattress on the floor and two metal shelves for a dresser. Everything else had been used for firewood.

He said, "Do you feel up for the five-dollar tour?"

"I'm wiped out. I know it's dumb." The brisk air had been good but her own apprehension had sapped her energy. Ruth met his eyes, tapped a finger to her lips.

James nodded. *Yes.* He said, "You should get a little sun. Your body needs the vitamin D."

She just wanted to nap. Let them listen to her breathing. But she was desperate for answers and didn't know when she'd have a chance to be alone with him again. "Okay. Yeah."

He left. To get permission? Wasn't the whole point to sneak out together and find a quiet corner? Ruth patted the duffel bag in her lap, a few personal effects retrieved from the *Endeavour* and someone else's reasonably clean clothes. The comfort she needed wasn't there.

James returned with another wheelchair, not as padded as her new one. It wasn't the room that he suspected was bugged, or not just the room. The chair, too. She nearly shouted. She nearly gave them an earful. But James saw it in her expression. His eyes widened and he spread his hands as if to catch her.

Ruth kept quiet, exactly as she had done with Ulinov.

The courtyard seemed like a dangerous place to talk, packed with idle soldiers. Too many heads turned to watch as James rolled her along the concrete path, hunched close to her ear. "I don't know if a directional mike could pick our voices out of all this," he said, "or if they're even equipped with anything like that, but let's make this quick."

"You don't trust Hernandez."

"I think he'd give his life to protect us."

"But then . . . You switched chairs."

"We don't know where he got it or who had it before him. And there are too many unemployed intelligence people trying to make themselves useful."

They passed a Winnebago, a bare-chested soldier mending his sleeve, a young lieutenant scowling at a clipboard.

"I trust him," James said. "I do. But it's not realistic to expect him to withhold information from his superiors or not cooperate with them."

By that logic I shouldn't even trust you.

"You need to be careful how you act and what you say. I know you like to push buttons. Don't do that here."

Ruth was bitter. "You sound like Kendricks."

"He came to see you? He was talking about it. I thought maybe I'd convinced him that I had you on a short leash, but shit, Ruth, you were nothing but trouble up there, mouthing off, always arguing. And the last month or so you just got worse and worse."

"Keeping me up there was a waste."

"It's not always about you."

Four soldiers jogged toward them down the walkway. James stopped her chair and a miserable frustration squeezed down on Ruth's thoughts like a cramp. She felt helpless on so many levels, physically, mentally.

The men dodged around her wheelchair and kept going.

James began pushing her again. Ruth wished she could see his face but it was like old times, just his voice at her ear. He said, "Kendricks isn't somebody you want to fight."

"No, I don't. I barely even knew who he was until he came and put his foot up my butt."

"This winter there was cannibalism in some of the mines."

He said this without changing his mild, scolding tone, and Ruth grabbed the wheel beneath her good hand, a beltlike sting of pain. James stumbled. Ruth craned her neck around.

"Yes," he said. "It's not just rumors. There's proof that it happened on a wide scale."

She tried to anticipate where he was heading. The habit of analysis was, as always, more comforting than dealing with her own emotional reaction.

The military and FEMA stocks, the thousands of cattle herded to elevation, the subbarrier-scavenging efforts—all of this should have been enough, even now, to sustain two-thirds of a million people.

"They held back most of the food from the start," she said.

James began rolling her forward again. "You can understand the decision. The council wanted to make sure that somebody, at least, would still be here in the long run."

Ruth shook her head. It was a very human phenomenon, making a fear real by taking action intended to be preventative. They had created a problem that otherwise might not have arisen for years, if ever. There had never been much living up here—short grasses and shrubs, rodents, birds, some elk—and by cutting off the supplies they had made a rebellion inevitable. No doubt it had started slow, with sneak thieves and hoarders.

"When did the opposition get organized?" she asked.

"Ruth, just listen to me."

The rebuke, his tired, paternal patience, made her wonder at herself. She didn't need to prove anything to James.

"The council had been doling out some food," he said. "It was a starvation diet but enough to keep people waiting, keep them dependent, even though almost none of it got too far up the canyons."

Some of the larger mines were more than five miles east of Leadville, she knew, deep in the snarl of gullies and peaks.

James sighed, an *mm-mah* sound she recognized as the verbal equivalent of a shrug. "I don't know that there was anything else they could have done, really, short of using choppers to fly supplies in that far. It's a lousy situation."

It was criminal. It was murder. But she said nothing. He was right—and it had been done in part to protect the labs.

The path forked and James chose to angle back toward the main building, squeezing past a pickup truck with a tall camper shell. "There have always been raiders," he said, "guys with hunting rifles, nothing that stood up to army troops, especially since the army was getting fed every day."

Words came out of her in a hush. "What did they do?"

"We're under martial law. We have been since the beginning,

for whatever it was worth. Not every place had a solid military presence." He made his shrugging noise again, *mmm*. "Last fall that changed. They sent out a third of the troops here, and moved other groups around to establish garrisons in key spots."

They had wanted control. They had wanted order. And they had simultaneously eased the local situation by ridding themselves of thousands of hungry bellies.

"It backfired," James said. "The first snow came early and a lot of those units got caught before they were ready. Scavenging efforts stopped. The chain of command was already a mess, with different groups from all over the country, different branches of the military . . . The first breakaway was the White River Plateau, in December, and Loveland Pass went over in February. They declared independence and then they declared possession of the nearest towns and cities below the barrier."

Ruth closed her eyes, a useless denial, and opened them immediately. The emotions inside her were like that dream of tornados and falling.

He stopped her chair beside two aluminum garden sheds, the nearest stamped with fake, curlicue ivy. Opposite them stood a wide tent. Half a dozen soldiers sat outside, doing nothing, not playing cards or tossing a ball, just resting right there on the ground. One man mumbled something and the others turned to look.

James knelt and pointed at the top floor of the college, as if they were discussing the labs inside. This was his life now. This was their life. She would always be onstage.

"It's not much of a war," he said. "Nobody has the resources, and we're too far apart."

The high region that Ruth thought of as Colorado actually stretched over what had been seven Western states, along the spine of the Continental Divide. It was separated from the Canadian Rockies by wide gaps in Montana, and humped as far south as Arizona and New Mexico before falling into desert. Much of this far-flung line of small continents and islands were set apart from each other by shallow channels or valleys that plunged away for tens of miles—but Leadville sat roughly in the center of the main bulk of the habitable zone.

The White River Plateau was a freestanding body between Leadville and the heights of Utah. Ruth didn't see how anything had truly changed if they chose to be their own small kingdom. Loveland Pass, on the other hand, lay only forty miles north.

That was why such an immense wall of steel had been built across the far side of town.

"So far it's been mostly harassment," James said, "patrols and scavenging parties chasing each other off. But there used to be some huge military bases in this state. Nobody's short on guns. The breakaways have been arming the refugees here and encouraging them to overthrow the government."

Gustavo must have known. He must have heard, he lived for his radios, but he had kept the truth from her. Why? On whose orders? All the while she'd been sharing everything she learned from the labs . . . and Gus had almost certainly reported her indiscretion back to Leadville . . .

It hurt her too that James was taking such risks for her.

His voice was low and relentless. "Unfortunately you can't just wall off an area this size, especially since people need to get in and out to the farms. The nearest mines are all army barracks now, and they've been stacking cars and stringing wire and placing guns. And hanging people. They—"

"Dr. Hollister!" A black-haired soldier ducked out of the big tent. One of the men sitting in front must have passed word inside. Ruth thought she recognized him as part of their escort. "Sir, you shouldn't be this close to the perimeter."

James had a smile for him. "Dr. Goldman is still adjusting to the altitude, she needed a little air."

The soldier glanced at her and then from side to side, clearly looking for an officer. His hand had gone to his collarbone as if to finger the strap of a slung rifle, though he was armed only with the pistol on his hip.

"We'll start back," James said and Ruth chimed in, too loud, thrumming with her own blood. "The sun hurts my eyes!"

The man watched them go, his hand still at his shoulder.

James didn't hurry. "Look, I think maybe half of why Kendricks voted to bring you down was that I sold him on the idea that it would increase his stature to have you under the council's direct authority rather than tucked away under NASA's umbrella. That's why it's so important that you don't rock the boat. It will reflect on him now, the space hero running around saying what a lousy job everyone's done."

Bitterness wormed through her again. "Then why not just leave me up there forever?"

"It's not about you, Ruth. It was never about you."

Could they really have only wanted her equipment? She knew they'd lost most of their gear when the locust broke loose inside NORAD, it was total chaos—

James said, "They evacuated the space station for Ulinov."

Enough. Lord knew she'd already heard enough. Ruth shut her eyes. "That doesn't make sense."

"Shit. I was hoping you knew why."

"Knew what?"

"I have connections but I'm not on the inside. I just hear things." James stopped her chair and leaned close, making a charade of pointing at the building again. "Rumor is, they need him for top-level negotiations with the Russians, because the Chinese are mobilizing."

Before the locust hit Asia, China had invaded and occupied much of the Himalayan range. They'd already possessed a foothold in Tibet, of course, and rose over this region like a human plague. Then they had stopped communicating with the world.

James turned his eyes to her face, then cut one glance back behind her. "India's provided too much work on the ANN for us to just forget about them," he said, "but there's no way they can hold off the Chinese by themselves. Not without going nuclear."

And even now, at the extreme, no one would want to take that step. No one could afford to contaminate the rare fragments of land above the invisible sea.

"They say India's agreed to a real estate deal in exchange for protection, and the Russians are in trouble. They've been pushed almost all the way off of the Caucasus and Afghanistan mountains." James got up and moved to the rear of her chair as Major Hernandez strode toward them, no doubt summoned by the black-haired soldier.

Ruth waved and smiled.

"Rumor is," James said, "American planes are going to airlift the Russians in to cut off the Chinese."

19

"**They're sending another search** team to California," Aiko said, propping her hip and both hands against the work counter too close to Ruth.

Ruth tipped back in her chair. "Where did you hear that?"

"Everywhere. It's for real. And this time a few of us have to go with the soldiers—they're deciding who right now."

Aiko Maekawa was a gossip, soft-voiced but insistent. Timberline had an incomparable rumor mill—too many big brains, Ruth supposed, all of them trained to hypothesize— and Aiko seemed to pride herself on being one of the main vectors of information. It let her be first, let her act the discoverer with each new person she approached. Lord knew she wasn't adding much to the development of the ANN.

The girl was very bright, and tireless and accomplished, and she had lost her mind all those months ago when her parents and two sisters didn't make it out of Manhattan.

That was the dirt on Aiko, at least.

This morning was Ruth's eighth day in the labs. She usually just nodded and let Aiko talk at her. Any remarks only prolonged the disruption, because Aiko confused attention with

approval and enjoyed repeating the highlights of each story—
and Ruth didn't always think it was smart to be talking.

The labs were riddled with listening devices.

Most of what Aiko had to say was harmless—Ted had a
thing for Trish, a married woman; the onions mixed into last
night's pasta were fresh, from below the barrier—but even
then Ruth resented the distraction.

The makeshift labs were already chaotic, overcrowded,
every surface jammed with machining hardware, PC and Mac
monitors arranged in stacks, all of it steel and chrome and
plastic.

Prominent in the cleared space before Ruth now stood a
multimode scope fitted with an atmosphere hood. These glass
sheaths were designed for experiments in gaseous environments, but in this case had been connected to a simple air
compressor. It also contained a fluid-heating unit set at body
temperature.

She sat within inches of active, living locusts.

"You know what happened to the last mission, right?" Aiko
glanced across the lab at Vernon Cruise, to make sure he
wasn't eavesdropping. Aiko would go through her little song
and dance as many times today as possible.

"They ran out of air and barely got off the ground," Ruth
said, hoping to avoid a gory rehash.

It was an uncharitable thought, but she suspected Aiko's
love of bombshells stemmed in part from her looks. Beautiful
girls grew up differently than everyone else. The way they
were adored had a distinct formative effect, turning many of
them into show-offs of one kind or another. Aiko was fairly
disgusting about it, always trying to position herself in front
of her victim, man or woman.

Ruth resembled a white pillow person in her wrinkled lab
suit, with no discernible breasts and only a trace of hip. Aiko
was too willowy to show anything either, yet she had a long
sculpted neck and almond skin and dark, exotic eyes. A contest between her and Doc Deb would have been no contest.

"At least two of us have to go," Aiko said. "This week for
sure, as soon as possible."

"What happened?" Ruth asked despite herself. "I mean, why now?" Maybe the FBI teams had reworked the sales records and pinpointed a new location.

"There's already a big stink in the parasite team," Aiko continued, teasing out her information. "They're sure some of their people will get picked since they're the farthest behind."

Ruth frowned. The situation in Timberline was remarkably like things had been aboard the space station, divisive and cold. During the past week she had seen many of the scientists here act as cruel to each other as only family can be, deriding rival concepts, trading insults over who was to blame for disorder or contamination in the shared labs.

Ruth tried not to care. Ruth had done her best to close herself to it all, using a smile and easygoing humor like a lab suit against the interpersonal grime.

Maybe if things had gone better with Ulinov, she would have felt differently. Maybe if . . .

But it was easier to limit her vision to the microscope. Easier to limit herself and stay uninvolved. She'd rather be lonely. She was used to that, at least.

She'd even ignored a conspicuous slap in the face.

While she was still in the hospital, Gary LaSalle and his development team had downloaded her files and begun examining everything they thought they could use. Before she was shown around Timberline, they'd run the first of several new refining trials on her machining atomic force microscope.

Ruth wouldn't have waited either. That wasn't the issue. She had hoped to solidify her name and reputation by formally presenting her research, and by showing off the MAFM and customized application modules—but she'd realized it wasn't safe to complain. She'd always meant to share her work anyway.

LaSalle wasn't sharing. The council had awarded him exclusive round-the-clock rights to her gear, at least initially, as well as first access to her records.

It was a rejection of everything Ruth had done.

Since the first days of the plague, she'd aligned herself with the hunter-killer group. In concept the HK ANN was a true weapon, specific and controlled. They had yet to perfect their discrimination key but the HK worked, if inefficiently.

As much a chemical reaction as a machine, LaSalle's "snowflake" ANN operated on natural atomic bonding. It disabled locusts by pulling them into nonfunctional clusters. Each compacted bunch then recombined around the original seed and shed more artificially weighted grains, which would attract other locusts—and since early April, LaSalle had conducted nineteen successful tests in lab conditions.

The HK ANN also tested out in prearranged environments, but with a best target rate of 58.8 percent. LaSalle's bug simply clotted everything within the test chamber.

Ruth had not been the only one to point out the obvious danger. Other prominent names in Timberline had raised the same objections, yet LaSalle insisted his snowflake would only affect locusts because it was fundamentally incapable of exerting force on larger, more complex molecular structures. Ruth didn't understand how he could make that claim, although she hadn't seen schematics of the snowflake since early March.

No one outside his group had seen anything recent either.

The development teams had normally been open with each other, because peer review was their only safeguard. That had changed, however, after the council gave LaSalle priority two months ago. A reorganization of the labs had isolated LaSalle's group on the third-floor wing, which they now claimed entirely. His people couldn't avoid the other scientists in the residence hall, yet they were close-mouthed about their progress.

Ruth didn't believe the council would be overconfident, not after everything that had happened. Their decision implied that LaSalle had indeed run favorable tests with rats or weeds and other things exposed to the snowflake.

Still, she trusted her instincts. LaSalle's bug could not work as advertised. It might disrupt the molecular integrity of all organic beings—mammal, insect, plant, even bacteria. Nothing would ever live on this world again.

She needed a breakthrough now more than ever. There was

no other option. It was too easy for nontechnical people to hear only what they wanted, and without something new to wow the president's council, without any shred of progress, she might never make them listen.

She glanced pointedly at her scope but Aiko was still reciting complaints. "It's not fair. All of us are busy. If someone has to go, it shouldn't be—"

Ruth ducked her head so that eye contact was impossible and made a business of worming her index finger into her cast. The itch of her unwashed skin was real but Aiko's reaction was more important.

Aiko raised her voice, trying to recapture Ruth's attention. "They're talking to somebody out there on the radio."

Ruth looked up.

"It's true. I swear." Aiko's dark eyes were intent on Ruth's face. "A guy who helped put the locust together managed to get to a mountain with a radio. He's alive, just barely, but his story totally checks out and he swears he can lead us to their records, their gear, everything."

"Holy shit."

Aiko laughed. "I knew you—"

"Vernon," Ruth called, "hey, Vernon, have you heard anything about this?"

Aiko blinked, her lips parting in surprise and hurt. Then she took a step back as if to shield Ruth from their colleague as he turned his head from a pressurized isolation system.

Vernon Cruise was a smallish man, five-nine, with thick sandy hair and glasses. He acted the grandfather to many people here, being old enough to retire, and was rightly proud of his contributions in mapping the locust's structure. Too bad he'd tried to tell Ruth all about it on her third day, and again on her fourth, pushing his laptop and his printouts in her face when she was hot to familiarize herself with the bug on her own.

They could have been friends, but Ruth remained leery. It wasn't just the monitoring devices—any of her lab mates might be doubling as a spy for the president's council, to stay in favor, to earn extra food or cigarettes.

Ulinov had done her a favor. Ulinov had made it all too clear where she stood in this place.

"The army's sending another plane to California!" Aiko blurted, before Ruth could say anything else. "The guy who built the locust is still alive."

Vernon's eyebrows went up but Ruth didn't bother to contain a rude sound. "Hah." Already this mystery man had gone from being a member of the research team to the lead designer, and so the rumor would grow.

"I hope it really is him," she said.

Hurrying to James's office took most of her strength. If he'd been on a different floor, Ruth would have needed to sit and rest. She had been in physical therapy for six days now, mere stretching at first, then light weights and a treadmill. She hated to break up her afternoons but recognized that she'd better rebuild her stamina if she was going to be mentally effective for more than a few hours at a time.

"Not now—" James called as she pushed through his door.

He was at his desk, spine straight, hands clasped together among the few papers set before him.

Senator Kendricks sat in the only other chair, also stiffly. "Well, speak of the devil," he said, turning his head and his white cowboy hat.

Beyond them was a gorgeous day, a clean blue sky and the near horizon of snow-topped peaks. The windows in the labs were all boarded over, and Ruth still felt confused whenever she walked in here during the day and found a rectangular hole in the wall full of sunshine and mountains.

"Dr. Goldman," James said. His formal tone was a warning. "My office has a door for a reason."

"No, no." Kendricks waved her in. "Might as well get her side of it." He stood, gesturing to his chair. "Please. I know you're still getting your legs back."

She didn't object. Let him do this tiny favor. Were they talking about California?

"Missed you the other day," Kendricks said.

Ruth smiled, a loathsome new reflex. She found herself being more and more false. "I hear it went great."

There had been a parade after all, two days ago, but Major Hernandez suggested it wasn't worth the risk of driving her into town and Ruth was glad not to waste the time. She was glad, too, to avoid Ulinov and Gus and Deb. It would have been satisfying to thank Bill Wallace personally, but he had yet to be released from the hospital.

"It was more than great," Kendricks said. "It was— It was something. Everybody cheering. Everybody coming together."

She nodded and forced another smile.

"You should have been there. All of you. Might have done your hearts some good, see what you're working for."

Pep rallies during the apocalypse. Crap. But it was possible, even likely, that Kendricks understood people better than Ruth. Morale inside the labs was erratic at best, and they had enough to eat and showers and lights and the chance to ignore the world beyond these guarded walls. How much worse was it in town, in the tents and trailers, in the mines? It was damned cynical to assume that the council had staged a celebration for the sole reason of bolstering their own leadership.

And yet she'd also had a new thought about their decision to change the calendar, declaring this Year One. Plague Year. The phrase was sensible and right and deeply manipulative all at the same time, if you looked at it from a certain angle—and Ruth found herself doubting everything now.

It was top-notch public relations, deceptive and smart. It played on expectations and fear and hope. It was a way to give the Leadville government even more legitimacy, to make themselves ever more necessary and important.

"I think everyone in the labs is getting close to some real success," she said, thinking to steer the conversation toward Aiko's rumor. "I honestly do. We just need a few more pieces to fall into place."

"Well, that's what we were talking about. Putting things in place." Kendricks rolled his head toward James and said, "Gary LaSalle has a high opinion of you, Miz Goldman, and James here has been saying the same thing for a long time."

Oh Lord. Ruth cut her gaze away from Kendricks for one instant but James didn't react, his watchful brown eyes framed by his short brown hair and short brown beard.

Kendricks said, "We'd like you to join Mr. LaSalle's team."

"No way."

James winced, a barely perceptible shift of posture, but Kendricks just shrugged. "I know you're not on the bandwagon, Miz Goldman. But I want to appeal to your patriotism."

"Sir, that has . . ." She shook her head. "I worked for the Defense Department with full clearance. It's not fair for you to . . ." It didn't matter what was fair. She tried again. "I'm totally committed to our work here."

"That's what we need. Total commitment."

"LaSalle's bug is wildly dangerous, sir. I'm not the only one who's been saying it."

James interjected, leaning over his desk, in a tone that remained uncharacteristically formal. "There are some aspects of the situation you're not aware of, Dr. Goldman."

Kendricks turned on him. "Don't you say another word."

"If it's about the guy in California," Ruth said, "the rumor's already going around."

James shook his head. *No.*

Kendricks continued to watch him for a moment before looking back at Ruth. "We'll see how California plays out, if that man can do what he says. But we have bigger problems."

"How could— *Bigger?* Than beating the locust?"

"The Chinese have developed weapons application nanotech," Kendricks said. "You're not okayed for any of this but Jesus Christ, I wonder what goes through your mind that you won't cooperate with us after everything that's happened. Do you realize we barely survived the plague year at all?"

That phrase again. He used it intentionally, like a gun, threatening and prodding her.

She was right. She had always been right. LaSalle's snowflake would not function as an ANN, affecting only the locust, and the council no longer intended to use it as such.

It would be a matchless weapon, given a strict governor to keep it from proliferating without end—and in her records, among the things she'd worked out during her endless wait aboard the space station, had been the basics of a control.

Ruth tried misdirection. "I couldn't help LaSalle even if I wanted to. My expertise is in a completely different field. It's apples and oranges."

"Now that's not true," Kendricks said, tilting his head again. "He says your ideas have been a big help."

So she would always own a part of it, if something happened. Lord God. The perfect weapon of mass destruction, more killing power than a nuke and no fallout or contamination.

It would be easy to safely deliver the snowflake, capsules kicked out of a helicopter, bomblets from a jet, American aircraft low over occupied Himalaya with a hundred thousand people reduced to jelly in each thundering wake . . .

Her heart beat so hard she felt her upper body rocking, a palsy of rising shame and anger.

Kendricks said, "I know you two aren't friendly. Let's say we don't put you directly under LaSalle. Work together, but be your own boss."

As if her ego was the problem.

"That's crazy. You're crazy." She didn't regret the words. "When we beat the locust it's over, all the fighting. We save everybody and the fighting stops everywhere. We don't need nano weapons! We can all go back down again."

Kendricks just looked at her, the lines in the tanned skin around his eyes deepening slightly.

Ruth raised her voice. "We can all go back down again."

"I think it was a mistake," Kendricks said, slowly, "to overprotect you people. The Chinese sure aren't babying their technicians." He turned to James, his chin and long hat brim aimed down in an aggressive posture. "Make her see. Tell her everything, whatever she needs to hear. This has got to happen."

James was respectful. "You're a hundred percent right, Senator. Shifting gears like this, all at once, nobody here is ready for it. Our entire focus has been defensive since the beginning." He glanced at Ruth. "It's a lot to take in."

She tried to play along. "I just don't understand. We're so

close. It's crazy— It seems crazy to take us away from beating the locust now."

"You might be surprised," James said, "to hear that the council evacuated the space station sooner than necessary not because of you but for Commander Ulinov." His expression never changed, and Ruth marveled at his daring. She nodded quickly. She didn't trust herself to sound convincing. He said, "We're joining the war in Asia, flying the Russians in to invade the Chinese before they complete their weapons tech. The Russians insisted on having Ulinov here as their representative."

"But so what? What does any of that matter if we can all live below ten thousand feet again?"

James made his shrugging sound, *mm-mah*, signaling her that he didn't really believe what he was about to say. "First, there's no guarantee we'll ever beat the locust. And second, the council has good reason to believe the fighting won't stop even if we do."

Kendricks nodded, grimly pleased by James's performance. "Things are too far gone. It's been total war for too long."

"There have always been wars," Ruth said.

"Not like this. Not with whole nations thrown on top of each other." He flexed his small hands, squinting past her at the window. "Not with armies eating each other's dead and keeping prisoners like cattle."

". . . what?"

His eyes came back to her. "You people aren't the only ones who've been studying the locust, Goldman." Kendricks had never called her *doctor*, and now forgot even the questionable honorific of *miz*. "They've been learning over there, too. We've been watching them close."

The spy satellites, Ulinov's cameras.

"It's going to be us or them," Kendricks said, "whichever side can strike first. They'll wipe out everyone else. I mean *everybody*."

One world. One people. She could see how the simplicity of this notion would appeal to a certain mind-set, especially after so much conflict and atrocity—and the chance had never been so attainable, with every enemy reduced to a fraction of their former numbers and gathered tightly together.

The victor could never forget the plague, not with so many animal species extinct and the environment crashing as it sought new balance, but they could forget recorded history.

It would truly be a new start. One culture. One peace.

Year One.

And yet James had made it clear that he did not agree with Kendricks, hinting at further complications. Fuck fuck fuck. Maybe he wanted her taken into the council's confidence, brought into the weapons labs, only to divert and delay LaSalle's progress. She could prevent an escalation to nano warfare long enough for the other scientists to beat the locust. Wheels within wheels. Where would it stop?

Ruth turned to her friend. James nodded. So she looked Kendricks in the eye and said, "Okay, I'll do it."

20

Her descent from orbit could not match the distances that Ruth had gone within herself. She would never help Kendricks prepare for a first strike. She had put her life into helping people, if for selfish reasons, for career gains, and for her own gratification—and the tragedies of the past year had sharpened this vague altruism into something like a fever.

She thought of Bill Wallace again, his body ripped open, staying at the controls of the *Endeavour*.

If she'd read James right, if she'd correctly anticipated his plan for her to become a mole inside the weapons labs, it would have been smarter to say nothing more after giving Kendricks her lie. But she had to know.

"What about California?" she asked.

"Well, we all have big hopes." The tension was noticeably going out of Kendricks and he bobbed his head in one of his contrived, friendly gestures.

Ruth persisted. "This guy is definitely who he says he is? I mean, where's he been all this time?"

James looked at Kendricks for permission, then turned and

grinned, a rare flash of teeth splitting his neat beard. "I talked to him myself. His name is Sawyer."

She didn't have to ask if James thought he was for real.

They got rid of her. Kendricks said he wanted to be back in town in an hour and had more to discuss with James.

He offered his hand before she left. They murmured polite nonsense, *glad you're on board* and *yes, sir,* and Ruth found that the charade was easy enough.

She strode back to Lab Four automatically, then almost walked on past. She almost went down to her room, to bed, to close her eyes and sort through her thoughts. But this might be her last chance to do anything productive.

Vernon Cruise cornered her again thirty minutes later, waddling back into the lab with a laptop and several folders. What in the world was this guy's problem?

Ruth supposed that word had spread. Vernon must have figured it was his final opportunity to show off before she moved upstairs to LaSalle's group. In a way it was flattering, and the smile she gave the old man was genuine. She wanted him to have his little moment. "Hey there," she said.

Vernon's gaze flicked to the other two people in the lab, exactly as Aiko had done to make sure she wasn't being overheard. Not long ago Ruth might have seen some humor in that. Instead, irritation crept into her feelings of tired goodwill.

"I know you wanted to get an unprejudiced look at the bug," Vernon said, "but give this a glance."

"I hear it's really great."

Vernon huffed, impatient, and Ruth managed to keep from rolling her eyes as she accepted three hefty folders.

He'd put the memo where she couldn't miss it, on top inside the first cover, a single page identical to the rest, with the same ordinary computer type, but the first line made her pulse jump up against her ribs.

"If you're caught with this we're all dead."

Ruth stared at him. Vernon's expression was . . . scornful? He had tried to establish a conduit of information for her almost from the beginning, though he hadn't been so bold as now. He hadn't been so desperate. It was a juvenile trick— No, it had all the sophistication of *grade school*, passing notes, but the listening devices throughout Timberline couldn't hear a piece of paper. Too bad she'd been too busy. It was almost funny—it was sad and awful—how often she'd been too busy in her life.

The memo was from James. Ruth was sure of that. She recognized his confident delivery, and halfway through it resumed their earlier conversation about the man in California.

Her heartbeat was in her neck now and in her broken arm. "Absolutely," she said.

Ruth stayed in Lab Four after Vernon left with her *yes,* pretending to read through the other folders. She wondered if he'd burn the memo. That seemed too conspicuous, an open flame. The conspirators couldn't run around routinely torching papers or someone would notice. Maybe he'd go straight to the bathrooms, drop it in the tank. Every week the soldiers hauled away five hundred pounds of scientist poop for the farms. Sure. Vernon was always muttering about his bladder.

She had to believe he'd take care of it. Their lives were both on the line. There was nothing on the paper to identify her specifically if Vernon was caught, but Kendricks would know. What would they do? March her into the courtyard and shoot her?

In another hour it wouldn't matter.

In an hour she'd be on the plane to California.

James owned more of the truth than Kendricks wanted any of them to know, the least of which was that Gary LaSalle had already developed a crude governor for his snowflake, using Ruth's ideas and machining gear to complicate its structure.

Because his ANN had no programming, the only way to

retard its replication process was to burden it with additional demands. The new, larger snowflakes were more stable than the original. They tended to glom on to each other as well as foreign mass, after which the chain reaction broke down as they became encased in free carbon of their own making—

The assault had gone much as Ruth envisioned, U.S. jet fighters spilling canisters that broke open on impact, a flourish of death that quickly died itself. Almost too quickly. In time, an improved version would be even more powerful. But they hadn't dusted the Chinese. China was years behind the design teams here in Timberline, and posed a significant conventional threat to its neighbors, yet nothing more.

Yesterday the council had given orders to hit the White River Plateau, the breakaway westward toward Utah.

Yesterday their quiet war had become something else.

Most of the U.S. spy satellites were controlled by Leadville, and coverage overhead was regular if not constant. White River must have known they were inviting an attack by preparing their own flight to the coast. They had no nanotech teams and in fact were short on basics like shelter and electricity, but the man in California would be an invaluable hostage and bargaining chip. They'd obviously decided it was worth the gamble, although they could not have anticipated such a weapon.

Casualties had been estimated at sixteen hundred, with several dozen more unlucky enough to have survived their wounds. The snowflake tended to liquefy the sinus cavity or lungs first.

After the strike, after ending any race to California, Leadville broadcast a warning to whatever remained of the rebel leadership. Leadville intended the warning for everyone. This man, Sawyer—he belonged in the capital.

White River had been an object lesson.

Ruth stopped paging through the second folder and actually looked at the diagrams there. Vernon hadn't given her these print-outs for show. This was a working file. The laptop he'd left must be similarly packed with data. She probably had a copy of everything they'd learned about the locust.

That would be too much information for him to have compiled by himself, unless he and James had been hoarding it together all this time, which seemed unlikely. How many others were in on the scam? With only thirty-nine scientists including herself, there couldn't be many left who weren't either spies for the council or allied with James and the conspiracy.

There was strength in that thought. She wasn't alone.

She hadn't been here long enough to gauge how far things had developed, but her guess was that most would side with James. These people were too clinical in their thinking, too independent, and every mentor in their lives had tried to instill a powerful sense of responsibility in them.

Ruth glanced at her lab mates again as she walked to her computer, but she had no way to know if either of them was aligned with her, no word, no signal.

Computer discs were strictly rationed. Ruth had just three for herself but there were others on a shelf, labeled *Iso* and *Plas286* in a looping cursive. She blanked them both. Then she downloaded her current analysis and everything else she'd done in the past week.

She might have told Vernon *yes* even if the note had ended with White River's fate, but there was more. There was worse.

The man in California swore he could beat the locust, given his equipment and a few capable assistants—yet he had no interest in improving their ANN. He had no plans to attack the invisible sea at all. The process of sweeping the planet clean might require years, he said, a figure Ruth couldn't dispute, and there was no guarantee it could be thorough. To repopulate an environment like that would risk encountering pockets of the locust that the ANN had missed, and new plagues.

He intended to take advantage of the locust's versatility.

The machine was biotech, as Ruth suspected. Its designers had hoped to teach it to isolate and destroy malignant tissues, dosing each patient with an individually keyed batch inside a sealed chamber—and when its work was done, they would spin a dial and drop the pressure, and out came the patient free of cancer and free of nanos.

He said he could reverse-engineer a new version of the locust, shorn of most of that extra capacity and therefore quicker, more responsive. With the work they'd already done on their discrimination key, he said he could create a model that would live inside a human host, powered by body heat, and disable the original locusts as they were inhaled or otherwise absorbed.

Targeting only the original locust type, using only those specific materials to replicate, it would be like an ANN on the inside, a vaccine, proof against the machine plague.

And it would spread poorly except by direct injection. The council could use this new nano to literally control the world, giving it only to a select population, ensuring loyalty, handing out territory and establishing colonies below the barrier as they saw fit. All of Earth. The prize was too sweet, after too much hardship, and they could secure it as easily as turning their backs, not an effort but a lack of one. Every dissident, every rebel, every other remaining nation—in less than a generation the squabbling, starving millions trapped in the highlands would dwindle into a few grubby tribes unless perhaps they agreed to come down as servants and slaves.

Kendricks would have his one world, one peace, one people.

Aiko almost blew it for them, shouting in the courtyard. "Ruth! Hey, Ruth, you didn't get tapped, did you?"

She should have known there would be a crowd. It wasn't that there was much to see—two jeeps and a truck, some different uniforms—but the days here were especially monotonous for the families of the scientists. These people were the lucky ones, well fed, protected, and they fought over the few chores available to them—gardening, laundry, water detail.

The confinement had been hardest on the seven children. The fifty-four civilians were allowed only in their rooms, the gym, the cafeteria, and outside on sixty feet of sidewalk and dirt. Ruth guessed that more than half had gathered along the building, as well as a dozen techs. Damn.

"Wait!" Aiko hollered. "Hey, Ruth, wait!"

She quit edging through the crowd just to get Aiko to shut her mouth. It was noon, the white sun hard on the olive drab trucks and green men, the spectators caught in a band of shadow under the building's eaves.

Aiko caught up but took an extra step too close. "I told you, didn't I? I told you." She seemed to have forgotten that she was mad, her dark eyes glinting with excitement. "Are you going along?"

"With this arm? How could I fit in a containment suit?" Ruth flopped her cast in its sling.

"Then what's in the duffel bag?"

"Files and a laptop." That was true. *Give her something juicy.* "D.J. screwed up and left the diagnostics upstairs, so I get to play nursemaid on the ride down. James wants to make sure they really have everything before they take off."

That almost made sense, and Aiko loved it. "What a shit assignment. Do you know who the other losers are?"

"I'll tell you later," Ruth said, stepping through the boundary from shadow to sun. She didn't look back.

They should have waited for lunch. With everyone in the cafeteria, there would have been few witnesses—and Ruth was hungry again, always hungry after the small portions. It should have been an insignificant worry, but she couldn't shake it. Was she going to have to skip a meal?

Unfortunately, James had had no control over the timetable.

James could only shape the situation to the limit of his authority. The expedition would include three techs, and Kendricks had visited this morning in part to confirm names. The council had no reason to rely solely on this man Sawyer. He was an unknown, and he refused to tell them the location of his lab until they'd come for him, and soldiers couldn't be expected to identify everything of importance among his gear and computers. The dilemma was whom to send. Risking the best and brightest was unthinkable, but sending low-level assistants or the ineffectual was a risk of another sort. They might miss something.

James had haggled with Kendricks over who could be spared versus who could do the job. He had agreed with the senator, and then he had drawn up a different manifest altogether.

"Goldman, check." The captain's orders were already well creased, perfectly creased, and he folded the sheet into his chest pocket. "Where have you been, ma'am? We're running late."

"Sorry." She'd hoped to rush out and avoid Major Hernandez. The security chief might wonder why one of Timberline's premier eggheads had been included and insist on making a call even though she was on the list. "Can you help me up?"

The truck bed was level with her chest. Three of the men in back had quickly stepped forward, taking her bag, reaching for her, but Ruth only had one arm.

Their fatigues were newer and cleaner than any she'd seen yet, and camouflage instead of the olive drab of Timberline's security detail. Hernandez and the others were Marines, she had learned. These men were Army Special Forces.

The captain half crouched and laced his fingers together over his knee, palms up, making a step for her. When he straightened, Ruth waggled her cast with all the grace of a chicken. She hadn't expected him to hoist her up, but he did it easily. She would have toppled if the soldiers in the truck hadn't grabbed her good arm.

"Whoa, hey, we gotcha." The nearest of them smiled, a light, honest, boy-meets-girl grin.

It didn't matter that Prince Charming here probably flashed the same look at every female over seventeen. Ruth saw an opening. She couldn't think of anything clever to say but that didn't matter, *you're really strong* or *thanks guys* would do the trick, start a friendship. Calculating, she smiled back, but there was a familiar voice behind her—

Major Hernandez. "Do we have it together, Captain?"

"Sir."

She pushed against Charming, driven by a spike of panic, but of course her sneakers and jeans were obvious among their boots and forest camouflage.

"Dr. Goldman," Hernandez said.

She thought of the story she'd told Aiko, that she was only riding down to the airport and back. But the captain had just checked her off on the manifest. She could hardly use that lie in front of him, and otherwise her mind was blank.

"We need to reach California before sunset," Hernandez said, looking up at her, "and nobody wants to wait another day. I'll expect you to do a better job of working with the group from now on. Understood?"

Ruth nodded dumbly and let out her breath.

They planned to do what White River had not—to keep Sawyer and his work from the council. They planned to divert north to Canada, develop the vaccine nano on their own, then spread it far and wide.

The substitution game would have been impossible for James to pull off alone. He had zero influence over the military command, and three scientists could hardly outfight or escape an escort of elite troops.

Some or most of their escort would be on their side.

James was not alone. Nor was he the top leader of the conspiracy. James had only hinted at this and hadn't dared to put a name on paper—there had been no names at all—yet Ruth had to believe it was one of the top generals if this person could switch units as he saw fit. At first glance it seemed odd that a military man would object to the council's actions, but Ruth suspected that career army were indoctrinated with much the same ethics as everyone in nanotech.

With great power comes great responsibility, and the sixteen hundred people killed in White River had been fellow Americans, or could have been again someday. Someday soon.

21

Ruth sat quietly through the short drive, head down, mouth shut. Fortunately, conversation was possible only in a yell. The big truck had no muffler and its shocks were blown. The slat benches in back rammed up or slammed down each time the wheels hit the slightest bump in the road, and she let the bass roar of the engine fill her head.

The airport was a dense and complicated scene, the short county runway surrounded by fat commercial airliners and smaller craft. Waiting on the tarmac now was a single-engine Cessna, civilian white and beige, and a much larger C-130 cargo transport painted olive drab.

They parked beneath the 130's tail but could have driven straight in. The rear of the plane was open—it dropped down and became a loading ramp—with a jeep, a flatbed trailer, and a bulldozer lined up nose to rear within its long body.

Ruth saw no more troops or specialists waiting to join them among the USAF ground crews, so the expedition would total fewer than twenty. She was the only woman.

Hernandez, the ranking officer, dispatched five Special Forces and an Air Force pilot to the Cessna, then hustled everyone else into the massive C-130. Was he trying to keep on schedule or was he, like Ruth, afraid that a voice on the radio would cancel their mission before they were in the air?

Her fellow techs were Dhanumjaya Julakanti, better known as D.J., and Todd Brayton, both from the hunter-killer development team. Both had helped design the discrimination key.

She got the acknowledgment she needed in their eyes and a nod from D.J., but there was no way to talk. Hernandez insisted everyone sit together close behind the cockpit. The bulldozer, trailer, and jeep were chained to the deck, but if anything snapped free during takeoff, it would drop toward the tail. Smarter to be up front.

A knife of panic bit into her again when the plane lunged skyward. The interior was a long, dimly lit drum. No windows. Too much like the *Endeavour*. Worse, the web seats ran alongside the edges of the deck, facing the opposite wall rather than forward, so that the g-forces drew her stomach sideways.

Finally they leveled off. Always courteous, Major Hernandez unstrapped and knelt before the three techs. Ruth watched his face intently, alert for a wink, a word, a tipoff of any kind.

"I know this all seems thrown together," he said, "but you're in capable hands. I don't want you to worry about anything except your job, okay?"

Hernandez and four Marines had been assigned to the expedition as their personal bodyguards, in addition to the seven men of the Special Forces team and three USAF pilots. Hernandez rattled off introductions, making a point of including the troops in the other plane—and Ruth noted that this hand-picked group was all chiefs and no Indians, entirely sergeants and corporals. It also seemed top-heavy, with Hernandez and the Special Forces captain. A lieutenant colonel headed the trio of pilots.

D.J. said, "Seems to me you're a little shorthanded."

"No point wasting suits," Hernandez told him, "or air, or jet fuel. And there isn't going to be anyone else there, if that's what you're worried about."

No, Ruth thought. *Not after they dusted White River.* None of the few regions still capable of getting a plane off the ground would dare.

The small Cessna was flying ahead of the C-130, since it required a shorter, narrower space to touch down than the cargo plane. If necessary, the men aboard the Cessna could do whatever possible to improve and mark the landing area.

After a flight of two and a quarter hours, the C-130 would have the fuel capacity to circle or even to return to Leadville in a worst-case scenario, but there was a sufficient stretch of road waiting. Satellite photography, backed by discussions with the Californians, confirmed a near straightaway of 2,500 feet along the slanting plateau of the mountaintop.

"Putting down in an urban area might be tricky if this guy's lab was in a city," Hernandez said, "but the C-130 is one of the toughest aircraft ever built. We can squeeze into a dirt field if necessary, then drive from there."

D.J. scowled at the bulldozer and began to open his mouth.

"We've got everything covered," Hernandez assured them. "We're in, we're out, we're home."

Home. Shit. There was her clue.

Major Hernandez was still loyal to the council.

"It's the Special Forces," Ruth said. "Think about it."

D.J. shook his head. "James and Hernandez are friends."

She shook her head right back at him. "That doesn't mean anything. James tries to get in good with everyone."

Privacy hadn't been a problem. The C-130 could hold nearly a hundred troops, and the vehicles formed a low, irregular wall down the middle of the deck. Ruth had opened her laptop and started arguing schematics with D.J., who caught on and made some loud comments of his own. After a minute she'd apologized to Hernandez for the disruption, then moved away with D.J. and Todd. They were still in view of the soldiers but buried in engine noise, which was bone-shaking here alongside the wings.

"I'll tell you what doesn't mean anything. One word." D.J.

didn't quite sneer, but his full lips held a condescending smile perfectly. "He could have meant home like home free."

"He would've said it another way if he was on our side."

"I don't think he'll say anything at all."

Dhanumjaya Julakanti had jumpy eyebrows, a dimpled chin, and a tendency to overenunciate, especially the words *I me my*. Some people couldn't see past his charisma or his IQ, a classic combination, and mistook his self-importance for leadership—but Lord knew she wasn't Miss Humility. Ruth recognized a piggish obsession with being right when she saw it.

Todd Brayton wasn't any help. Young, maybe twenty-five, straw blond with brown eyes, Todd was fidgety, too quiet, more nervous than Ruth and D.J. together. When they first met the week before, she'd tried to avoid staring at his blister scars. Todd made that difficult. He touched the blotch on his nose often, and constantly rustled his burned fingers together. He had been one of the last techs out of NORAD and Ruth admired his willingness to face the locusts again. Yes, they'd be wearing suits, but exposure was more than a nightmare to him.

Todd was the bravest of them.

He seemed to have already hit his limit, however, with nothing to spare for any conflict outside himself.

"Look." Ruth strived to keep her voice friendly, which was impossible, half-shouting over the engine noise. "Hernandez would have preferred a full platoon of his own men. There's no reason to send a mixed group except that our guy plugged in a separate unit. And he made sure to stack the deck while he was at it, seven to five."

D.J. waggled his chin at her. "You're just making assumptions again. Maybe they planned to send all Special Forces originally and Hernandez is the one who was switched in."

"It doesn't matter," Todd said. "We can't hint around about it, we might tip off the wrong side."

D.J. kept shaking his head. "They wouldn't tell us anyway."

"You think they'll wait to see how things play out," Ruth said. Sure. Whether it was the Special Forces team or Hernandez and his Marines, they didn't care about her peace of mind.

They'd want to keep their options open until the last minute, and couldn't rely on her not to slip up.

James would be in trouble no matter what happened, she knew. Imprisoned? Banished? Ruth was only beginning to understand his sacrifice. But if this mission was a bust the soldiers could all go back to Leadville, no harm, no foul.

She and D.J. and Todd would have a harder time claiming innocence. In fact, they might be better off instigating a showdown between the two halves of their escort, stay out West.

It was a dangerous thought. Even if the right soldiers won, they might execute her for making them outcasts.

Ruth went back to the front of the plane and chose a seat in the small crowd where she could see a wedge of sky through the open cockpit door. She managed a smile, thinking that the crash of the *Endeavour* had been preferable to this flight. At least it had been over quickly. Her anxiety was a restless jitter in her fingers and in her mind.

Below, outside this thin metal shell, lay an environment only marginally less lethal than the vacuum of space. The dead zone stretched without interruption from Utah to the mountains in California—and west of the Sierra range it blanketed a full third of the planet, unblemished and absolute except for the volcanic peaks of Hawaii, until the high points of New Guinea and Taiwan rose up across the Pacific.

The plane rattled and dropped left, and Ruth yelped as the nose stayed down. But it was only turbulence. They leveled out again, and nearly every man present said something nice to her or smiled and nodded. Ruth couldn't even meet their eyes, silently cursing herself.

She was a damn poor choice to save the world.

Landing was uneventful. The plane bounced once, a shuddering impact followed by a quick, gut-fluttering arc, but Ruth managed not to embarrass herself again.

Then they taxied for fifteen minutes, which was maddening.

Where was there to go? The plane moved at a crawl and stopped three times. Hernandez made her remain in her seat. They were going to jockey back around into a takeoff position, he said. Ruth kicked her legs. At last the pilots were satisfied, and the two Special Forces troops aboard went to lower the tailgate. Again Hernandez made her stay put, but she could smell pine trees and earth as soon as the plane opened.

Hernandez had already conferred by radio with the USAF pilot and five Special Forces in the Cessna, who'd touched down forty minutes ago. They reported everything as expected, no tricks, no traps, only a handful of malnourished survivors. Still, Ruth was ordered to keep close to the Marines.

Some instinct tensed in her hindbrain when she emerged into sunlight. At first she blamed Hernandez for this paranoia, but then D.J. said, "Top of the world, eh?"

That was it. In Leadville the close horizon of giant peaks manufactured the illusion of being protected. Here there was only the pale sky. They were up on the tallest point and their view appeared infinite. To the west, beneath the late sun, the land tumbled away in a zigzag maze of ridgelines and cliffs and rounded granite slopes.

The habitable zones in California were little more than a chain of flyspecks. Yosemite offered several large patches not far from here, but this peak seemed alone above the barrier. Her eyes went again and again to the tangle of ravines and dusky green forest below as she moved with Hernandez and the Marines.

Lord only knew where Sawyer had come from. If that ragged knuckle of lava southward across the valley poked above ten thousand feet, its surface area looked no bigger than two or three football fields.

The C-130's tires had left inky skid lines like claw marks on the asphalt road, very near the only structure in sight. Glancing back at the plane was a mistake. This mountain was barren of trees, but she saw a rock outcropping down the road that their starboard wing must have cleared by a matter of feet—and they'd have to squeeze past it again to take off.

The building, originally, had been a two-room cabin with

a stubby chimney. It was old, maybe 1950s. Another room had
been tacked on years ago, and a modern whisker antenna rose
alongside the chimney. More recent additions consisted of
two-by-four framework and blue tarps, and behind it Ruth saw
three low huts skinned in clear plastic. Greenhouses.

Five adults and a boy stood together away from the cabin,
out on the road with an equal number of Special Forces in
camouflage and an Air Force man in gray-blue. The two
groups did not mingle. The soldiers all held assault rifles, long
barrels tipped casually toward the ground.

Ruth frowned. Was this really how they planned to treat
these people, herding them?

"Flank," said the Marine beside her, like a swear word, and
motion drew her eyes back toward the greenhouses— Two
shapes, scuttling for cover— One of them thrust out its arm,
and the men around her raised their weapons—

A woman up the road screamed, *"Lindsey, God no!"*

Her shrill fear was immediately lost in male voices: "It's
just kids!"

"Kids—"

"Stand down," Hernandez said. "For Christ's sake."

The Marines surrounding Ruth lowered their rifles as a
young girl's laughter reached their ears, clear and breathless.

"Lindsey!" the woman shrieked, but the girl danced back
into the open and pointed her stick at them, making *buh buh
buh* sounds before ducking behind the cinder-block foundation of a greenhouse.

Ruth stared, even after Todd had nudged her and they'd
started walking again. The girl looked to be nine or ten,
dressed in yellow rain gear that hung on her like thirty-gallon
garbage bags, and she was obviously delighted by the soldiers.

Ruth shook her head and smiled. The emotion in her was
too complex to articulate, but that girl was hope. That girl was
a future. Given the chance, mankind would rebound from anything. Human beings were too adaptable.

The soldiers blocked her from the six Californians as Hernandez introduced himself, so Ruth edged her good shoulder
in between two Special Forces. Five of the six, two women,

two men and the boy, were haggard and dirty and therefore completely normal. It was the last man who froze her attention.

Piebald blister rash peppered his face and neck, distorting his black beard, old scars intermingled with larger, healing patches and hemorrhagic bruising. His dark eyes showed his suffering, and Ruth believed she could see his guilt. This was someone who had helped decimate an entire planet, accident or not. Atonement was beyond him. He had paid horribly, and strived now to do more, and he would always be lost inside his pain—and yet the feeling in Ruth was not hatred or even base revulsion. It was awe. It was respect.

"Mr. Sawyer," she said, extending her hand.

His fingers were rough and nubby but his smile was a fragile thing. "No," he said. "My name is Cam."

22

"I'm Ruth," the lady told him, holding on to his hand for another moment. Whether she was proving something to him or to herself, Cam appreciated the effort.

He knew he was a monster and his hands were the worst. His right pinky had been eaten down to the bone at the first joint, and ruffles of scar tissue prevented him from bending that finger more than a little. Nerve damage had robbed him of sensation in his ring finger as well, leaving his grip uneven.

"You came across with him," Ruth said, softly, carefully, but her intelligent brown gaze was unwavering.

One of the other civilians got loud, a dark guy with a dimpled block chin. The man's eyebrows rose in a display of impatience. "Where is Mr. Sawyer? Is he all right?"

"He's sleeping," Cam said. "At least he was."

"Sleeping!"

The officer, Hernandez, was more tactful. He said, "We need to see him, *hermano*." *Brother.*

Cam felt a smile cross his lips again. Those three rolling syllables evoked so much that he had lost. "Let's wait a couple hours, okay? He's better when he's rested."

Hernandez glanced at the sun and then at the cabin.

"Really," Cam said. "He's not having a better day."

"All right." Hernandez turned to one of the men in camouflage. "Captain, why don't we make these folks a solid meal and see if there's any medical attention we can provide."

Hollywood's name was Eddie Kokubo. Edward. But that was the only thing he'd lied about. This island could have sustained them all easily and the people here had been eager to help, eager for new faces, eager to rebuild any semblance of a community.

Cam had regained consciousness inside their home, in brilliant yellow lanternlight and the wretched noise of a woman's sobbing, crushed somewhere beneath his own agony. There was space in his body only for a flicker of understanding— and the confused, recurrent terror that they would cook him.

He drifted in that place for days, surfacing irregularly but all too willing to retreat from himself.

Eighty-one hours after reaching elevation, he woke as they were changing his bandages, alone in a real bed. Dr. Anderson was so much like he'd pictured from Hollywood's descriptions that he forgot they'd never met. Mid-forties, graying, Anderson wasn't quite overweight, but his oval cheeks and stubby fingers gave him a look of contentment, which was reinforced by his slow way of moving. His wife, Maureen, was less gentle, a redhead with creases on her forehead and alongside her pointed nose.

"Doctor A," Cam said.

Maureen jerked back at his croaking. Anderson merely paused and then looked up from Cam's left foot. "You're awake," he answered, simple encouragement.

It went like that for another two weeks, Anderson babying him with calm pronouncements and broth, fighting the onset of fever with judicious amounts of aspirin and irreplaceable one-use chemical cold packs. Nearly half a square yard of Cam's skin had been turned into open, oozing wounds, and Anderson kept him isolated for fear of infection.

They also wanted to see if he and Sawyer told the same story. They questioned him a bit at a time. Anderson was mostly accepting but Maureen probed for inconsistencies, her green eyes like jade, and his condition proved an excellent excuse to avoid answering too quickly. He would look away or take a deep breath, not needing to fake grief and exhaustion, thinking as best he could until he was convinced he had his half-truths straight.

He and Sawyer were the only ones talking.

Hollywood had bled out within an hour—and laid beside him now were two additional graves. Jocelyn Colvard and Alex Atkins had also crawled up that night, too long after Cam and Sawyer dragged Hollywood to the barrier. A stroke killed Jocelyn instantly but Atkins hung on for almost seven days, groaning, coughing, a restless coma that gave way to rasping death.

Cam would never know how Jim Price had fallen. Life wasn't like TV, where hero and villain were inevitably, neatly brought together for a stylish mano-a-mano duel. It wasn't even possible in this situation to determine which of them was the hero.

Price must have gotten stuck too far east up the valley. Driving out of Woodcreek had been the wrong choice after all, and Price and the rest had died for that decision.

Sawyer, as always, had been right even in the final extreme. The few people on this mountain had listened to the shoot-out in the valley and assumed there were good guys and bad—and by carrying Hollywood with them, Cam and Sawyer had cloaked themselves in the illusion of his friendship and his trust.

They'd fought, they said, because Price planned on making himself king. Price and his supporters had raided a gun shop in Woodcreek, and they stood up to him despite being outnumbered, and their friends died for it. Erin. Manny. Bacchetti.

Maureen softened as he described Hollywood's days with them. "So Eddie finally got someone to call him that," she said, lowering her eyes to the floor, and she traded stories of her own to help Cam through his healing.

In the next room Sawyer wept and Sawyer screamed, waking Cam, a constant disturbance, but Cam's sympathy was for himself and for the dead and for these good, generous people.

Sawyer deserved to suffer.

Eddie Kokubo had invented greater reasons for fighting across the invisible sea, but Maureen believed that his first and most powerful motivation had been heartbreak. Eddie just hadn't fit in here. The four adults were married couples, the youngest of them thirty-three, and the oldest of the children was only eleven. There had been another man but during the first spring he had finally succumbed to liver damage, and none of the other people who'd staggered up onto this mountain at the outset of the plague had lasted more than a week, devastated by internal injuries.

From the beginning, eighteen-year-old Eddie was never purposely excluded—except when the kids were caught up in games that were too silly for him; except when the adults did their real planning; except each night when everyone went to bed.

They were not completely alone. They saw smoke from cookfires on a bump to the northeast, and watched Cam's group to the south through binoculars.

Cam had fretted at that, but didn't ask. *Did you see us butchering each other?* When he got outside he peered southward himself. His favorite cliff was visible, along with several crests and ridgelines, yet the majority of that small peak canted west and south away from this mountain. He detected no hint of the stay-behinds, no smoke, no motion, but they would be saving fuel for the winter and in any case he spared few glances for his old home after being sure that even more of his lies were safe. The valley between hurt him too deeply.

Month after month Eddie had wasted batteries trying to raise them on the ham radio, wasted wood and grass making smoke signals. He built flag towers and laid out giant words in rock—and then one morning he was gone, leaving only a note signed with his bold, chosen name. *Hollywood.*

That night they lit a row of bonfires to alert the people across the valley or to help poor Eddie find his way home. His journey was both foolish and grand, of course—it was entirely adolescent—and yet he'd been vindicated beyond even his wildest imaginings.

Without Eddie, Sawyer might never have reached a radio.

The two Special Forces medics examined Cam first in the semi-privacy of the cargo plane, while the other soldiers let the kids get in the way as they set up tents and dug a fire pit. If these corpsmen were less educated than Dr. Anderson, their supplies made up for it. They re-dressed the stubborn, swollen divot of rash under Cam's right arm and gave him wide-spectrum antibiotics that they warned could cause diarrhea, Anderson agreeing that the risk of dehydration was better than relying on his wasted immune system to overcome the infection.

The medics didn't even attempt to deal with his dental problems. Across the valley they had eaten all of the toothpaste they'd found on scavenging trips, and Cam had been chewing lightly on a cavity for months now. The bits of floss he'd shared with Erin and Sawyer, the few brushes they'd worn down to nothing, had probably kept him from developing worse trouble—but toward the end of his climb, nano infestations had destroyed his gums along the upper left of his mouth. His eyetooth and the molar behind it were loose, dying. Both would need to come out soon, and the gap would further deform the contours of his face.

When he emerged from the plane, Ruth and the other two scientists were questioning Maureen. They turned, however, and the loud one, D.J., immediately hammered at him: "Where is Sawyer's lab? Do you know the street address?"

Cam had expected impatience, but this guy was nervous. All of them. Why? Not for a lack of guns.

And that wasn't a question they should have asked.

Ruth quickly intervened, glaring at D.J. "I need to sit down," she said. "I'm tired. Can we all just sit down and talk?"

Cam nodded, and they walked with D.J. and Todd to the downhill side of the road, not far from the planes or the cabin—or the two Marines who followed the scientists over. This berm of hardpack and crumbling granite had become Cam's favorite spot; favorite because the kids came here often, noisily rooting for quartz; favorite because the views were west, away from Bear Summit.

Neither D.J. nor Todd was much for conversation, though. D.J. didn't know how to listen and Todd didn't open his mouth, scratching and scratching at the blot of old scarring on his nose, looking anywhere except at Cam's ruined profile.

"We're going to beat the plague," Ruth said, "I swear," but Cam barely glanced up from the rock he'd picked up, a shard of milky quartz shot through with orange-black veins of iron.

Sunset would be unspectacular today, no clouds, the yellow sun falling to the edge of the world without changing in hue or strength. The grasshoppers sang and sang and sang.

"We were already close," Ruth insisted. "Close enough to test out in lab conditions."

He nodded. It was everything he wanted to hear. But his reaction to their arrival was not what he'd hoped, and he turned the gleaming white rock over again in his gnarled hands.

He had thought he was beyond self-pity, yet found himself avoiding Ruth's eyes. She stared at him with the same open wonder as the children, and spoke with compassion and an astonishing deference, which affected him in ways that D.J.'s disgust did not. Because it was undeserved. Because disgust was all that he felt for himself, for his appearance, for his past.

This bright, daring woman would never have been so respectful if she knew the truth.

Few men would have considered Ruth pretty, but she was healthy and trim and dedicated. Cam wanted to like her, which was exactly why he couldn't trust her. Not yet.

"You're with the rebels," he said matter-of-factly, just to get a reaction. It didn't matter. Sawyer was theirs, unless somebody flew in and shot all of these soldiers. Jesus. No wonder they were in such a rush.

Ruth seemed startled, but didn't shy away when he lifted his gaze. "What? No, we're from Leadville."

"Then you should know."

D.J. interrupted. "This is bullshit. Just tell us."

"You should know." Cam didn't have any idea where to find Sawyer's lab, and he had been definite about that fact with his radio contacts. Sawyer refused to share the location until they came for him, until they treated him, until they took him wherever he would be well fed and protected and clean.

Cam had begged Dr. Anderson to call Colorado before he even told them his own name, identifying Sawyer first. Unfortunately, ham radio wasn't like picking up the phone. The family who'd lived here kept a transceiver for recreation and for emergencies, and it had more-than-sufficient wattage to bridge the distance—but unless there was someone waiting at the right time on the right frequency, a broadcast was no more effective than a prayer. And these days, nearly all radio traffic was on military and federal bands. No one was monitoring amateur channels.

The International Space Station would have been an ideal relay, and the survivors here had spoken to the astronauts several times during the past year, so they began transmitting on a diligent, revolving schedule, certain that they'd intercept one of the rapid orbits overhead. But the ISS never responded.

They had also developed several contacts on the ground, both near and remote. Within ten days they'd raised some again. None could help. Most were just as helpless, stuck on scattered high points along the coast, while those in the Rockies had strived all this time to remain uninvolved with Leadville or its enemies.

Cam was aware of the slow-developing civil war along the Continental Divide. Hollywood had shared his limited knowledge of it, a distant curiosity, but those hostilities confused their attempts to reach across seven hundred miles.

The silence became an invisible sea in his mind, wide and desolate, into which they ventured each night when reception was best—but nights passed while atmospheric activity prevented them from sending a clear signal. Nights passed in which they chased down intermittent contacts only to be dismissed as a hoax or simply too far away.

Finally, three weeks after their arrival on this mountain,

Cam and Sawyer spoke with a nanotech expert in Leadville named James Hollister. Open broadcasts could be intercepted by anybody on the same wavelength, however, and Cam had been prepared to see someone other than Leadville fly in—someone who might have heard only parts of their conversations.

"Seems like Hollister would've told you what we told him," Cam said, and D.J.'s eyebrows rippled in anger.

"You'll get your price," D.J. said. "Whatever you want."

"I want to know where you're from."

"Hey, come on." Ruth tried to elbow D.J. with her cast and shrug at Cam at the same time. Busy lady. "We're all on the same side here," she said.

He remembered when he had played the peacemaker.

"James told us only Sawyer knew what city," she explained. "We just hoped you were holding out. We weren't exactly Miss Manners about it, though."

A joke? Cam glanced up, but she'd turned to D.J. now, directing her sarcasm at him. Then Ruth and D.J. both looked over their shoulders, hearing footsteps that Cam's bad ear perceived a moment later.

Maureen moved softly across the road behind them at a funny, sidestepping angle, avoiding the two soldiers nearby.

"He's awake," Maureen said.

23

Ruth was uncomfortable with her sense of fate and its grip on her increased as they walked toward the cabin. Mostly this odd mood was rising anticipation, a conflict of relief and worry that at last it was time. But there was something more. She identified with Cam—so cursed, so lucky—in ways she was still only beginning to realize.

Maybe she would have felt this same quiet empathy for anyone in his place, but it was an extensive chain of events that had brought them together. Her step-father would have called it providence. Too much circumstance, too many choices and accidents outside their individual lives.

"You're going to have to take this slow," Cam told D.J., and Ruth immediately said, "That's not a problem, whatever you want."

"Just follow my lead."

And yet, she thought, the prime factor in her being here now, this evening, was really only the dumb force of nature. Until the plague year humankind had forgotten, in their cities, in their comfort, the godlike hand of the seasons.

It was winter that had dictated this encounter.

Only spring thaw had allowed Cam and Sawyer to cross the valley, and only spring thaw had allowed the shuttle to touch down. Thaw had allowed the Russo-Muslim and Chinese-Indian wars to resume on the other side of the planet.

Cam limped, favoring his right leg. At the cabin's front steps he stopped and turned, blocking their way, not even looking at D.J. yet sticking an arm out to corral him as D.J. tried to go around. "Wait," Cam said. He was watching Hernandez and the two medics hurry over from the cargo plane, followed by Dr. Anderson and all four children and several more soldiers.

D.J. took offense. "We don't have to—"

"I said wait." Cam's burned face lacked expression, and his tone was level, but his shoulders canted forward and D.J. shut up and moved back.

Both of their Marine guards closed in, the nearest bumping Todd in his hurry. She saw Cam's gaze flick between the soldiers once, twice. Then he dropped his arm from D.J.'s path.

The grasshoppers filled the quiet, *ree ree ree ree ree*, as busy and insistent as her thoughts.

Lord knew he was a mystery, his inconsistencies. He had been firm with Hernandez, overriding the major's initial request to see Sawyer, and he had been equally tough with D.J., and clearly he was dangerous. Yet he was gentle with her. Because she had been so polite or merely because she was female?

It would be impossible, she supposed, for him not to have become horrendously self-conscious.

D.J. acted like he couldn't see past the scarring but Cam was smart enough, aware enough, to concern Ruth. He had guessed after just thirty minutes that something was off between them and Leadville. How? Could he be that sensitive to tensions?

He was young, Todd's age, but he had kept himself alive where so many others had died, and she imagined that was an education of a kind that few could match.

Plague Year. In this place, the name was fitting, and Ruth felt that cold sense of distance in herself again. She had been lucky. It was a strange thought after so much hardship and death, but she had been very lucky all this time.

"Major," Cam said, as Hernandez arrived with his small crowd. "We can't take all these people inside."

Hernandez was affable. "The kids aren't going, *hermano*."

He'd used that word before. What did it mean, *sir* or some equivalent of *gentleman*? Ruth knew *amigo*, that was *friend*, but she believed it would be more like Hernandez to treat Cam formally even as he tried to manipulate him.

Hernandez had done the same with her.

Cam shook his head once, an efficient *no*. "Two or three people besides me, that's it. That has to be it. And the camera and stuff stay out here."

One soldier had brought recording equipment, a handheld family minicam, a larger video camera, a tripod, a batch of wireless clip microphones and extra tapes and batteries.

Hernandez studied Cam briefly. Then he shook his head, too. "I'm afraid I'm on orders," he said.

They compromised. Hernandez was adamant that the three scientists go in, but reduced the support staff to himself and the audio/video gear to one camera.

Ruth followed Cam into the shadows of the front room, the living room, and crossed through with only an impression of neatness. Then he held out his hand again and ducked into an adjacent bedroom alone.

Beneath the not-unpleasant reek of woodsmoke, she smelled old sweat and grime. Hernandez raised his minicam and thumbed the record button with a small chime, apparently as a test. He lowered it five seconds later. D.J. glanced around with one eyebrow up and Todd rocked on his heels, sort of pacing without really moving.

Much like Ruth's quarters at Timberline, this cabin seemed empty of furniture. No couch, no chairs, all used for firewood. A pair of sleeping bags lay folded on the hardwood floor near the fireplace, no doubt for two of the children, and on some shelving built into the wall was the ham radio.

The sight of it filled her with that quiet, uneven sorrow again. Gustavo might have heard these people directly if he had only monitored amateur frequencies in the first week and a half of Cam's attempts to make contact. Evidently Gustavo's voice had filled this room more than once. But in mid-April, Gus had been occupied with military transmissions and preparing for their landing—and then the ISS had been empty.

What if they had spoken? She wouldn't be here, maybe none of them, not even the Special Forces unit substituted into their escort. The council would already have Sawyer and his equipment.

It could still happen. James would cover for them, telling Kendricks that she was busy if the senator asked, dampening any rumors in Timberline; but the listening devices throughout the labs would inevitably catch word of who was missing, and Ruth had to assume the tapes were scanned daily.

New orders could come at any moment, alerting Hernandez to the traitors around him.

Or there might be another plane flying out right now.

"Okay," Cam said, turning Ruth's head. He gestured with one scabby claw. "He's doing okay."

Albert Sawyer was a slumping wax candle of a man, shrunken and malformed. He had sat up, or had asked to be propped up, against the wall alongside his bed.

He must have wanted to appear as robust as possible, but repeated cerebral events had robbed Sawyer of muscle control down most of his right side—drooping eye, slack cheek, head tipped over his fallen shoulder. He had also lost too much weight, so that what flesh he'd kept was taut and hollow against his frame, and whereas Cam's brown face looked abraded or burned, Sawyer's whiter skin had turned into a blood purple hide, clotted and pebbled. His long bullet head grew hair only in wisps.

Cam and Maureen had warned them, but Ruth caught her breath and Todd froze in the door, bumping Hernandez with his elbow as he involuntarily reached for his nose.

She saw their reaction mirrored in the living half of Sawyer's face. His left eye widened, bright with emotion.

"Look at these pretty fucks," Cam said, too loud, in a brash voice she hadn't heard before. Sawyer's gaze rolled furiously and Cam spoke again, drawing that one baleful eye to himself. "You ever seen anybody this fucking well manicured?"

Sawyer's mouth worked. "Swee'ovem vizza."

"Real sweet. They were gonna do black tie."

It was a gamble, she thought, making their relationship adversarial, but Cam knew Sawyer best and they hadn't left him much choice, humiliating Sawyer on first sight.

If this destroyed man wanted to show them up, he might finally relinquish his secrets.

Hernandez sketched a salute, hiding the minicam down by his hip in his left hand. "I'm Major Frank Hernandez," he said, "USMC Second Division and expedition commander."

Nice. Overkill, but nice. They had to make Sawyer feel important, make it clear they'd brought their best.

Even D.J. was courteous. "My name is Dr. Dhanum—"

"Yaowp!" Sawyer lurched, both eyes blinking shut. For a moment Ruth thought it was a word she hadn't understood, but Sawyer wasn't interested in hellos. She supposed Cam had explained who had come, and that was plenty for him.

She watched his loose mouth, analyzing his sounds.

"Ayuhn'velah annabuh bee, a'cos assigned the way."

"I can develop an antibody," Cam told them. "*Archos* was designed that way, as an adaptable template—"

"Yahp!" Sawyer barked again at Cam's elaboration. " 'Dadable templut," he said, with all the petulance of a three-year-old who has ritualized a favorite story.

Cam carefully repeated it. "An adaptable template."

Ruth looked away, a slow cringe, the horror in her still growing. The others were also silent.

Sawyer's brain had been ravaged as badly as his skin.

He glared at them, defiant, challenging. Cam made a patting gesture and Ruth knelt to the scuffed wood floor, putting herself below Sawyer's bed rather than continuing to stand over him. Basic psychology. They might lessen his agitation by demonstrating that they were a willing audience. Hernandez and Todd followed suit, but D.J. glanced at Cam. Cam stayed on his feet. D.J. reluctantly hunkered down.

Sawyer mumbled again and Cam said, "We were going to cure cancer in two years. Maybe less."

D.J.'s brow wrinkled. "This was all in our—"

Ruth hit him, slapping her knuckles against his leg. Yes, they already knew these basics, but they were damn well going to let Sawyer brag. The name *archos* was new and possibly useful, another angle for the FBI to take with their research, patent records, incorporation files. They might be able to out-fox Sawyer if he gave them enough clues but still wouldn't co-operate.

Or if he was unable to cooperate. Lord only knew what was happening inside his head.

He lectured them on the mechanics of the nano, slurring, staring down at his bedsheets or dragging that lopsided gaze across their faces. But he was either still unaccustomed to or refused to accept the condition of his body, and repeatedly coughed for air in midsyllable. Once he started to retch. After each fit he pulled his good arm over his mouth, wiping away drool—and he began to bump the back of his hand against his lips compulsively.

Cam translated with determination and patience, though after a while he sat on the edge of the bed and stretched out his knee. His intonation was sometimes uncertain but he did not hesitate over technical phrases. He had been the one who spoke with James, she decided, although Sawyer probably ad-dressed the microphone directly on occasion.

Ruth had wanted to feel the same sympathy she'd experi-enced for Cam, but it was a very different emotion inside her now. Sawyer must have been a great man, capable of great things, to have played any part in developing the *archos* pro-totype, yet his decision to withhold the location of his lab was unforgivable. It was a threat to her. It didn't matter that it might not have been a wholly conscious decision.

Sawyer had not let his guilt become the burden that was so evident in Cam. What remained of him seemed possessed by the bitter rage of an invalid, and he was crippled further by his awareness of everything he'd lost.

He erupted with that rough shout again and again, at himself when his body failed, at Cam for guessing the wrong words or even for correctly anticipating what he planned to say next.

Hernandez filmed the two men, the minicam tucked against his body. The angle looked poor and the room was darkening as twilight settled outside the square window, but a good audio recording would be the most important thing.

Sawyer was selling himself.

Did he think he needed to convince them of his identity, or was he only striving to keep his past straight in his own mind? Ruth supposed he'd prevented them from making introductions so he wouldn't have to use their names. He knew his limitations. His short-term memory was unreliable, yet he remained canny enough to try to conceal this weakness.

He was excusing himself.

Twice more he laboriously explained that *archos* had been designed to save lives. Four times he insisted he hadn't played any part in allowing the prototype to get loose.

Ruth was reminded of a toddler again, attempting to make something real by chanting it over and over.

"What was your specialty?" she asked, after twenty minutes. She didn't know how Sawyer would react to the interruption, but already he was tiring and she was afraid he'd keep them captive all night even as he grew more incoherent. Maybe it would have been better to let D.J. grill him from the start.

"The rep efficiency is mine," Sawyer told them, through Cam, and his pride was fierce enough to mold his slack, eroded face into what she thought was a smile.

It was that simple. The wreckage of his self-esteem was propped up on who he had been, and only on who he had been, and he was terrified that they would exclude him after retrieving the files and equipment.

There wasn't anything else left for him.

"Replication speed is going to be our biggest hurdle," Ruth said, which wasn't untrue. "James told you we have a working discrim key, right? You'll have to look it over, but the vaccine nano won't hold up if we can't streamline the rep process."

He regarded her quietly, perhaps judging her sincerity. She wondered how well he could see now in the shadows.

D.J. shifted on the hard floor and managed to put his hand down with a slap, drawing everyone's attention. "I'd say it's worth redesigning the heat engine," he said. "We don't need the fuse and that's another way to shave some additional mass."

Sawyer's smile returned. This must have been his first opportunity to talk shop in fifteen months. He jabbered and Cam said, "Right. Except the design work is already done. Freedman added the fuse later. We can build straight off of the original schematic."

"Fantastic," Ruth said. That would save them days or even weeks—and he'd given them another clue. *Freedman.*

Cam spoke for Sawyer again: "We'll fly out tomorrow?"

Ruth straightened, barely able to contain her excitement.

Hernandez said, "Yes. Tomorrow morning."

Sawyer nodded, satisfied.

But the silence lingered. Sawyer dabbed at his mouth and D.J. shifted his weight once more. Hernandez said, "It would be better if you told us where tonight."

"Whar?"

"There's a lot of planning to take care of."

"Col'ado!" Sawyer's eye rolled with confusion and fury, and Ruth clenched her fist.

He expected them to take him east. Why? What did he think was waiting for him there? Safety, food, intensive medical attention—but no doctor would ever be able to fix him.

Maybe that was the problem. Maybe he had no interest in saving them if they couldn't save him.

Hernandez kept calm. "Not a chance," he said. "That was never the deal. We can't waste the fuel going back and forth, and we need you to make sure we recover everything important."

"Fuhgyou. Col'ado."

"They told us," Cam said, but Sawyer whipped his head back and forth in a stiff motion that bent his torso. One leg kicked up beneath the blankets as he lost his balance, and Cam grabbed his arm.

Cam shook him. "They told us you had to show them first."

"L'go!" His voice was a screech. "L'go me!"

Cam obeyed. Cam pulled his gnarled fingers from Sawyer's shirt but then reversed direction, surging his weight into the other man, shoving his open palm against Sawyer's ribs. It looked spontaneous. It looked like an act of long-suppressed misery, and Cam's regret was obvious and immediate. He grabbed at Sawyer again as Sawyer collapsed on the bed, mewling in pain. "Aa aaa! Aa!"

Hernandez jumped to his feet, the camera left on the floor, yet he stayed back as Cam leaned over Sawyer, patting his side and murmuring, "Sorry— Hey, I'm sorry—"

Sawyer's response surprised her, not spite, not more of that cruel glee at his own power. He answered Cam with the same apologetic tone. "Na'now, 'kay? Na'now."

"Not now, okay, you bet." Cam turned toward them, but with his eyes averted. "No more right now."

The feast was a disaster too. Leadville had included fresh meat in their provisions, a slab of ribs large enough to identify as cow. They'd also brought charcoal and the soldiers layered a broad, shallow pit with two full bags of briquettes. That smoky aroma was torture by itself, the ghost of summertime family gatherings, and the smell became unbearable when they placed the meat on a grill set low over the embers.

Everyone clustered around the fire pit except Sawyer, the two medics, and Dr. Anderson. Cam had also stayed inside, in case Sawyer was uncooperative, and Hernandez double-checked that their portions were held back for later.

The sky deepened enough to show the first stars. Todd said the brightest dot was Jupiter and one of the soldiers said it was Venus. The kids pushed through the small crowd, yelling. Ruth sat right up front, dulled by exhaustion and disappointment, alive with hunger. Her back was cool, her face too warm. Her arm ached inside her cast.

Maureen's strident voice lifted her gaze from the sizzle and pop of the meat. "You have to take us with you!"

Across the fire pit, Hernandez had been talking quietly with the Special Forces captain and two of the pilots. Maureen stood behind them now, having edged close enough to eavesdrop.

Hernandez turned and shook his head. "We don't have enough containment suits, and we might be down there for hours."

"But come back for us. Take us back with you."

"We won't want to risk an extra landing or use up the fuel."

"You landed fine!"

The four children, parading among the soldiers with their stick weapons, had gone still and silent at Maureen's outburst. Now all of them fled, ducking through the taller adults.

"You can't just leave us here!"

"I'm sorry. We'll give you as many supplies as—"

"You can't! You can't!"

Ruth returned her gaze to the fire pit as Maureen pleaded in a lower voice and the other California woman began to cry. They didn't realize they were so much better off here, even if the planes had been headed back to Leadville.

It was interesting that Maureen seemed to have the same false ideal of Colorado as Sawyer, and Lord knew Ruth had created her own unrealistic expectations while she was still aboard the ISS. Maybe everyone needed the possibility of a safe haven, somewhere, to keep them going. Ruth didn't know how to feel about that. It made her sad and it made her afraid.

She rubbed her eyes to hide her face and wished again that there was another way.

The meat was phenomenal, crisp fat, nearly raw against the bone, and she ate too quick, trying not to wolf it down but not entirely in control of herself.

Hernandez made sure Ruth had her own tent, a low two-man dome made for backpacking. The soldiers staked it down between the long body of the C-130 and their own, larger tents.

She washed her face and hands at a plastic tub, wanting at least to pull off her top and sponge her neck and armpits. A bath would be better. But she had no privacy, walled in by soldiers, and water was a carefully measured resource here. Unlike Leadville, surrounded by mountain ranges and snow-pack, this little island had only two dribbling springs, one of which dried up each summer. Maureen had warned Hernandez about rationing twice in Ruth's hearing.

She lingered over the tub, dripping, reluctant to settle in for the night despite feeling totally depleted. She wasn't sure she'd be able to sleep. The bugs here were creepy, pervasive, and loud—and her fear was the same, nonstop flickers of adrenaline. Hernandez had relayed their clues over the radio, the names *archos* and Freedman, but it might be days before the FBI produced anything useful.

The conspiracy would be uncovered long before then.

If Hernandez had included her name in his report, even just to praise her efforts, it might be soon. Tonight. What would happen? Fuel was so precious, would they fly her back? Would there be a gunfight as one group of soldiers turned on the other?

She was glad when Cam banged on a supply crate and yelled, "I have to see her!"

From her perspective the knot of men were a single, com-plicated shadow, their flashlights aimed into Cam's body. The soldiers appeared ready to turn him back. Ruth hurried over and said, "Hold on."

"I want to try again with Sawyer," he told her, "just you and me so he's not so outnumbered."

"I'll go," D.J. said, striding up beside Ruth's shoulder.

Cam shook his head. "Didn't ask you."

He moved through the dark like he was born to it, not at all hindered by his limp. Ruth and her Marine escorts kept to the bobbing white cone of their flashlights, staring down, sweeping the smooth asphalt road for nonexistent hazards. The fifty yards between their camp and the cabin were enough distance for Cam to leave them behind.

Two windows shone with lanternlight, at the cabin's front

and at the side. Sawyer's room. The night, so absolute, might have made Ruth uneasy but instead heightened her sense of inclusion. The cool dark seemed so much smaller than daylight, hiding the miles of empty land that fell away below them.

She heard the boys inside, faintly, then the deeper voice of a man. The soldiers' flashlights jabbed up and caught Cam and Dr. Anderson standing together by the front door. Their hands rose to shield their faces.

"Thank you," she said to her two soldiers. "Why don't you wait here."

"Ah, no ma'am." Staff Sergeant Gilbride shook his head. "The whole point is to keep from overcrowding him—"

"We'll stand outside his room. He won't know we're there." Gilbride started forward, gesturing to Cam, and the rich lanternlight spilled over them as the door opened. They stepped inside, Ruth caught between Gilbride and the other soldier.

What had Hernandez told his men, to be careful that these people didn't take her hostage and demand to be flown to Colorado? Sawyer was more valuable than she, and they had done everything in their power to make him available . . .

The three boys had several decks of cards laid out on the floor beside their lantern, a game she didn't recognize. Dr. Anderson knelt among them. Cam led the two Marines and Ruth toward the short hall at the back of the room, pausing there.

"You seem like you have your head on straight," Cam said, making eye contact, and Ruth shrugged at the compliment. Then he lowered his voice. "Flirt with him."

"What? Yeah, okay." She had been carrying her laptop at her side in her good hand. Now she brought the thin case up against her chest, smiling—and irritated—at the idea that the real reason he'd chosen her was for her boobs. Wrong woman.

He didn't smile back. "I'm serious. Don't go overboard, let's just see what happens."

"It's not a problem."

Sawyer's room had a rancid stink. His guts were a mess and his digestive process was inconsistent. Dr. Anderson had said that breaking down solid foods took nearly as much out of him as he gained in nutrition, describing lumpy stools and bloating and screaming fits, and Ruth wondered if this flatulence was the result of tempting him with beef ribs. She wondered if Cam had done it deliberately, to hurt and distract him.

The relationship between these men was one she might never fully comprehend, brother, enemy, each of them dependent upon and simultaneously dominant over the other.

"Hey, buddy," Cam said, "you feel better?"

"Nuh." Sawyer lay on his right side, his withered side, knees drawn up beneath the covers. His other hand shifted along the edge of the mattress, crablike, groping and pausing and groping again. His eyelids were low, his attention drifting.

A part of her wished she wasn't here. She had no idea what to do. Her impulse was to shout and beg, but there was so little they could offer someone in Sawyer's condition. She thought ruefully of Ulinov, poor Ulinov, who had tried for days and weeks to make her return to her work when she would only stare out through the lab module's viewport.

Sawyer surprised her again. "Came back," he said clearly enough, in a voice that was contrite, almost childishly so.

Ruth felt worn down to nerves and bone, but Sawyer, being so much weaker, had been reduced to an utterly vulnerable state—and Cam had expected it, planned for it.

"She wants to hear more about your ideas," Cam said.

"A lot more." Ruth hefted the laptop. "I'll show you mine if you show me yours."

"Hah." Sawyer's grunt was ambiguous to her, but he tried to raise his head, a tremor in his neck muscles quickly becoming a shudder. He slumped back down onto the mattress with a sigh.

Cam hauled him up into a sitting position, untangling his strengthless legs. Sawyer cried out. Ruth knelt away from them and busied herself with her laptop, sneaking glances. Finally he was settled. Too bad Cam had positioned himself on Sawyer's left side, his strong side—probably by habit, because it was easier to talk to the living half of his face.

Ruth sat close, her bulky cast like a weapon or a wall

between them, his drooping eye and cheek a barrier of a different sort. "This is the best we've put together," she said, placing the open laptop on her legs.

The first graphic was Vernon's, a simplified progression intended to wow nontechnical big shots. It had four squares across the top and four across the bottom, like the panels of a Sunday paper cartoon. It showed an oversized, two-dimensional star of an HK ANN attacking and then breaking down an oversized fishhook of an *archos* nano. The written description for each panel was ten words or less.

"Yuh yusing th'now?" Sawyer asked, blurting his sounds, and Cam said, "You're using this now?"

"No, we're still in trials. It's a mock-up. But the groundwork is solid, we've hit 58 percent effectiveness. There's no question that the discrim key is functional."

"Fif'y hey sno'good." His slur remained incoherent but the smugness in his tone was unmistakable.

"Fifty-eight is awful," she agreed, "but if we can operate faster than *archos*, it might not matter if the error rate is through the roof."

Sawyer shifted, grunting again, and Ruth mourned his speech impediment. Was that *yes* or *no* or something else altogether? How much wasn't he saying because it was too much effort? She looked across his misshapen profile at Cam, needing help.

It would be right to warn him, recruit him into the conspiracy. Cam would be instrumental in continuing to control Sawyer, and they might need another pair of hands during the takeover—but there was just too much at risk. She hardly knew him, and the chance existed that he might take her confession straight to Hernandez.

Always alert, Cam noticed her glance and seemed to interpret it as a prompt. "Maybe you can make this thing better," he told Sawyer, "make it a hundred percent."

"Yah." Sawyer bobbed his head.

"I have proofs and schematics," Ruth said.

"Lemme see." Sawyer fumbled one-handed with the computer and Ruth tried to help, equally limited, her cast blocking her way. Cam reached in and the three of them managed to set the laptop on Sawyer's thighs.

He scrolled through the data Vernon had assembled, sectional diagrams and test series analysis. He muttered. He beat his good hand on the bed. Cam stared at the screen as he translated Sawyer's growl, maybe hoping to increase his own understanding of their terms and concepts: "Just the fact that we're putting this ANN tech inside the body should improve its targeting ability. It will congregate in the same places as the *archos*, in the extremities and scar tissue."

Ruth nodded with all the caution of someone in a minefield. "Sure." She didn't want to argue. What if he shut up for a week just to punish them? But human beings were not empty containers. A living organism was many times more complex than any equivalent area outdoors, tightly packed with miles of veins and tissue. The blood system might bring most vaccine nanos into proximity with most *archos* nanos, but every stray *archos* tucked away here and there would be free to replicate . . .

Sawyer was ahead of her. "The problem is the ones we miss," he said, through Cam, "and this discrim key looks like good work. You could probably keep everyone you've got sweating over it for another year before you pushed that percentage up. So we add a new component."

"More bulk will slow us down." The criticism was out before she could catch it, even though she'd just reminded herself not to antagonize him.

But Sawyer seemed to enjoy the challenge. He made a throaty bullfrog laugh and said, "Iffah wurks awurks."

Cam shook his head. "Sorry, what?"

"If *fit*," Sawyer repeated, loud with anger, and Ruth said, "If it works, it works. Absolutely."

The *archos* nano generated marginal amounts of waste heat, a fraction of a calorie, when it first awoke inside a host body and then seventy-one times more during replication. By modifying the vaccine nano to detect this signature pulse as a backup to the discrimination key, Sawyer thought they could ensure that it located every *archos* that hadn't been destroyed while still inactive. The person whose body was this battle-field might experience some pain and a long-term accumulation of injury, but the best way to improve the vaccine nano would be to have a working prototype that could be tested and refined.

It was chancy, innovative. And it would be quick. Sawyer insisted they'd need only a bit of integral coding. There would be no new design work. He could craft a thermo-sensor from a single port of the heat engine, and his team had used EUVL fabrication gear—extreme ultraviolet laser—with machining capacities well beyond the MAFM or electron probe in Leadville.

"But a lot of Stockton burned," Ruth said. It was the perfect opening, assuming the FBI report targeting that city was accurate. "What if your lab got wiped out?"

Sawyer turned stiffly, bringing the animate side of his face around to her. His pebbled lips drew back in a thin, numb smirk. Then he shook his head and carefully formed four syllables, pleased as always to correct her.

"Sacramento," he said. "We move'tuh Sacramento ad for'y f 'reven six'y hey streed."

Forty-four Eleven 68th Street.

Ruth caught her breath, unable to hide her elation. His good eye never left her face, though, clear and aware and so very weary. She hadn't tricked him. He had chosen to give up his secret, after first impressing her again with his skill set.

It was not surrender but a change of strategy. He jabbered for another ten minutes, his cadence rushed, desperate to explain himself as his body failed him. Fatigue reduced his mumble to a slur and he soon became unable to follow his own thoughts. He repeated himself, slapping his hand on his leg, closing his eyes or staring at her with uneven, fading intensity.

Sawyer had one more surprise for them.

24

Kendra Freedman expected to live forever—two or three hundred years, at least. Destroying cancerous cells was only the beginning. The *archos* nanotech had the capacity to rid the body of all disease and pollutants. The potential existed to overcome age itself, scouring away plaques and fatty deposits, rebuilding bones depleted by osteoporosis, replenishing the tissues of the heart, liver, stomach.

Their parents' generation might be the last to die.

Given two hundred years of good health in which to continue their work—and to allow other medical technologies to advance—they could become true immortals.

Four years before the plague, Al Sawyer jumped at the chance to work with Freedman. It wasn't that he bought into her immortality rap. The field was full of enthusiastic kooks proposing everything from heads-up computers mounted inside the optic nerve to cold fusion in a Coke bottle. He joined Freedman because she was independent and because she offered him all the latitude he wanted and because she had money.

Nearly two decades of sky-high promises followed by more realistic, incremental advances in nanotech had dried up

venture capital funding as investors grew disillusioned, but
Freedman had a sugar daddy, a rich man who didn't want to
take it with him.

She offered Sawyer a six-figure salary and at least rented
time on any equipment he wanted. It was a sweet deal, maybe
too sweet for a freshly minted Ph.D., and Sawyer soon found
out why. His contract was strict on intellectual rights. He
would own anything he designed, but Freedman would always
have free license—and in the meantime he was forbidden
from publishing. Sawyer didn't care. If he'd wanted to be
famous he would have learned to play the guitar.

Freedman was a genius engineer and didn't need help
building her device. She hired Sawyer to teach her baby
to multiply. His thesis had been on replication algorithms,
like those of so many of his contemporaries. Flawless self-
assembly was the last great hurdle in nanotech, and there were
hundreds of hotshots around the world filing for patents on
every marginal improvement and new theory. Soon somebody
would take that breakthrough step and leave everyone else
buying the rights, shaking their heads for the rest of their lives
and mumbling about how close they'd been. He didn't want to
be one of the losers.

A black woman in a white man's world, Kendra Freedman
actually had a few more chips on her shoulder than Sawyer did
himself. It was a starting point, something in common, and fos-
tered an us-against-them attitude that was its own motivation.
She was already working sixty-hour weeks before he came
along, and an unspoken competition kept them both in the lab
for seventy or eighty or more as they pushed on through nights
and weekends. The man-woman thing played little part in their
relationship. They were both too tired and anyway Freedman
was five-foot-two and 170 pounds, shaped like a pear. That was
surely some part of her drive to create body-adjusting nanos.

At the time they were located on the outskirts of Stockton,
because she had family nearby and because she was saving serious cash on her lease. Freedman had seen too many com-
petitors burn through their funding and suddenly end up on
the auction block.

Everything changed when Sawyer ran his first successful computer simulation, three short years after signing on. Her backer was becoming impatient—the man was sixty-two—and while Freedman had continually improved the components of her device, not enough progress had been made on its programming, in part because they had a limited number of prototypes available for trials. She pulled everyone from their specialties to support Sawyer's work, including herself.

His script was initially error-prone but always quick. It was also the forward leap that Freedman needed to renew her backer's interest. He brought in old friends, new funding, and Freedman blew tens of millions upgrading her computers and fabrication gear. Yet even as this equipment was delivered, her backer insisted on uprooting them. His new partnership had secured superior lab space in Sacramento, not far from the university, as well as a loose affiliation with the school that would allow Freedman to take advantage of computer science grad students. Moving her into a major city would also make it easier to bring other potential investors on walk-throughs.

The new lab included a new isolation system, a hermetic chamber large enough to encompass their working lab. Sawyer's replication script had a "start" but no "stop," and in fact they hoped not to encumber his program with an end command. Ideally a well-integrated *archos* would devour all cancerous cells, and only cancerous cells, and therefore quit replicating when the diseased tissue was gone. For the moment, however, their half-finished nano appeared able to multiply endlessly, which was both marvelous and frightening.

Freedman was prudent. She'd built the hypobaric fuse into the heart of her device early on, and as a safeguard it was foolproof. Test series would be run inside atmosphere hoods inside the larger chamber, for double insurance. It was unlikely that *archos* could escape the hoods, but the pressure within the hermetic chamber was maintained below self-destruct and the only way in and out was through an air lock.

She chose two-thirds of a standard atmosphere as her trigger because it was a significant drop yet still tolerable for test animals and people. For simplicity she debated rounding down from 66.6 percent to 65, but her frugal habits led her to settle on 70 percent instead, since it would take slightly less time to cycle the air lock to that level. Every month they'd save themselves a few hours, and save on her electric bill.

There were larger dangers, so-called acts of God—earthquake, fire, flood—but they set their atmosphere hoods to purge at the first hint of any threat to containment.

It was the head of their software team who brought *archos* into the world, a man named Andrew Dutchess.

At fifty, Dutchess was the oldest member of their group, a onetime refugee from the tech stock collapse of the late 1990s. He had been chief operating officer of a major corporate branch advancing new methods of screening for prostate cancer. He had been a paper millionaire and rich in family as well, married and the father of a boy and a girl.

The recession and his company's failure could not be blamed entirely for his divorce—like all of them he worked too many hours—just as no one else could be held responsible years later for his decision to steal *archos*. But Dutchess had never experienced Sawyer's success. Dutchess had been under increased strain as Freedman pushed him to meet expectations.

Too late, ravenous and cold on the desolate rock island above Bear Summit, Sawyer decided that Dutchess probably didn't really do it for the money.

Dutchess wedged a desk chair between the outer doors of the air lock, and the inner doors could not be opened until the lock equalized. Freedman and Sawyer were still inside. There was no mistaking what Dutchess had done but neither of them understood at first, rapping on the three-inch glass and shouting.

They would never muscle their way out. The pressure differential produced a force of five tons on the doors. Given the right codes, the chamber's pumps would increase the air density inside to match the world outside, allowing them to escape—but Dutchess had disabled the override by smashing its computer chip. The phone line was missing altogether. A cut wire might have been spliced, so he'd removed it entirely.

He glanced back at them often as he fed discs into the many computers outside the chamber, not only downloading files but then wiping the hard drives. Meanwhile Freedman counted sample cases. Several were missing, along with most of their software and a few items that didn't make sense, like Sawyer's personal PDA. It looked like Dutchess had panicked—the hermetic chamber was not huge, and he would have been only a few yards from them as he filled his pockets—and apparently he'd grabbed whatever was nearest before slipping out through the air lock.

It was Friday evening. Dutchess had made his move at the best possible time. No one else was expected in the lab until Monday, and it wasn't as if either Freedman or Sawyer had dates who would realize they'd never left work. Dutchess had planned for a head start of more than fifty hours—but it was only Sunday afternoon when the power failed.

Emergency batteries and then backup generators kept the lights on and the chamber secure. Twice more the public grid came up again, and failed again, and night fell before the lab's independent system depleted its fuel reserves.

Sawyer and Freedman had been digging at the doors' rubber seals all that time, hands cramped around metal brackets torn from the mice cages—and without the constant efforts of its pumps, the chamber had gradually lost its negative pressure.

They pried the doors open just after 3:00 A.M. Monday morning and emerged into chaos.

There wasn't—couldn't be—a person alive who knew exactly what had happened. During their wait inside the lab, Freedman theorized that Dutchess must be on a plane to Europe or Asia, but *archos* was loose in the heart of the Bay Area even as she and Sawyer argued or worked at the air lock doors or took turns urinating shamefaced in the corner.

Maybe Dutchess sold the nanotech to someone who then

opened a sample wafer despite his warnings, verifying possession. More likely it was something as ordinary and stupid as a
car crash, Dutchess nervous and speeding, the wafers fractured
in the collision. Possibly he ran across a street without looking.

The first reported infections were in Emeryville and
Berkeley, and there was never any chance of containing it.

Kendra Freedman stayed to alert the authorities. Sawyer
last saw her driving west, deeper into the city, through an easy
March rain and insane traffic. He went east.

If she reached the capital buildings or even a police station,
no record survived. The machine plague hadn't yet reached
Sacramento but panic was its own disease, ravaging the city.
Her effort was wasted.

Sawyer kept enough of his wits about him to realize that
Interstates 80 and 50, the main routes up to Lake Tahoe, were
not a good bet. People still hadn't made the connection between elevation and safety, but thousands were fleeing in all
directions and the streets were a mess—and he knew that 80
could be a bottleneck even in normal conditions.

Andrew Dutchess had been a sometime skier, taking his
kids to the mountains when he had them for the weekend.
Back at work he'd complained about the drive every time.

Sawyer went south, lucking past a National Guard road-
block before it was complete, then eventually turned east
again on Highway 14 after inching past several wrecks and
jams. This small highway was uncrowded compared to the In-
terstate and he made better time.

Above 6,500 feet the rain was falling as snow.

More than once he nearly told Cam or Erin or even Manny
the truth, to better the odds that his knowledge would survive,
but the risk to himself was too great. In any case, Sawyer had
always known that the majority of the *archos* schematics and
prototypes were forever lost.

25

Cam found Ruth waiting for him outside the cabin. She'd
left twenty long minutes ago—the time it took to clean
Sawyer and get him settled down again—but apparently she
also had questions she didn't want Sawyer to hear. She sat
sideways on the lowest of the three front steps, using the highest as a desk for her laptop, and when she looked up her expression was clear in the blue shine of its screen.

Her excitement calmed him. It was answer enough to most
of the things he wanted to ask.

Sergeant Gilbride stood behind Ruth, but the other soldier must have run over to their camp with the news. The big
plane radiated light now, white and red beacons on its high
tail and wings, the illuminated square of its rear door busy
with people. Flashlights bobbed among the shapes of their
tents, too, as if stirred by the wind that had risen over this
plateau.

Cam hesitated in the doorway, letting the cold shove past
him into the cabin, afraid to step on her equipment.

Ruth said, "How is he? Sleeping again?"

"I hope so." As Cam watched, four silhouettes carried a

box up into the plane. He didn't think it was any later than eleven. "You can't take off in the dark, can you?"

"Probably." Her eyes and smile were large, high-spirited. "But I'm sure they wouldn't chance it."

"We won't go until it's light," Gilbride informed them, with the same assurance as Major Hernandez. "We're gonna need sat photos to figure out where we can land."

Ruth pushed her laptop aside, clearing the top step, then stood as Cam descended, her face eclipsed in shadow except for one cheek and the springy curls of her bangs. "Thank you," she said. "Thank you so much."

He thought he felt her body heat on a fortunate brush of wind. He thought of Erin. Her scent was marvelous, subtle, female. He looked away at the plane and said, "Is this vaccine thing really going to work?"

"Yes. And maybe in a hurry, if it's as simple as uploading our discrim key into the original template."

"What if that guy took all that stuff?"

"There's not a lab in the world that doesn't keep backups of everything, samples, software. We'll take apart the whole lab if we have to. And it's almost for sure that their gear is still there, the fabrication laser. The main components are all the size of a refrigerator, so he couldn't have taken it by himself. As long as we have the schematics and the hardware, at least, you could help us re-create it."

Cam nodded, fighting his pessimism. So little had gone right for him. The last thing he wanted was to be tied to Sawyer indefinitely, a month, a year, serving as nurse and translator. His hatred for his old friend had thickened as they healed, as he became sure they'd survive when everyone else had died, as he realized how completely Sawyer controlled him.

He believed that what they'd heard tonight was accurate— the son of a bitch was too wasted and senile to lie convincingly, not in such detail—but Cam would be a long time incorporating this truth into his thinking.

Sawyer was not at fault for the plague's release.

"What about all that other stuff," he asked, "everything about fixing the body and living forever?"

"Absolutely," Ruth said. A favorite word, he'd noticed. She prided herself on being direct and decisive. "Once we have our feet back under us . . . Everyone in nanotech knows a hundred times more than we did a year ago. I think it's possible."

She seemed to understand what he wanted to ask next. *Will you people be able to fix me someday?*

"It's very possible," she said, and reached for him in the chill darkness. Her fingers bumped his forearm, traced down and clasped his hand. But she let go before he could react.

The gesture, small as it was, stunned him utterly.

Cam had lost the hope that anyone could ever be so casually intimate with him again.

The morning sky had a color that he didn't remember, a rich, placid blue. Sacramento, nearly at sea level, lay beneath 10,000 more feet of atmosphere than the mountaintop they'd left just thirty minutes ago. Standing beside Sawyer's wheelchair, Cam glanced up into this deep tint again and again. Sunlight detailed the fine gray whorls of two fingerprints that someone had left on his Plexiglas faceplate, and he smeared the delicate grease away with his glove.

Tension beat in all of his weakest points, his hands, his ruined ear, the dying teeth at the upper left of his mouth. That he was unable to rub or scratch these wounds only increased his restless fear.

It was an alien place. The cargo plane had no windows, and to step from the rough mountain onto a freeway eight lanes wide had been startling. Bracketing this elevated stretch of midtown Business Loop 80, the buildings of Sacramento formed a dense, unrelenting jigsaw of flat surfaces and lines, block after exacting block. There was no horizon on this level earth.

His suit and radio headset deafened him to anything outside himself, and he was glad. Outside was only silence. Amidst miles of concrete and glass and steel, they were alone.

But the city lived for Cam in a way that could not be shared. He had been here before many times. Sacramento was only an hour's drive east from his childhood home, and he wondered if any of his brothers had made it this far during the exodus to the mountains—

"For Christ's sake, just cut them both. We aren't taking the 'dozer back with us anyway." Hernandez overrode the exchange of voices on Cam's headset, uncharacteristically terse. The soldiers had already backed out their jeep but the chains securing the bulldozer to the flight deck were snarled.

"Sir, we can probably just snap 'em if we rev it up."

"You might snap the brake lines or something too." The massive vehicle had heavily ribbed monster tires instead of tank treads. "Find the bolt cutters."

"Yes, sir."

Major Hernandez had not objected to Cam's sitting in on his briefing this morning, had in fact solicited Sawyer's opinion through him. And on learning that Cam knew the area, he'd questioned him as well. Hernandez definitely seemed like the right man for the job. In the predawn his troops had set out three crates of supplies he'd chosen to leave behind, and fifteen minutes after sunrise he'd downloaded his first orbital photographs via commsat link.

The greater Sacramento metropolis had been home to 1.5 million people, congested, smoggy, crime-ridden—and with an unparalleled abundance of parks and wildlife areas. The urban sprawl was interrupted nicely by two rivers, several freight canals, and a dozen lakes both natural and man-made.

Cam was certain that the river channels still teemed with life, no doubt the larger parks and playgrounds as well, and he had warned Hernandez of his encounters in the valley with the mosquitoes and the grasshopper swarm. Ant colonies numbering in the millions might have filled every apartment complex and grocery store, prospering first on bodies and decaying food, then on carpet glue and upholstery. The expedition members probably wouldn't attract insects, being scentless in their containment suits, but if they walked into a horde they could have trouble. He needed Hernandez to be alert for strange threats.

The city might kill them in a hundred ways, collapsing structures, slow leaks of flammable gas. This place was silent but not at rest—and everywhere around them, swirling with every step and movement, was the invisible sea.

He felt too close to success, after so much pain and loss, not to dread that this might also be taken from him.

Last night everything in Cam had changed. Until last night his greatest goal had been somewhat external—to help others in a late, hopeless effort to balance all the wrong that he had done. Now it was more personal. Now the chance existed, however slight, that *archos* could to developed into a new-generation nano capable of making him whole again, and the possibility alone had influenced his mood.

The larger goal was still real. He would always owe a debt for surviving, but it was the personal hope that was the loudest in him now.

He did not want to end up like Sawyer, ruined and helpless. The damage to his own body would become crippling as he aged—he might only have another five or ten years—and this morning his impatience and his caution felt like a collision in his mind.

Dehydration would be another hazard today. Cam was already moist with sweat, skin sticking on rubber, even though he was wearing little inside his suit, and as the morning warmed his outfit would become a body-shaped oven. They didn't have enough air to periodically cool themselves by purging the suits.

Each person wore a rigid pack of twin oxygen tanks, narrow cylinders weighing more than ten pounds apiece. Sawyer's hung from the handles sticking out from the rear of his chair.

One tank, one hour, unless they used it up more quickly in exertion or in fear. Leadville had game-planned for an average of fifty minutes per cylinder. There were six extra tanks for each person, but eight hours total struck Cam as a dangerously thin margin of error.

It was difficult to put his faith, his fate, completely in the hands of these strangers.

As the capital of a world-class economy, Sacramento had no less than three airports and a major U.S. Air Force base. All were near the city's outskirts, though, which was unfortunate since their target lay within the core of downtown on 68th Street. The expedition planes would need to refuel before heading back to Colorado, but the nearest airport was five miles from the lab and the streets were hopelessly clogged.

This open stretch was an unusual find. As quarantine efforts failed, most of Sacramento fled for elevation. So had the 5 million people living farther west in the heavily urbanized Bay Area, yet in this case a blockage worked to their advantage. A northbound tractor trailer had tangled with two cars and rolled, and a third car plugged the only opening between the big rig and the median divider when its driver did a poor job of shooting the gap. Nearly all of the vehicles that were already past had continued up the highway to a cluster of traffic, leaving a half mile of generally free room.

The Cessna had landed first again, its crew removing five cars, then cutting two overhead signs with a welding torch.

They were still thirty-eight blocks from their destination, but instead of asking Hernandez to bulldoze straight across, military analysts had mapped out a jigsaw path through residential back streets and, at one point, across two neighboring yards. The detail work was impressive but Cam thought their estimate of seventy minutes to target was bullshit.

They hadn't even started moving yet.

"Got it!" The Marine's shout was a relief and Cam turned from staring into the thick blue sky.

"Okay, clear the axle—"

"—reach across?"

Their headsets broadcast and received continuously, which made for some confusion on the general frequency yet left their hands free from toggling SEND buttons.

"All right, saddle up." Hernandez again. "*Hermano*, that's you, let's move it out."

"You bet." Cam had rolled Sawyer's chair ten yards from the cargo plane, out of the way, positioning him to face back toward the aircraft instead of the dead city.

Four men in beige containment suits hustled down the loading ramp, making way for the 'dozer. Hernandez might have been any of them. Another soldier stood by the jeep, untangling a yellow tie-down. They had arranged their crates, fuel cans, and spare tires in rows across the long trailer's front and rear, which looked like a defensive arrangement but was more likely constructed for balance and safety. Many of them would travel sitting on the trailer, and six troops had jogged up the freeway with gas cans and a starter kit to find a truck or a station wagon that could carry everyone else.

Ruth and her two colleagues had crowded into the jeep as soon as it was clear, a choice that reminded Cam uncomfortably of the way Jim Price insisted on staying with the pickup. Two of them sat in back, helmets bent over her laptop, and the third had twisted around in the passenger seat to participate. They were silent, relegated to their own frequency. Hernandez had put the scientists on channel four not long after takeoff, when it became apparent that they were going to talk talk talk.

The odd shape on the left was Ruth. Her cast prevented her from using her sleeve or from wearing her air tanks correctly, because that arm was tucked inside the chest of her suit, so the soldiers had rigged an extra waist strap, neatly folding up and taping her sleeve. Still, Hernandez had cautioned her to be careful, and Ruth said he could guarantee she wouldn't move at all if he piled another five hundred pounds on her back.

Cam admired her style and her rare ability to shine. He would have liked to talk more, to be close to her again, but he had been stuck in the role of babysitter and she was totally absorbed with D.J. and Todd.

The bulldozer rolled out at a crawl, then accelerated around the far side of the plane, its fat, ribbed tires sending a tremor through the asphalt. Beyond the plane's nose, it angled across the freeway more nimbly than Cam would have believed.

He leaned into Sawyer's range of vision. "You ready?" The faceplates in their soft rubber helmets were broad but still hindered the peripheral vision—

Sawyer had his eyes screwed shut, lips open, jaw working, a hideous fish in a tight-fitting bowl.

Cam patted his shoulder, his textured glove rasping on the smoother material. "Hey." Could he be trying to clear his ears because his suit was overpressurized? "Hey, Sawyer. Jesus."

During the plane's descent over the city, their beige suits

began to collapse and cling at their bodies. The C-130 could have maintained the same pressure as the mountaintop, the same safe pressure, but Hernandez hadn't wanted to subject their outfits to the real test after they were on the ground. Instead, two Special Forces soldiers had hurried among them, adjusting the pop valves on their backs to equalize with sea level. Was it possible that Sawyer had only pretended to follow directions to yawn and swallow to keep his eardrums from hurting?

It had been one of Sawyer's worst days from the start.

His belly had yet to recover from the beef ribs and he'd shaken his head at breakfast, squalling when Cam put a spoonful of freeze-dried eggs to his lips—and there was no way to eat or drink inside a containment suit. Cam only hoped he'd mellow as he weakened instead of becoming more irritated.

The son of a bitch had struggled as best he could when they fit him into his gear, because he hated having so little control over his own body or possibly because he recognized that he'd be forced to wear the same diaper as long as he was inside it. The suits came with bladder pockets and a relief tube that could be slipped onto a penis much like a condom, yet Cam had been guaranteed that this device would slip off, with no adjustment possible, leaving him filling his boot. All of them had chosen adult diapers instead. There was no alternative.

Cam's diet had been so limited for so long he was normally constipated, but the antibiotics had upset his gut. Not long after getting up he'd endured two loose, wretched movements, then prayed that his body was done. Any embarrassment would be a small thing compared to the day's potential, but he didn't want anyone to regard him with the same disgust that darkened their eyes when they looked at Sawyer.

He didn't want Ruth to look at him that way.

Sawyer had kicked again when their suits began to collapse during the descent, and after he'd dislodged his headset he'd thrashed all the harder, confused and half-blinded by the light aluminum frame. Hernandez ordered the plane back up to safe altitude, where they'd unsealed Sawyer's helmet and pulled his radio altogether. Cam had suggested that Sawyer would only get tangled in it again—and the headsets weren't necessary. The suits muffled voices but the last thing they needed was Sawyer battling loose gear instead of focusing on his job.

"Hey!" Cam prodded his shoulder again, rough with concern. "Do your ears hurt? Look at me."

Sawyer turned his head slightly, not upward at Cam but down toward where he'd been touched. His eyes did not open and his lips continued to work in that weird chewing motion.

"I think I need help." Cam waved at the soldiers so they'd know who was speaking. "Hey, help."

Hernandez lifted one arm in acknowledgment. He had been exchanging gestures with another suit, talking on the command channel, but switched to the general frequency in midsyllable. "—ield." He strode toward Cam, his glove still at the radio control on his belt. "What's the problem?"

"Sawyer's suit might be giving him trouble, the pressure."

Hernandez glanced into Cam's eyes before ducking to check on Sawyer. The major's lean face was hard, measuring, yet eased slightly even as he moved past.

Words could not have conveyed his assessment of Cam any better. Hernandez had worried that Cam was panicky, imagining failures in their equipment now that they were deep into the plague—and his decision, his confidence, made Cam proud. It made him feel stronger and more complete.

Hernandez gingerly squeezed Sawyer's arm, testing the suit's rigidity, then stepped behind him to examine the gauge on his air hose. "Captain," Hernandez said. "Over here."

A shriek of metal cut through them, abrading steel. Cam jumped, his helmet loud with voices, then shuffled to keep his balance for several heartbeats before he realized that it was the ground vibrating instead of his legs. The bulldozer. "Jesus—" But the radio had quieted immediately and he shut his mouth, mimicking their discipline. He tried to look over his shoulder, limited by the suit, and shuffled his feet again as he bent his entire upper body.

The exit ramp they planned to use was thick with vehicles.

Nosing into the jam, the 'dozer rammed its iron blade underneath a burgundy sedan and lifted it onto its side. The sedan bashed into another car, its roof crumpling like a wad of paper. Then the bulldozer shoved into the sedan's belly and powered both vehicles aside. Strewn behind were gleaming patterns of glass, plastic, and chrome.

Hernandez had jumped too, throwing his arms out from his sides. Beneath his mustache was a rare smile, which he must have thought no one else could see. It was gone when he looked around. "I think we're okay here," he said, stepping back from the wheelchair to make room for the Special Forces captain.

Sawyer was blinking inside his Plexiglas, aroused by the tremendous noise; the screech of steel on asphalt; the groaning bass roar of the bulldozer's engine.

Cam knelt clumsily, rocking his head from side to side until he drew Sawyer's attention. "How do you feel? Your ears hurt?"

"The suit's fine," the captain said, softly enough that Sawyer wouldn't hear since he lacked a radio.

"Mm tired." Sawyer stared at Cam with puzzled misery, perhaps blaming him.

"Try to rest." He stood before his anger could show.

The ski patrol had not been much of an elite, with never more at stake than a broken leg or some kid separated from his parents. These men were of an entirely different class. Highly trained, highly motivated, with everything in the world on the line—it was a privilege to be associated with them and a disgrace to have wasted their time.

Hernandez started toward the plane and Cam took one step after him, leaving Sawyer. Hernandez turned back.

Cam said, "I'm sorry, sir."

Hernandez studied his face again, quickly, then gave a nod. "Shout out anytime, *hermano*. We need to keep him happy."

"*Lo que usted diga*," Cam said. *Whatever you say.*

He wanted so much to be one of them.

26

Ruth realized she had been right not to trust Cam with the secret of the conspiracy. He was too close to Hernandez. Too bad. She liked him. He tried so hard. But the strength of his commitment was its own liability.

Crammed into the back of the jeep with D.J., writing new code and arguing over every line of it, Ruth managed to ignore her anxiety until the bulldozer began crashing around. Lord knew she had always been able to hide in her work—and using the keyboard and ball mouse with one glove-thickened hand was a real chore, enough to keep her occupied.

"I can't see when you do that," D.J. said, reaching across her to steady the laptop. Ruth bumped his arm, grabbing at her belt and changing frequencies.

She needed to hear what Hernandez was saying.

It was unfair to doubt Cam for a choice he hadn't made, of course. He didn't know that two sides existed, and it was only natural for him to respond to the resources and the sense of control Hernandez had brought into his life.

He was a good man but profoundly wounded—and so he might disbelieve everything she'd say about the atrocities of the Leadville government. The quickest way for him to be done with this mess was to fly back to Colorado. He would be a champion. He could in some way consider himself whole again. Ruth wasn't sure he would be *able* to choose a path that led anywhere else, a path that meant more running, more effort, as they diverted north into Canada and reorganized a working lab and tried to gather enough allies to hold off the inevitable assaults as Leadville pursued them. It was too much to expect.

Nevertheless, tension and guilt had kept her awake most of the night. Her brain ached from the blunt rubber stink of the suit and her body felt heavy with exhaustion even as it twitched with nervous energy, ill and uneasy.

D.J. pulled on the laptop and complained again, a muted buzz outside her suit. She'd caught Hernandez midsentence: "—ooner we get you on the trailer." He made a sweeping motion in her direction and Cam rolled Sawyer after him toward the jeep.

The bulldozer punched into another vehicle. *Ka-rang!* One of the car's tires popped as the 'dozer shoved it sideways, the metal rim digging into the asphalt with a hair-raising wail. It didn't stop until the car tottered over the embankment at the top of the exit ramp, tumbling down with three distinct impacts.

"Lowrey, Watts." Hernandez raised his voice only slightly. "We're lifting this chair up onto the trailer."

"Yes, sir, I was gonna put him up front against that crate."

"Fine. Let's move it. The ramp will be clear in a minute."

Cam noticed Ruth's attention and lifted one glove. She thought he might have smiled but the low sun was on his faceplate, obscuring the middle of his expression. She turned away.

In her uncertainty, some part of her actually wanted to find the labs stripped clean. Once they had Sawyer's schematics, the Special Forces would instigate their takeover—and Hernandez would fight. Ruth was sure of that much.

No matter the odds, Hernandez would fight them.

* * *

Overall the city appeared only lightly damaged. Commercial buildings loomed above them, impassive weight, a thousand white glints of sunshine on unbroken glass. If they failed, if Sawyer's files and prototypes were truly lost and the machine plague held sway over the planet forever, this place was a monument that would exist in some form until ultimately the continental shelf rolled into the Pacific Ocean. Concrete and iron would withstand quakes, fires, and weather for eons.

Ruth gazed all around, gripped by dark wonder.

The frozen traffic here surged only one way—west, toward the freeway, every car nosing into the next. They came up onto sidewalks. They diverted through parking lots and hedges and fences. They were full of stick shapes, and the crowded street itself had become the grave of hundreds, color-fast rags on yellowing bone, screaming jaws and eroded fingers, the skeletons of dogs and birds scattered among the human remains like strange half-grown monsters.

The carnage looked even worse in contrast to the commonplace icons of America, most of which survived untouched. Rising on poles, bolted to storefronts, were the garish plastic signs of Chevron and Wendy's and 24 Hour Donuts.

Their progress eastward was a crawl at first, the jeep hanging back with the big white pickup truck the soldiers had gotten started. The man in the bulldozer had a lonely job. He thrust into the packed cars, always a half block or more ahead of the group, and he was even more isolated by the metal slats that Leadville mechanics had welded to the operator's cage to protect him from the shrapnel that sometimes crashed up.

With each roar of the bulldozer's engine, each shriek of metal, echoes rattled against the high faces of the buildings and fled into the silence, sometimes returning to them from odd directions. Sometimes the sounds that came back did not match those that had gone away, lower in pitch or delayed too long.

Ruth wasn't the only one who kept looking over her shoulder.

Dangerous hooks and teeth lined their path, torn hoods, bent fenders, windshields mashed into opaque spiderwebs.

Debris gritted beneath the jeep's tires as it advanced, scattered dunes of safety glass and chunks of bone. They rolled over puddles of antifreeze and gasoline—and Ruth instinctively drew a long breath through her nose, though of course she could only smell the thickening odor of her own sweat.

It would be appalling for them to have made it this far only to lose their lives to one spark, fifty cars igniting around them like explosive dominos. The image shocked her, veins of fire throughout the city . . . but good engineering prevented most of the vehicles from leaking fuel as they were smashed or overturned, and the man in the bulldozer exercised some care when pushing his blade into a vehicle's underside.

Ruth saw patterns in the devastation. The people who'd left their cars to continue on foot had collected in drifts on the far sides of the standstill traffic. Obviously they'd kept fighting toward the freeway, every skull and arm leaning forward as if to meet her, but why had so many died in groups?

She understood suddenly and was nauseous. Those stained bones, settled now, would have been a real barrier with flesh and muscle on them, stacked waist high in places, slick with fluids, perhaps still moving. Hemorrhaging or blind, thousands of men and women had staggered through the maze of cars until they reached obstacles they couldn't pass . . . and it had been bodies that filled the spaces between the never-ending vehicles . . .

Ruth was glad for her containment suit. At first, in the plane, wearing it had been like wrapping herself inside a small prison, prickles of goose bumps lifting against the rubber skin, but now it helped her feel removed from her surroundings.

Now she knew better than ever that her solitary, stubborn focus on her work had been correct. There was no doubt that she had been right to come here. The hard question was if she would be good enough, smart enough, quick enough.

A distant shriek turned her head again, a living sound, high and ragged. A cat? *No.* Her gaze darted over the colorful jam of cars, the tall face of an office complex. Was it some trick of the breeze? Then she noticed Cam patting at Sawyer's shoulder and realized the sound was his, muffled by his suit.

But was the son of a bitch mourning or—it was cruel to think it—was he only frustrated with his suit, his own stink, the isolation of being without a radio?

Hernandez and his Marines made a great business of reporting each landmark and reading quadrants off their maps, as if they might get lost despite moving at a near crawl. The pilots, who'd stayed with the planes, were relaying both the general frequency and the command channel back to Colorado. Ruth supposed the theory was that another team could benefit from their observations if they didn't make it out.

The constant chatter was also a way to overcome the desolation, concentrating on each other instead.

But it too was a danger. She didn't think Senator Kendricks would listen himself, not hour after hour; he was too busy, too important, but if she were in his shoes she would insist on regular updates—and her name would be mentioned. It was not an *if* but *when*.

Kendricks would know that something was wrong.

After four blocks—after more than forty minutes—they escaped the main thoroughfare and turned north on 35th Street, into residential streets leading nowhere except into a warren of low-rise apartments and duplexes. These narrower roads were spotted with stalls, but the residents here had mostly escaped their immediate neighborhood and left these streets passable. The 'dozer ranged ahead as they pointed eastward again.

"Keep it under thirty," Hernandez told Gilbride, who sat at the jeep's wheel. Hernandez himself had picked out a spot on the trailer with his map unfolded, sitting alongside Cam and Sawyer and Marine Corporal Ruggiero, Corporal Watts, and Sergeant Lowrey.

The Special Forces unit followed in the pickup truck, minus Staff Sergeant Dansfield, who was running the bulldozer, and Ruth worried that by segregating themselves they'd alert Hernandez, if only subconsciously. Were they making plans, their radios off? What if he realized they'd shut down their headsets?

She knew they'd made one obvious blunder. When they left the plane, most of the soldiers brought only their sidearms. In this place, guns were just something else to carry. But two of the Special Forces had grabbed their assault rifles, and Hernandez must have noticed—

Ruth squirmed, shifting her cast inside the tight pocket of her chest and making a fist. The strain hurt her still-healing break and helped her center herself. *Stop it. Calm down.*

Hernandez didn't know. He couldn't. If Leadville sent warning he'd confront her immediately, along with D.J. and Todd, or arrest the Special Forces depending on the extent of his information. Only the conspirators had reason to hold back, but if they waited too long and a warning came— If they decided to back out because Sawyer's lab was stripped clean—

Stop. Just stop. Ruth clenched her fist once more and held it, hurting, furious with herself.

They went nineteen blocks to 55th Street quickly, but then the frozen traffic crowded in again. Weaving south, they managed another block before the road was impassable. As planned, the bulldozer swung into a driveway and crashed through a six-foot fence, then another. They cut across two lots back toward 54th. One yard was a small Eden, ivy, brick, sun chairs. The next was carpeted with dead lawn as dry as cereal. Dusty particles wafted up behind the 'dozer, and Todd, in his fidgety way, brushed his suit clean and then tried to smooth the folds in his sleeves.

"We're eight minutes over our mark," Hernandez said. "Not bad, gentlemen." They had expected to reach this point after three-quarters of an hour. Ruth felt like she'd aged a month.

"How are we doing on air?" Todd asked.

"Lots of time," Hernandez told him.

"Look at my gauge, okay?" From his gesture, Todd intended these words for Ruth and D.J., directly behind him, but Hernandez said, "I'm not going to endanger you unnecessarily, believe me. Let's hang on until we reach the labs."

Ruth leaned forward and put her glove on Todd's shoulder. Twenty-plus minutes in flight, ten more unloading the vehicles, another sixty to come this far— He was still outside the red, which surprised her. "You have twelve minutes," she said.

They drove south on 54th and then swung eastward again on Folsom, another main thoroughfare that was comparatively open for several blocks.

The jeep blew a tire just past 64th Street. They had been about to stop anyway, to allow the 'dozer to clear the thickening stalls, and now Hernandez said, "Buddy check, buddy check. We change out the man with the lowest gauge first."

Two of the Special Forces guys wrestled with a spare tire and car jack, moving deliberately to keep from snagging their suits. Captain Young and two others began switching air tanks, Sawyer first, then Sergeant Lowrey, then Todd. A person alone could not have done it. The hose attachment was shut, leaving the wearer with no more than the air in his suit. Simple brackets held the canisters into their packs, easily freed and easily screwed down again—but the threat of contamination had a complex solution. A semi-rigid plastic hood attached to a compressor pump was fitted over the hose and tank spigots, then taped to secure the seal. The pocket of low pressure destroyed any *archos* that had gathered there, before Captain Young reopened first the hose connection and then the tanks.

A suit alone contained maybe fifteen minutes of breathable air, but Ruth clenched her fist each time they began the process, no matter that they never took longer than two minutes. She was fourth. She kept from babbling her phobia only with concentrated effort, staring down at an orange shard of taillight plastic rather than the men around her.

The tire change was done before Young finished with her. Meanwhile, the 'dozer had cleared Folsom Boulevard down to Sixty-eighth Street. Hernandez got them organized again and they rolled on through the dead traffic, three more blocks.

Highway 50 stood to the south like an immense wall, forming a straight horizon beyond every gap in the buildings. So damned close. But there hadn't been any room to land there.

Two hundred yards down 68th Street, the 'dozer bashed its

way into a narrow parking lot that was empty except for a red VW Beetle. Dansfield shoved the car into a hump of brush and left his machine in that corner, out of the way. Beyond the small lot lay an L-shaped, two-story structure, both levels banded in dark gray brick and silvered glass.

Inside the nearest wing was the *archos* lab.

Hernandez made her wait. He wanted his men to enter the building first, but renewing everyone's air supply took priority.

Ruth stepped out of the jeep, stamping her boots and hugging her laptop. She stared at the mirrored face of the building yet did not recognize her reflection or the emotions inside herself. No. This moment felt as if the last flight of the *Endeavour* had been condensed into one tremendous pulse, faith and doubt, excitement and terror.

Young changed out Dansfield and Olson immediately, because they were in the red, then took care of D.J. and Cam next after the rest of the soldiers volunteered to wait. Still thinking of *Endeavour*, Ruth also re-experienced the stunning respect she had known for the rescue teams.

These men were astounding, all of them, to have fought across this wasteland with such competence.

It was wrong that they needed to be enemies.

She looked for Sawyer. Watts and Ruggiero had lifted his wheelchair down from the trailer and Sawyer made a flopping gesture with one arm. Ruth started toward them, stopped. She was afraid of her own agitation. Sawyer angered too easily, and he had been like an idiot child all morning. She couldn't afford to rile him.

The soldiers with fresh tanks approached the building and found the door secured. Its electronic locks had seized when the power went off. The delivery entrance around the side was open—Freedman and Sawyer had left that way—but to get the jeep and trailer there would involve clearing another street. Hernandez elected to go through the wall instead. Along the inner faces of the building's L-shape, overlooking what had been low-maintenance landscaping of shrubs and river rock, the walls alternated waist-to-ceiling windows of reinforced glass with floor-to-ceiling panes.

Lowrey put four pistol shots through the nearest full-length section at downward angle, aiming his bullets into the floor rather than the lab space beyond. Then they bashed out the weakened glass with tire irons and carefully rubbed the frame clean of shards.

"Let's bring them in," Hernandez radioed, after scouting the interior for no more than a minute.

D.J. bumped her armless side, hurrying to be first. Ruth almost clubbed him with the laptop. Instead, she studied her footing as she crossed ten yards of loose rock, Todd matching her step for step with his glove extended, ready to help.

Moving inside should have been a triumph. It felt like a trap. Her eyes, accustomed to daylight, seemed dim and weak.

Ruth assumed the offices and admin were on the second floor. Labs tended to be at ground level because it was silly to haul equipment up and down. That would make their job easier. So would the six-foot hole in the wall. They'd come straight into a large rectangular space, with a glassed-in section filling almost half of the right side. The hermetic chamber. It was a lab within a lab, since the main area was definitely a clean room itself, hard white tile floor, white paneling, the ceiling lined with recessed fluorescent lighting. Ordinary PCs sat along the left wall with an assortment of multimode scopes.

A monitor had been knocked off the end of a counter, a chair overturned. For an instant she thought Hernandez and his men had already begun ransacking the place, but those small signs of disorder had existed for fifteen months now.

Please, God, let us find everything we need.

The glass box was maybe nine hundred square feet, with the long phone booth of the air lock protruding from its left face and bulky steel manifolds scrunched between its right side and the wall of the main room. The box itself was fairly crowded with another set of computers and microscopy gear including the fabrication laser—three squat monoliths in a row.

Ruth strode toward the glass barrier, her radio busy with the soldiers cautioning each other as they carried Sawyer's wheelchair in behind her.

"Don't drop him!"

"He keeps rocking around—"

"Science team, listen up." Hernandez. "We need you to identify everything in this place with a rough score from most important down to least important. We definitely don't have room to take it all back. Come over here. Sergeant Gilbride has grease pencils you can mark—"

Ruth interrupted. "Look for generators first," she said. "Major? Have someone look around for generators. There's an independent power system on-site. We can run a few trials."

"There's no time for that."

She turned from the glass box and quickly spotted him among the beige suits. Hernandez held both arms overhead and waggled his hands, a *this way* gesture.

"You don't know what you're—" Ruth stopped herself, and ended in a hush. "We have to try." Drawing attention to herself on the general frequency was a terrible risk. Senator Kendricks would be listening now, if at all, to learn whether or not their mission had been worth the jet fuel.

"Dr. Goldman," Hernandez said, and she cringed at her own name. "We have a limited amount of air and a great deal of heavy loading to accomplish. The drive back will go a lot faster than the ride here, but let's not count on it."

She blundered on. "What's the point of driving back if we're not positive we have what we came for?"

"I think she's right." That was D.J. "We have six hours. I say let's allocate half of it to test series before you start throwing things on the trailer."

Lord God, had she sounded even half as arrogant herself? There was so much to think about— Ruth hurried for a more diplomatic tone. "We're not asking you to waste time standing around, there's plenty of gear to load up in the meantime."

"What makes you think there are generators here?"

"Freedman knew what she was working with. Look at this isolation chamber. You don't build something like this without putting in backup power. The public grid is too unreliable. You lose electricity, you lose containment."

"All right." Hernandez adjusted as easily as that, even though his plan must have been like clockwork in his mind, ticking smoothly ever since they'd left Colorado. "We'll give you two hours. No more. No argument. And one of you starts ID'ing equipment right now so we can get the ball rolling."

He was a good man, better than Leadville deserved. What had James said? *I think he'd give his life to protect us.*

Very soon she would betray him because of his integrity.

"Captain," Hernandez continued, "locate the generators and have your guys look them over. *Hermano*, how's Mr. Sawyer?"

The beige suits rearranged themselves and several moved toward the only door out of the lab, Captain Young instructing his team to switch to channel six.

Cam rolled Sawyer forward as he answered Hernandez. "He wants to talk to Ruth, sir," Cam said.

She was obvious in the group, one-armed, her torso misshapen by the cast. Cam aimed Sawyer right at her. Ruth hunched down and took another deep breath, frantic to compose herself.

Sawyer's faceplate was marked with odd, ghostly streaks. Finger smudges. He'd dirtied his gloves on the tires of his wheelchair and then tried repeatedly to scratch at his lumpy scars, or to hide from their surroundings, or possibly even to take off his helmet as he forgot himself.

Ruth saw awareness in him now. That one bright eye glared out from his slack, lopsided expression.

"Wuh'ere," he said, faint without a radio. "Yuhgamme'ere."

"You got me here," Cam translated.

That he needed to have it confirmed spoke volumes about his mental state. "Of course." She made a smile. "We're going to turn on the power, take your hardware for a little test-drive."

"Yuh." He jerked his head in approval.

"I've been in nanotech more than ten years and never seen anything like this." Small talk in the graveyard.

But Sawyer's head convulsed in a side-to-side motion

rather than up and down. He didn't want coaxing or compliments. He had finally set aside his ego.

"Ubstuhs," he said, blinking. He'd lost sight of her when he shook his head, and his eye tracked feverishly before he found her again. Was it desperation in his gaze? He grumbled and Cam said, "Look upstairs. Freedman kept dupes everywhere, at home, in her office. I think Dutchess only cleaned out the lab."

Ruth resisted the urge to turn and go herself, still wary of upsetting him. "D.J.?"

"I heard it. Ask where exactly—"

Sawyer remained cooperative. "Freedman's office is the second door from the top of the stairs," Cam said for him. "On the left. Try her desk or her file cabinet."

D.J. and two Marines hustled away as Special Forces Master Sergeant Olson came back on radio. "Olson here. Looks like the generators ran dry, sir. Probably start up if we refuel."

"Give it a shot," Hernandez told him.

Cam spoke again in tandem with Sawyer: "If there's nothing upstairs, try those computers beside the scanning probe. Dutchess wiped just about everything but a good hacker should be able to reconstruct deleted files from the hard drive. You'll have at least preliminary designs on the *archos* components."

There was motion behind Ruth, as Todd or maybe Hernandez stepped toward those PCs. She kept her attention focused on Sawyer, wondering at the change in him.

He continued to speak and Cam echoed him: "If you have full data, use model R-1077 as your base. R-1077. There's no fuse and its mass is under one billion AMU. Less than a quarter of that is programmable space but it should hold the rep algorithm and your discrim key."

You. Your. He was putting everything in their hands. He must have felt that he was losing the war against himself. His unusual strength of will, his rage, his private terror—these were all useless against the wet touch of spittle at the corner of his mouth, the clumsy meat that had been his arms and legs.

He might hang on another five years but in the truest sense he was dying, and he knew it, and in this lucid moment he wanted most of all to escape his own bitterness.

Ruth managed another smile, more genuine this time, and Sawyer's intense gaze flickered from her eyes to the sad quirk of her mouth. He nodded—and then the lab came to life around them in a cacophony of beeps and buzzing. Many pieces of equipment had still been on when the electricity went out, and the overhead fluorescents winked and then smothered them in furious white.

The distractions broke the wordless communion between Ruth and Sawyer. He glanced away and Ruth saw his expression loosen, tense as he fought to hold on to his thoughts, then ease again as he was overwhelmed by new stimuli.

Already his concentration was fading.

D.J. returned downstairs with a small zippered packet of CD-RW discs and a smaller, flat metal case like a gentleman's cigarette holder. He made quite a show of his finds, proudly holding them out. The Special Forces unit had also returned to the main lab and D.J. created an eddy through the gathered suits as their curiosity led most of them after him for a few steps.

Ruth forgave his self-important grin.

Lined with form-fitted sponge, the case held sixteen vacuum wafers no bigger or thicker than a fingernail. A container intended to be manipulated by human hands was of astronomical proportions for a batch of nanos, even compartmentalized, but the microscopic structures within would be fastened to a carbon surface for easier location under the microscope.

This was not *archos*. Freedman would never have brought complete, programmed nanos outside the hermetic chamber. But the sectional components would help them to intuit the full potential of this technology later on—and the base prototypes might serve as their vaccine nano with only minor adaptations.

The discs offered more magic. Sawyer perked up again

when D.J. showed him the CD packet, which was lurid pink and sported the too-cute, doe-eyed face of a PowerPuff Girl. Somehow, fleetingly, that made Freedman real to Ruth as an individual for the first time, a woman who'd spent a few extra bucks on a vibrant case instead of buying a plain one.

"Series twelve," Cam said, still diligently translating. "The series twelve discs are the replication program."

Someone caught Ruth's arm and she looked up. Beyond the few suits clustered around Sawyer, the rest of the group were now getting ready to haul equipment outside, pushing chairs back into the far corner, unplugging computers and disconnecting keyboards.

The man who'd grabbed her elbow was Captain Young.

"You have it?" he asked, his voice muffled. The Special Forces team leader had shut off his radio. He thrust his face close and Ruth leaned away, startled, but Young pulled on her again and pressed his helmet to hers. Conduction improved the transfer of sound waves.

He spoke more precisely. "Do you have what we came for?"

She hesitated. She nodded.

Young bobbed his head in response and then turned, releasing her arm, reaching for the radio control on his belt. His voice filled the general frequency. "Green green green," he said, and unslung his rifle from his shoulder.

27

Cam glanced away from D.J. and Sawyer at the strange announcement, "Green green," and saw at least half of the men raise their left arms in what appeared to be a choreographed movement, their gloves balled into fists. It was a gesture of identification. Then they stepped toward the other soldiers with their sidearms drawn.

"What—!" he shouted, but the radio filled with chatter.

"Freeze fucking freeze right there *crazy what are you* freeze *hey Trotter* hold it don't move!"

The coordinated action took just seconds. There must have been a prior signal he'd missed. Each of the attackers stood close to one of the others, and none of the attackers had anything in hand, whereas most of the rest were encumbered with a computer monitor, an armload of cords, a stack of electronics.

Each attacker put his Glock 9mm in his opponent's face and grabbed at the man's waist, seizing not the man's holstered pistol but his radio control. Their wiring ran safely inside their suits except for a short length that extended from every left hip to every control box, which allowed their headsets to be unplugged and jacked directly into another communication system like that of a plane. Now the attackers silenced the other men.

Something shut off in Cam as well. Confusion, dismay, anger—the shock wave through his head left him empty and clear, tuned entirely outward. He absorbed details into his body like oxygen. It was the fluid, immediate thinking of an animal, disassociated from logic or emotion.

It decided him. He ducked sideways like a blitzing cornerback angling for position.

During the past hours Cam had become able to distinguish among his companions in spite of the suits—some of them, at least; Dansfield because of his height; Olson with grime on his sleeve; Hernandez because of his clipped stride and his tendency to be the group's focal point. Instinct said that it was the Special Forces who were taking over and Hernandez who was in trouble. Given time, Cam might have reached the same conclusion with a quick count. The crush of beige suits was five on five and two more attackers hung back with assault rifles, wicked black metal in their suit-thick arms. But he had forgotten numbers. And he knew that they had forgotten him.

The nearest rifleman stood three paces from Ruth, his M16 pointed at the ceiling. Captain Young. His helmet shifted as he reiterated his code, "Green two green tw—"

Cam hit him in the ribs, shoulder to body, and like a cornerback striking a ball carrier he chopped down at the captain's arms.

"No!" The only female voice.

Then another rise of male shouts: "What did *shit* look out!"

The M16 rattled, four shots into floor. Spent casings leapt against Cam's chest as he and Young tumbled together, their momentum increased by the weight of their air tanks.

Another, heavier gunshot reverberated through the enclosed space of the lab. Then they hit the tile, Young underneath him. But the air pack kept Young from falling flat. Its bulk punched his body up as Cam slammed down on top of him, and Young didn't fight when Cam tore away the M16.

Slipping, crawling, Cam stabilized himself on his left hand and his knees and brought the weapon level. He couldn't have

fired. His fingers were splayed over the flat base of the trigger
guard between the rifle's grip and the magazine.

Details— His finger pad on smooth metal, moving for the
trigger— The suits across from him now four on five instead
of neatly paired— Hernandez and the Marines had used his
surprise move to counterattack. One man lay crumpled on the
floor. Another guy had been knocked onto his butt. *But where
was the second rifleman—?*

Then a boot punted into the right side of Cam's faceplate.
Impact drove his jaws together and twisted his neck and he
dropped the M16, thrown all the way around onto his back.
The air tanks bit into his shoulder blades but his pain centered
around the unnatural bulge beneath his lip. His dying teeth
had wrenched forward from his gums, two lumps, enormous
and wrong. They seesawed loosely on their broken roots as he
coughed blood against his faceplate.

The rifleman stood over him, M16 pointed into Cam's body.

"No *no* he doesn't know!" Ruth had been just a step or two
from the Special Forces soldier but she ran anyway and continued that frantic motion once she'd reached his side, waving
her only arm like a wing, elbow out, still clutching her laptop.

She was impossibly brave, confronting the soldier. But her
words were strange. "He didn't know, he didn't— We need
him!"

The rifleman held his pose. Cam also remained motion-
less, sprawled cockeyed on his tanks, although his hands
curled with the need to come to his face and a different fear
crashed through his chest and arms. *My suit Christ what if my
suit is ripped?*

The rest of the room seemed quiet too. Cam swallowed
blood. Beyond his feet were Todd and Sawyer, Todd hunched
toward the wheelchair in a manner that looked protective and
D.J. retreated several paces past the near corner of the hermetic chamber, sidling away from everyone.

Her words didn't make sense.

"Stop, he didn't know," Ruth babbled, and there was a shuf-
fling motion on Cam's other side as Captain Young groped up
from the floor, panting audibly in short, choked breaths.

"She's right," Young gasped. "We need him."

A new voice cut in. "Green green, what's happening—"

"Green two, green two, we're okay," Young said. Who was he reassuring, another group of soldiers? Could they have flown in another plane? No, the pilots waiting across town on the freeway had radar and would have warned Hernandez— The pilots—

Right. The pilots were in on the deal and must have shut off the radio relay to Colorado at the first code from Young.

There could only be one thing they wanted, one reason to take over. The nanotech. But what was the point of stealing it? What could they ask for, not money—

Bitch. The sneaking bitch.

Ruth had been using him all this time; she'd even smiled and held his hand and meanwhile she'd known—

Cam arched his head back, a grating spike in his vertebrae. Through speckles of blood, he saw how the struggle had been lost.

The suit crucified limply over its pack was Marine Corporal Ruggiero. He carried a map case on his belt, which is how Cam knew him because the Plexiglas over his face opaqued by fracture lines and a veil of gore. When Cam tackled Young, when the assault rifle discharged, the Special Forces soldier guarding Ruggiero had flinched. Point-blank, the 9mm round exploded Ruggiero's skull inside his helmet.

The fight was not completely one-sided. The person Cam had glimpsed on his butt, now upright and rubbing his neck, was a Special Forces soldier named Trotter—but with guns already drawn, the Special Forces had rapidly taken control again.

Except that now a man was dead.

The beige suits were in nearly the same positions as ten seconds ago, five on four, but their postures had changed. They leaned away from Ruggiero's body and Cam felt the same tilting horror. One murder in this tomb of millions, and it changed everything.

"Oh shit," Olson said. Among them he was alone, unmatched by a Marine prisoner. He held his pistol low beside his hip as if hiding it. "Oh shit I wasn't— I just—"

Lacking a radio, Hernandez yelled to make himself heard. "What are you doing, Young, going over to the breakaways?"

"We never planned to hurt your guys," Young said.

"I never figured you for a traitor."

"Swear to God. We didn't want anyone hurt."

Ruth interjected like always. "You don't understand." Her pale face shifted away, searching for Hernandez, then quickly returned to Cam. "We had to do this. We're the only chance there is for people to get the vaccine everywhere."

Hernandez ignored her. "You've got the pilots?"

"I'm sorry, Major," Young said. "I swear. Don't give us any more trouble and your guys will be fine."

It was too much for Cam to separate, the new emotions in his head—alarm and doubt and old, old guilt. In the space of a heartbeat he'd gone from empty to overfull. What the hell could she mean, *only chance*?

"You won't make it." Matter-of-fact, Hernandez sounded like he was the one holding a gun. "All of you better think. Where are you going to go? Anyplace you try for, we'll have fighters on you. Anyplace you land we'll bring in troops."

Young turned from him. "Tape them up, hands to feet."

"You can't win."

"Olson, did you hear me?"

"Y- yes, sir. I got it." Still contemplating Ruggiero's body, Master Sergeant Olson stuck his left arm up as if beginning the attack all over again. "We're on six."

Olson took charge of the men with the prisoners, switching off the general frequency. They began to disarm the Marines one at a time, unbuckling their prisoner's gun belts altogether rather than only taking their sidearms.

"Watch them," Young said, and the rifleman swung his M16 away from Cam's belly at last and went to reinforce Olson.

Ruth knelt instantly, off-balance. "I wanted to tell you—"

"What a fuck-up." Young might have been cursing himself. He didn't look down at Cam until the words were out.

"Leadville was going to keep it for themselves," Ruth said, but Cam stared at Young instead, unable to look at her. One more murder, and for the wrong reasons. For nothing.

His tongue dug at the hole in his gums, fleshy tendrils, embedded rocks of enamel. Already the cloying soup of his own blood was making him nauseous.

He coughed. "Why would they . . ."

Young also knelt, so that there was one of them on either side of Cam. He'd drawn his pistol and hefted it now, a silent display, before reaching across Cam's belt with his other hand.

Ruth said, "What are you doing?" Then her voice was only a mumble. "Let me explain!"

Young had disconnected him, and said, "I can't have him on the radio."

"Then how is he supposed to help us with Sawyer? He didn't know. Let me explain. We have to be able to talk. They're essential to building—"

"Whoa. We're not sticking around here. Are you serious? I thought you were just delaying to give us more time."

"We have to stay. This is our best chance."

"Dr. Goldman, we're going to take whatever you tell us."

"What if something gets broken? What if it turns out we left one little app module we didn't realize we needed?"

"You know we have to get out of here."

"Two hours!" she said. "We can stay at least two hours like Hernandez said. Leadville doesn't know, right?"

Young paused, perhaps aware of how closely Cam was listening. They would never trust him again. And in recounting what had happened, in rethinking his mistake, Cam noted how similar this conversation was to the one she'd already had with Hernandez. Young had even taken the same patient, parental tone in response to her unswerving mania.

Her bravery and her commitment were real.

"My guess is we probably pulled it off," Young answered slowly. "They haven't said anything."

Ruth hammered at him again. "Then we're okay."

"I don't think you understand the risk. We still need to get back to the planes, we still need to refuel, we need a lot of things to go right before we're back in the air."

"This is our best chance. This is— It's everything we've been fighting for. Don't waste it. Please."

Cam almost said something too, and Young noticed. Young's eyes narrowed and he stood up, away from them both. "All right, we stay until we switch out these tanks. That's it."

"What? That's barely an hour and a half!"

"That's it," Young told her.

But they were still working twenty minutes into a new set of tanks. Young had ordered the scientists to gather their stuff together as he changed them out—"Time to move," he said— but Ruth and D.J. barely acknowledged him, in the thrall of their own excitement, and Young had wavered.

Cam thought they probably wouldn't have gotten away with it if Hernandez was still in charge, but now this behavior was a rebellion inside a rebellion. Young could never be the authority that Hernandez had been. He might have shut off the electricity or physically dragged them out, except that he wanted as badly as anyone for them to succeed.

Early on, while Todd and D.J. were still booting up all systems, Ruth shut off her radio and pressed her helmet against Cam's, her earnest face close as she described the reasons for the conspiracy; the weapons application research under way in Leadville; the sixteen hundred Americans killed in White River; the fear that the Leadville government intended to use the vaccine nano to recolonize the planet as they saw fit.

"That's genocide the easy way," she said. "Leave everyone else to die off and they'll rule forever."

Cam had pledged his loyalty again—too late. It was a waste of manpower, but Young put Iantuano in the crowded chamber to stand guard, to make sure Cam didn't reconnect his headset and shout a warning to Leadville, or maybe wrestle down one of the scientists and cause a disturbance that couldn't be explained.

Red red. At a third signal from Young, the pilots across town reestablished the audio relay to Colorado. There had been only four minutes of silence from the expedition group, and during that time the pilots continued to provide secondhand updates while "working around a bad wire in the relay." No

cause for alarm. The mission was on target, on time, and prepared to stay put for a while.

They had maintained that fiction. Most of Leadville's attention was on the science team now, prompting or questioning them. D.J., Ruth, and Todd were supposed to describe
their every action, yet often became distracted by each other's
commentary or fell quiet as they obsessed with their thoughts.
Ruth especially was untalkative, using gestures whenever
possible.

The plan was to keep the lie going until early afternoon if
possible, until they abruptly pointed their C-130 north from
its path back toward Leadville.

On the half hour, every half hour, Major Hernandez spoke
to his superiors while Captain Young aimed an assault rifle not
at Hernandez but at the rest of the Marines. Young was visibly
reluctant, shamed by this role, but he had sworn that Hernandez would watch the rest of his squad die before getting it
himself if he said anything wrong.

It was also necessary to make a show for the satellites, despite a forty-minute gap in coverage. The takeover had occurred safely under a roof, hidden from orbit, but once there
were eyes overhead again, Leadville would have questioned
why they weren't seeing an effort that matched what they'd
been told—so the Special Forces exhausted themselves loading the trailer and bustling in and out of the lab simply to look
like a group of twelve men instead of seven.

There hadn't been time yet for Cam to settle things in his
mind. Too much was happening too fast, although they spoke
with him less than he'd hoped, questioning Sawyer rarely now.

His disappointment verged on panic. He needed them to
need him, but most of the work had already been done,
apparently—in Colorado before they'd flown out, late last
night on Ruth's laptop, and more this morning.

Their efforts were going well. That much he knew. That
was good. Still, it frustrated him to be pushed aside. He had
never been their equal but now he wasn't even a useful tool.
His big contribution had been to confirm Sawyer's identification of each vacuum wafer. He'd also made certain that they

understood two passwords for the computers, *powerpuff* and *Mar12,* the birth date of Kendra Freedman's favorite niece.

Sawyer also seemed afraid of becoming irrelevant, yet devalued himself by burying each bit of worthwhile information in meaningless personal background. The niece's name. Her visits. He squawked and rambled, rubbing and rubbing at his armrest with his good hand, trying to be a nuisance.

Twice the science team exchanged a round of high fives and several times Ruth laughed, a satisfied, barking *ha* that carried through her helmet.

Cam watched them and he waited, his torn gum aching, aware of the bruises along his back, arms, chest, chin. Aware of the numb scars covering his face and his body. In many ways the growling in his belly was also a memory, ugly and alive.

The fabrication laser didn't look like much, three fat blocks like refrigerators that would be a motherfucker to get through the air lock, never mind the wires and pipes joining them together. The third one was missing a shallow inset from its middle, where the gray paneling gave way to a white console that held a display grid, a keypad, and two joysticks.

Nothing the scientists did looked like much, either. They typed. They patiently monitored their equipment. They consulted with Leadville.

Almost two hours ago D.J. had fitted a pair of vacuum wafers into a thin tongue that eased out of the console, exactly like the tray of a DVD player. Retracted into the body of the laser, automatically sealed within an atmosphere hood, the wafers were opened by delicate waldos after a decontamination procedure swept dust and debris from the working space. The laser was also equipped with atomic point manipulators and a scanning probe, and D.J. activated autoretrieval programs that found and then arranged a single proto-*archos* from the first wafer alongside a heat engine component from the second.

It was a painstaking process. Each wafer held a dozen samples of a common type but with minor variances, since they had been individually machined rather than produced by self-replication. D.J. rejected the first three engine fragments.

Meanwhile, Ruth and Todd solved a protocol issue between her laptop software and that of the lab computers, then began uploading their files. They had also popped in several of Freedman's discs, ordinary CD-RWs.

The actual beam of the extreme ultraviolet laser, despite its giant name, would have been imperceptible even if it wasn't hidden inside the machinery. On the video monitor it appeared only as a symbol, a computer-generated slash, even tinier than the lattice shapes representing the nano-structures.

Unable to use a touch pad well with his gloves, D.J. sketched the parameters he wanted with a joystick and then sat there, hands off, as the laser cut unnecessary materials from the engine component, paring it down. Then he gave instructions to graft this nub into the heart of the proto-*archos*.

He ran adjustments on the same program six times before he had it right. This took eighty minutes.

"Great, looks great," Ruth said.

Still cutting, the laser began to alter the molecular composition of the nano's core. By eradicating select atomic particles, they could create a semi-solid state microprocessor encoded with the replication algorithm and their hunter-killer discrimination key, as well as coding for the thermal sensor.

There were two serious complications.

First, it was a sequence that could not be corrected, either done perfectly the first time or, with faults, a waste of their entire effort. Before trying again they would need to build a new nano, and odds were that D.J. would average another six tries to re-create this hybrid structure.

Worse, the second complication was that faults were statistically guaranteed. Even as the laser stuttered and lanced into the nano's core, free radicals were expected to damage these unimaginably fine pathways.

It would never be a hundred percent.

The question was whether they could fabricate a vaccine nano that retained enough coding to function, and how well, because whatever they created would assemble more nanos with exactly its own limitations—and it was imperative for the vaccine to operate with a low number of flaws. Otherwise it would be overwhelmed by the *archos* plague. It would be useless.

Twenty-six minutes into their fresh tanks, Young thumped on the glass of the hermetic chamber again. Without a radio jack, Cam couldn't hear his words at all but the message was obvious.

Get out.

"Soon," Ruth said. "I promise. We really can't stop the etching process after—"

Young struck the glass again, his mouth working. Beyond him, Cam saw two of the Special Forces troops bend stiffly to look at the ceiling, although the fluorescent lighting seemed steady. Were they shutting down the power?

"What! When?" Ruth's voice was high, frightened, and D.J. stood up from the EUVL console. Young had swiveled his head and Cam realized he was talking to Iantuano now.

That ready animal calm fell over Cam once more but he resisted it, even as he sidestepped away from Iantuano and turned to confront him, making sure his legs were clear of Sawyer's wheelchair. "What's going on?"

"Get your buddy out," Iantuano said.

"They're almost done."

"Get him out. Two jets just came over the mountains."

28

Leadville command had known all along. Ruth should have guessed. James had not been among her counterparts on the radio, advising and encouraging her. Delaying her. He wasn't knowledgeable about their hunter-killer tech or familiar in any way with laser fabrication, but as the head of their labs, he should have been in the background.

James's absence itself was the warning that Leadville had tried to prevent him from giving, and Ruth had been too caught up in her work to understand. It might have cost them everything.

Young was right. They should have run for the plane.

Were their suits bugged? No, microdevices couldn't transmit that far. Hernandez had said something, an innocent-sounding phrase, preset signals for degrees of trouble.

"Young?" Ruth waved her palm back and forth against the glass wall of the chamber. "Young! You cut the radio relay!"

Slightly to her left, outside the glass, Young turned.

"Let me talk to them," she said.

"I've got it covered, Doc. Move your ass."

Cam was already rolling Sawyer through the air lock, pushing Sawyer's arm down as he grabbed at the wall.

Ruth said, "Listen to me. We have the ultimate hostage."

"No kidding." Young shook his head, not in disagreement but in harried exasperation. "Iantuano, clear them out."

"Yes, sir."

"Wait!" Ruth slapped at the glass but Captain Young had already started toward the far corner of the main room, where his prisoners sat against the wall, their boots and wrists bound with silver duct tape.

He'd sworn he would slaughter them—

"Young, *no*! I meant the nanos and all the hardware!"

He didn't answer. He'd switched off the general frequency. What channel had Olson used? Ruth grabbed at her controls. Static. Static. Band two was the command channel, and the pilots across town had kept this relay open:

"—down now, stand down and surrender your weapons to Major Hernandez." The voice from Leadville was a woman's, cool, inflectionless. "There's no reason for more bloodshed."

"And I'm telling you." That was Young. "Back off."

"Stand down, Captain."

"Back off. We'll blow it all up first. Understand? We've got enough gas cans here to have a real party, so back off. You don't want to—"

The sky hammered against the building in two screaming sonic waves as the F-15 Eagles cut overhead.

Leadville had sent an overwhelming force. That was what they claimed, at least, and the pilots across town confirmed that radar showed another C-130 lumbering after the two fighter jets. Leadville boasted that it held sixty troops.

Young repeated his only threat—"We'll blow it up, all of it!"—then instructed the pilots to cut the relay entirely. He said, "Can you block our stretch of highway, put your planes in the middle?"

"Already moving." The USAF man did not call Young *sir* or *captain*, Ruth noticed. Was that significant?

The next nearest landing space was the Sacramento city executive airport, five miles south from where they'd touched down, and the roads between were jammed with stalls—and it would be another fifteen minutes before the Leadville plane covered the distance from the Sierras, another ten or more before they were on the ground.

"We'll be most of the way back before they even set their brakes," Young said.

But Ruth wondered. Even if they weren't captured on the ground, even if the breakaways mustered air support or if Canadian fighters intervened on their behalf, would Leadville permit anyone else to keep the *archos* tech? Men driven by greed and fear might not understand that spin-off nano types could be to their benefit as well. Men fixated on war might disbelieve that a vaccine nano would also save them.

One air-to-air missile, that was all Leadville needed to erase a slow-moving cargo plane forever.

"No!" Ruth tottered back from Iantuano, struggling ineffectively with her single arm. "Not yet! If we don't have this we have nothing—"

He caught her wrist. "Are you crazy? We have to move."

"I'm done, I'm done, I'm wrapping up," D.J. yammered behind her and Ruth shifted back and forth, trying to be larger, trying to block Iantuano from the EUVL console.

"Let us secure our prototype or all this time was wasted!"

"Ma'am, we're moving out."

"I'll go," Todd said. "Sir? Look, I'm going."

"Got it!" D.J. shouted. "Let me extract—"

Thump bump. Captain Young had come back to the outside of the chamber, his rifle cradled in one arm, his other hand on the glass. At the same time, two soldiers were hustling in through the air lock. Cam had already pushed Sawyer's wheelchair across the larger room, his head turned over his shoulder to watch.

"If I didn't know better I'd say you were playing both sides," Young said, looking for Ruth's eyes through the many layers between them, the glass wall, their faceplates.

She held his gaze. "That's ridiculous."

D.J. stepped to her side and showed Young his fist. "I have it, okay? I have our sample. Let us make sure we've got all the software and we can go."

"Do it fast," Young said, making a rolling gesture like a traffic cop. "I want to bring that laser but you're in our way."

The soldiers who'd come into the chamber were pulling a dolly. None of the EUVL components weighed more than two hundred pounds, but the soldiers also had a stubby blue cylinder, not an air tank, connected by a coil of line to a slender, blackened nozzle. The welding torch.

Ruth said, "You have to be careful how you take it apart!"

"Doc, anything that's not on our trailer in fifteen minutes gets left here."

"You can't just cut the cooling lines, we'll never fix—"

"Fifteen minutes."

"I can minimize the damage," D.J. said. "Let me show them where to cut and I'll pull as much wiring as I can."

"Sure," Young answered. Already one soldier was helping the other, Dansfield, fit a heavy welder's mask over his helmet.

Ruth hesitated, arguments swarming her brain. The third component—the power supply and computerized electronics—was tied to the others only by a bevy of cables, easily yanked. Unfortunately the second unit—cooling system, fans and filters—was connected to the first by several heavy-duty pipes. If they hacked through those lines, they would lose most of the coolant and badly contaminate the decon system. But better that, she supposed, than to risk damaging the laser optics in the first component by smashing the bolts free.

She seized her laptop. Todd was gathering up the CD-RWs and D.J. had zipped the case of vacuum wafers into his chest pocket. Ruth bustled into the air lock, Todd close behind.

There were still so many tests and refinements necessary before they had a dependable vaccine, more than anyone ever could have accomplished within the limits of their air supply.

They'd probably run through the whole process fifty times. They needed days, even weeks, and she closed her eyes and cursed herself.

The rationale for preliminary checks had been sound, but they should have stopped as soon as they were sure they had the essentials. Maybe they could have finished refueling at Sacramento International before the jets rose over the horizon.

Ruth had honestly thought she was beyond pride, beyond anticipating her place in history—yet the temptation to be first had been too great. Temptation and weakness.

She'd never completely escaped her fear as they worked— there were too many reminders, the clinging skin of her suit, the weight of her pack and the cramping discomfort in her shoulder—but she had used her diaper standing right there among five men and thought little of it, spellbound, possessed.

Now she prayed to God that there would be a place and time for her to lose herself again. Not for her own sake. Not ever again for her. The millions of people left in the world didn't deserve to starve and fight through the next thousand years because of her selfishness. Shouldn't that count for something?

Please please please. The litany was her heartbeat.

"This is Dansfield, I'm lighting up—"

She looked back. Stupid. Three of the four men behind her in the hermetic chamber had turned outward, and she saw Iantuano's lips part in surprise at her reaction. Then her gaze shifted naturally to the fourth man, a kneeling shape, just as the welding torch in his hands spat out a holy blue-white flame. She flinched.

Please God.

Afterimages clung to her eyes. "Todd," she said, "will you double-check the trailer? I'm going to look over what's left in here and then we can triple-up on each other, okay?"

"Sounds good."

"Let me help." That was Cam, jacking his radio back in without permission. Ruth paused, afraid for him, but surely Young wouldn't object now that Leadville knew everything.

His scarred, broad features had swollen between his nose

and mouth, though the extent of it was tough to judge because the interior of his faceplate was flecked with dry blood, thickest over the bottom half. Beside Cam, low in the wheelchair, Sawyer blinked up at her with a frightened chimpanzee grimace. No doubt he'd also looked at the welding torch.

"Why don't you give that guy a hand?" she asked, motioning outside the lab where a soldier was lashing equipment onto the trailer. "We can't afford for anything to fall off."

"Right." Cam turned and trotted after Todd, leaving Sawyer in the middle of the floor.

Ruth strode alongside the counter, regarding the jumble. If there was room, if they had a fleet of trucks, they would leave nothing except the chairs and desk lamps. But other items didn't matter, picoammeters, a signal generator—

She was standing in Corporal Ruggiero's blood.

She clenched her fist and kept moving, although she angled back from the counter to walk on clean tile. Then her gaze lowered again with the same reflex curiosity that had nearly blinded her.

The puddle had smeared when they dragged Ruggiero from the room, a broad trail now turning black and sticky.

Captain Young was in the far corner again, where he'd gone after each interruption, standing over the prisoners with another Special Forces soldier as a third man wrapped more tape around the prisoners' legs. They were already immobilized. Why bother?

Ruth fumbled for her radio control, careful not to drop her laptop and unwilling to set it down.

"—or own fault. Otherwise you'd be riding back with us."

"You can't just leave us here." Hernandez. They must have plugged his radio in.

"I can't bother keeping an eye on you or messing around with an extra vehicle," Young told him. "I'm sorry. We'll tell them where to find you."

"What if they don't get here in time?"

"You have almost two hours. And you can survive for almost two more after that before you really start to hurt."

"Not if we suffocate in these suits."

"We'll leave you a knife," Young said. "You should be able to get everybody up and moving in ten, fifteen minutes."

Longer than that. But Ruth didn't say it. The Marines would need to be very cautious to avoid cutting open their suits, and now she realized why the soldier with the tape was looping it around their shins and knees instead of reinforcing the bonds at their feet. More surface area meant more exacting surgery.

"Wait." Hernandez spoke faster now. "You know Timberline has the best chance at putting together a bug that really works. If you take this technology to the breakaways—"

"Good-bye, Major. Good luck."

"—you're playing with more lives than you—"

Young knelt and yanked Hernandez's jack himself, as the soldier with the tape leaned over. He also held a folding knife. They cut Hernandez's wire and then did the same to the other three Marines, irreparably muting them.

It was a mercy, giving Hernandez and his squad a chance, and it was smart. Ruth approved. If Young had executed them, he couldn't expect any better for himself if things went bad.

Leaving them here to be rescued was also, she thought, a calculated move to draw away some of Leadville's forces.

More than fifteen minutes passed before they were driving—the EUVL components barely fit through the air lock one at a time—but Young held up until the last piece was aboard the trailer.

Their shadows were small and huddled beneath them, the noon sun suspended near its highest point.

Dansfield led off in the 'dozer, Trotter kneeling on the roof on the operator's cage with one of their two assault rifles, and Olson stood behind him on the bulldozer's body. The five civilians and four remaining Special Forces crammed into the jeep and among the tightly packed gear on the flatbed, Sawyer and his wheelchair wedged into the back. Iantuano sat on top of an EUVL component with the second rifle.

Newcombe had disabled the pickup with three pistol shots,

both driver-side tires, the radiator. They'd also dumped most of the equipment they'd brought here, keeping the remaining air tanks and the pressure hood—and Ruth noted that among the abandoned gear were the gas cans Young had sworn he'd use to destroy the lab machinery if Leadville pressed too close.

His quiet choice made her proud and sad at the same time, a feeling that was wild and lonely and *right*. Even worse than the Leadville government controlling this nanotech would be no one having it at all. Young had no intention of blowing up what so many people had struggled so hard to attain.

They were slow, the jeep straining to pull its load, but even at twenty-five miles per hour they were up Folsom Boulevard and moving north on 54th before they heard the planes again.

The fighters crossed overhead, a sky quake. Pressed between D.J. and Cam at the rear of the jeep, not down in the bench seat but perched on the rim of the vehicle's body, Ruth tried to look around but lowered her head before she lost her balance.

They bumped through the adjoining yards, briefly dodging eastward, then continued north on 55th. Half a block later they pointed west. From this point on it was a straight shot back through nineteen residential blocks until they approached the highway, and Jennings accelerated to keep up with the 'dozer.

"We're going to make it," Young said.

The enemy C-130 came head-on over square shapes of the city horizon, low and lazy, and Ruth twisted her head around again to look for the sun, completely disoriented.

Were they driving the wrong way? "Where are—"

Other voices made a confusion of the radio: "*Jesus they're* the airport's south of *right at us!*"

They couldn't be lost. There was only one path back through the ruins, so the big cargo plane must be flying out of the west rather than eastward from the mountains. Soon it would pass over the freeway directly toward them.

Objects tumbled down behind the aircraft. *Canisters of the snowflake nano-weapon.*

Ruth tried to scream and couldn't, lungs caught, already

dead— No. The snowflake would be useless against people in containment suits. The tumbling objects were men, thick with gear, and long appendages whipped upward from each human figure and rippled and spread. Parachutes.

Already there were half a dozen rectangular gliders see-sawing down in the C-130's wake.

29

A wet shock of blood hit Cam's faceplate as Jennings lurched back from the steering wheel. The snap of the man's head was abrupt and vicious, and Cam jerked and shouted as gunfire rolled over the street.

Dead, helmet torn, Jennings bounced forward again from his seat and fell across the wheel. The jeep swerved left at thirty-five miles per hour, slowing as his boot slid off the gas but rammed on by the trailer's weight and inertia.

The shift of momentum was a steepening terror in Cam as his thinking exploded.

Past the Thirty-eighth block, Olson had spotted an olive drab glider hung up in a cluster of trees, its harness open, the paratrooper gone—and Captain Young had shrugged and said to keep going. They knew they were surrounded. They knew they were outnumbered. Counts varied but they agreed that more than forty chutes had swept down from the C-130, gathered mostly in a large batch ahead of them and a smaller group behind.

Young hoped to bluff their way through, but the sniper's kill shot had been timed with at least one other marksman.

Eyes wide, *mind* wide, Cam saw Trotter spin off the roof of the bulldozer's cage ten yards ahead. Farther on, muzzle flashes erupted along the squat brick wall of an apartment complex and from behind the corners of a condominium building, more than a dozen erratic bursts on and off like a firing of synapses.

The 'dozer took the brunt of it. Sparks and yellow paint dust jumped up from the hard iron and Sergeant Olson fell with Trotter. In the driver's seat Dansfield bucked and shook, shredded as a few rounds chanced between the slats of armor and then pinwheeled back and forth.

Riding shotgun in the jeep, Young shouldered against Jennings's body to straighten the wheel. Too late. He kept the jeep and trailer from jackknifing—and maybe from turning over as the trailer's mass continued forward—but bad luck had a red Toyota minivan angled across their path.

They struck the van doing twenty-five or more, their right fender punching the corner of its rear end. Both vehicles rocked and the smaller, heavier jeep butted against the minivan's side.

No one was wearing safety belts. Jennings and Young couldn't fit into theirs, unable to sit properly because of their air tanks, and in back Cam and the three scientists were perched together above the bench seat.

Impact threw Cam sideways into Young's back. Todd, opposite him, began to topple out of the jeep but was hit by the side of the van at the same time that Ruth and D.J. were carried forward over Cam in a tangle of bodies. Someone's arm mashed his headset against his skull.

Pinned beneath them, against the dashboard, Young squirmed out through the open side of the jeep.

On the radio a man wept—who else had been shot?—and they were all breathing like dogs. Cam dragged himself into the space that Young had cleared, then dropped onto the asphalt. Blunt jigsaw chunks of safety glass rolled like pebbles under his forearms and belly.

The minivan and the jeep had come to rest in a cockeyed T-shape, the trailer bent around to make something like a triangle, and to Cam's widened perceptions the little import van felt like a huge bulk between himself and the paratroopers.

Then a knot of rifle rounds tore through the dented panel above his head and slammed into the jeep. *Tink tak tak.*

"Cover cover gimme anything!" That was Young. His face-plate had a stress fracture across his brow and he looked past Cam at the trailer with one eye shut, the skin on that cheek-bone and temple rubbed raw. "Newcombe!"

Two minutes ago Cam had considered asking for a pistol. They had extra guns stripped from the Marines, but Young had been off the general frequency, communicating with their pilots and maybe Leadville as well, and the spare gun belts were on the trailer with Newcombe and Iantuano—

Jennings. There was a gun on Jennings's corpse.

Even as Cam thought it, crabbing onto his knees, Young and someone on the trailer managed a small amount of return fire—the sporadic, heavy bark of Glock 9mm pistols. Young didn't even bother to aim, his arm thrust under the minivan.

The paratroopers responded and Cam stayed flat as a shower of glass clattered over him, mixed with slower-falling shreds of paint, plastic, and upholstery. But the rifle fire didn't sound as concentrated as before. Some of the troopers were advancing, he realized, and must have ducked at the pistol shots.

Young was slowing them down but probably not by much.

Cam rose from the asphalt against all instinct, overcoming his own fear-stiffened muscles. Any safety the ground provided was a lie. If Leadville had been negotiating with Young since their first exchange, it was only a ploy. This ambush was Leadville's true response, and showed a willingness to pick up whatever pieces were left rather than risk recapturing nothing at all—and if Cam and the others were overrun here in the street, they could all expect a bullet in the head.

So close, the troopers would kill them out of self-defense, to prevent them from detonating the explosives Young had threatened to use.

Cam hunched into the side of the jeep and clawed at Jennings. He screamed when a bullet sang off of the jeep beside him, near enough that the vibration went into his chest. Then he ducked back to the ground, dragging Jennings by the neck.

He glimpsed Todd above him, still lying in the rear of the

jeep and using his body to shield Ruth and D.J. Todd's voice was a mantra, a mumble, his headset either damaged or knocked off somewhere inside his suit: "Down, down, stay down!"

Twice now Cam had seen him protecting others.

Beyond the jeep, Newcombe stood on the trailer where he'd been riding in a narrow slot among the computers, pistol out, and the invaluable hardware around him might have been the best protection. Maybe no one was shooting at Newcombe. Sawyer had likely also come through the crash okay, his chair wedged into the rear and facing backward, but Iantuano was missing from his perch. Either the snipers had nailed him in that opening volley or he'd been thrown onto the street.

"We gotta move! Move now, move south, let's get behind that white building!" Young rallied them with well-trained authority, but spoke as if organizing people scattered over a vast distance instead of a few yards. "Where are the scientists? Newcombe, can you reach—" He stopped.

Cam held a Glock 9mm in one hand, even as he tugged the gun belt away from Jennings.

Young stared at him. Young was reloading, vulnerable.

"Captain? Hey, shit." Newcombe obviously thought Young was wounded or dead, and assumed command after no more than an instant's panic. "Shit, uh, we're running for the white house!"

"They're still in the jeep," Cam said, answering Young, and Young was talking again even before Cam had finished.

"Make sure they have the nanotech," Young told him. "Newcombe, can you reach the extra belts? Grab 'em all. We're gonna have to hike it out."

Abandoning the lab equipment was a good sacrifice, and should hold many of the paratroopers here. But how close were they to the freeway? Had they even reached Thirty-fifth Street?

"Science team, listen up!" Young was fiercely methodical. "I want you over the driver side of the jeep, that's away from me. We're gonna run south to that white building on the closest side of the street *and I need you to bring all of your gear*, the laptop, the samples, *all of it*!"

Cam tried to think through the math. Christ. They were at least seven blocks from the plane, two down and five over.

Young continued. "Iantuano, you still with me?"

"'Round back of the trailer, yeah. I think I busted my arm."

"I need you to carry Sawyer. Can you slide your sixteen down to Newcombe? We go on my mark."

Seven blocks unless they were cut off.

Cam belly-crawled after Young between the trailer and jeep as Todd scrambled down onto the asphalt, then Ruth. Looking from side to side for D.J., Cam saw Iantuano punch Sawyer in the gut three times to stop him from fighting, swinging awkwardly with his left because his other arm was broken.

"Where's the other one, the other scientist?" Young shouted at Ruth even as D.J. yelled, "Give up! We have to give up!"

He was still in the jeep. Cam might have left him. There was no time. But Ruth and Young both argued with D.J. even though they couldn't see him, crouching together alongside the vehicle. "Goddammit it's not that far," Young said, and Ruth yelled, "We can make it!"

"It doesn't matter if we don't have the laser—"

"The software is the most important thing!" Ruth shouted. "The software and the samples! We can make it!"

Iantuano inched toward them, parallel to the trailer, with Sawyer over his shoulder in a fireman's carry. Meanwhile the rifle fire came in short, controlled bursts, picking over the minivan. Only Newcombe was shooting back and Cam could sense the Leadville troops shifting closer—

Young turned and fired point-blank into the jeep, five quick rounds. D.J. cried, "No, no, *wait*!" But every shot went into the front wheel well, destroying the tire and striking the engine. Crippling the jeep would make it harder for their enemy to move the lab gear, which might keep at least some of the paratroopers from chasing them. These shots also sounded like return fire from their position, and solved the problem of D.J. as effectively as Iantuano had controlled Sawyer.

"No, *wait*," D.J. pleaded. "I'm stuck! I can't!"

"Help me grab him." Young glanced into Cam's eyes before he rose, and Cam couldn't leave him up there alone.

Standing over the jeep felt like leaning into the path of a train, expecting a bullet, and Cam tore a ligament in his shoulder as they hauled D.J. out of the backseat and put him on the street with rough adrenaline strength.

"Green green, we are inbound on foot!" Young hollered, and clearly their pilots had been waiting, listening.

"I am holding position. I am holding position." The Air Force man spoke with cool precision, then added, "Get your ass back. We're not going anywhere without you."

They were lucky— It was a crazy thought— Cam realized they were lucky their radio channels hadn't been jammed. Their headsets were basically just walkie-talkies, and Colorado was a long goddamned ways off to affect local communications, but the paratroopers surely had the same equipment as they did.

A transmitter on the enemy C-130 could have flooded their headsets with music or white noise.

But maybe the paratroopers were listening too.

"*Now.*" Young led them into the open, his Glock popping. At the same time, Newcombe ducked around the minivan and swept the road with their only M16.

Ruth and Todd went next, together, like two kids on a dare—but first they wasted a precious moment jittering, hesitating, glancing back and forth from Young to each other's pale faces. They still seemed to be looking at each other when they took their first steps.

Iantuano lunged after them, hampered by Sawyer's weight. Cam moved with the Special Forces man, his pistol shots too high as recoil pushed his arm up. Newcombe followed with the rifle.

D.J. was the last to emerge, although he'd been told to stick with Todd and Ruth, and possibly he would have stayed behind if they hadn't left him alone with his fear. Something propelled him after everyone else.

"Wait! Wait!" he shouted.

It was ten feet from the minivan to the sidewalk, twenty more to get behind the boxy white fourplex. The bulldozer and several stalls provided obstacles between them and the Leadville troops, and a sagging fence would also partially conceal them once they hit the yard—but a squad of five paratroopers had advanced much, much closer than anyone had guessed.

Rifle fire pounded over them in a deafening tide.

Just as quickly, the noise turned away. Sprawled behind the 'dozer, Olson was still conscious, his ruptured suit bloodied at the abdomen and one foot. Olson had grabbed Trotter's M16 and squeezed off the full magazine in a wild, chattering upswing.

He wounded three of the nearest troopers. Then the others shot him dead, point-blank.

The paratroopers wore olive green containment suits with combat helmets of the same color, on top of hoods with long insectoid eyes rather than faceplates. They were thick-bodied, encumbered by flak jackets and a third air cylinder.

Cam wouldn't have hit those dark, scrambling shapes at thirty-five feet even if he had been standing still. Charging sideways, twisted over to make himself small, he kept shooting anyway and nearly killed Newcombe when the man dodged in front of him. Cam yanked his pistol back and lost his balance.

Young, Ruth, and Todd had already run past the corner of the building and Newcombe made it as Cam stumbled, his knee folding. Six feet, three— Cam flopped onto the weeds and soft dirt and squirmed to get his gun around—

The majority of the paratroopers, whether maintaining their positions up the street or also advancing, were restricted in their field of fire by the squad that Olson had surprised. A few shots ripped across the front of the building overhead but for the most part the rifles had quit.

A sniper found Iantuano, the largest, slowest target. On his shoulder Sawyer convulsed, drilled through the chest, and

Iantuano buckled three-quarters of the way across the yard. The man was near enough for Cam to see the dismay in his eyes and he expected Iantuano to fall dead, hit in the neck or torso by the same bullet. But the round must have bounced inside Sawyer's ribs and exited at an odd angle, because Iantuano was wounded low on his side and only lightly. He pushed himself up on his arms—both arms, even the broken one— then clutched at Sawyer.

D.J. was unable to make the decision to go left or right around them and paused there, high-stepping over Iantuano's legs.

The sniper winged him. D.J.'s forearm flapped out from his body and he twisted after it, staggering. He kept his feet just long enough to collapse beyond Cam.

Iantuano could have rolled the last yard and saved himself. Instead he tried to improve his grip on Sawyer, worming forward with both legs, his face distorted by effort. But his bloody gloves slipped loose and a shadow of a new emotion altered his expression as he glanced down at Sawyer. That shadow was miserable doubt, almost wistful.

The sniper put his next round through Iantuano's helmet.

Sawyer's wounds were mortal. Where the bullet had exited through his abdomen, the tough rubber suit was peeled open in a fist-sized flap. His stronger arm beat irregularly on the ground but weakened to a twitching as Cam gawked.

He faced in the direction they'd fled, upside down, bent over his air tanks. Whether he saw them and the safety that he could never reach was impossible to know. His one glaring eye shifted toward Cam and passed on, still lively in his misshapen face.

They left him out there like an animal. And it was wrong and it was right. A bad death was nothing more than Albert Sawyer deserved for all of his selfishness and his savagery— and yet those traits had also been Sawyer's best, his force of will, his adaptability. There was no final equation.

Cam left him out there to die alone and turned and ran.

* * *

Todd helped Cam with D.J., who was clumsy with shock and wanted to sit down. "I can't, I can't," D.J. said, but that he was talking was a positive sign.

Captain Young ranged ahead, not bothering to sneak a glance around the rear of the fourplex before crossing an alleyway. Nor did he make any attempt to find cover as he jogged through a nearly empty parking lot. If there were paratroopers in front of them, it was over. Their only hope was speed.

Ruth moved like a drunk, swaying as if her air tanks were solid steel weights. But whether she'd sprained an ankle or simply exhausted her legs, she never complained.

"I can't—" It was a hideous wound. The impact through D.J.'s forearm had broken his elbow as well, and bone chips from his shattered ulna had acted like shrapnel inside the muscle. Blood dribbled from his sleeve over his hip and his leg, and also painted Todd. Cam thought he could fashion a tourniquet from one of the spare gun belts Newcombe wore like bandoleers, but they'd need to stop running and that wasn't going to happen.

"Squeeze your arm with your other hand," Cam said. "Squeeze on it or you'll keep bleeding!"

"I can't, I can't."

"Almost there," Todd said, muffled. "Almost there." His headset was loose in his helmet, poking his neck, broadcasting every bump and scrape like footsteps.

Newcombe brought up the rear in an awkward skipping stride, turned halfway around with the M16 at his hip. "Nothing," he reported, "nothing, still nothing, *where are they*—" He banged against Cam's pack and stopped.

Beyond this block of apartment housing lay the outskirts of the business district from which they'd detoured on the drive in, and the street before them was endless with traffic. Many cars had come up onto the sidewalk and wave patterns showed which vehicles had stopped first, other drivers swinging around them into the lots of a dry cleaner's and a used-book store.

"Move move move," Newcombe said, pushing his hand into D.J.'s lower back. Young and Ruth were already ten yards into the standstill traffic, angling left and then left again through the smooth, colorful shapes. Windshields caught the noon sun, obscuring the ghosts slumped inside.

"Let me go!" D.J. wrestled away from Cam.

"What? We're just—"

The maze of vehicles was more difficult for them, too tight nearly everywhere to stay in a row together, and D.J. wouldn't cooperate. "*I'm not dying for it!* Let me go!"

Halfway across the street, Young turned to look and Ruth sagged onto the blue hood of a commuter car, her breathing loud in their radios. "Calm down," Young said. "It's always an hour or two before the plague actually wakes up and we'll be there in ten minutes if you just keep moving."

"They'll shoot you! They'll shoot your plane down!"

"Maybe not."

A skeleton in moldering rags folded around Todd's boot as he kicked into its pelvic bone, watching D.J.'s face instead of looking where he was going—and his hands, carefully placed on D.J.'s shoulder, jarred that shattered arm.

"Haahhh!" Twisting, D.J. drove his air tanks into Cam's chest and threw him against a silver four-door. D.J. kept turning, ready to run, but Newcombe blocked his path.

Cam knew too well how pain affected the mind, and in one sense this injury was bigger than D.J. He couldn't see past it.

D.J. swung his good arm at Newcombe, who took the punch and held his M16 up in an entirely defensive position, making a fence of himself.

D.J. sobbed, crazed, hateful. "They'll kill you!"

"Fuck. Let him run." That was Young.

Todd said, "We're almost there! D.J.!"

But Newcombe stepped aside and D.J. surged past him.

"Don't, no!" Ruth yelled. "*He has the samples!*"

They tackled him after just two yards as the F-15s raged overhead. Within the trembling roar, Cam snagged at D.J.'s pack and Newcombe swatted his mangled arm. D.J. collapsed, his piercing wail lasting as the jet engines faded.

"Get it, get it!" Newcombe shouted, his rifle leveled away from them back toward the apartment buildings.

D.J. fought as Cam rummaged through his chest pockets, not to keep the sample case but to regain his feet. He rolled upright again as soon as Cam released him, shambling, clutching his arm with his other hand.

He was still tottering away when Cam glanced back from the far side of the street.

Why hadn't the troopers enveloped them? The lab equipment was a prize but Leadville had men to spare, and any pursuit should have closed in by now—

"Green, do you copy?" Their pilot. "Green, green!"

"Here," Young said. "We're here."

"Shit news. I got a bunch of guys taking up position out on the freeway."

Young stopped and raised one fist, as if they could possibly miss him. He had outpaced the group and was the only animate shape within the canyon of buildings.

As they surrounded him, Ruth knelt, heaving for air. Cam turned to watch the way they'd come and Newcombe did the same, though it seemed more and more like a bad guess to expect troopers behind them.

"How many you got?" Young asked.

"Nine or ten." The pilot sounded apologetic. "Some of them are rushing the plane."

"Can you—"

"We are not resisting," the pilot continued, formal again. He must have been simultaneously transmitting these words to the men outside his door. "We are not resisting."

They'd counted at least forty troopers chuting down, likely fifty, and riding in the jeep Young had supposed that the last ten were kept as a reserve aboard the enemy C-130, unless Leadville had misrepresented the size of their force, a common trick. Of those fifty, a few would have been hurt in the drop. Young had comforted his team with the fact that impact traumas routinely hobbled 2 percent of gear-heavy troops landing in an open field, and the confines of the city must have upped that number drastically, no matter that these soldiers were an elite and outfitted with gliders instead of regular chutes. A sky crossed with power lines, the streets treacherous with cars—if they were lucky as many as a dozen men had been immobilized.

Let's be pessimistic, Young had said. *Assume forty-five effectives.* That put maybe fifteen troops about three miles east of them, dropped at the *archos* lab to prevent a retreat, to secure any files or gear they'd missed, to help Major Hernandez and in effect become reinforced by his Marines—and Cam had assumed the other thirty or more all took part in the ambush.

Leadville, however, correctly figured that twenty riflemen in a box could decimate their small, lightly armed party. And as they drove into the waiting guns, the remaining ten troops had already been hustling toward their plane.

The three men wounded by Sergeant Olson were likely the difference between a squad pursuing them now and Leadville deciding instead to regroup. The wounded needed care. The trailer needed to be guarded and moved. And why bother risking more casualties in a building-by-building mouse hunt? Leadville knew they'd run out of air. Leadville also knew exactly where they were. The spy satellites must have tracked them since they'd left the lab.

It was over, all of it, and the feeling was like carrying Erin as she bled out with four thousand feet of elevation still between them and the barrier.

Cam saw the same weary dread in Ruth's flushed, sweating face as she blinked up at Young. Todd had also frozen, his expression locked in a grimace, one glove at his helmet as if to fidget with the minor scarring on his nose.

But Young was shaking his head. "Update me on high ground."

"Why don't you give it up?" the pilot said, gently now. "There's no way—"

"Update me on high ground!"

A code name. Did they have more planes heading in from the breakaways or maybe Canada? The entire fucking world was going to be here on top of them soon, until the fighting became a small war and cost a hundred lives, a thousand.

Cam was willing to take it that far to win.

"Last call was affirmative but I cannot confirm," the pilot said. "They jammed my downlink as soon as the F-15s showed on radar. Either way it's no good, man, they got us, we're opening our doors—"

"Radios off!" Young shouted. "Everyone shut your radio off, they'll track our broadcasts."

Cam was willing but Todd was more rational.

"Sir," Todd said carefully, "they've got us." He did not obey the order, holding both hands wide now in a shrugging motion. "What difference—"

Ruth turned on her friend. "If there's any chance—"

"Radios off," Young repeated and Newcombe echoed it, checking their belts. "Radios off. Radios off."

Todd was patient, as if speaking to madmen. He was, Cam realized, still trying to protect them. "Even if you bring in another plane there's no way we're going to sneak off somewhere to meet it. They can see everything. They can—"

"The satellites are down," Young said, and the spike of exaltation that Cam felt was new energy and strength.

High Ground.

Six hundred miles away in the heart of the fortress that was Leadville, a man—or maybe two, maybe a woman—had taken action that was almost certain to be traced back to its source. The number of technicians monitoring the spy sats was too small.

Maybe their co-conspirator was already on the run. Maybe he had already been identified and shot.

Sometime in the past hour, corrective sequences had been sent to the five KH-11 Keyhole satellites still under Leadville's control, deliberately misfiring their jets, pushing the sats down into Earth's atmosphere where they tumbled and burned.

* * *

"Leadville is blind," **Young** said, leading them farther south. A clump of skyscrapers rose from that horizon.

Ruth also seemed to have discovered some reserve of stamina. She kept up the pace but Todd needed prodding. Newcombe, still at the rear, repeatedly pressed the stock of his M16 against Todd's air tanks with a mute chiming.

"But they're not," Todd argued. "They still have radar. Even if your plane comes in below this side of the mountains all the way from Canada, they have fighters—"

Young said, "Nobody's flying in for us."

"What?" Ruth slowed abruptly. "Then what are we—"

Young waved them close to a panel truck before he paused and swung around. His cheek had swollen, and the fine crack through his faceplate seemed to split his right eye into unmatching halves. "There are three hospitals and a med center right in this area of town," he said. "We can find air, enough to get us to the mountains."

"Christ." The word was out before Cam knew it, an honest reaction but one he wished he'd suppressed.

"I know it's a long shot," Young said.

"Long shot!" Todd glanced at Cam for support. "Even if our tank fittings match up, even if you figure out how to make the switch without contamination—"

"We can rig something."

"Even if you filled a car with a hundred extra tanks—"

Young did not use physical intimidation, although it would have been easy for him to gesture with his pistol or merely to lean too close. He did not even raise his voice. "You want to talk yourselves into giving up? Five of my guys are dead."

"It's just not feasible," Ruth said, reluctantly, and she also turned to Cam. "How long do you think it would take us to reach elevation from here with the highways jammed?"

Cam didn't answer—there was an idea in him—and Todd said, "It's too far. It would take us days. I don't know if we could even drive out of the city."

"We have an hour," Young told them. "Two or three hours before we really have to give up."

Todd's hand went to his faceplate again, his nose.

"Maybe we can take over the plane," Newcombe said.

"We gotta try something." Young studied each of them in turn. "We gotta see what we can do."

"I, no—" Todd visibly shuddered. "They'll know the hospitals are our only option! They'll be there anyway just to raid for oxygen while they're down here, medicine, all of—"

"Bullshit. They're gonna have their hands full collecting their people and getting the lab equipment on board."

"What if they leave us here?"

"It's better if we give up," Ruth said, slowly. "Better than if we get caught. And you were smart about Major Hernandez. They won't hurt us."

"They won't hurt *you*," Young corrected her.

"The vaccine," Cam said. "Let me at least try to—"

Behind them, a high screech of metal echoed up the street like a living thing in flight.

The paratroopers loped by in two pairs, the second trailing the first at an interval of nearly sixty seconds. What the noise had been Cam could only guess, the shriek of a damaged car door pushed out of the way, some other wreckage. It saved them.

So did Young, again, motioning for everyone to keep quiet after the first men had gone. The next two were well positioned to catch anyone emerging from hiding, thinking it was safe. Young seemed to expect them and he was right.

The optometrist's office was a lousy place to disappear, down on the ground floor with a big window—a broad waiting area that doubled as display space, lined with mirrors and revolving stands of glasses. But the entrance was locked and the film of dust over the front room was undisturbed. They'd found their way inside through an open side door after taking cover behind a Dumpster.

The paratroopers barely glanced in, a ripple of silhouettes across the window and then nothing more.

"The vaccine," Young said. He looked at Cam but turned to Ruth as he continued. "Is that even possible? I thought you needed a lot more time."

All of them sat on the firm carpet, scattered unevenly behind two freestanding counters and a desk. Overhead the walls held posters of beaming young white people, close-ups that might have been more appropriate in a hairstylist's except for the inhuman sapphire blue of their contact lenses.

A genuine strangeness walked inside Cam, measured and intent. He was too calm, and the mood had grown as they waited. He felt the shape of it on his numb face and he saw it in Ruth as well—in her steady, solemn gaze.

She was uncharacteristically mute.

Todd said, "It's just a first-gen. We'd be better off running for the goddamn hospitals while they're out there hunting us down."

"No, you were right about that," Young said. "The nearest hospital is five blocks and they gotta be everywhere now. But it's good odds we won't see another sweep through here. They've got too much ground to cover."

Outside, the F-15s grumbled southward.

"We're probably safe to hole up in this place," Young added, and Ruth stirred at last.

"It might work," she said. "If it doesn't it's harmless."

"If it doesn't he'll be infected!" Todd's glove bumped at the lower half of his faceplate restlessly, obsessively. "How do you even expect to deliver it into his system—is he going to eat the wafer?"

"It can be breathed in."

"He'll get a lungful of plague at the same time."

"Yes," Ruth said.

"Then what?" Young asked, and Newcombe said, "Yeah, what about the rest of us?"

"If it works, he'll incubate."

Young said, "But what does that mean?"

"We—" She dropped her eyes. "It could be passed from one person to another via body fluids. Blood."

"Let me try." Cam pulled the sample case from his chest pocket and held it out, meaning for her to identify which vacuum wafer contained the prototype.

"We should draw straws," she said.

He pulled it back from her. "No."

"No way, Doc," Young agreed.

Cam pressed the case against his chest. "It has to be me."

"That's wrong," Ruth told him. "We're all in this, we should all—"

"I'm your best bet. I know better than anybody what an infection feels like." It would collect first in his oldest and worst wounds, his ear, his hands. "I'll know if the vaccine is working or not before you're out of air."

She shook her head. "Yes. Okay. I'm sorry."

He was glad she said the last. He shrugged for her benefit and said, "I've got the least to lose."

He had the most to gain. Ultimately, his decision was the same choice he'd made after Hollywood had struggled up to their barren rock peak.

It was what he wanted to be remembered for. Succeed or fail, this was who he wanted to be.

His collar locks were loud and the air sighed out of his suit up over his face as he lifted his helmet, suddenly and unbelievably rank in comparison to the atmosphere inside the shop. Musty and stale, the shop was still far sweeter than the baking stink of himself. Ruth had instructed him not to breathe but Cam tasted the change even with his mouth shut, the brush of wind at his nostrils like a promise.

"Ready?" she asked, and Todd brought the vacuum wafer up to Cam's lips. Ruth hadn't wanted to chance the operation herself, having just one hand, and Cam had needed both of his to remove his helmet. "One, two, now," she said.

Todd pushed his finger and thumb between Cam's open teeth and broke the wafer, pinching it, as Cam inhaled sharply. They'd agreed that he might as well swish it around his tongue and actually swallow it too.

"Okay, hold your breath as long as you can." Ruth offered him a strip of sturdy white fabric, cut from a jacket exactly like medical doctors wore on TV. Newcombe had found it hanging in back after Ruth suggested that they'd better try anything to minimize Cam's initial exposure.

He wrapped the dusty fabric over his nose and mouth with practiced movements, then slipped free from his air pack, feeling soreness and bruises all through his shoulders and back, and along his hips and stomach where the waist belt had sawed against him. He would have liked to lose the suit completely. His body itched and hurt in a hundred places, and the smell was like wearing a toilet. Unfortunately he was dressed only in a T-shirt, to reduce chafing from his pack, along with the damp adult diaper and socks and boots, and there didn't seem to be any more clothing available in the shop.

They were long past modesty but he couldn't afford to reveal his many abrasions to the machine plague, though it was likely that some of the *archos* nano had already wafted inside his suit.

They arranged another bundle of fabric around his collar, a bunchy scarf. Young took Cam's pack, triple-checked that the spigots were off and then studied its gauge. He inspected Todd and Ruth before trading exams with Newcombe.

Then there was nothing else to do.

"Forty-six minutes," Young said. After that, Todd would be out of air and Ruth would be well into the red.

Cam pushed his broken teeth out of his gums, mashing his glove-thick finger against his mask. The eyetooth peeled free easily but he winced at the pain that the molar caused as one of its roots clung to him. His stomach reacted wildly to the warm new trickles of blood he swallowed, and he burped and burped again. Absurd.

Young turned on his radio and switched repetitively through the few channels, trying to intercept enemy communications, but there was only an open broadcast meant for them: surrender. He clicked off but was soon listening again, his map spread beside him, obviously planning the quickest route back to the planes and the Leadville troops.

Newcombe prowled the shop, searching through drawers and cabinets for anything useful. The receptionist's desk held a can of Pepsi and two cheese-and-cracker packets. In back he found a tray of snorkeling goggles with plastic insets that could be replaced with prescription lenses, and brought one to Cam.

Ruth and Todd sat on either side of him protectively, resting, trying to make their air last. There was so much to say but at the same time nothing at all.

None of them wanted to act like last words were necessary.

Inside Cam's bloodstream and throughout his body now, either *archos* was beginning to multiply uninhibited, devouring his tissues to form more and ever more of itself—or the vaccine nano was disassembling the invaders and remaking this material into more defenders, a war of tides.

At first *archos* would replicate freely even if the vaccine prototype worked, just by sheer force of numbers, yet without this machine cancer the vaccine would have nothing upon which to grow itself.

He thought of Sawyer and the long year behind them. He thought too much.

For the vaccine to fail totally would not be the worst scenario, Cam knew. If it was somewhat effective, slowing the spread of the plague but eventually, inevitably allowing lethal damage, they might wait and hope and understand too late that he'd committed himself to a lost battle . . .

"Okay," Ruth said.

"What?" Cam had forgotten them, absorbed with the pace of his own heart and the rhythm of his breathing. Could it really have been most of an hour?

She stood up. "Okay, let's get ready. We're going to have to do this in the next five or ten minutes."

"What do you need?" Young asked.

"Your knife. Some kind of container."

"It hasn't been long enough," Todd said, his hand at his faceplate again. "You can't—"

"I won't just sit here."

Cam intervened. "I think it's working."

Todd's voice became a shout. "It hasn't been long enough, there's no way you could know!"

"He's right," Ruth admitted, but she smiled at Cam, a tired little slant. As a gesture it was identical to the shrug that he had given her earlier, a show of resolve. "We're doing it anyway," she said, accepting a blade from Newcombe.

"Leadville says they have decon tents," Young said, "to take care of casualties. And we can move pretty fast if we have to once we're out of these suits."

Todd was very quiet now. "Do you know what *archos* does when it burns out inside you? The nanos don't just shut off."

"I'll go first," Ruth said.

"The more there are in your tissues, the longer we stay here—" Todd couldn't seem to bring himself to be explicit. "It's not too late. We should go now. We can be partway there before our tanks run out!"

Ruth knelt in front of Cam as Newcombe stepped to her shoulder, holding a dirty old paper Burger King cup taken from the trash.

Cam extended his left arm. She carved through his sleeve and removed his glove. The air was cool on his palm. He flexed involuntarily. She looked up into his eyes and he nodded. Her mouth was set again with that tight, brave smile, and he wondered what she saw in his face.

She sliced deep into the pad of his index finger, then slit his middle and ring fingers as well. The pain wasn't bad. He had long since sustained too much nerve damage.

Ruth popped her collar locks and removed her helmet, her curly hair tangled and limp with sweat. She closed her eyes briefly and lifted her face, either reveling in the feel of fresh air or praying or both.

Cam's blood pattered into the paper cup, teeming with the *archos* plague and also—maybe—a host of vaccine nanos.

They drank from him.

30

The stillness was incomplete. The hush that embraced the city was disturbed by a spring breeze and the banging, here and there, of untrimmed tree branches against buildings; the low creak of structures still losing the night's cold; the mindless buzz and clack of flies and ants and beetles.

The early sun drew shadows on the street, the great square shapes of high-rises and odd little talons cast by finger bones and ribs.

A plastic grocery bag strayed eastward, given flight by an updraft yet quickly sagging down again.

Ruth Goldman stood level with the crinkled white bag on a second-story office balcony, impulsively cheering its surge into the morning sky. "Hey—" But the bag descended and snared on a rooftop air-conditioning unit. She looked away, trying to hold on to the elation that its random, dancing movements had evoked in her. Irrational, yes, to have such a strong reaction to a piece of garbage, but merely by disturbing this wasteland it had become a cousin to her.

Her hope was fragile and yet savage at the same time.

"We're ready," Cam said behind her, through the door

she'd left open. Ruth nodded, hesitating as she tried to settle her emotions, and Cam stepped outside. She thought he would say something more but instead he only joined her at the railing, gazing out over the wide street.

She wished she could see his face. She would've liked to share a smile. They were a matching set, both with their left arms in a sling—but they were also identically hooded and masked and goggled and gloved.

The five of them had been exposed to the plague for thirty-three hours now and it was an advantage that Leadville could not match, the ability to wait.

Captain Young thought Leadville was still a long way from maxing out on containment suits and oxygen and jet fuel, but the price of the hunt had grown too steep and the last planes had flown out yesterday evening.

They had won. The vaccine nano worked. Ruth had no doubt that it could be improved upon, yet their prototype functioned at a level that exceeded the minimum requirement. Freedman and Sawyer's fabrication gear might have been more finely calibrated than she'd guessed, or maybe it was only that for once the cards had fallen in their favor, allowing them to build the nano correctly the first time.

Occasionally they did feel some pain, especially after eating. Every bite of canned peaches or soup concentrate carried *archos* into their systems. So far, however, no one had suffered worse than brief internal discomforts or a faint itching beneath the skin. If they chanced upon a particularly thick drift of the plague, Ruth suspected they would experience real damage before their antibodies responded, but the fact remained that they were able to move freely through an environment in which their enemy was limited.

They had won. They could wait.

Leadville was going to be a constant problem, Young warned. He expected surveillance planes, and Leadville still controlled a thermal-imaging satellite that would pass above this area twice each afternoon—and out in the open they would be comparatively easy to spot, given the total lack of any other animals or industrial heat sources.

But they could wait. They could hide. And their odds would improve as each day passed, as they hiked farther from Sacramento and the search area expanded.

Across the street, the bag blew free of the air unit and tumbled over the roof of the auto parts store. Childishly pleased, Ruth hummed to herself. "Mm." At the building's edge the bag dropped, however, sinking toward a delivery entrance where three skeletons huddled against a chain-link fence.

Weird veins of black bristled along the concrete there, roping an anklebone, sweeping up the wall and disappearing into the edges of the delivery door. Ants. The bugs were crazy for something inside the store, some chemical or rubber.

Late yesterday, scavenging for food and clothing, they'd repeatedly avoided ant swarms and Newcombe had opened the door of an apartment to a brown mass of termites. Flies harassed them until the day began to cool, and as night fell Cam had suggested that this second-story office would be a safe place to camp. The building was brick and there were stairwells on either end if it became necessary to run.

Insects would be another constant threat, as would the hazards of the wreckage-strewn roads, mudslides, weather.

They had won but they still had so far to go.

The distance between Ruth and her companions also seemed much greater than was right. She glanced sideways, conscious again of that desire to share. Strange, to be strangers. They were blood kin, and she would be a long time forgetting the warm, coppery taste of him—and yet they had been too busy foraging and catnapping and keeping on the move to talk about anything more than their immediate plans.

That would change. There would be time to know each other better as they traveled, but it felt awkward and wrong that they could be at all shy with each other now.

"I," she said, and when Cam turned she ducked her head and gestured away from herself. "Young really wants to split up?"

Inside the office space, the other men were on their feet, both Young and Newcombe wearing day packs. Fortunately there wasn't much to carry, the nanotech samples, weapons, two radios, batteries, small items like matches and can openers. They would find food as they went and sleep among the dead.

Cam said, "No one else likes it either." He shrugged. "It just makes too much sense."

"Yeah."

If some of them were spotted, the others could carry on, assuming that Leadville sent troops to capture them instead of dusting the entire valley floor with the snowflake nano. Their vaccine was protection against only the *archos* plague. But Leadville wouldn't indiscriminately dust a wide area for the same reason that their enemy hadn't hit Sacramento after evacuating all forces—it would be stupid to kill Ruth and the others without knowing exactly where to find their bodies, to recover the phenomenal machines inside them.

I'm glad I don't have to say good-bye to you, she thought.

The three–two division had been obvious. Ruth and Todd needed to separate, to improve the chances that a nanotech expert would escape. Young and Newcombe would also split up, each of them acting as a bodyguard, and because both Cam and Ruth were handicapped—his hand, her arm—it made sense to put them together in the larger half so they could help each other.

The soldiers' training and Cam's long experience with this world gave them an edge, a good edge, and Ruth didn't think she was crazy to feel optimistic.

It would literally be an uphill battle, trudging on foot from here to elevation and then onwards from peak to peak, carrying immunity to the scattered survivors. Lord knew some of those people would also be a danger, too hungry or too full of hurt to understand why or how they had come. Others would help them, though, perhaps a majority, dispersing in all directions, reclaiming the low ground between the coast and the Continental Divide and someday beyond . . .

And if they succeeded, if they discovered peace again, who could say what might come of the *archos* technology and everything else they'd learned?

Before too long she might make Cam whole again, and heal the burns and internal injuries of all survivors.

She might find the immortality that Freedman had chased.

Ruth turned again and smiled, even though he couldn't see the lower part of her face. She knew the expression would affect her eyes and her voice. "I guess this is the easy part."

"Walk in the park," Cam said.

"Absolutely."

They spread north along the Sierras first.

Acknowledgments

Most of all I want to thank my best friend, Diana. (She was also kind enough to marry me a few years ago.) Without her patience and support, this book would not exist.

I'd also like to thank my father, Gus Carlson, Ph.D., engineer, former department head at Lawrence Livermore National Laboratory, and all-around smart guy. He's been an excellent sounding board in my research and brainstorming, not just with the nanotech featured in *Plague Year* but for a good deal of the concepts in my other stories as well.

Kudos also to my bright and tireless editor, Anne Sowards, and to Ginjer Buchanan, Susan Allison, and everyone else who's been so great at Penguin USA. Also a tip of the hat to my agent, Donald Maass, and to Cameron and Stephen in the office there.

There are other people deserving of mention for their contributions and friendship: Patti Kelly and Ute Kelley, both super grandmas; Meghan Mahler for her maps; Peter Kelley for his amazing work in my corner of the Internet at www.jverse.com; Derek, Troy, and Darren for the skiing; and of course, Steve and Naomi.